England's Janissary

England's Janissary

PETER COTTRELL

ROBERT HALE · LONDON

© Peter Cottrell 2012
First published in Great Britain 2012

ISBN 978-0-7090-9330-5

Robert Hale Limited
Clerkenwell House
Clerkenwell Green
London EC1R 0HT

www.halebooks.com

2 4 6 8 10 9 7 5 3 1

Typeset in 10½/13½pt Plantin
Printed in the UK by the MPG Books Group

For my mother, Pamela Dorothy Cottrell (nee Mockett)
6 March 1932 – 15 October 2009

PROLOGUE

Saturday, 9 September 1916, Ginchy, the Somme

KEVIN FLYNN WAS not a religious man, however, from the scant shelter of the shell-crater it felt like a titanic petulant toddler was randomly pounding the ground with an invisible hammer and all he could do was crush himself further into the chalky soil and pray to the long-forgotten deity of his childhood.

He fumbled for the words of prayers buried deep in the darkest, neglected recesses of his mind and between explosions he could hear the man huddled next to him muttering desperately: 'Hail Mary, full of Grace ... Jesus! ... blessed art thou ...' Elsewhere he could make out less noble sentiments whilst another man moaned, clutching his shattered face as blood oozed slowly through grimy fingers. Others just stared ashen-faced at him, waiting for him to tell them what to do.

When the German defensive bombardment had begun he could count the heartbeats between the guns firing and the shells striking the ground. Now the barrage was in full swing and sounded more like a deranged drum roll shredding the Irish Division's attack. Above him, over the lip of the crater, a German machine gun groped across no man's land, scything the legs from under anyone foolish or unlucky enough to cross its path.

Everything was noise and Flynn drowned in it; blood pounded in his ears and echoed around his head whilst every fibre of his body throbbed. The ground groaned under each impact and despite being drenched in sweat he felt as if even the moisture in his body was withdrawing deep within him to escape the chaos all around him. Even the urge to urinate had long gone – or at least he could no longer remember whether he had surrendered to it or not. His tongue felt as if it had grown to twice its size and stuck to the roof of his mouth, a mouth so dry it felt like sandpaper. It tasted bitter – acrid, dry, coppery with fear and adrenalin.

He sucked down gulps of sulphurous cordite-laden air in deep calming breaths and stared at his rifle's sights, focusing on the numbers stamped into the blue-grey metal. The rifle's furniture felt hard beneath his grip as strength returned to his aching limbs. He knew they had to move. 'Right, lads,' Flynn shouted, 'if we stay here, we are as good as dead. When I say, we move – clear!'

Flynn slithered up the slimy side of the crater, hugging the ground, and as he peeked over its ragged lip he felt hot air kiss his cheek as a bullet brushed past his face, sending him tumbling back into the squalid hole. 'Shit!' he cursed as fear rippled anew through him and he knew he had to get a grip. Christ, how he hated the sergeant stripes that squatted expectantly on his sleeves, mocking his resolve and self-control.

'Ye all right, Sarge?' called a big open-faced Dubliner, his slum accent brittle with fear, and Flynn forced himself to grin despite his own welling desperation, staving off the moment when terror would overwhelm his rational mind. They were all scared and he knew that the others were looking to him, as an NCO, to tell them what to do, to take away the burden of choice and make decisions for them.

The army was good at that, at ingraining instinctive obedience into impressionable young men. He knew it, they knew it and he felt such a charlatan, cursing the stripes he'd once flourished before giggling Grafton Street shop girls. Flynn felt his heart sink; he was a sergeant whether he liked it or not and despite his obvious inexperience the others expected him, in their innocence, to know what he was doing, even though they were all of an age.

'Right, lads, listen in,' he said, affecting his best sergeant's voice, clear, calm, in control, play-acting. 'Jerry's got a machine gun about a hundred yards up on the left. If we move right, it looks like there is a trench about thirty to forty feet away. If we can get into it then we're home and dry. You, Corporal—' He pointed at a burly lance-jack on the other side of the crater '—I want you to give covering fire. When I shout, you follow.' The lance-jack nodded and sloshed, thigh deep, across the shell hole to take up a fire position and slipped off the safety catch.

'When I say move you go like hell and don't stop until you reach the trench and if you find any Jerries in it when we get there then give 'em what for, clear?' Flynn barked. 'Remember your drills and you'll be all right.' He couldn't believe that he was spouting the same claptrap as the instructors had back at the depot and he wasn't sure who he was trying to reassure – them or himself. He gave them one more cursory glance and turned back towards the German lines. 'Prepare to move!' The lance-jack began blazing at the machine-gun nest. 'MOVE!'

Flynn lunged forward, his legs pumping, adrenalin and fear tunnelling his vision so that all he could see was the ruined parapet of a trench forty feet ahead of him. Muttering another Hail Mary, Flynn stumbled forward, feeling as conspicuous as a turd on a billiard table before tumbling to his knees behind the meagre cover of broken iron barbed-wire pickets and blazing wildly at the enemy, sensing rather than seeing the others running hell-for-leather towards the sanctuary of the trench.

He was in hell, a chaotic, random pyrotechnic hell littered with tattered khaki corpses, lying deceptively peaceful amid the carnage. Flynn blazed at the enemy, palming the bolt in exactly the way he had been told never to as he screamed 'Move!' over his shoulder at the rifleman behind him. He waited until the man was past him before he sprinted after him and crashed into the trench, home and dry.

He skidded and crashed full-square onto his backside, sending pain shooting up his body, and looking down saw that something was caught on the mud and nails of his ammo boot. It took a second or two for it to register that it was the shredded remains of a face. He grimaced and fought back a gagging sensation before throwing the wet, rubbery thing away.

Biting back his fear in hard, laboured breaths, he took in his surroundings. The air was foul, a cloying cocktail of cordite, rotting matter and a hint of phosgene. The lance-jack was there, the Dubliner and another three pallid, shaken youths. The others were gone. There was nothing more to be said. 'Follow me!' Flynn said and without a backward glance trotted down the trench. Moments later they passed an ashen-faced German corpse slumped staring blankly into space, its skull gaping and leaking brains.

A warm mug of discarded coffee steamed, tugging seductively at Flynn's taste buds as bloated flies feasted on the greying cadaver, but without a second glance they ran on, bombing bunker entrances as they passed with neither a backward glance nor an attempt to inspect the results. He could hear the thud of boots on duckboards but it always seemed to be just around the next traverse. Always out of sight.

Flynn prayed that his pathetic band wasn't all that was left of the company or even the battalion, let alone the brigade, and he was becoming desperate to find someone to report to, someone to take away the burden of responsibility. Someone else must have made it into the German trenches. They had to. They just had to.

Skidding to a halt, he grunted as the others thudded into his back. There were muffled voices and the scuffle of boots around the next traverse. Gulping for air, he strained to listen – the voices had dropped away. Clutching a grenade to his chest, he blinked the fear and sweat from his eyes as he began to ease the pin loose. Psyching himself up for what had to come next, he darted his head around the corner. A bullet gouged into the woodwork next to his head as he lurched back into cover. 'Jesus Christ! We're British!' he shouted at the top of his voice.

'Come out slowly if you don't want to get shot,' ordered a firm commanding voice.

'We're coming out. There are six of us – Ninth Dubs! Don't shoot!' Flynn called as he stepped slowly around the traverse. The saucer-eyed youngster who had shot at him relaxed visibly, exhaling heavily as the tension poured out of him. Behind him a dozen or so Dublin Fusiliers watched him nervously and stood aside as a young officer approached him.

Selfishly, Flynn's first thought was relief, not because he had found some other members of the regiment, fellow survivors, but that he had found someone who outranked him, someone to abdicate his burden of responsibility to. The officer, little more than a boy himself, beckoned Flynn forward. 'Good to see you, Sar'nt, whoever you are,' he said with a forced air of studied calm. 'We could use your help.' He paused, awaiting a response but none came. Flynn was looking down at the corpse lying at his feet. 'You know him, Sar'nt?'

'Knew him, sir,' Flynn corrected, regretting his words as soon as he said them. 'It's Mr Kettle, sir,' he added, almost matter-of-factly. 'My company commander. Least he was. B Company.' Someone had once told Flynn that Lieutenant Kettle was a home ruler, the Irish Parliamentary Party's MP for South Tyrone up in Ulster and that he taught at some Dublin college, God knows which one.

Strain was etched across the officer's face as he ran his fingers through his matted blond hair before plonking his battered helmet back onto his head. 'I know, he was a friend of my father. You know it was him who said that us Irishmen were not fighting for England but for the rights of small nations,' the officer said in middle-class north Dublin tones not dissimilar to Flynn's own.

'Lieutenant Dalton, acting OC C Company. I guess I'm OC B as well, now,' the officer continued, holding out his hand. Flynn shook it firmly but as he opened his mouth to speak a shell crashed into the parapet, sending both men sprawling into the muck as dirt, chalk and debris rained down on them. Flynn cursed and Dalton smiled boyishly. It was then the shooting started.

'You lot, hold your position here, we'll be back in a minute,' Lieutenant Dalton shouted over the din. 'Sar'nt, you come with me.' They scurried down an old communication trench and moments later they were up and out over the sandbags into the shattered moonscape of ruined buildings where they lay catching their breath, gathering their thoughts, desperately trying to get their bearings and locate the enemy.

'That way!' Dalton whispered and darted off. There was so much gunfire that it was virtually impossible to tell where it was coming from – in front, behind, left, and right, above. Thankfully, none of it seemed to be very effective but still they kept low in an attempt to avoid stray rounds until they squatted behind a ruined wall. Dalton raised his index finger to his lip, appealing for quiet – at once bizarrely childlike and deathly earnest – then pointed off to the right. Flynn lay flat and poked his head around the corner. There were coal-scuttle helmets bobbing nervously in the crater up ahead whilst a German officer was frantically snapping out quick battle orders. 'On my word, we attack,' Dalton whispered, pulling out a grenade.

Flynn nodded as the officer smiled reassuringly. Now who was conning who, Flynn thought. Strangely, he didn't feel as scared as he thought he should be; maybe it was because he wasn't making the decisions anymore, maybe it was because he was way beyond scared already.

The attack was swift and violent and over almost as quickly as it had begun but it did the job. Flynn's ears were ringing as he stood on the lip of the crater staring down at torn bodies and the huddled mass of wretched, frightened, broken boys holding up their hands, wide-eyed and pleading for their lives. Their German officer, bleeding profusely from a torn cheek, slowly unbuckled his pistol belt and let it drop to the floor wordlessly, raising his hands. Flynn squatted down and picked up the gun belt, briefly examining it before tossing it over to Dalton. The lieutenant deftly dropped the pistol, a Luger automatic, into his jacket pocket and let the belt drop. 'A keepsake for my little brother,' Dalton said.

'Best be getting them back, sir. Before they work out there's just the two of us,' Flynn prompted and prodded his bayonet, none too gently, into the German officer's back. 'C'mon, Jerry, let's go.'

Scrabbling for the right words, Dalton trawled the depths of his rusty schoolboy German. '*Soldaten, hande hoch! Raus! Raus! Schnell! Mitt me kommen! Raus!*' Meekly their sheep-like mass of captured Germans, pale with shock and fright, quietly did as they were bid whilst stray rounds zipped by.

Dalton frantically shouted for the others to cease firing and Flynn resisted the swelling urge to run for cover, focusing instead on herding their bag of prisoners into the captured trench. Even his prisoners seemed keen to reach safety and be out of the fighting that had begun so bloodily in July. Some, especially the younger ones, appeared to have a bit of a spring in their step and even their officer looked relieved to have let slip the weight of having to make decisions. Shed, in the end, as easily as his pistol belt.

'Twenty-one of the little buggers, by my reckoning, sir,' Flynn told Dalton as they flopped down on the fire step. Flynn felt his hands tremble and balled his fists to try and control it but he could feel it beginning to overpower him as it always did when the adrenalin drained away. Even Dalton was having trouble reloading his revolver as his hands shook too. They looked at each other and started to laugh, like teenage boys usually do after they have done something unfeasibly stupid, something that sounded like a good idea at the time, and had only just got away unscathed. It was then that the sergeant noticed that the young officer was bleeding and suddenly Dalton seemed to notice too as his own adrenalin rush subsided. 'Stretcher bearers!' the sergeant cried. 'Mr Dalton's been hit, stretcher bearers!'

As Dalton was bundled onto the waiting stretcher, he turned to the sergeant. 'What is your name, Sergeant?'

'Sergeant Flynn, sir. Kevin Flynn.'

'Well, Sergeant Flynn, it looks like you're in charge now.' And with those three words Flynn felt the weight of responsibility crash down once more on to his tired young shoulders as he riffled through his pockets and pulled out a small tin of ration cigarettes and plucked one from it. Momentarily he glanced at the legend in tight blue letters – 'If you don't like these then bugger off and buy your own' – printed down its side. He lit it and sucked in the rank blue-grey smoke, feeling it fill his lungs, feeling it take away his sense of smell, and sighed.

'Bugger! Why can't you find a bloody sergeant major when you need one?'

CHAPTER 1

Tuesday, 6 January 1920, Drumlish, County Longford, Ireland

'FOR GOD'S SAKE, woman, will you not keep your noise down? The lads will hear you!' Sergeant James McLain barked in frustration.

'I will not!' bristled his wife Mary, as she rounded angrily on her husband. 'I don't want to go to Dublin! I like it here in Drumlish!'

'For the love of God, Mary, how long have we been doing this? I've got nigh on thirty years behind me and when they say it's time to move it's time to move.'

'But Dublin's full of eejits with guns!' she shrieked.

Flynn woke with a start. He was afraid, his face slick with sweat; his wet shirt stuck to him. His temples throbbed painfully as he sat up and he was momentarily disorientated by the stink of flatulence mixed with stale sweat that seemed to pervade every barracks he had ever lived in.

'I don't want to go to Dublin!' Mary McLain shrieked through the thin plasterboard wall, sending daggers lancing through Flynn's hungover brain and making him nauseous. He knew he drank too much but sometimes it felt like the only way to blot out the memories that stalked the shadows of his mind whenever he tried to sleep, whenever it was quiet; the only way to curb his fear.

'There's no talking to you, woman!' McLain shouted, slamming the door and stomping into the duty room below. Flynn's hobnails scraped on the bare floorboards as he fumbled open the top drawer of his bedside cabinet. As he pulled out a worn, leather-bound hip flask, bedsprings groaned from across the room and Constable Jim O'Leary poked his ashen face out from a mass of grey blankets to peer through the gloom at Flynn.

'The usual?' O'Leary muttered and Flynn nodded. 'You know, Kevin, my boy, you look like shit,' O'Leary added, before disappearing back beneath the blankets. Flynn shook his head and smiled and unscrewed the flask's cap, sniffing the contents. His nose hairs tingled. It was good stuff; you could always count on policemen to get the best poteen – illegal potato whiskey. He sighed and replaced the cap, tossing the flask back into the drawer.

Downstairs, Constable Gary O'Neill's dark, watchful eyes followed Sergeant McLain as he stomped about, his greying moustache bristling, his worn, round face red with impotent rage. O'Neill's sharp, weathered features broke into a sympathetic smile as he handed McLain a mug of tea. 'Will you be having a brew, Sarge?' The Ulsterman's harsh Antrim accent seemed oddly out of place in County Longford.

'Do they not teach you Prods to make tea?' McLain grimaced as he sipped the mug of tea and calmed slightly as he raked his thinning hair.

'Mrs McLain doesn't want to go to Dublin then, Sarge?' O'Neill asked quietly.

'She's got it into her head that I'll get shot if I go to the depot. She says she likes it here and to tell the truth, O'Neill, so do I, but orders are orders and you'll be in good hands with your man Sergeant Willson when he gets here. He's a proper peeler. Not like some I could name!'

O'Neill rolled his eyes theatrically, ignoring McLain's dig at him for having served in the Irish Guards during the war. 'At least it's not to Cork they're sending you,' O'Neill added.

'Aye, so they're not, thank God,' McLain said, as he strolled over to the barracks' front door and opened it, silhouetting himself perfectly in the light. 'I knew Jim McDonell, you know, and Paddy O'Connell, the two lads the Shinners murdered in Soloheadbeg when all this bloody nonsense kicked off. They were proper peelers too. Thank God nothing like that will happen here, eh?'

A lone figure loomed out of the gloom, hunched against the damp chill, his collar up and his cap down, casting deep shadows. His hands were stuffed deep in his pockets and McLain tensed. In some parts of Ireland it was an offence to put your hands in your pockets just in case you were hiding a gun but McLain thought that was all nonsense; anyway, even in the dark he knew the man's gait. 'Good evening to you, Sergeant McLain,' the shadowy figure called through a haze of pipe smoke.

'Good evening yourself, Mr Kelly,' he replied in a ritual that they repeated at the same time every day.

The tip of the rifle's foresight hovered neatly over McLain's round chest. The sight alignment was perfect and as he lay in the dark field opposite, the rifleman's breathing was controlled, serene even. Slowly, unthinking, he clicked off the safety catch and took up the pressure of the trigger.

'Not yet,' a voice hissed in his ear.

'But I've a clean shot,' the rifleman stated quietly.

'Not yet!' Joe Maguire repeated and the rifleman reluctantly reapplied the safety catch with a gentle click, slumping out of his fire position with a disappointed sigh. Maguire, the local IRA commander, patted his shoulder; he could sense the man's frustration even in the dark. 'There will be plenty of time to get him later,' he whispered reassuringly and the silent rifleman nodded, the moonlight glinting in his cold, hard eyes. Maguire was on tenterhooks. His boss was tucked away in an alleyway further up the street and the last thing he wanted was for everything to go wrong with him watching.

Waiting until Mr Kelly had disappeared around a corner, Maguire slowly inched his way closer to the barracks through the damp meadow. The shutters were still open. He could see the policemen talking inside, a clear shot, whilst fifty yards behind him half a dozen nervous young gunmen lay concealed in the cold, wet grass, clutching an odds-and-sods collection of firearms, awaiting his command.

Maguire's stomach churned with that familiar sensation of anxiety and excitement, just like it always did, before the feeling surged into his chest and groin. Unthinking, he slid his pistol from his coat pocket and cocked it as he watched a young policeman pull on his coat. The weapon was cold in his hand, like death. It was intoxicating, frighteningly so. His skin tingled.

McLain stepped back into the barracks, abruptly cutting out the light, and O'Neill looked up, releasing his pen from his slender hand. 'It'll be a beautiful night for paperwork, Sarge. I suppose you'll be out on your rounds soon, Sarge.' It sounded more of a statement than a question. 'Shall I come with you?' O'Neill asked hopefully.

'It's not like you to be wanting out and about,' McLain replied, plucking his overcoat from its peg.

O'Neill licked his lips. 'Ach, it's this bloody paperwork! It's just such a shame that HQ doesn't have more forms for us to fill in, eh?' McLain shook his head and, sighing, O'Neill slumped in disappointment.

'I'll take the new fella, Flynn, with me. He needs to get to know the place, especially as I'm away soon,' McLain said.

O'Neill glanced down at the pile of papers on the desk and,

resigned, picked up his pen. An off-white enamel mug sat steaming in front of him, thick with the red-brown tea that generation after generation of policemen seemed to be able to make but never managed to explain how.

'Evening, Sergeant, Constable O'Neill,' Flynn said on the stair, buttoning his tunic and feeling better for a wash and the smell of tea.

'Get yourself to the armoury, Flynn, we'll be off out in a minute,' McLain said gruffly. It amused Flynn that the backroom could be graced with the epithet 'armoury'. It was farcical, a bit like calling their police station – a substantial detached house – a barracks!

Flynn smoothed his dishevelled brown curls and scratched his chin. The armoury smelt of gun oil as he squatted over the strongbox, rhythmically sliding cartridges into the drum of his revolver. He felt like he had been around guns all his life and had grown to hate them with a passion. They were a means to an end, a necessary evil, nothing more, nothing less.

As he entered the duty room, O'Neill looked up and smiled. 'There's a brew on if you want one,' he said, nodding towards the brown china teapot squatting on the stove, and Flynn helped himself to a cupful.

Watching the two men, their medal ribbons adding a splash of colour to their rifle-green uniforms, McLain thought they were an odd couple, an Ulster Protestant and a middle-class Dubliner, both in their own way outsiders in the ranks of the Royal Irish Constabulary, but he sensed that the shared experience of the war had created an invisible bond between the two ex-soldiers.

Flynn looked older than his twenty-five years. A thin scar tugged across his face from the tip of his right ear to the corner of his eye, giving him what some girls may have thought was a rakish, swashbuckling look, yet his pale grey eyes looked tired, like a man who had done too much too soon, and whilst McLain guessed he was about six foot tall it was hard to tell because Flynn stooped when he relaxed, making him look shorter than he was.

'Where did you get that?' O'Neill asked Flynn, nodding at the pale scar, and McLain noticed Flynn's eye twitched when deep in thought.

'Opening a tin of bully beef,' Flynn finally quipped, making O'Neill laugh. When McLain finally got round to asking Flynn where he'd won his Military Medal, the reply was brief, one word – Ginchy – betraying nothing of the turmoil behind his eyes. Ginchy meant nothing to McLain but O'Neill's reaction showed that it meant something to him, another shared rite of passage.

'Here you are, Sergeant, you'll be wanting this on a night like this,' Flynn said, as he shrugged on his greatcoat. There was a distinct nip in the damp air and the coat felt warm and dry. 'You know, Sergeant, there was a time I'd've killed for a coat like this!'

'You're not wrong there, Flynn, my lad,' said O'Neill, smirking, barely looking up. 'In fact I think I did!' McLain paused momentarily as he buttoned his coat around his thickening middle, unable to tell whether O'Neill was joking or not.

'What I need is a decent pair of gloves to go with it,' Flynn mused as his aching joints anticipated the damp night air. At least the cold would clear his head and if he had to go out he may as well be snug, he thought. After all, any fool can be uncomfortable. McLain felt uneasy watching the fluid motion of Flynn's hands as he tugged his .38 Webley revolver from its holster, checked the cylinder and slipped it into his greatcoat pocket in one swift, practised motion. 'Better to be safe than sorry, eh, Sergeant?' Flynn stated flatly.

Flynn could tell that McLain disapproved of guns, but back in training he'd been told never to go out at night without a weapon and he had no intention of becoming another statistic on the Inspector General's monthly report. Times had changed, even in Drumlish, whatever McLain may have thought. 'Let's go then,' McLain said, straightening his cap and nodding towards the door.

'After you, Sergeant,' replied Flynn, as he smoothed back his brown curls, plonking on his own cap and bowing slightly in mock deference. It struck McLain that Flynn always called him Sergeant, not the more familiar Sarge like O'Neill and Constable O'Leary, but then they were old constabulary hands, whilst Flynn still had much to learn.

McLain gave a brief cursory glance around the room before both he and Flynn flipped up their overcoat collars in unison against the night. Flynn patted his pockets, as if to reassure himself that he had his electric torch and his revolver, and as McLain yanked open the door a shaft of light slashed through the darkness, like a knife scarring the night.

CHAPTER 2

Tuesday, 6 January 1920, Drumlish,
County Longford, Ireland

MAGUIRE FROZE AS the two policemen strolled down the barracks path chatting. He felt light-headed and painfully exposed, he could hear himself breathing and his grip tightened on the pistol in his coat pocket but the two policemen, as yet unaccustomed to the dark, didn't notice him.

'You see them flower beds there,' he heard McLain say. 'A neat garden works wonders to give any nosey head constable or visiting district inspector a warm fluffy feeling and not poke their nose into my barracks. The first bite of every meal is with the eye they say!'

Flynn laughed. 'So the constabulary's not much different to the army then, Sergeant!' It was obvious from McLain's look that he did not approve of such comparisons.

'We'll take ourselves up to St Mary's,' McLain continued, rubbing his hands together against the cold. 'Who knows, we may be fortunate enough to be treated to one of Father Keville's rants about the evils of the British Empire, God save us!'

'Now there's a thing – a churchman with a political opinion. And there was I thinking that we didn't have enough of those!' Flynn chortled, as he followed the sergeant towards the church.

As their voices faded into the dark, Maguire could hear McLain muttering about the state of Irish politics and, relaxing slightly, he steeled himself to dash across the road towards the open barracks door. Somewhere a dog barked and he thought that he could hear the thud, thud, thud of a football being kicked against a wall.

'Get ready,' Maguire whispered to the rifleman behind him, but as he rose silently to his feet, the barracks door slammed shut with a loud thud, plunging the street into darkness once more. Maguire instantly flopped back down onto his knees, ignoring the sharp pain that shot up his thighs as he landed on the cold, hard ground.

'What now?' the rifleman asked. Maguire looked up the street and then back at the barracks, the shadows obscuring his expression, his eyes two points of light in the starlight.

'Work your way around the back. Take Doyle with you and see if you can get at the back door. Don't do anything until you hear the signal, though.' The rifleman nodded and melted into the darkness as Maguire loped off up the street. The dog barked again.

Something moved in one of the barracks' upstairs windows and MacEoin waved frantically at Maguire. 'Get back!' he hissed from the shadows. Maguire stopped and looked back at the barracks and, to his horror, straight into the eyes of a middle-aged woman watching him from the window. Maguire forced himself to glance casually at his watch before continuing on up the street. When he reached MacEoin he could see the anger etched on his face. 'I told you to go back!' MacEoin hissed.

'McLain's wife saw me from the window.'

'And?'

'I don't think she suspects anything.'

The upstairs light went out and MacEoin relaxed slightly. 'Go back to your lads, quick! We'll jump McLain and his other fella as they get back,' MacEoin ordered, before turning to his stocky bodyguard, Brendan Fitzgerald. 'Stick with them, Brendan, but don't get too close, mind. I don't want them to see you.'

Fitzgerald nodded and padded soundlessly away, masked by the strains of an old rebel song drifting from a nearby drinking den melding with the thud of a football. Maguire tried to look as casual as possible as he strolled back towards his men, fighting to control his anxiety. He would be a long time on the toilet when this was all over, when the adrenalin wore off and the stress kicked in. As he reached the edge of the field, a faceless voice hissed, 'Quick, boss, they're here!' The two policemen had just rounded the corner. Thud! Thud! Thud! The sound of the football was beginning to grate. Then it stopped.

It was only when the thudding stopped that Flynn noticed the footsteps and did his best to look behind without making it too obvious. The hairs prickled on the back of his neck and his mouth suddenly felt bitter and dry as he thought he caught a movement in his peripheral vision. He felt sick. 'Don't look back, Sergeant, but I think we're being followed.'

'That we are, Flynn, my boy, that we are. Yon fella's been dicking us for the last five minutes at least,' McLain replied, as he strolled casually along with his hands clasped behind his back, as if all was well.

Sensing that there were others skulking nearby, Flynn carefully slid his hand into his coat pocket, feeling for the handle of his pistol, slipping it into his palm before easing back the hammer in the muffled depths of his overcoat pocket. He fought back the urge to run and as they reached the barracks' gate, a shadowy figure slipped into the light, its face hidden by a cap pulled low and his hands thrust deep into trenchcoat pockets.

They stopped and, hooking his thumbs behind his lapels, McLain studied the stranger with a detached air of professional curiosity, whilst Flynn gently slid back his left foot so that he stood at a slight angle to the stranger, making a narrower target. His pulse raced, his hangover completely gone. Like an echo from his past, the queasiness in his gut told him what was coming. Instinct kicked in and a quick glance down the street confirmed that at least three others were making their way up out of the shadows behind them.

'Evening, gentlemen, a terrible night for it.' The stranger spoke softly in a calm Longford accent, dark eyes glinting in the moonlight. 'If you would be so kind, please put your hands in the air, both of you. You are now prisoners of the Irish Republican Army. Now, Sergeant, tell the others inside to come out with their hands up and no harm will come to any of you....'

Maguire slowly extracted his right hand from his pocket, betraying no urgency. After all, his rats were well and truly trapped. Flynn tugged at his own revolver, catching the hammer on his pocket and accidentally discharging it into the ground at Maguire's feet. Maguire skipped, snatching off an unaimed shot in the direction of the policemen. There was a soprano yelp of terror. Maguire stood rooted to the spot, staring in horror at the rapidly deflating football in the hands of a trembling, dumbfounded boy. 'Ma!' the boy screamed, wailing into the night.

Flynn shouted as he shoved McLain towards the barracks, cursing his sloppy weapons handling. He snapped off another two shots before a fusillade rippled from the dark in reply, kicking up dirt around his feet, spurring him on. Somewhere, a window shattered and a dog joined in the cacophony as McLain crashed into the barracks' door, bowling O'Neill backwards, followed by Flynn who banged off his last two rounds into the dark. 'Get that bloody door shut!' McLain barked, as he slumped against the main desk.

His backside was numb; his pants felt sodden and for an awful moment McLain thought that he had wet himself. In fact, he almost felt relieved when he heard O'Neill shout, 'Sarge, you've been shot in the arse!'

'Never mind that!' McLain winced through gritted teeth. 'Get the bloody door shut!' There was a flurry of footsteps on the stair and O'Leary, all dishevelled blond hair and bleary eyed, stumbled down, buttoning his tunic.

'Get the shutters closed as well!' snapped McLain as another window shattered. A bullet thudded into the front door. 'It's the bloody Shinners, they're attacking the barracks!' O'Leary blanched, the blood visibly draining from his face. 'Mary!' McLain bellowed towards the door to his private quarters and, moments later, a frightened middle-aged brunette, her hair shot with slivers of grey, poked her head out. McLain's backside was beginning to sting like hell and he did his best to hide the fact from his wife, as warm blood trickled down the backs of his legs.

'Get yourself and the children into the cellar and stay there till I tell you to come out.' She opened her mouth to speak but hesitated as another bullet thwacked noisily into the front door, splintering the weathered wood. 'Do it, do it now!' McLain barked, and his wife nodded before disappearing. He could hear her herding their children into the cellar followed by the thunk of its heavy door banging shut.

'Jim, quick, make sure the back door is locked!' Flynn shouted. O'Leary just made it, slamming the door and bolting it against a flurry of muffled kicks and curses. It shuddered from the impact of several bullets and then the back yard fell quiet. More glass shattered and lead smacked into woodwork and pinged off stone as O'Neill raced around the barracks, slamming closed the heavy wooden shutters on the ground floor.

Flynn frantically searched for the armoury keys, his sweat-soaked body beginning to react to the surge of adrenalin and fear that coursed through him. He had hoped that he would never feel like this again in his life. He forced himself to control his breathing and, hands shaking, he unlocked the heavy chain that secured the station's four carbines to their rack.

'Come on, you bastard! Come on!' he cursed. Dropping the padlock, he yanked four carbines off their rack and swung them onto his shoulder, tearing the button from his left epaulet. It pinged across the slate floor as he hefted a box of .303-ball ammunition. The handle felt as familiar and as uncomfortable as ever in his hand.

He momentarily toyed with the idea of taking the box of grenades, but decided against it; the less opportunity he gave the others to blow themselves up the better. It was bad enough that they had to deal with the IRA without giving explosives to men who were barely competent with firearms. He'd leave the bayonets as well. If it got that close then something really had gone seriously wrong!

'Sergeant! O'Neill! O'Leary!' Flynn shouted as he tossed each man a carbine. They had received rudimentary firearms training at the RIC depot, but only Flynn and O'Neill had ever had to use them in anger. Weapon-handling drills and firing on the ranges were one thing, but using them for real, well, that was another entirely. 'Gary, with me!' Flynn shouted, loading his police carbine, a cut-down version of an army .303 rifle, and bounded towards the stair with O'Neill in hot pursuit.

'Eejits with guns! Dublin my arse!' McLain muttered bitterly, as he hobbled stiff-legged towards the front door to take a peek out of the hatch. Behind him, O'Leary did his best to bite back on his smile at the irony of the sergeant's comment but the tea towel stuffed down the back of McLain's trousers and his wincing gait weren't helping.

'Keep back from the windows and if you see anyone give them a swift couple of rounds. Remember to move after you've fired or they'll get you – you know the form,' Flynn shouted at O'Neill, who simply nodded and disappeared into the back bedroom.

Flynn burst into the spartan dormitory. Their kit boxes were stacked against the wall and behind him, a dartboard, obscured by a tatty poster, banged against the door as it swung shut, a cluster of darts skewering a wanted poster for the notorious gunman Dan Breen. McLain had noticed the poster was missing but did not know that the others used it for darts practise. It was Breen who had killed McLain's friends at Soloheadbeg and, consequently, had a bounty of £1,000 on his head. It was a princely sum by any standards but the problem was that anyone giving information on such a prominent IRA man was unlikely to live long enough to enjoy it.

Flynn eased himself next to the window, ducking back, as a stray round shattered the glass, flooding the room with bitter night air. Logic dictated that there had to be at least twelve gunmen out there but then the IRA rarely seemed to comply with the basic tenets of the military art and Flynn didn't know whether to admire or pity the man who was standing pathetically in the middle of the street, imploring them to surrender.

Watching Maguire wave his arms, Flynn took aim. 'Ah, got you,' he muttered as he steadied his breathing and gently squeezed the trigger. Instinctively, Flynn palmed the bolt, re-cocking his rifle and raising it back to his shoulder, but a round brushed past his face and ploughed into the ceiling, dusting him with plaster. Two more shots crashed into the room and Flynn hit the deck.

'You two up there, what's going on?' McLain shouted up the stairs.

'Not sure, Sarge, it's all gone quiet. There's no movement out back!' Flynn heard O'Neill reply as another shot crashed through the window.

'They're still out front!' Flynn shouted. He felt light-headed as blood pulsed through his ears like waves crashing on a distant shore and he lost all sense of time. A loud bang and a whoosh invaded his thoughts and a red distress flare hung momentarily in the air before drifting gently downwards under its parachute. McLain was summoning help but God knows how long it would take to arrive.

The flare sucked Flynn back to the squalid trenches and even the tea and bacon sandwich that Mary McLain brought him in the early hours did little to distract him from their awful predicament. He could feel the presence of death. It felt like someone had stuffed an egg whisk into his gut and turned it.

Maguire knew that he stood out like a turd on a billiard table, haranguing the policemen to give up whilst his men plugged away in impotent frustration at the barracks. Lights were beginning to go on all down the street as the gun battle shattered the tranquillity of the night. 'Did you shoot at my son, you bloody eejit?' Maguire looked up in disbelief at the woman who hung from a nearby doorway, shouting at him.

'For Christ's sake, woman, this is army business! Away with you now!' he snapped. It was bad enough that the entire attack was turning into a monumental cock-up, without having an audience as well. Cursing, the woman slammed her door. 'All of you, get back!' Maguire shouted at the other villagers who had come out to watch and he could see MacEoin and Fitzgerald cajoling them inside as they came down the street.

'Well, this could have gone better,' Maguire muttered and as he turned back towards the barracks he felt a heavy weight smash into his hand, hurling him to the ground. His arm was numb, as if it had been hit with a sledgehammer, and he couldn't feel his fingers. He heard the crump of boots next to his head as he lay paralyzed on the damp, wet ground and felt hands tug at his shoulders.

'Joe, are you all right?' a voice pleaded desperately by his ear and, close by, a rifle barked from the shadows, deafening him as the muzzle-flash blinded him.

'It's my flaming arm!' was all he could say as someone dragged him back into the safety of the shadows. The numbness was receding now. Pain! Violent ripples of searing pain shot up his arm straight into his brain and, whilst he couldn't see his hand, he could feel warm sticky liquid running down it. The air tasted coppery with the tang of blood.

'Me gun!' Maguire hissed. 'I've dropped me bloody gun.'

'Leave it!' MacEoin shouted, heaving Maguire to his feet and shoving him towards a waiting volunteer. 'Get him out of here!' Maguire felt himself stumbling, half running, half dragged across the damp, dark field to safety. MacEoin ordered Fitzgerald to keep the policemen's heads down and cover their retreat before dashing off after the others.

Alone in the dark, time dragged for Fitzgerald and he was just about to give up his lonely vigil when he noticed something moving through one of the upstairs windows. 'One for the road, eh?' he muttered as he took aim at the shape and, smiling, squeezed the trigger before slipping away, without a backward glance.

Flynn allowed himself a flicker of hope as the first weak tendrils of dawn began to grope into Drumlish. If any of the IRA were still there the light would strip them of their cover. He steadied his nerves and squeezing his carbine until his knuckles blanched he poked his head cautiously out of the window. Nothing happened; the street was empty and even the drizzle had gone. His eyes were drawn to a dark stain in the road and what looked like a revolver.

'Here goes nothing,' he muttered and stood up. On the landing he checked on O'Neill who was slouched in an armchair, cradling his rifle, relaxed but alert, every inch the combat veteran. 'Any sign, Gary?' Flynn asked.

O'Neill shook his head. 'I think they've done a bunk, Kevin ...' He smacked his lips thoughtfully 'You know, I could murder a brew and some scoff,' he said, with studied nonchalance. 'First things first, though. I need a flaming leak!'

Flynn forced a smile and went back onto the landing, battling to control the tremors that were building, threatening to seize control of his hands. He always got the shakes after a fight and to be honest he hadn't met many who didn't. O'Neill was probably sitting on the bog shaking like a jelly too but at least it was in private.

Climbing down the stairs, Flynn noticed dusty shafts of light latticing the gloom of the duty room. McLain slouched against the desk, his rifle across its top, keeping his weight off his backside whilst O'Leary slumped by the stove, his blond hair tangled and his face pale with shock. Both men were pallid, unshaven, dishevelled and visibly knackered. McLain looked up with red-rimmed eyes at Flynn, who frankly looked as bad as he felt. 'And?' he asked expectantly, his usually round face pinched and drawn with stress.

'Gone,' was all that Flynn could manage. It sounded inadequate somehow.

This was the first time for McLain and he fought to control his bladder. At fifty-five he was far too old to be playing cowboys and Indians and too close to retirement to get shot. 'Does it always feel like this?' McLain asked tonelessly. 'Do you ever get used to it?'

'No,' Flynn said as he eased open the barracks' door and stepped into the street, nerves jangling, anticipating a bullet. His boots crunched on broken glass as he slowly walked over to the bloody oil-smeared pistol lying on the damp ground. Cautiously, he scanned the area, looking for any signs of life as, all along Main Street, heads poked out of windows and doors and in the distance he could see Father John Keville walking briskly towards him.

Cautiously he squatted down amongst the soiled brass cartridge cases scattered in the dirt. The front of the barracks was pock-marked, every pane of glass shattered and, cradling his rifle in the crook of his arms, he slowly dropped his eyes. 'Sergeant!' Flynn called. 'Best you come and have a look at this.'

McLain eased himself out of the front door and, doing his best to conceal his injuries, he stepped gingerly over to Flynn, wincing at every step. O'Neill was at his shoulder, rifle at the trail. 'Well, Constable Flynn, get yourself over to the post office as quick as you can and telegraph District about last night,' McLain ordered.

Flynn looked up and nodded. 'Very good, Sergeant,' Flynn replied, barely suppressing a grin as O'Neill winked at him over McLain's shoulder.

O'Neill smiled at McLain. 'Well, someone won't be thumbing his nose at the law for a while.' McLain looked puzzled and glanced back at the pistol. Next to it, in a splash of darkening dried blood, lay the remains of a thumb. O'Neill pocketed the pistol and as he picked up the severed digit in his handkerchief, he saw O'Leary, white as a sheet, tumbling out of the barracks' door.

'Sergeant!' O'Leary shouted, his voice trembling. 'They've shot Mrs McLain!'

CHAPTER 3

Greville Arms Hotel, Granard,
County Longford, Ireland

'I'M SUPPOSED TO be in command of you lot, so Christ knows what they'll be thinking in Dublin!' MacEoin growled, his mask of studied boyish charm slipping as he struck the table, making the tobacco smoke swirl and the tea cups and stout bottles rattle. He was exhausted and angry and like most senior IRA officers lacked any real training for his job. He was a blacksmith by trade, compact and muscular.

'Aah, you'll be fine, yer man Mick will see to that!' the man next to him said, referring to MacEoin's friend, Michael Collins, the real driving force behind the IRA's campaign. 'You know as well as I do that the big fella looks after his own.'

MacEoin gave the speaker, a local solicitor called Paul McGovern, an angry stare. 'Those bloody Keystone Kops have made us look like a right bunch of culchie eejits. Mick won't like that. If you ask me, someone grassed us up. How else could the attack have gone so bloody wrong?' MacEoin barely contained his anger. He resented the implication that his rank was purely on account of Collins and the others knew that despite his youthful looks he was a hardened, committed and ruthless revolutionary.

'Sod the Keystone Kops, perhaps we should have got Charlie Chaplin to lend a hand? You want to know why we messed up? Because it was an arse plan, that's why,' Maguire interjected and the four men at the table looked around at the cigarette-smoke-shrouded speaker slouched in the deep shadows of a floral-embroidered armchair, his hard, dark eyes burning dangerously like coals.

'It was you who mucked it up, Joe, not Charlie fecking Chaplin!' butted in MacEoin's right-hand man Sean Connolly. 'You shot a fecking football and a peeler in the arse! If you hadn't danced around in the street playing at Tom Mix we could have got the bastards!'

'Don't try and blame me for your cack-handed plan. It was you and Sean here,' Maguire growled angrily at MacEoin and Connolly, his face pale and dangerous, 'who dreamt up this flaming masterplan! 'Twas a bad business with the woman.' MacEoin darkened like a storm cloud, struggling to ignore Maguire's barb. 'How do I know one of yous two didn't blab about the attack? After all, people are always coming and going from your forge and there's a constabulary barracks just down the road. You could easily have been overheard!'

MacEoin snorted. 'You know damn well that none of my boys would blab to the peelers.'

Maguire brandished his bandaged hand. 'But you'd happily say that one of mine did? You know they shot me bloody thumb off! Damned near wrecked the rest of me blasted hand as well. Jesus, just look at it. I don't see any of yous getting wounded. If one of my boys was a tout I'd know about it!'

MacEoin laughed. 'Jesus, don't we all know it! I guess your thumb is now in Longford helping the peelers with their enquiries!' Maguire scowled at the weak joke; he didn't like being laughed at. MacEoin paused again and looked at Maguire. 'Well, now, I've got a few contacts in the constabulary. I think I'll have a word with some of them and find out whether they were tipped off or not.'

'How do you know you can trust your pet peelers?' McGovern asked.

'Because I can,' MacEoin replied tersely.

'I don't trust peelers,' Maguire cut in. 'They're all the same, even the ones on our side. If they can betray their own I can't see that they would hesitate to stitch us up when it suits. Once a traitor always a traitor if you ask me!'

There was a scraping noise outside the door and the men froze suddenly. Lawrence Kiernan, the young owner of the Greville Arms, stood up and walked towards the door. Connolly placed his hand on the pistol in his jacket pocket. McGovern held his breath as Kiernan stretched his hand towards the door knob. The door burst open and an attractive young woman swept into the room carrying a tray of fresh tea and sandwiches, disarming the room with a cheery smile.

'Kitty,' Kiernan said to his sister, 'you nearly scared the life out of us!'

Kitty Kiernan laughed as she looked at their startled faces. 'Will you just look at the state of you all? You look like you're plotting a revolution or something,' she teased, flashing another mischievous smile, knowing full well what they were up to. Besides, she had been listening at the door for the last few minutes.

'Kitty, darling,' said McGovern, who was married to her sister Helen, 'what is it we can do for you? You just shouldn't go sneaking up on people like that. Lord knows what could happen to you.'

She placed the tea tray on the table in the middle of the room and made a show of tidying up the dirty dishes. 'I was just wondering whether you were hungry, that's all.'

'Of course you were, Kitty,' said MacEoin, 'but this is army business and your Mick wouldn't forgive me if you got dragged into it.' Kitty Kiernan was Mick Collins' girlfriend.

'I'm sure that Mick would understand that I want to help,' she said. 'I don't want to be a glorified camp follower traipsing after the drum,' she huffed but MacEoin raised his hand.

'Please, Kitty, you do more than enough already and besides Mick really wouldn't be happy with me if anything did happen to you. Now please, we have business to attend to and it's best you know nothing about it.' Kiernan stood by the door holding the handle with barely disguised impatience, waiting for his sister to leave. 'It's for your own good,' he said quietly as she passed and he closed the door as she shot him an angry look.

Connolly sighed, looking at Sean. 'Joe may have a point. You don't think that one of your pet peelers is playing fast and loose with us and spilled the beans about our plans?'

MacEoin shook his head. 'No, I don't think so. Only one of them knew anything about it and I can trust him absolutely. No, it wouldn't be him.'

Maguire snorted angrily and shook his head. 'How do you know? What's so special about this peeler then?' he asked, leaning forward.

'Trust me,' was all that MacEoin said, dismissing his questions.

'Whatever went wrong, Sean,' Connolly continued, 'we underestimated the opposition. It's as simple as that. That pompous old duffer McLain wouldn't have put up a fight if it wasn't for that new fella. What's he called, Joe?' He looked over at Maguire. 'He's on your patch. What's his name?'

'Flynn, I think,' Maguire replied. 'Another bloody traitor. He only arrived a week or so ago and I will take great pleasure in helping him retire from his new career at the first opportunity!' The others laughed.

'Amen to that,' said MacEoin.

'Anyway,' Connolly pressed on, 'we need to do something before our friends back in GHQ decide that we are useless culchies! That is if they don't already, God help us. We assumed too much and, Christ, don't we all know what assumption is the mother of.'

'I'll sort this Flynn,' Maguire said coldly, matter-of-factly.

'You better,' MacEoin replied equally flatly.

Maguire was unimpressed. 'Ach, Sean, I really don't like the way that you lot seem to be trying to pin this on me. Especially when I was only following your orders – yours, Sean, not mine. If you'd told me to gun the bastards down, I would have done it. Didn't Jerry McNamara have a clean shot at McLain and I stopped him taking it because of your plan? If he'd taken it we may not have got their guns but one more of them would be fertilizer by now! You told me to take them all prisoner and now I've lost my flaming thumb! What have you lost, eh, a bit of face?'

'All right, all right, calm down, Joe,' MacEoin soothed. 'It's war and shit happens. We've sent a message and that is what really matters, even if it was only to shoot a peeler in the arse!' There was another ripple of laughter.

'Christ, don't I know people die in war, Sean, but it's all over the papers about the woman and it looks bad!' Maguire opined.

'Sure, Joe, 'tis regrettable but aren't the Brits and their lackeys panicking now. Every attack makes them panic even more. Every time they declare a state of emergency they piss off the people even more with their cack-handed attempts to crush the rebellion. Our job is to make sure they fail.'

'And you, Joe, must keep the pressure on in your area,' Connolly interjected. 'Now McLain's gone we need to keep the pressure on and let the peelers know no one wants them. They can either resign or we'll retire them ourselves. The suits in the Dáil have ordered us to step up the boycott of peelers and their families. No one is to have anything to do with them—'

'And if they do?' Kiernan interrupted.

'If they do, then we have a polite word with them and if that doesn't work then maybe stronger measures will be needed. Sure, the McLain woman tells them that ...' Connolly smiled knowingly 'I think that once the people see what happens to traitors then we will have few problems.'

'The message has been sent.' MacEoin looked at Maguire. 'I want that shite Flynn dealt with, understand? Have him followed and when you get a chance, cap him.'

Maguire nodded and smiled a cold, mirthless smile. 'Sure, boss, I'll get on to it. I'll do it myself if you want.'

'Whatever,' MacEoin said dismissively. 'There is something else I need you to deal with first, Joe. I've had a message from Mick that there is at least one informer in your area who needs to be dealt with.'

Maguire looked up at MacEoin in surprise. 'You don't think that this one had anything to do with last Tuesday's fiasco?'

'No, I think not,' MacEoin replied. 'But this one is just as dangerous so be careful. The Brits have stepped up their patrols and as most of their soldiers are trigger-happy teenagers, I don't want any of you taking unnecessary risks or we will all end up with our arses in gaol or worse and I'm sure none of us want that.'

'Sean, we'd best be on our way,' Connolly said as he flipped his fob watch back into his waistcoat pocket.

'If you will excuse us, gentlemen,' MacEoin said. 'Sean is right, I've a meeting in Longford and I really don't want to be late.' He looked at Kiernan. 'Thank Kitty for the tea, won't you, please – Lawrence, and Joe, keep an eye on the enemy in your area. Hold back from Flynn for the moment but I sense that one will be trouble, so keep an eye on him. Well, you have your orders. I'll let you know when we will meet again.'

He said something in Irish but neither Kiernan, McGovern nor Maguire had a clue what he had said; none of them spoke the language. To be honest, Maguire wasn't convinced that MacEoin did either.

CHAPTER 4

Drumlish, County Longford

'CHRIST, WHY DOES it have to always rain in this miserable flaming country!' cursed the sodden shape hunched into the rough collar of an ample khaki greatcoat. A moustachioed sergeant major barked from the front of the lorry, his voice harsh with natural authority. 'I suppose you'd rather be in Iraq or Afghanistan waiting for some rag-head to cut your balls off, eh, Purton?'

'It's just that even Catterick has got to be better than this shithole,' Private Purton answered sheepishly.

'For God's sake, Purton, all you do is bloody drip!' snapped the sergeant major, rolling his eyes in mock horror. He knew that soldiers always complained; it was only when they stopped that he should worry. No, in a strange way whinging was good for the young British soldier.

Purton sulkily slipped further into the depths of his worn khaki greatcoat as he was jolted into his neighbour, who grunted in protest. It was what the Irish called a soft day, damp and miserable with a gentle breeze coming down into Drumlish off Cairn Hill, but at least the rain had stopped, for now.

Looking around at the other soldiers, Purton sighed. When he'd heard the news of the Armistice he was in a flea-bitten dug-out somewhere near Ypres and had visions of swanning around India with doe-eyed houris sipping chota pegs and watching the cricket from some sun-drenched veranda, not freezing his bollocks off in Ireland. If only he'd known then what he knew now, he wouldn't have signed on as a regular!

As ever it was cold, it was wet and it was well past lunchtime and Purton had long lost all interest in Ireland's troubles as he fantasized about bully beef and chips. He was getting sick and tired of trundling around Ireland in a clapped-out old lorry waiting to be ambushed and he sometimes thought that it was a sad testimony to his lot that even cook-house fare had become the stuff that dreams were made of. So far he couldn't work out why the hell anyone would fight over Ireland; the Fenians were welcome to it. 'Where the hell are we?' Purton asked and the sergeant major looked around once more.

'This wonderful example of the Irish rural idyll nestled in the heart of our sovereign king-emperor's demesne is called Drumlish, Purton. Now be quiet, there's a good lad, before I have you on a charge!'

A pedestrian shouted angrily as the lorry bounced through a pot-hole, splashing him with muddy water, and Flynn touched the peak of his cap as the convoy passed. The lead truck skidded to a halt and the sergeant major leant out of the cab. He glanced at the medal ribbons on Flynn's tunic and asked the way to Cartrongolan.

'Just down this road and turn left at the crossroads. You can't miss it, sir,' Flynn said, bracing up slightly as he spoke to the warrant officer. Sergeant majors were demi-gods in any British army unit and he knew that this man had not only earned but truly deserved respect. Officers were all well and good but it was men like him who were the real glue that held any unit together, the backbone of the army.

Flynn didn't miss the army; he missed some of his mates but he didn't miss the bullshit and bluster. He didn't think of himself as a proper soldier, anyway, not like the sergeant major who'd oozed regular army. Besides, peacetime soldiering was nothing like war service anyway. He wasn't really sure where he belonged anymore.

He saw a tall sandy-haired stranger hawk into the gutter as the convoy passed and resolved to ask O'Neill if he knew him. McLain would have known but the sergeant was long gone and his replacement, Sergeant Willson, was still settling in.

'Well, now, Constable Flynn, don't you look like you were wishing to be in them trucks with the soldiers.' Surprised, he spun around to face the speaker, pulse racing, subconsciously preparing for trouble. The space was empty and, confused, he dropped his gaze slightly and looked straight into a pair of clear, green eyes, sparkling with amusement.

The young woman's head was cocked to one side as she laughed, flashing him another warm, bright smile as she studied him. Flynn prided himself on his ability to think clearly, but he was lost for words, his thoughts in tatters, a strange feeling welling up in the pit of his stomach as well as elsewhere. It was a sensation he hadn't felt in quite a long time. He wasn't good with women but her smile and gentle curves captivated him.

She casually pushed a damp stray lock of unruly wavy red hair away from her eyes. They were clear and bright, full of laughter, and they held his eyes as he drank in the contours of her face, studying every detail. Yes, it was a pretty face, he decided. He chewed the inside of his lower lip and narrowed his eyes, his brain racing to put a name to the alluring face.

'I'm … I'm sorry, miss, I was miles away. What was that you said?' he stammered pathetically. His right eye twitched and she giggled gleefully at his lack of composure.

'I said, Constable Flynn – it is Constable Flynn, isn't it?' she said without waiting for a reply. 'You looked like you were after going with them soldiers rather than staying with us here.' She smiled mischievously. 'I was just doing the messages for my ma when I noticed you. They say you were a soldier yourself once. In the war, was it? My oul'fella said you won a medal, for bravery, so they say.'

'Do they now?' he managed to reply. That was villages for you – everyone knew everyone else and everyone was related to everyone else – unlike Dublin where no one gave a damn about anyone, but that was cities for you too. She touched her hair again, gathering in her shawl against the chill, smiling.

She was shorter than him by a head, five-four at a guess, about twenty or so and she looked familiar, but then everyone in the village looked familiar. Right now he really wished that he had paid more attention to McLain's many attempts to impart his extensive local knowledge before he left. McLain seemed to know everyone and everyone knew him. That was sergeants for you but McLain was long gone.

'Excuse me, miss, but have we met?' He instantly regretted his absurdly brusque tone. 'I'm sorry, but I don't think we've met. I'm sure I'd remember if we had …' He hesitated again, realizing how that sounded as well. 'Er … met.'

'Call me Kathleen, Constable, Kathleen Moore. It's my oul'fella's store up on St Patrick's Street, and you'll be Constable Flynn from Dublin.' Her eyes sparked playfully. 'There now, we've been introduced.'

'Miss Moore,' he replied, touching his cap slightly theatrically. 'I am Constable Flynn, and if I may say so, Miss Moore, you seem to know quite a bit about me.' He smiled; it felt strange.

'Do you not have a first name then, Constable Flynn?' she persisted.

'Kevin. My name is Kevin, Miss Moore,' he stuttered.

'And you were in the war then, Constable Flynn?' She went on, nodding at his ribbons. He paused momentarily, suddenly conscious of the scar on his face. 'My big brother Davey, he was in the army, too. Done for at Gallipoli he was,' she stated, quite matter-of-factly, almost as if she was talking about someone else's brother rather than her own. 'Missing presumed killed they said.'

'I'm sorry to hear that, Miss Flynn. I wasn't at Gallipoli; I did my time on the Western Front, me and thousands of others. I was in my local mob, the Dublin Fusiliers. It seemed like a good idea at the time.' He suddenly felt stupid for making that throwaway comment. 'Yes, I was in the war, Miss Moore, like many others ... Look, miss, it's been a pleasure meeting you but I really must be on my way.' He glanced at his wristwatch, growing uncomfortable with the direction of the conversation. 'Sergeant Willson will be waiting on me and I'm late.' He paused. 'Another time, perhaps?'

Kathleen looked up at Flynn and smiled as he touched his cap again, in another mock salute before stepping off with a forced air of faux purpose. Behind him he heard her voice softly chase after him. 'I look forward to it, Constable.' He risked a glance behind and caught sight of her waving before he turned away, unsure of exactly what it was she was looking forward to.

Fitzgerald watched the pretty red-haired girl chatting with the policeman and was disgusted by the way that she was so blatantly flirting with the enemy. 'I can see that I will have to have a wee chat with you about your choice of friends!' Fitzgerald muttered, before disappearing into a nearby bar.

Kathleen was rather pleased with herself for finally managing to speak to the handsome young policeman and there was a slight skip in her step as she strolled along, thinking about him. She didn't notice the two men emerging from the pub following her with their caps pulled low, heads down stiff with malice. She still didn't notice them following her down the back lane behind her father's house either. In fact, she was so caught up in her thoughts that the first time she noticed them was when she felt a hand seize her arm and spin her round.

'Quiet now, you treacherous bitch, if you've any sense left!' Fitzgerald hissed. 'You better be after taking more care over who you talk to, d'ye hear,' he added softly. 'People might be getting the wrong impression, you chatting to a peeler an' all. Shame on you for fraternizing with the enemy.'

'Away with you now,' she retorted, pushing Fitzgerald, oblivious of her danger. 'And you, Mick Early,' she added to the man's companion.

Early leant forward. 'It'd be such a shame should anything happen …' He left the threat hanging unsaid and suddenly she realized how alone she was. She was afraid; the alleyway was deserted. Fitzgerald drew close. His teeth were stained and crooked and she could smell the cheap tobacco on his breath. 'Stay away, if you know what's good for you.' And then with a violent shove they were gone.

She felt a surge of cold, naked fear creep up her spine like some malevolent spider and, trembling, her legs gave way as sweat exploded from her pores and tears welled in her eyes. The back gate latch scraped, making her jump.

'Kathy?' She heard an anxious voice from the back yard. 'Kathy?' Her mother emerged from the back gate. 'There you are. And who was that with you? I thought I heard voices. What are you doing down there?'

Kathleen quickly wiped her eyes with her hand and stood up. 'No one, Ma, just me. I slipped,' she lied.

For a fleeting moment Flynn wondered if the girl's interest was a honey trap; after all, why would a pretty girl be interested in him? He'd been warned about honey traps whilst in training but somehow it didn't ring true. She didn't seem like a Shinner, but then that could be wishful thinking. He made a note to himself to find out whether the Moores were 'traced players' or not.

He was suddenly very conscious of the scar on his face and he traced its length with his fingers as he walked. Sometimes, the war seemed a lifetime away, as if it had happened to someone else. At times he wished that it had but it hadn't and in the dark of the night it all came back to him in its vivid, lurid glory: the sights, the sounds, the smells.

He hated being alone in the dark, alone with his memories, but that's what whiskey was for. He had survived but, whether he liked it or not, part of him was still there, trapped in the trenches, and it dawned on him that maybe the girl's brother's death had trapped her there too. Perhaps he was the only person she had met who could give her a glimpse at the world her brother had inhabited. Maybe she thought that he could help her come to terms with what had happened. Perhaps they had that in common. Then again, was it possible she just fancied him, he wondered, and as his thoughts drifted he noticed a tatty piece of paper fluttering against a telegraph pole, touting for attention. Distracted, he didn't notice the two men following him.

He didn't notice when they ducked into a doorway, suddenly intently interested in something or other in the window, when he stopped to read the poster. 'Spies and traitors beware!' it boldly declared in the large black 'Gaelic' script that the nationalists so loved. 'Fraternizing with English soldiers and the traitors of the Royal Irish Constabulary is punishable by death! By order of the Irish Republican Army.' Flynn thought that it was ironic that it was written in English despite the rebels' enthusiasm for Gaelic. Hardly anyone spoke it anymore and it wasn't for nothing that people jokingly called it 'Gaolic' because most rebels learnt to speak it.

He tore the poster down and stuffed the paper roughly into his jacket pocket. This was the fifth such poster he had found in the village in so many days and he half expected to find another one tomorrow. Someone in the village was putting them up and Flynn was curious to know who. 'Constable Flynn! There you are!' Sergeant Willson, McLain's replacement, called as he bowled along purposefully, accompanied by O'Leary.

'Me and Constable O'Leary here were off to old Tom Muldoon's farm but something has just cropped up, so I'm needed here.' Willson shoved a bike at Flynn and smiled smugly. Willson was maybe ten years younger than McLain and none of them knew much about him, except that he was old school like McLain and exuded the same calm, quiet confidence – but it was too soon for Flynn to tell whether it was a front or not.

'I want you to have a wee chat with old Tom Muldoon. I'm told that since his missus died he's been a wee bit too fond of the drink, so he has, but I have it that he's a good man and his heart's in the right place, if you get my meaning,' Willson said quietly. 'Truth be known, O'Leary here is a wee bit worried about the old fella. Says he was blathering on about something he needed to tell Sergeant McLain, but he wouldn't say what to O'Leary here. Something important he said. Have a word with him and if he won't make any sense then bring him in to see me, understand?' Flynn nodded. 'Oh, and tell the old fella that if he's let his cattle go wandering on the king's highways again, I'll be having him up before the magistrate!'

'I'll tell him,' Flynn replied. 'Oh, and Sergeant, before I forget, I found this on yon telegraph pole.' He showed Willson the IRA flyer. 'Another one of those bloody IRA warnings.'

Willson looked at it and sniffed distastefully, a look of melancholy disappointment in his eyes. 'Jeez, when will the flaming Shinners give it a rest,' he replied, shaking his head slowly.

'So, what will we do about it, Sergeant?' Flynn asked.

'Well, Constable Flynn, my boy, I guess that O'Neill and I will be having a wee one-to-one with that young Mick Early fella.' Flynn furrowed his brow, unsure what Willson meant. Willson gave Flynn a wry grin. 'Sergeant McLain was kind enough to point out the local troublemakers for me and Early's the little Fenian gobshite who's been putting the things up.'

'How on earth do you know it's him, Sergeant?' asked Flynn.

'Because I watch him do it,' laughed Willson. 'The wee eejit is too thick to realize that I can see him from the barracks' window! That's him up there in the doorway with that other fella pretending not to follow you.' Flynn blanched. 'Don't worry yourself – he's a useless beggar and I think me and O'Neill will be having that wee chat now,' he said chirpily.

Fitzgerald looked around just in time to see Willson striding up the road towards him and he grabbed Mick Early by the lapel. 'Let's get out of here,' he said as they raced off up the street.

CHAPTER 5

The Muldoon farm near Drumlish, County Longford

'JOE, LOOK! PEELERS!' Paddy Doyle pointed towards the road.

'Will you calm down!' Maguire snapped. He knew that he shouldn't be so short with Doyle but his inexperience irritated him as did the youth of most of his troops. Doyle's open features were flushed with fear and excitement as his knuckles whitened on the stock of his old Howth Mauser.

'Some bastard has grassed us up!' Doyle shrieked.

'I don't think so. If they was onto us there'd be a damn sight more than two of them,' Maguire replied, licking his lips, watching the two policemen pedalling casually towards the farm, before looking around at the three gunmen standing behind him and flashing a grim, humourless smile. 'If you ask me I think yon peelers may well come to regret their wee trip in the country!' His companions brayed, trying to mask their fears, putting on a front.

'Paddy, you stay up here with me,' Maguire ordered Doyle, before turning to the others, two brothers with a long track record of fighting, and killing, for Ireland. 'Jerry, Mick, get down to the lane there and find a good position for a shot. We'll cover you from up here.' As the McNamara brothers loped off down the hill, Maguire called after them. 'Oh, and boys, don't do nothing until I say, understand?'

He glanced at his watch. It was just gone one o'clock and gossamer wisps of cloud scudded across the skies, banishing the last vestiges of the morning's drizzle as he caressed the familiar butt of the revolver nestling in his coat pocket. 'Right, Paddy.' Maguire watched the policemen get closer, their rifle-green uniforms looking almost black in the feeble sunlight. 'Stick with me and do what I say and you'll be all right!' he said, patting Doyle reassuringly on the shoulder before heading towards one of the outbuildings. Relieved, he noticed that neither policeman had a carbine and reasoned that he held the advantage.

Stray cattle blocked the policemen's path and a large brown heifer stared at them with huge, rheumy, dark eyes. 'You'll be at home with all these cows then, Jim!' Flynn shouted, as O'Leary slammed on his brakes.

'Away with you, city boy,' O'Leary called as he leapt with a practised flourish from his bicycle straight into a fresh, green, steaming cowpat. 'Shit!' O'Leary muttered half to himself.

'You don't say, Jim! You'd best be careful where you step there!' Flynn chuckled as he quickly scanned the ground, stepping gingerly from his bike, doing his best to avoid the steaming cowpats littering the ground like squidgy landmines. 'Christ, what a flaming dump!' he sighed, looking up at the rambling, moss-strewn dry-stone walls and the unkempt pastures before him.

'Will you stop whinging, you miserable jackeen, and get yourself up to the farmhouse. Go find old Tom and I'll get these bloody cows off the road,' O'Leary called as he scraped the clinging muck from his boot.

'All right, you culchie git, I'll fetch the old bugger,' Flynn replied, propping his bike against the shabby wall and looking up at the dilapidated grey-stone, slate-roofed buildings ahead. As he struggled through the muck, Flynn glanced back at O'Leary's lamentable attempts to herd the cattle into a nearby field and laughed, shaking his head. O'Leary may have been a country boy once but he'd definitely lost his touch with cattle, if indeed he ever had one.

Ahead a dog barked. The track was ankle-deep cloying mud that splashed up the legs of his trousers as he squelched up it. The sensation of cold slime seeping into his boots, oozing into his socks, felt vaguely familiar, and in the back of his mind it reminded Flynn of trudging up to the front but that seemed ages ago, another life.

As Flynn neared the farm building, his nose hairs tingled from the stink of chicken droppings. The dog was still barking, a persistent bark, an attention-seeking bark, short, sharp, repetitive and anguished, and a vaguely familiar feeling grew in the pit of his stomach, churning deep inside, and in a dark, half-forgotten recess of his mind. Unthinking, he loosened the stiff leather flap of his pistol holster, exposing the wooden grip of his revolver.

The front door was ajar and squinting into the gloom Flynn gently pushed it open and carefully stepped inside. 'Hello there, Mr Muldoon!

Are you there? It's Constable Flynn! Sergeant Willson from Drumlish sent me! Mr Muldoon?'

Nothing stirred. The room was still and the barking more anguished, intense, close by. The air reeked of smouldering turf, an old chipped enamel-tin mug of tea sat on a sturdy old oak table, a tatty crucifix adorned the wall above the fire-blackened mantelpiece and a tired old chair lay upended on the ochre-tiled floor. He gently patted the mug with the back of his fingers. It was stone cold.

His gun rasped on his holster. 'Mr Muldoon?' The silence made Flynn feel alone, vulnerable, afraid. The hair rose on the back of his neck. He was back in no man's land. The hammer of his pistol felt stiff under his thumb – 'Click!' Instinctively his tread became cautious, on the balls of his feet, alert – ready.

Maguire watched the young policeman step from the house and into the farm's back yard. Heart racing, he rolled back the hammer of his pistol with the heel of his left hand before pressing himself into the shadows. Doyle was as white as a ghost and trembling with fear and excitement. The dog's bark was grating on both men's nerves and Maguire regretted not shooting it when he had the chance.

The ancient mongrel saw Flynn first and pogoed in excitement, straining against its leash as he crossed the yard. Flynn grimaced as his boot skidded in a fresh dog turd. The stench of the decrepit outhouse reinforced the pervading air of atrophy. 'Easy, old fella,' Flynn said, trying to calm the animal, ruffling its matted pelt. 'Where's your master, eh, boy?' he asked as it lolled its tongue, its meaty breath warm and rank on his face until it quietened and wetly nuzzled his hand.

Maguire shifted his position and aimed his pistol, resting the barrel across his left forearm. Doyle blinked nervously, his mouth suddenly dry and coppery as he eased the butt of his ancient single-shot Mauser into his shoulder. Oblivious of the danger, Flynn knelt by the dog.

Something caught Flynn's eye in the shadows of the byre opposite and he stared at it intently, trying to work out what it was. It seemed strangely familiar and then he realized that it was an old brown boot, worn and caked in mud. Close by, a second lump began to take on the shape, then a pair of legs and then a lump wrapped in a soiled threadbare tweed jacket. It was a body.

Cautiously, Flynn rose and walked towards it and nudged the corpse with the toe of his boot. It was heavy; a dead weight that rocked slightly and slumped back. Its hands were bound behind its back with faded green twine. A small hole oozed in the back of its head and most of the face was gone, torn away by the exit of a heavy-calibre bullet, scattering gobbets of flesh, bone and blood on the ground. A disembodied blue eye watched Flynn from the filth. He ran his finger across the entry wound; it felt slick, still fresh. The gunshots shattered the silence and Flynn realized he had walked into a trap. 'Jim!' he shouted as he ran back towards the farmhouse and the road beyond.

Flynn tore through the cottage and off down the track, spraying mud behind him, praying that he could reach the road before his pursuers managed to shoot him. Ahead, he saw two men standing on the nearside of the wall, peering over at something on the ground in the lane. His heart sank. Where was O'Leary? He loosed off a couple of rounds and kept running. They were too far away for him to have a hope in hell of hitting them but he'd startled them and knew that he only had seconds to turn the fight around.

A bullet brushed past Flynn's face and he dove behind a twisted brown lump of rusting farm machinery by the trackside, banging off another couple of rounds. He plunged down. Another bullet ricocheted off what looked like a spoke near his head. 'Shit!' he yelped.

Maguire was as startled as Flynn by the gunshots and shifted his position into a classic duellist stance, aiming at the policeman. He squeezed the trigger – Click! Click! Click! Three misfires. 'Shit! Shit! Bloody Brit bullets!' he spat, fumbling frantically to empty the dud cartridges onto the ground and recover some fresh ammunition from his pockets whilst Doyle hopped from foot to foot trying to get a bead on Flynn's retreating form. 'Well, drop the bastard!' Maguire barked angrily.

'I would if you got out of the bloody way!' Doyle wailed, barging Maguire aside and jerking the stiff trigger of the ancient Mauser, sending his shot high and to the right. The bullet tore through the rotting lintel of the back door in a shower of splinters and Maguire saw Flynn flinch as he darted into the cottage, a reflex response to being shot at.

'Quick! After him, don't let him get away!' Maguire cried, skidding erratically on soggy manure after Flynn. Behind him, Doyle fumbled with his rifle bolt and stumbled off after Maguire. Hard as he tried, Doyle found it difficult to stay calm; it was his first real operation with the IRA and he could already feel his nerves shredding. He cursed his lack of skill with his rifle and didn't relish the thought of killing. He wasn't a killer.

He knew that Muldoon was a traitor but the sight of his brains pouring out had made him feel sick. Doyle thanked God he'd missed the kill – the McNamara brothers had executed the old man before he and Maguire had arrived at the farm – but he had been shocked at Maguire's angry outburst at their not waiting for him. Doyle knew he would never be as hard as Maguire or the others.

O'Leary felt like he had been struck by a sledgehammer. His left arm was numb and there was a shooting pain in his right leg. His nose and mouth were full of a bloody, coppery taste mixed with shit. Somewhere, far away, almost dreamlike, he heard a succession of bangs. Slowly, as his senses returned, he realized that he had been shot and agonizingly he levered himself onto his side, looking groggily around. He began to make out the shape of a blurry figure in a shabby suit and flat cap plugging away at someone. Trembling with exertion, O'Leary lifted his gun and, summoning up a final burst of effort, squeezed the stiff trigger before blacking out once more.

The shot was high and clipped the back of the man's head, throwing up a fine spray of blood and hair as it tore the cap from his head, forcing the chin down into his chest as he crumpled onto the ground with a groan. His dead hands clenched violently, snatching off a stray shot into the muck at his feet.

Maguire saw Jerry McNamara go down; he also saw the British army Crossley tenders approaching, soldiers bobbing nervously up and down, weapons ready, bayonets glistening in the embers of the day, Lewis gunners protruding from cab roofs, scanning the horizon for targets. 'Shit!' he cursed. 'It's a bloody army patrol; they must have heard the shooting.' Doyle hefted up his rifle, preparing to open fire, and Maguire quickly batted the weapon down. 'Are you stupid? The bastards'll slaughter us. Let's go,' he snapped.

'What about Jerry and Mick?' Doyle asked anxiously. 'We can't just be leaving them, can we?'

Maguire hesitated for a moment before he looked at the whey-faced youth staring at him. 'There's too many, we'll not stand a chance.' He waved in the direction of the road. 'Only a fool throws his life away, d'y'hear? We've enough martyrs already – it's soldiers we need! Unfortunately those two have just become casualties.' The lad's head jerked awkwardly as he took one last fearful look at the enemy before scuttling off after Maguire, who was already out of the cottage and into the fields beyond.

★

Flynn cursed his stupidity. From the moment he had tumbled behind the rusting machine he realized that it was a dead end – a death trap. He was stuck. He couldn't move forward or back without risking being shot. 'Bloody fool!' he cursed again as he shrank as small as possible, watching the two gunmen in the field.

O'Leary's gunshot startled him and it barely registered when the gunman nearest the wall collapsed in a welter of gore. His companion seemed unable to take it in either and looked frantically around before making a half-hearted lunge for his brother's rifle, then losing his nerve and fleeing, snapping off a few wild shots from his Browning automatic. 'Not so funny now, is it, you gutless shit,' Flynn shouted, as he levered himself up onto his knees and took aim at the fleeing gunman. Click! Nothing happened. 'Shit! Count your bloody ammo!' he cursed in frustration. It was a schoolboy error and he knew it.

He heard engines roar and several NCOs barking orders. It all seemed so familiar and placing the derelict machine between himself and Muldoon's shanty, Flynn called back over his shoulder: 'Police! Don't shoot!' A young officer poked his helmeted head over the wall and looked in askance at Flynn, who indicated that there were still enemy nearby.

'How many?' the officer shouted.

Flynn shrugged. 'Don't know, sir.' The head ducked back and he could catch snatches of a muffled conversation, quick battle orders. He recognized the gruff tones of an NCO dishing out orders and the sounds of boots, rifles and webbing on the move. His nerves were ragged as he crawled back towards the wall, trying to press himself as flat as possible, trying to become part of Mother Earth, and it felt like an eternity before he slid behind the wall's solid cover. All along the lane soldiers crouched in nervous anticipation, high on adrenalin, sweating fear. He could almost taste the excitement, taste the fear. He half expected to hear a whistle blow followed by the anguished tear of machine guns.

O'Leary lay on his back with bandages swaddling his arm and leg. He groaned as a medical orderly tied them off and Flynn scurried over to him. 'How is he?' he asked anxiously. O'Leary watched him wearily.

'I'm not flaming dead!' O'Leary muttered.

The medic looked up at Flynn and puffed out his cheeks in thought. 'He'll live,' the bemedalled lance corporal grunted and Flynn knew that his friend was in good hands. 'He's caught one in the shoulder and one above the knee. He's a lucky bugger. It could have been much worse but I think his dancing days are over!'

Flynn nodded, relieved, and looked down at his companion, patting him gently on the shoulder. 'You know, there was a time I would have jumped for joy to catch a Blighty like that.' He pointed at O'Leary's bandages. 'Hey, look on the bright side – at least you've got a good excuse to get out of dancing with the sergeant's wife next Christmas!'

O'Leary smiled weakly and beckoned Flynn to come closer. He leant forward, placing his ear close to O'Leary's mouth. 'Good job I can't dance, eh?' O'Leary coughed with a crooked smile before slumping back onto the ground.

'Constable!' someone shouted somewhere behind and Flynn spun around sharply to see the young officer strolling casually towards him. He looked very young and unconcerned with taking cover, which confirmed Flynn's building suspicion that the danger had passed. 'Well, Constable, who the devil are you?' the officer asked.

'Constable Flynn, sir, Drumlish RIC Barracks,' he replied smartly, chopping off a sharp salute. 'To be honest, sir, I wasn't expecting to see you either but I must say I'm glad I did! My colleague over there is Constable O'Leary,' Flynn continued, pointing at O'Leary.

'Well, Constable … er … Flynn.' The officer paused as he caught a glimpse of Flynn's medal ribbons. 'I'm Lieutenant Crawford, First East Yorks,' he replied, holding out his hand. Flynn shook it firmly. 'My men have just about cleared the area and it looks like any Shinners up there—' He pointed at the farm '—have scarpered. We bagged one of the little blighters though,' Crawford said with a boyish grin. 'Caught him trying to slink away. Haven't had a chance to have a little chat with him yet though. Care to join me, Flynn?' Two soldiers shoved a forlorn figure towards one of the lorries. 'Sorry about your chum, by the way,' Crawford said. 'Rotten luck, what, but Corporal Johns says he will live. That's something at least. By the looks of it we must have got here in the nick of time, old chap!'

'Just about, sir. A few minutes longer and I think me and Jim, I mean Constable O'Leary, here would be in real trouble!' he said, pointing his thumb at O'Leary. 'If you don't mind me asking, sir, why are you here? After all, you really did arrive, as you say, in the nick of time.'

Crawford carefully weighed up his response. 'We had a tip-off. Our intelligence boys said that something was going on over here and that we should gatecrash the party! So we did. Would have been here almost an hour ago if it hadn't been for these bloody country lanes. Doesn't anyone believe in road signs in this place?'

Officers and bloody maps more like, Flynn thought. 'It's funny, though, it looks like your people were on to something all the same. When we got here I found the farmer, Tom Muldoon, trussed up like a chicken and shot in one of his sheds. My sergeant said that he had something important for him but it looks like the Shinners got to him first, poor bugger. The whole bloody area is riddled with Shinners.'

A hard-faced sergeant stamped crisply to attention in front of Crawford. 'Farm's clear, sir. There's a body out back. Old fella. Some sort of execution by the look of it, sir.'

Crawford nodded, the information confirming Flynn's story. 'Thank you, Sar'nt Eastbury. Start getting the men back in and get some tea on.' The sergeant nodded, saluted and doubled off smartly – every inch the professional he undoubtedly was.

Flynn felt his hands beginning to tremble as he fumbled his revolver back into its holster and walked after Crawford towards the skewed body lying in the field. A red-faced corporal was riffling through the corpse's pockets when they arrived. 'Dead, sir,' the corporal said matter-of-factly, a statement of the obvious. 'No ID on him, sir. Sar'nt Eastbury told Purton and Buscott to guard the other body. One of the lads told me he saw two blokes legging it but he couldn't get a clear shot.'

'Thank you, Corporal Wyatt. No matter, one of the other patrols will get them.' Crawford sighed and ran his fingers through his tousled blond hair. Flynn looked down at the corpse, trying to work out if he'd seen the man before.

'Sar'nt Eastbury!' Crawford shouted.

'Sir!' Eastbury replied sharply.

'Get Purton and Buscott to bring the body down here, please!' Crawford commanded.

'Sir!' Eastbury shouted in affirmation.

Grimacing with obvious distaste, Crawford jabbed the corpse with the toe of his boot. It rocked and blood slopped from its shattered skull onto the grass. 'Know him?' Crawford asked. Flynn shook his head; he had never seen the man before in his life.

'Maybe his mucker over there can tell us,' Flynn said, sliding back into military slang.

The officer nodded. 'Let's hope so, eh?'

CHAPTER 6

The Muldoon farm near Drumlish, County Longford

MICK McNAMARA LOOKED down at his brother's shattered head and felt sick, shuddering involuntarily. His face was bruised and ached like a bad day at the dentists, his mouth was bitter, awash with blood, and cold drizzle seeped through his clothing. He felt miserable, wretched, trapped, alone ... betrayed.

Nearby a tight huddle of squaddies hunched around a reeking kerosene stove brewing up tea, leaching its heat. McNamara's eyes burned with cold, homicidal fury as he watched the officer and the grey-eyed policeman approach. A young soldier leapt up, proffering a tin mug full of orange-brown tea to the officer.

'Constable, tea? The lads have brewed up. I'm sure there's plenty, there usually is,' Crawford added nonchalantly, before gingerly sipping the scalding liquid from the metal mug. It was a chipped white enamel mug, a typical army tin mug, the sort Flynn had slurped from a thousand times before, the sort that made drinking tea some sort of macho endurance test.

The thin pressed metal almost scalded him and in the chill damp it was perversely comforting to feel the searing heat, teetering on the brink of being painful, taking his mind away from what had almost happened. What was it his army instructors had told him in training – pain was God's way of letting you know that you were still alive! It was a sensation, and all sensations were made to be enjoyed!

'So what about this one?' Crawford asked, pointing at McNamara. 'Recognize him then?'

Flynn sipped his tea and looked at him thoughtfully, his head cocked to one side. 'Nope. He looks a bit like the other bugger though. Rebellion seems to be a family affair hereabouts, sir. My sergeant would probably be able to place him.'

Crawford slid his swagger stick under McNamara's chin and shoved his bruised, swollen head up. 'Well, who are you?' McNamara pulled away and hawked a gobbet of blood onto the floor, desperately trying not to look as scared as he felt, and glared with ill-concealed contempt at Flynn. He was furious with Maguire. He felt let down, betrayed.

Images of interrogation, torture and the gallows swirled around McNamara's head as he fought to retain control. He wrapped his arms around himself, partly in an attempt to comfort and partly to keep out the rain as he watched the policeman and the British officer chatting casually as they sipped their tea. He could murder a mug of tea; his mouth felt dry and gritty. All in all, Mick McNamara was thoroughly miserable; he was having a bad day.

'Well, say something,' Crawford said quietly, his cut-glass English public-school accent grating on McNamara. McNamara spat again.

'Oi, you bloody Shinner git, answer when an officer speaks to you!' Eastbury bellowed as he slammed his fist into McNamara's head with a meaty thwack. White-hot pain shot through McNamara's skull as his knees collapsed beneath him like a puppet whose strings had been cut. An ammo boot cracked into his ribs followed by another. His ears were ringing, blood pounding. Flynn winced; his eye twitched.

'Now, now, no need for that, Sar'nt,' Crawford rebuked quietly. 'Now, pick him up, please.'

'Very good, sir.' Eastbury responded with ill-concealed disappointment and jerked McNamara back to his feet by his scalp. 'Answer the officer when he addresses you!' Eastbury snarled as he wrapped his scarred fist around the man's lapels but still McNamara said nothing.

'Refusing to speak isn't going to help you, you know, my man,' Crawford continued. 'You were caught running away from here. My men saw you throw away your gun and this constable saw you trying to shoot both his colleague and himself. Even worse, a man has been murdered here and if you cannot or will not explain why you were here, then I am afraid that you are in serious trouble....'

'I am a soldier of the Irish republic. I'm not afraid of you or your murdering thugs ...' McNamara snarled.

Crawford cut him short. 'Murdering thugs, eh? Captured under arms against the Crown and out of uniform, all the rules of war say that I can shoot you right here, right now. Rebel, traitor, soldier, common bloody criminal – it's all the same to me, old chap. If you think gunning down unarmed old men is soldiering, then you are much mistaken. You'll be lucky if you don't end up at the end of a rope. If I had my way we'd do it right now but sadly …' He left the rest unsaid. McNamara's face paled. 'Now tell me, who else was here with you and who is this fellow?' Crawford enquired, pointing his stick at the corpse at his feet and prodding it disdainfully.

McNamara tried not to betray his feelings as he stared down at his brother's corpse, its matted blood and brains seeping into the grass. He clenched his mouth shut; he hugged himself and stared defiantly at the officer. 'Very well,' said the young officer in a measured tone, shaking his head with feigned disappointment, like an adult speaking to a miscreant child. 'Sergeant, put this … er … gentleman in the wagon, if you please. We'll let the intelligence boys have a word with him when we get back to base.'

'Very good, sir,' Eastbury replied sternly and, nodding towards the two Tommies flanking the IRA man, barked, 'You heard Mr Crawford – put the prisoner in the wagon! Jump to it!'

Flynn knew that the sergeant was playing a part, doing what the lads expected, being what the lads wanted – a quintessential British NCO, just like Flynn had done when he was in the same situation. The soldiers seized McNamara roughly by the arms and ankle-tapped him all the way to the lead vehicle. Flynn knew that the soldiers would probably give their prisoner a good kicking in the back of the lorry, out of sight of the officer. Intelligence officers euphemistically called it pre-interrogation conditioning but to a layman like him it just seemed to be kicking the crap out of someone to make them shit scared of what was coming.

'Excuse me, sir? But this man belongs in police custody. He's a suspect in a murder enquiry,' Flynn said to Crawford.

The officer looked at Flynn in feigned surprise. 'I'm sorry, Constable, but he's army property for the moment. When our chaps have had a chat I'm sure that he'll be handed over,' he replied.

Who was responsible for what, and who had jurisdiction where, had become a real pig's-ear since the government had given the army emergency powers, and whilst they were supposed to help support the police, it was never that clear cut. The politicians called the IRA common criminals but they refused to let the police treat them as such. Flynn shrugged, there was nothing he could do and he knew that in this case possession was nine tenths of the law. 'You do realize, sir, that by not handing prisoners to the police you just help encourage these bastards to think that they are soldiers, not just a bunch of bloody gangsters and crooks.'

Crawford shrugged. 'Sorry, old chap, but I have my orders.' Jerry McNamara's body was rolled into a gas cape and then slung unceremoniously into the back of a truck with a thud, sprawling carelessly at his brother's feet. The officer strolled over to the lead vehicle and, glancing back, shouted, 'Come on, Flynn, we'll give you a lift back to Drumlish,' before hopping into the cab and banging the door shut. Flynn sighed; he had a feeling that an already long day was about to get longer.

CHAPTER 7

The Muldoon farm near Drumlish, County Longford

MAGUIRE LAY PRESSED into the shadows of a patch of wind-blown gorse scrub peering at the soldiers through a chipped pair of Zeiss field glasses, concealing his silhouette behind a straggling gorse bush, fully aware that he had got away just in time. It was a good position; he could see and shoot at any approach route. Only a determined hunter would find him.

Doyle sprawled in the grass nearby, wet and miserable, cradling his obsolete 1871 pattern Mauser as groundwater seeped into his jacket, soaking his shirt, trembling like a frightened cornered animal. Doyle's guts churned and he felt like he needed to defecate. He farted. Maguire groaned. Doyle had never been so afraid in his life and now he was terrified. He felt like his bladder was on the verge of giving out as well. He licked his lips in a pathetic attempt to moisten his bitter-tasting mouth and looked at Maguire. 'What do we do now, Joe?'

'Shut up!' Maguire hissed. He could see that Doyle was close to cracking.

'What's happening, Joe?' he asked, almost pleading, cursing the fact that he too didn't have a pair of binoculars to spy on the Brits. 'Joe, what's happening?'

Maguire sniffed contemptuously. 'For Christ's sake, shut up, will ye, Paddy!' He made an exaggerated show of adjusting his field glasses. Doyle glowered sulkily at him but said nothing. From his vantage point he could see the soldiers climb back onto the lorries and Jerry's body being slung onto the back of one. 'Let's hope that Mick doesn't blab,' Maguire said, almost to himself.

'He'd not do that, would he?' Doyle protested. 'He's a good fella. He'd not grass on us!'

Maguire shook his head. 'Sure, they all talk in the end, they all do. That you'll learn, so you will.'

Doyle blanched. In his inexperience he had imagined that everyone else was the hard man and that he was the weak link. It had all seemed so different when he had joined the Volunteers, the IRA, with all its fighting talk and heroic songs. Somehow the reality of war seemed squalid, shabby, utterly devoid of glory.

Without looking, Maguire heard Doyle's sharp inhalation of breath as he prepared to speak again. 'For Christ's sake, will you shut it! Right, who else knew about today's job? It's bloody obvious that either someone shot their mouth off in the pub or we've got a tout on our hands.' Doyle could see that Maguire was furious – yet another operation had gone wrong and he was desperately trying to think who could have grassed them up. Informers were the bane of the republican cause.

'Why do you think someone grassed?' Doyle asked.

Maguire shot him a glance. 'Something I heard at HQ and now I'm minded to think that there is something in it!' Doyle's pathetic blank stare reminded Maguire of a wet sheep and he could see that the boy was terrified. Doyle was trying to think how they had been compromised. He was an ordinary Volunteer and knew almost nothing of the army's plans. He'd been collected the night before, he'd had his tea and said goodbye to his parents and told them nothing about why he was going out. They had not asked, but they knew. His republicanism had come to him in his mother's milk and he knew that his parents were sound.

'Do you think that is why the peelers were here? Do you think they heard Mick shooting that informer?' Doyle asked.

'Jakers, it's not the peelers that worry me, you eejit, it's them fecking Brit soldiers. If they hadn't shown up we'd've seen to the peelers easy enough,' Maguire spluttered. 'Besides, the peelers'd never have heard the shots away in Drumlish on a wet day like this. No, they were on their way here anyway.'

'If Mick talks, what do you think he'll tell them?' Doyle was worried.

'Everything, I guess. We'd best get away from here. I need to let HQ know what has happened,' Maguire said quietly.

Suddenly, a terrible thought began to shape in Doyle's mind: maybe someone would think he'd betrayed the others, that he was a tout. Worse still, maybe someone would believe it and his short life would suddenly become shorter, ended in some dank cellar or country lane with his trousers full of excrement and a placard around his neck declaring that he had sold his country for English gold.

'Let's get out of here,' Maguire whispered, as he stuffed the binoculars into his jacket and, still on his knees and elbows, shuffled away from the edge of the shrub before rising slowly into a crouching squat. Rainwater dripping from the peak of his flat cap, he cast a quick glance around himself before rising to his feet in the dead ground.

Doyle loitered a few moments longer before following. He drew some comfort from Maguire's apparent calm but was still more afraid than he had ever been before in his life. His legs were like jelly and despite himself he couldn't help glancing behind, half expecting to see a crowd of British soldiers come charging over the horizon, all bayonets and blazing guns.

'Wait up, will you!' he called after Maguire. He regretted not bringing an overcoat as the drizzle thickened into a steady rain and more filthy water seeped into his boots, soaking his socks and chafing his feet. He just knew that his feet would be raw with blisters by the time they got to wherever Maguire was leading him. Doyle had no idea where they were going and part of him dreaded finding out. Even if he had asked, he doubted that Maguire would or could be bothered to tell him anyway and every step sucked Doyle further and further into his own little bleak, miserable world.

Every now and then the rain eased up and once or twice the sun feebly probed through the cloud, taunting Doyle as he stumbled along, his hands thrust deep into his pockets. He fell into Maguire, who staggered and gave him an angry, pregnant, sidelong glance. 'Watch how you go, you!' Maguire rebuked and then turned back towards what had made him draw up short in the first place.

Part obscured by mist, a low, rambling, shambolic grey-stone croft squatted in a shallow depression. Here and there, ancient slates had fallen from its rickety roof and a battered weather-blistered door hung precariously from dark rusty hinges. The door, like the shuttered windows, was firmly shut whilst nearby a lively, peat-brown, rain-swollen burn frothed angrily past the dismal cottage. The place looked like it had seen better days and save for the lazy wisps of grey turf-smoke struggling from its single crooked chimney, it looked deserted. 'We're here,' muttered Maguire. 'Stay there, cover me. I'll call you over when I know it's safe.'

Doyle slumped down on one knee, grimacing as muddy water instantly soaked through his damp trousers, compounding his cold, wet misery. Ignoring him, Maguire stepped off towards the cottage, cap low, hands thrust deep into his pockets, looking for all the world like a petulant child, huffily paying scant attention to any semblance of a tactical approach and making no attempt to conceal his disgust at what had transpired back at the farm.

Despondently, Doyle watched Maguire reach the front door and rap on it with his fist. After a brief pause the door opened and Maguire gave a quick, almost furtive glance around before he disappeared inside like a man entering a brothel. Doyle felt miserable. Soon the entire company, if not the entire battalion, would know that he'd been found wanting. Worse still, he had an awful feeling that Maguire thought that he was an informer to boot!

The rain thickened and without a watch Doyle couldn't tell how long he knelt against the crumbling dyke. It could have been a few minutes but it was probably longer; it seemed like an age. He was sodden, water cascading down his back when the door swung open and Maguire shouted, 'Paddy, get yourself in here, will you!' Despondently Doyle struggled to his feet and trotted towards the croft, his thoughts giving way to tea and a fag, maybe even something to eat.

Inside the croft was dark and as he pushed his way through the door it reeked of burning turf, tobacco smoke and tea. He salivated. A copper kettle steamed on an iron stove and a rough wooden table dominated the main living space. Around it sat a couple of shadowy figures. 'Fetch the lad some tea,' a strange voice stated authoritatively and moments later a chipped china mug of strong, sweet tea found its way into Doyle's cold, numb hands. The warmth was comforting and he noticed his clothes beginning to steam, adding to the gloomy fug around him.

'Sit down, Paddy,' the friendly reassuring voice continued. Doyle plonked himself down on the nearest chair and looked around. Maguire was there, sipping tea, looking thoroughly pissed off. There was another man opposite, his features barely perceptible in the shadowy room, whilst one more stood by the stove, warming his backside. Above them the rain rattled off the roof slates like dried peas in a tin.

'Paddy, this is Commandant Sean MacEoin,' Maguire said, gesturing at the shadow opposite. Overawed, Doyle gulped. The legendary blacksmith of Balinalee, the IRA's main man in the county! Flustered, Doyle plonked his mug down on the table with an audible thud. MacEoin smiled reassuringly and sat back in his chair.

'All right, Paddy, take your time. Joe here has already told me some of it but I want you to tell me what happened. You're amongst friends here, Paddy, so you tell me what you think happened.'

Doyle watched Maguire rise from his seat and leave the room. He also noticed that Maguire had taken his rifle. Doyle was alone with the two men. Suddenly he felt very frightened and very alone. His hands began to tremble. He slurped his tea nervously and began to talk.

CHAPTER 8

Drumlish, County Longford

'Y OU BEEN OUT long?' Purton asked, disturbing Flynn's strange sense of nostalgia as he sat nestled amongst the huddled Tommies. It was almost as if he had come home again after a long absence; he sort of felt like he belonged even though he knew he didn't.

'Last year. Since January 1919,' Flynn replied, without looking at the wizened old private.

'I was at Wipers, what about you?' Purton continued, valiantly trying to spark up a conversation with Flynn. He was reluctant to talk; he wasn't sure why, he just was. Maybe it was because McNamara was glaring at them with ill-concealed hatred. The less the IRA knew about him the better, Flynn thought, sensing that behind his empty dark eyes the IRA man was calculating the odds, waiting for his chance to make a break for it.

Around them, squaddies sat chatting quietly, smoking, and eventually Purton leant over and offered Flynn a cigarette. Reaching for it, Flynn glanced at the dead gunman's foot poking out from under the gas cape and couldn't help noticing that they were well-made boots. A flicker of a smile crossed his face. During the war, boots like that would have been long gone by now.

'Bloody traitor!' McNamara shrieked, unable to control himself when he saw Flynn smile. His boot lashed out and caught the policeman across the shin. 'You'll see how funny this is when I get out of here! You're a dead man, you bastard!' Clutching his shin, Flynn's eye twitched as he studied the gunman's face.

A soldier drove his rifle butt hard into the side of McNamara's head and he dropped like a stone beneath a flurry of blows. 'Leave him!' Flynn shouted, shoving the soldier back before heaving McNamara back onto the bench, his head lolling, blood gushing from his nose and mouth.

'Be a good boy, Paddy, and sit still!' Purton said to McNamara and then, realizing that Flynn was also Irish, added, 'No offence, mate.' Flynn just shook his head slowly and said nothing.

'Judas!' McNamara hissed, as he regained his senses. 'You should be ashamed to call yourself Irish, selling your country to the bloody English!'

'I warned you!' Purton snapped, raising his bony fist, but Flynn seized his forearm.

'Leave him,' Flynn said quietly, then released the soldier's arm and sat back to look at McNamara. He met his gaze and spoke quietly. 'There is only one person here who should be ashamed,' he said, 'and it's not me. So Ireland is a better place for murdering a lonely old man, eh? You'll build a better country on a pile of corpses, will you?'

The IRA man stared at him sullenly and resolved that he would kill this traitor the first chance that he got but first he needed an opportunity to make a break for it. He looked down at his brother's corpse and said a silent prayer to himself. 'I'll pay the bastards back, Jerry,' he mouthed silently, 'if it's the last thing I do. I'll make sure they all bloody pay.' The silence that followed was oppressive and Flynn felt strangely relieved when the convoy bumped into Drumlish: he was almost home.

'How on earth do you put up with a dump like this?' Purton asked Flynn.

'It's not so bad, they're good people.' Flynn glanced at McNamara. 'Saving a few bad apples and ...'

'Piss off back to Dublin, you jackeen shite,' McNamara spat, recognizing Flynn's Dublin accent.

'Oi, matey, I bloody told you once!' Purton barked, as he firmly burrowed his size ten boot into the prisoner's shin with a solid thunk. McNamara shrieked and clutched his leg in pain. 'Flaming jessie, hark at him shrieking like a girlie!' Purton laughed and the squaddies joined in.

'Well, so much for national solidarity, eh?' Flynn added as McNamara, smarting from the pain and mockery, scowled at him.

Strains of soldiers singing 'We're here because we're here because we're here because we're here' wafted from ahead as the convoy trundled down Main Street and Flynn caught a glimpse of the pretty redhead, Kathleen, strolling down the street chatting to her mother, an older version of herself. The girl looked up and smiled when she noticed Flynn in the lorry. He nodded briefly.

McNamara saw the girl wave and a cruel, mocking smile tugged at his mouth as he made a mental note to get word out about the girl with her wavy red hair. There was obviously something going on between her and the Dubliner and maybe she would provide the opportunity for him to wreak his revenge. If she was anything to do with the policeman he would make sure that she lived to regret it. McNamara noticed that the policeman was watching him.

'So tell me what gives you the right to go shooting people then?' Flynn finally asked.

'The Irish people, that's who, and the government of the Irish republic,' McNamara replied sullenly.

'Jesus,' Flynn snorted, 'the government of the Irish republic, elected by whom? If round here is anything to go by, the election was a fix. I don't remember Sinn Féin saying anything about turning the country into a bloody slaughterhouse either!' Before McNamara could reply, the lorry crunched to a halt outside the bullet-scarred RIC barracks and Flynn saw Sergeant Willson hurrying down the path. Lieutenant Crawford had already sprung out of the lead vehicle and was striding purposefully towards Willson, meeting him halfway.

'Good afternoon, sir!' Flynn heard Willson say earnestly, giving the officer a brisk salute. 'Sergeant Willson,' he added, offering his hand to the officer.

Crawford shook his hand firmly and replied, 'Lieutenant Crawford, First East Yorks.'

Flynn jumped out of the tender to join the two men who were now engrossed in a heated conversation. As he approached he overheard Crawford regaling what had transpired at Muldoon's farm. 'Constable Flynn!' Willson said, looking worried. 'How's Jim? Will he live? Mr Crawford here says he's shot up bad.'

Flynn nodded. 'Yes, but I have an awful feeling that he'll be losing his leg. His knee is broken. The medical orderly said that he'd live but I can't see him coming back.'

Willson hung his head and sighed wearily, the worries of the world suddenly on his shoulders. 'And us a man down already. Now we're two men down.'

Crawford butted in. 'If it's any consolation, Sergeant, he is in good hands. Our doc's a pretty decent fellow – he'll do his best for your chap, you'll see.'

'Old Tom was dead when we got there,' Flynn continued. 'Jim got one of them though. Mr Crawford's lads here caught another one. He's in the back of that wagon there, Sergeant. Won't say who he is. Perhaps you know him?'

Willson sniffed disdainfully at the corpse under the gas cape. 'That's Jerry McNamara,' Willson said. 'Nasty piece of work. And that's his younger brother Mick. Right pair of troublemakers they are. Well, c'mon, Mick, me boy, let's get you in the cells.' Crawford shook his head, raising his cane to block Willson's way.

'I'm sorry, Sergeant, but he belongs to the army for the time being.'

Behind them O'Neill was coming down the barracks' path and he sidled up to Flynn. 'What's all the fuss about?' the Ulsterman asked, cocking his head towards Willson and Crawford's heated discussion. Flynn could tell that O'Neill had obviously just finished bulling his boots yet again and his uniform was sharply pressed, making him look every inch the guardsman he used to be.

'The Shinners shot Jim. He's in a bad way but I think he'll live,' Flynn said. O'Neill nodded gravely. 'You know, Gary, I feel like I let him down.'

O'Neill raised his hand. 'Now don't even go there, Kevin, you know better. Christ, you and me, we've seen enough of this nonsense. There was nothing you could do about it and you know it. He just got unlucky, that's all.'

Flynn nodded, still unconvinced. He felt guilty that he had not done enough to keep O'Leary safe just like he felt guilty about all the others he thought he'd let down during the war.

Suddenly, Willson stomped past Flynn and O'Neill, cursing. He was livid. Flynn heard the tenders' engines spluttering back to life and watched Crawford climb back into the lead vehicle. He guessed that as McNamara was still sitting next to Purton in the back of the second lorry that Willson had lost the custody battle.

The IRA man stared down at Flynn. 'I'll get you, you little shite,' McNamara sneered at Flynn. Purton smacked him hard with the back of his hand. 'Shut it, Paddy!' Purton hissed before smiling down at Flynn and adding, 'No offence, mate,' once again.

Crawford waved cheerily as the convoy lurched off in the direction of Longford and, as the soldiers departed, the clouds parted once more and the sun struggled to warm the fast-fading day. Pale sunbeams danced across the puddles, reflecting off the dull brown steel shutters newly supplied by the local railway company to protect the windows and those behind them from IRA bullets. It was a funny place to call home, thought Flynn.

CHAPTER 9

Drumlish, County Longford

'LET'S GET YOU inside.' O'Neill smiled, placing a reassuring hand on Flynn's shoulder. 'You look like shit.'

'Cheers,' Flynn replied with a wry smile and the two policemen plodded back towards the noise of Willson slamming about the duty room, muttering darkly to himself about soldiers.

'Flynn!' Willson shouted. 'Get yourself in here! I need a full report and I need it now!' He flung a blank incident report form down on the duty desk. 'Right, lads,' he continued, fighting back his frustration. 'Constable O'Neill, I need you to take a statement from Constable Flynn here before I telegraph District and let them know what has happened. Tell me, boys, are all army officers like that little gobshite?'

Both old soldiers laughed as Willson stomped off to see his wife without waiting for a response. Flynn had never seen the usually stoic Willson so incandescent with rage before but then he'd never seen anyone defy the sergeant in the heart of his own little fiefdom before either. O'Neill sighed, settled in the duty chair and picked up his pen. 'He'll be fine,' he said quietly as he pulled out an incident report form. 'Let's go over what happened then.' He dipped his pen in the inkwell and sat poised to jot down notes.

Flynn looked out of the window and watched the fading light as dusk inched its way inexorably into the precincts of the town. O'Neill looked up from his scribbling and looked at Flynn. 'We'll be after closing the shutters up soon,' O'Neill said. The Ulsterman paused in thought. 'It reminds me of being back in a dug-out with these shutters.'

Flynn smiled wearily. 'It's a pretty cushy dug-out we have here, Gary, and you know it. We've bivvyed in worse. Well, I know I have.'

O'Neill laughed. 'But it's a dug-out nonetheless, Kevin, my boy.'

In the end it took O'Neill just over half an hour to take down Flynn's statement and then the Ulsterman strolled off to telegraph District HQ in Longford at the post office.

'Do you think you should be going out on your own?' Flynn had asked.

'Ach, I'll be all right, I'm from Antrim,' O'Neill had replied dismissively as he strapped on his pistol belt and headed for the door. 'Any Fenian who crosses my path will wish he'd not, Kevin, my boy,' he'd added with a reassuring smile and stepped out into the darkening street.

Wearily, Flynn climbed up the stairs and walked into the dormitory he shared with the others. He looked at O'Leary's bunk, knowing that his colleague would never be sleeping in it again. In a strange way he would miss O'Leary's sawmill snoring and constant nocturnal flatulence. It's funny what you got used to, he mused as he slid open his bedside cabinet drawer and pulled out his worn hipflask. He unscrewed the cap and took a long swig of poteen; the fiery spirit burned his throat. He took a second long gulp before closing the cap and tossing it onto his bed. 'You really are getting too old for this shit,' he said to himself as he got up and pulled an old cardboard Army suitcase from under his bed.

It felt strange to be wearing civilian clothes again and he barely recognized the face that stared back at him from the mirror as he pulled on his old beige trenchcoat and battered hat. The brim cast a deep shadow over his face, masking his eyes as he slipped his revolver into one pocket and his hipflask into the other. The stairs creaked as he picked his way down them and it struck him how disturbingly quiet his footfalls were in shoes rather than hobnail boots.

It was cold beneath the glittering stars strewn across the empty heavens and Flynn's thoughts were clouded. He needed to think, to decide what to do next. He turned up his collar against the breeze and slipped into the shadows. The gravel crunched beneath his feet, letting them take him where they would.

They took him to Cairn Hill, an ancient Bronze Age burial mount that overshadowed Drumlish, which unsurprisingly for the time of day was deserted. Flynn lost all track of time as he sat alone atop the old pile of rocks, staring into the darkness, all whispering noise and dancing shadows. The poteen sustained the illusion of warmth as he replayed the day's events over and over again. Could it have been different? It was a stupid question. What was done was done and there was nothing he could do about it but he always got scared after the event.

Darkness flowed over him as he watched the glittering lights of the village dancing below. He realized that he had never really looked at the place after sunset. It was beautiful. Since the IRA attack on the barracks it was too dangerous to go wandering about at night, especially on your own, and suddenly Flynn felt very foolish. He took another swig of poteen. He didn't like the dark, the shadows brought back too many memories, memories that he fought hard to bury; memories that only drink seemed to fend off.

He had looked into the abyss and knew that it had also gazed into him, soiling him somehow. He hated what he had become, what he had done. He had dreamt of peace and yet still it evaded him. He shivered, it felt like he was lying out in no man's land awaiting his prey and his joints seemed to ache in recollection. Everything was a mess. Yet life had somehow been simpler during the war: you were either alive or dead. It was black and white and at least you knew who the enemy was, not like now.

A soft crunch in the undergrowth startled him and Flynn leapt to his feet, yanking his revolver from his pocket, pointing it at the centre of the shape that was looming out of the shadows. Click! He cocked the weapon and snapped, 'Who's there?'

'Are you always waving your weapon at people in the dark?' a mischievous female voice quipped as the shadow stepped closer. Flynn tensed, his eye twitching as the moonlight reflected from the stranger's smile.

CHAPTER 10

Cairn Hill, Drumlish, County Longford

'HELLO, CONSTABLE FLYNN,' Kathleen said, looking up at Flynn silhouetted against the night sky. She ignored the gun. 'And how are you? I thought you might be wanting some company, so I've brought a thermos of tea,' she added with a smile.

'Evening, Miss Moore, I'm tearing away,' Flynn laughed, feeling suddenly calm as he self-consciously uncocked his gun and slipped it quietly back into his coat pocket. The girl sat down and then patted the grass.

'Come on, Constable Flynn. Sit yourself down here.'

He could smell her as he sat and she quickly poured a steaming cup full of tea. She handed it to Flynn, who accepted it without a word, their hands grazing as he took it. He held the Bakelite mug to his lips and breathed in the aroma. It was hot and sweet and he savoured its warmth before swallowing. It never ceased to amaze him how the simplest pleasures could often be the best; a dry pair of socks or a sheltered spot out of the icy wind, so unappreciated by those who had never experienced the privations of prolonged exposure to the elements.

'They're saying in the village that the IRA have shot old Tom Muldoon. Bernie Carolan told my da that he seen a dead body under a blanket,' she said with a sigh. 'So much suffering,' she added quietly and Flynn turned to look at her, drinking in the details of her face in the gloom.

'You know,' he began without knowing quite why, 'I hate guns, hate them. I had enough of them in the war.'

'But you've shot people?' she asked. 'You peelers have your guns too,' she added.

'You know, it's a terrible thing to see a man shot,' he said quietly, avoiding giving a direct answer. 'To take away everything from him: his past, present, his future. Everything he could be. You know what I'm saying, everything, a terrible thing.' He sighed. 'Jesus, of course you don't, why should you?' He sipped his tea.

'Was it bad?' Kathleen asked as she propped her chin on her knees, watching him drain the last of his tea. In the halflight she could just make out his features as he fiddled with the now-empty cup. Flynn didn't know whether she meant the war or Muldoon's farm and he struggled to find the words to answer her. They felt like lead in his mouth. Kathleen smiled quietly. 'You know they say that some men don't like to talk about the war.'

'It's not that,' he replied.

'What is it then?' she asked.

He thought for a moment. How could she understand what it is like to scrape human flesh from the welts of your boots or try to get to sleep with the cries of dying men ringing in your ears? To eat and live amongst the dead and kill without giving it a second thought. How could she understand? He shivered. How could anyone understand? Why the hell should they?

'You know when I speak to folk like O'Neill, words seem to come so easily, but …' He hesitated. She placed her hand on his thigh. It was warm. She looked up and traced the line of the scar across the side of his face. The skin tingled and self-consciously he began to draw back.

'It's all right,' she said, comforting him, caressing the line with her finger tips. 'How did you get this?' she asked.

'I walked into a door,' he said lamely but her eyes shining up at him in the moonlight told him she was unconvinced. She smiled nonetheless. 'Have you ever seen a corpse?' he asked suddenly, unsure why he asked.

He saw her cock her head to one side and then nod. 'I saw my grandma all laid out,' she whispered. 'When I was wee. She looked pale and like she was just asleep.'

'You know, sometimes we'd find men huddled together like that, like waxworks, without a scratch on them, stone dead, all the same from shock or blast or even fright. Sometimes they looked like they were asleep.' He paused to gather his thoughts. 'Yes, old Tom Muldoon is dead. Shot through the head.' He could still see the old man lying face down, trussed up and slaughtered like an animal. He'd seen plenty of dead men, too many, but somehow this felt different. It felt wrong and it sickened him deep inside.

'They shot Constable O'Leary too.' His tone was slow and measured as he spoke. 'He's lucky to be alive and I'll be amazed if he doesn't lose an arm or leg or both.' He rubbed his face with his hands. 'What sort of war is it when old men are taken out and shot in their own back yards? I'd really hoped that I would never see another shot man in my life,' he added. 'What the hell did Muldoon or Jimmy do to anyone, eh? That's what I want to know. We caught one of them too. Little Shinner gobshite stood there bold as brass giving it all that "I'm a soldier of the republic" blarney, like that made gunning down two men in cold blood all right. At least Jim managed to shoot one of the bastards.' He stopped abruptly. 'I'm sorry, Miss Moore, I really shouldn't use language like that, there really is no excuse.'

She took his hand and squeezing it gently, moving closer, it felt like ice against her skin and she was relieved when he didn't pull it away. She held it tightly in her own, warming it against her lap. 'It's all right, Constable Flynn, I've heard worse. If you don't mind me asking, why did you join the constabulary, Constable Flynn?' she asked him quietly.

'You know,' he replied, after one of those brief pauses that felt like an age, 'I'm not sure that I had anywhere else to go really. I came out of the army last year, came home, or so I thought. The problem is home isn't all it used to be. I'm a city boy, Miss Moore, a Dubliner born and bred. Dublin was in a right mess when I got home. The GPO in ruins, Sackville Street too! Christ, it was worse than I'd expected, it was like being back in France, rubble everywhere and people pretending everything was normal. But it isn't, is it? Not anymore.'

'I suppose not,' Kathleen murmured quietly, as she snuggled closer.

'I hate them for what they did to my town. It was beautiful, like an old friend – Grafton Street, College Green, Bachelor's Walk, Sackville Street, Parnell Square, the lot. The haunts of a misspent youth. The ghosts of my past hang about on every street corner.' Flynn went quiet, choking down the emotions that were unexpectedly welling up in him.

'You know, when I was a lad I played soldiers with the others on my street but I never thought I'd ever end up a soldier. Why should I? It's not what my family's menfolk do. I had a cousin join the Volunteers but we all thought it was a bit of a joke really. The Boy Scouts, full of politics and popguns and a load of pipe dreams and nonsense.'

'Our da wasn't happy when Davey joined up. Said we were respectable shopkeepers not soldiers,' she said quietly. The moonlight shone in her eyes.

'I was a shipping clerk down in the docks before the war. I used to watch the ships come and go and listen to the sailors' stories. I was fascinated by all those languages, the strange words, and I dreamt of travelling the world, going on adventures but always I knew I would come home. Home to Dublin's fair city—'

'Where the girls are so pretty,' she interrupted, stealing a line from the old ballad 'Molly Malone' and Flynn chuckled.

'You know, Miss Moore, you'd like Dublin, it's a grand city. The second in the Empire, so they say. If you're ever there, you should have tea at the Gresham.'

Kathleen sighed. 'You know, I've an aunt outside Dublin and I stayed with her once or twice, by the seaside with its fresh air and boats bobbing on the waves with their little blue flags on them. I love the sea. I used to stand on the pier and look at the beach. I never really took to the city, full of dirt and people and noise. Not like here.'

Flynn smiled. ''Tis a grand place all the same. You just haven't looked at it properly.'

Kathleen shuffled up closer still. 'Maybe you could show it me?'

'I'd like that,' he replied, suddenly feeling warm inside.

'You've a lovely smile,' she said and Flynn felt his cheeks flush. He was glad it was too dark for her to see. Kathleen shifted again. 'You know I've never really left this place.' She paused. 'And our Davey'd never been away before the war. Thought it'd be an adventure. Off to see the world, but he never came back.'

'Christ, we got an adventure all right!' Flynn said, his voice brittle with bitterness. She was close enough for him to feel her warmth, the smell of her hair. 'I joined up at the start, me and my pals. We were cocky so-and-sos but the Somme changed all that.' He paused. 'War isn't a game, it's … it's …' His voice trailed away. 'It's something I'd hoped I'd never see again, but ever since that bloody rising, it's just not been the same. Bloody hero when I left and when I got home …' He gestured around him.

'Did you ever think of staying away?' she asked him.

'Sometimes, but why should I? This is as much my country as any flaming Fenian! Why should I stay out of my own home just because I couldn't give a damn about their flaming republic! Anyway, where else would I go, where else?'

'Was coming home really that bad?' she asked.

The memory was still vivid, like yesterday. He'd been so excited by the thought of getting his old job back. His old boss Mr Byrne was a decent enough sort and had even given him five shillings when he joined up, but looked worried when he came back. 'You're a good fella,

Kevin,' Mr Byrne had said with a weary sigh, 'but things have changed since you left and there isn't a position for you here anymore.'

Things had changed! Too bloody right things had changed, Flynn thought, seething with fury as he stomped out of the shipping office. He passed a gaggle of young office boys furtively smoking on the steps and recognized one or two of them. One, a lad called John Riley, turned and spoke through a stream of smoke. 'What about you, Mr Flynn? Back from the war, is it?'

'I am that,' he replied, 'but that old bugger Byrne won't give me my job back!'

'Have you not heard?' Riley continued. 'It's the Shinners. The old fella would have you back if it were up to him, but it ain't, Mr Flynn, it truly ain't.'

Flynn stopped and turned to Riley. 'What's that?'

'It's them Shinners. They told him; told everyone hereabouts.'

'Told him what?'

'That those who went to fight for the English are traitors to Ireland and that anyone who gives them a job is a traitor too. Some fellas came by and told Mr Byrne so. I heard them talking and this one fella tells Byrne that anyone who betrays Ireland best look out.'

Now the memories were coming thick and fast. He looked at Kathleen and smiled. 'The Shinners ordered a boycott of ex-soldiers. Dublin's not like here. All those people, it's easy for them to hide in the crowd and frighten poor folks from the shadows.' If he closed his eyes he could still picture the graffiti as he ambled from the docks along Eden Quay towards the O'Connell Bridge and the town centre past the grey-stone buildings. 'Up the republic!' it declared, or 'English go home'.

Yeah, right up the effing republic, thought Flynn angrily and although he didn't care much for politics it made him angry that anyone thought of him as less than Irish just because he wasn't a republican. 'Half the lads in my mob had been home rulers before the war,' he told Kathleen, 'but the Fenians treated them like traitors just the same. Why is it that people in this bloody country think that it's all right to murder people just because they disagree with you?'

Kathleen frowned. 'My da says that if you take the gun out of politics, you may as well take politics out of Ireland.'

Flynn burst out laughing. 'He's a wise man is your da! If you ask me, I don't really care how the country's governed as long as we don't keep killing each other. Every bloody rebellion seems the same, an excuse to pick on little people, the ones who can't fight back, eejits playing the big man,' he said bitterly. 'There were men like that in the army. Give them a little power and it goes to their heads. If you don't stand up to them they walk all over you. Gutless buggers.' He stopped abruptly. 'Sorry, I shouldn't talk like this.'

'It's all right, I don't mind,' she said in a soft voice. He looked down into her eyes and his train of thought wandered again to more pleasant, less salubrious pastures. 'You were saying?' she said, squeezing his hand and laying it in her lap. 'When you came home?'

Flynn looked at the stars. 'My father tried to help but he couldn't get me a job.' He didn't want to tell her that he wasted his days hanging around street corners or drowning his woes in a glass of stout and whiskey. 'I almost went back, you know, to the army. I used to stroll down to Royal Barracks and stare at its grey-stone walls. Sometimes I thought that I'd be safe there, sort of going home.'

'So why didn't you?' she asked, as she gently stroked his hand.

'The recruiting posters make it look such fun: "Join the army and see the world." What they don't say is, go overseas and get shot at! Jesus, you can stay at home and do that these days and still get to sleep in your own bed! Why bother travelling halfway around the world to die, eh?'

'Davey liked the army; he said so in his letters. He was always writing letters was our Davey,' she said.

'What's not to like?' Flynn said. 'It feeds you, clothes you, looks after you, it even gives you friends to look out for you. It's the making of some fellas.'

'Did it make you?' she asked.

He didn't know how to answer that one. Had it been the making of him? Was that all he was, an ex-squaddie? Is that why when he'd been demobbed all he'd done was hang around with other down-on-their-luck ex-Fusiliers clinging to each other like shipwrecked sailors trying not to drown? How could she understand what they had been through, he thought, how could anyone who hadn't been there? He'd grown up in the trenches and he wondered if Kathleen would ever truly grasp the enormity of that – an adolescence of unspeakable violence.

'Sure, I missed the fellowship of it all,' he said. 'Danger, hardship, grief, it pulls people together. It's the killing I don't miss.' He went quiet. 'I'd rather hoped that I'd be coming back to a better life. You'd have thought people would have had enough of killing these last few years. Sadly, sometimes I think some people fall in love with it.'

'Did you?' she asked. He didn't reply. Somehow he couldn't. 'Why did you join the RIC?' she asked again as he sat quietly mulling over the question, unable to answer. Then, as if some invisible floodgate had been opened, the memories came thick and fast. He'd been drinking in one of the few pubs that welcomed ex-soldiers when he'd noticed a stranger moving through the crowd talking quietly, a smile here, a pat on the back there. The man sidled up to Flynn as he was finishing his fourth glass of stout. 'Can I fetch you another?' the man asked in a comradely tone and gestured at the barman for two pints without waiting for a response. 'Would you be the Kevin Flynn who won a medal at Ginchy?' the man had asked in hushed, conspiratorial tones.

Flynn plonked his empty glass down before peering at the stranger's pock-marked face with renewed curiosity, still sober enough to be a little alarmed. How did he know who he was? He suspected that someone had told him. After all, the bar was full of ex-Dubs and it wouldn't have taken long to find out who Flynn was but it still worried him. These were, after all, worrying times. 'The army could do with men like you, Sergeant Flynn,' the stranger continued, causing Flynn to laugh bitterly.

'And which army would that be? Haven't you noticed the war is over?' Flynn slurred slightly.

'Oh no, mister, the war has just begun to get the English bastards out of Ireland for good,' the stranger said, eyes shining fanatically as he warmed to his theme, 'and the army needs experienced soldiers like you, Sergeant Flynn.'

Flynn looked at him with barely disguised contempt. 'You know, I don't have a flaming clue who you are. I don't remember seeing you at Ginchy or anywhere else for that matter.' He looked around the smoky bar as the murmur of conversation dropped away amongst the ex-Fusiliers. 'You're not one of us. What do you and your bloody army know about war? This isn't a war, it's boys waving guns and playing soldiers. If you had the slightest clue what war was like, you wouldn't be so keen to fill the streets of your own country, my country with blood! Now do yourself a favour and piss off before I kick the shit out of you, you pathetic shite!

'Where were you when I needed a job, eh? You people called me a traitor when I wanted my old job back, we all were.' His words slurred as alcohol fuelled his anger and frustration welled up inside as he shoved the man towards the door. 'But good enough for your army now, am I? That's a joke. You think I'd fight for you when you people treat me … us,' he added with a wave of his arm, 'like something you've flaming trodden in?'

Flynn felt one of his comrades touch his arm. 'Leave him, Kev,' he said and turning to the man added, 'Get away whilst you can – you're not wanted here.'

The street was dark and as Flynn staggered home, his alcohol-befuddled mind didn't notice the footsteps closing on him from the shadows. Nor did he get the chance to fight as his assailants put him on the ground, raining kicks as he curled into a tight ball, his mouth full of bitter, coppery blood. Then, as he lay bruised, bleeding, throbbing with pain, a familiar voice, close to his head said, 'Kick the shite out of me, will you, soldier boy?' and then another boot in the ribs and then he was alone. When he woke up the next morning, hungover and covered in bruises, he decided to join the Royal Irish Constabulary.

In the thickening dark, Flynn turned to Kathleen. 'Why did I join the police?' He paused and smiled at her. 'I guess I don't like what has happened to my country. I fought for something better and I came home to this pile of …' his words faded. 'And besides, like I said, in the circumstances I'm not sure I had much choice. Maybe I just like the uniform!'

Abruptly he stood up. 'Well, young lady, I think it is time that you and I got back where we belong,' he said as he tugged Kathleen up onto her feet. She felt light in his hands and she could feel his strength as he pulled her up close enough for her to look straight up into his pale grey eyes reflecting in the moonlight. Flynn could feel her breath, warm, playing on his cheek, sensed her face close to his. Something stirred as he sank into her eyes. It was the closest he had stood to anyone in years without trying to kill them. On impulse, he kissed her, pushing her mouth open with his tongue.

'I'm sorry!' he spluttered, as he pulled back from her, embarrassed.

'No, it's all right. I hoped that you'd do that!' she said, smiling up at him as she cupped his face in her hands and on tiptoe kissed him back.

'Well, Kathleen, let's get you home before your da starts worrying where you are.' He sighed as they finally fell apart and he led her by the hand towards the lights in the village below.

CHAPTER 11

Drumlish, County Longford

SERGEANT WILLSON TORE open the dog-eared brown envelope that had arrived in the morning post before tugging out a sheet of crisp white constabulary-headed paper and read it quietly. 'Well, lads, it looks like Jim won't be coming back after all. They managed to save his arm but he's lost his leg below the knee. We've to send his things on. It says here that he will be heading over the water to Cardiff to stay with his sister. Any of you ever been to Cardiff?'

'What? That's in Wales! You must be bloody joking! At least he'll be getting his pension so he should be all right, eh, even in Wales?' O'Neill said from behind his desk.

'At least Wales isn't crawling with fellas waving guns all over the place. Mind you, he might get sick to death of all that close-harmony singing! Every time I came across bloody Taffs in the army they were always bloody singing!' Flynn said.

'I'd best pack his things,' O'Neill said, rising from his seat.

Flynn held up his hand. 'No, I'll do it. After all, I was with him when he copped it.' O'Neill didn't protest and Flynn wearily climbed the stairs. He knew that O'Leary had been too badly injured to resume his duties but it hadn't seemed real somehow until it was there in black and white, as if paperwork made rumour and supposition true. It was a bit like when he used to fill in casualty returns; somehow it all seemed so final written down.

'Now, I really do have to get by with just you two clowns,' he heard Willson chuntering to O'Neill. 'By Christ, they better be sending me some replacements soon.' He'd heard it a thousand times before in the army, in the police yet short handed as they always seemed to be, they always managed somehow. War was like that, he thought as he began to go through O'Leary's things.

He didn't have much and it didn't take Flynn long to pack. He folded everything neatly into O'Leary's kit box and it dawned on him that he too had very little to show for his brief time on the earth. When he had finished, he carried the laden box down to the duty room and placed it quietly in the corner to await the day when it would be sent across the water to Cardiff.

The dormitory seemed bigger somehow, the nights quieter without O'Leary's snoring and farting, especially as O'Neill was usually on duty whenever Flynn was off, and it felt strange to have the room to himself. There was a time he would have relished the prospect but now he feared being alone in the dark, alone with his dreams, and even the ones about Kathleen didn't quite keep his demons at bay.

Flynn was finishing his lunch, one of Mrs Willson's substantial stews, when the lorry arrived carrying their long-overdue reinforcements. One of the policemen who jumped out was tall and thin and in his late thirties. He nodded at Willson and it was obvious to Flynn that they were old acquaintances. The other, a dark, thick-set war veteran in his twenties, looked around, somewhat unimpressed with his new surroundings.

'Boys, this here is my old friend, Constable Mick Reidy,' Willson said, introducing the tall policeman to Flynn and O'Neill. 'He's an old hand, so it'll be good to have a real policeman around for a change, not like you two eejits, eh? That is unless the good life in Longford hasn't made you soft, eh, Mick? And you must be?' Willson said, turning to the other new arrival.

'Constable Mullan reporting for duty, Sergeant,' the new arrival declared in a heavy County Tyrone accent.

'God save us! Not another Ulsterman!' Willson said, rolling his eyes in mock horror before tossing a sly wink at O'Neill. Mullan's humourless features darkened momentarily and Flynn guessed that he was not one of those northerners blessed with the same dry wit as O'Neill.

'So not all Ulstermen have a sense of humour after all,' Flynn muttered, gently elbowing O'Neill in the ribs.

Willson scarcely gave the men's papers a glance and absent-mindedly passed them straight to O'Neill. 'You can get this sorted,' he said to O'Neill, before turning and walking back into the barracks. O'Neill shrugged and popped the folded sheaf of papers into his tunic pocket.

'Don't mind him,' Flynn said, 'he's not been the same since one of our lads was shot. It hit him really badly. I guess it's getting us all a bit down. Anyway, my name is Kevin Flynn and this here is Gary O'Neill. He thinks he's a bit of a comedian. We just play along with him. It spares his feelings. Anyway, c'mon, let's give you a hand with your kit.' The men exchanged perfunctory handshakes and then, between them, picked up the kit boxes.

'So who were you with?' Flynn asked, nodding at Mullan's ribbons.

'Ninth Skins,' he replied, meaning the ninth battalion of the Royal Inniskilling Fusiliers, part of the notoriously or famous, depending on your viewpoint, Irish Unionist 36th Ulster Division.

'Irish Guards me,' O'Neill butted in and, nodding towards Flynn, added, 'Ninth Dubs him!'

Mullan seemed comforted by O'Neill's thick Ulster brogue. 'The Micks, eh,' Mullan said, referring to the Irish Guards' nickname. 'Now there's a fine bunch of lads. Were you at the Somme?' he asked O'Neill.

'That I was and so was Kevin here. He got that Military Medal at Ginchy,' O'Neill replied softly, nodding at Flynn's medal ribbons.

'Aye, you lads done well at Ginchy, not bad for a scurrilous bunch of home rulers,' Mullan said without malice, 'but Thiepval, now that was a real ruck.' Flynn ignored the obvious dig at the politics of his old unit.

Reidy rolled his eyes. 'Will you lot give all this old soldier nonsense a rest and get this lot inside before it starts tipping down!' The others laughed and they lugged the kit boxes inside.

Now there were four constables in Drumlish life was a little easier but the barracks seemed suddenly overcrowded, especially at night, and when the steel shutters were closed up, the atmosphere became oppressive, claustrophobic even. Ominously, it reminded Flynn of being cooped up in a dug-out, awaiting an enemy bombardment.

'What did you do before the war?' Flynn asked Mullan one evening when they were out on the beat.

'Belfast docks,' he replied tersely, giving little away, and Flynn noticed that it was hard to strike up conversation with the taciturn man. The docks were a hotbed of sectarian bigotry dominated by working-class Unionists and Flynn had an uncomfortable feeling that Mullan disliked being stuck in a rural backwater full of taigs.

Unlike O'Neill, it was obvious that the unsociable Mullan was deliberately keeping himself apart from the others and, after a while, it became apparent that even his fellow Ulsterman found it hard to get on with him. One day, Flynn had been cleaning the weapons in the armoury when he overheard the two Ulstermen talking in the back yard.

'Yer know, O'Neill, I'd hoped they'd've sent me to a decent barracks, somewhere up north after Phoenix Park. Didn't I put in for Belfast but they sent me to here. Tell me, don't you miss being up north amongst decent folk, your own kind? How do you do with all these taigs hereabouts and the sergeant himself a taig too! How do you do it?'

'Listen here, Mullan,' O'Neill snapped irritably, 'I'd keep my views to myself if I were you. This isn't some Orange Lodge!' Flynn had rarely heard such venom in the usually chirpy Ulsterman's tone. 'Hereabouts they're mostly taigs, as you so bloody charmingly put it, but they're decent folk. So they're mostly Catholics, so what? They're Irish like you and me, just the same. This isn't Belfast and don't we have enough problems without some eejit stirring up any more?'

'Are you calling me an eejit, big fellah?' Mullan bristled and Flynn heard O'Neill just laugh as he walked away, then the back gate slammed and Flynn could hear Mullan muttering menacingly to himself. 'The sooner I get myself back to Belfast the better!'

'You and Mullan don't seem to have hit it off?' Flynn said to O'Neill when he saw him next.

'You should take yourself up north,' O'Neill replied. 'You'd see why I left. Belfast is full of Mullans, wee men with wee minds and big prejudices. Tell me, Kevin, why do we spend so much time hating each other when we could be building one of the finest countries in the world?'

Flynn shook his head. 'Ah, that would be politics, Gary, and you should know by now, that's not my strong point!'

O'Neill laughed and shaking his head strolled over towards the pot-bellied stove in the duty room. 'Tea?' he asked, holding up the pot.

Through the open door to the sergeant's private quarters, the two policemen could hear Willson and his wife arguing much as McLain and his wife had. 'I'm telling you, Will, it's unbearable. Half the shops won't serve me and the other half would rather I'd go away,' Joy Willson lamented.

'It's this blasted boycott, darling, and I can't help it if the Fenians've put the fear of God into folk hereabouts. I'll have a word with Father Keville after Mass and see if he can help,' Willson said earnestly, trying to placate his wife.

She rolled her eyes. 'And what good will that do? I've already spoken to the man and he just said that we're not from this parish, so he can't help it if people won't be civil to me!'

'And what am I to do, darling?' he asked her. 'Arrest them? You know that half the folk round here are only doing it because they're afraid of the Shinners.'

Even buying supplies for the barracks had become a bit of a pantomime with one of his constables 'requisitioning' supplies in the king's name and leaving the money on the counter or surreptitiously collecting them from a back door after dark. It depressed Willson that life in Drumlish was increasingly far from normal but it depressed his wife even more.

'What am I to do? Is that all you have to say for yourself? What am I to do? Do you want to end up like poor Tom Campion and leave the force in a hearse or something?' Joy Willson said bitterly, referring to the barracks sergeant over in Granard who had managed to accidentally shoot himself whilst pumping up the tyres of his bicycle.

'Ach, that was an accident and poor Tom was never any good with a gun,' Willson replied.

'And you are?' she threw back at him. Willson sighed. She was right. She knew how much he hated guns and it still amazed him that he had not managed to do himself a mischief with his own. 'You could always resign. You'd get a good pension,' Joy persisted, brandishing a tatty leaflet under his nose.

'And what do you have there?' he asked, taking the piece of paper. It was a leaflet from the 'Resigned and Dismissed Members of the Royal Irish Constabulary and Dublin Metropolitan Police Association' headed by an ex-RIC sergeant called Tom McElligott who'd been forced to resign because of his overtly republican sympathies.

'Jesus, Joy darling, I wouldn't wipe my arse with anything that bugger McElligott's had a hand in – it's just Fenian lies. If I jack this in, what do you think would happen to us, eh? The Shinners'd make sure no one gave me a job and we'd end up living on the parish. Is that what you want?'

Joy Willson looked up at him, concern written across her face. 'Well, at least you'd not be shot by the Fenians or yourself!'

Willson shook his head. 'No, darling, the country's no place for an ex-policeman. We just have to sit tight until this madness passes, like it always does, and things go back to normal.'

'Could you not transfer to another force?' she asked him.

Willson paused, momentarily in thought. 'I've been with the

constabulary these twenty-five years. Where else could we go, eh?' He had to admit a transfer had crossed his mind a few times in the last few months.

'My cousin Andy transferred to the Liverpool City Police before the war; he's a sergeant now. Perhaps I could write to him and find out who you speak to? Maybe we could go to one of the colonies even. I've seen recruiting ads in your *Police Gazette* before now. You're an experienced sergeant; sure they'd love to take you? And besides, anywhere has got to be better than here, love?' Mrs Willson pleaded.

'I'll think about it, Joy, darling,' Willson said quietly, 'but I can't promise anything.' Joy Willson looked reassured and smiled at her husband. She was terrified that one day one of the others would walk into her little home and tell her that her Will had been shot by the IRA.

As Willson entered the duty room he thought that Flynn and O'Neill looked suspiciously busy for a change, although he couldn't put his finger on what they were up to. 'So,' he said, with a sharp intake of breath, waving the leaflet at the two men, 'which one of you comedians brought this masterpiece of literature into my barracks?'

O'Neill smirked, snatching the paper from the sergeant's hand. 'That'll be me, Sarge. I saw it when I was out on my rounds the other day and besides, that's good paper, that is. Anyways,' he quipped, as he unslung his braces and headed towards the lavatory, 'I thought that I could find a use for it, Sarge, and after all it looks so absorbent!'

Willson's face broke into a broad grin. 'Well, at last you've said something sensible for a change!' The three men laughed but laughs were getting fewer as the IRA's campaign intensified, even in a sleepy backwater like County Longford.

'Have you seen the latest *Hue and Cry*, Sergeant?' Flynn asked, as he slid the police newspaper over the desk to Willson. 'Attacks are on the up. It says that over sixty of our lads have been killed since this terrible business began last year.'

Willson nodded gravely. 'I don't know what the rebels are trying to prove by it but without the constabulary this country would be a right mess.' Flynn thanked God that the worst of it was down in the south-west and that so far things had been relatively quiet since Tom Muldoon's shooting. If all they had to put up with was name calling, graffiti and people letting his bike tyres down, he thought that he could cope.

'Did you manage to visit Jim in hospital?' Willson asked.

Flynn nodded. 'He's not taken it well and who can blame him? His leg's gone and he's lost part of the use of his hand. Christ knows what he'll do when they discharge him.'

'He'll have his pension,' Willson added.

'I think he'd rather have his leg back!' Flynn retorted.

'Aye, you're probably not wrong there,' Willson said wearily. 'It's a bad business.'

'Did you hear the Shinners raided the Upper Military Barracks in Longford, the cheeky bastards?' Flynn asked.

'Aye and the police barracks at Ballymahon. Buggers got away with a handful of guns and some bullets too. Lord help us, they'll be giving them back to us soon enough!' Willson added grimly. 'Maybe the army and these auxiliary fellas will put the wind up them. They've been joy-riding round here more and more recently. You know, Flynn, this flaming country always seems to be lurching from one bloody crisis to another. I'm tired of it, so bloody tired.' Flynn could not remember seeing Willson look so old.

'What do you make of that business down in Listowel?' Flynn asked. Willson and the sergeant's face darkened.

'Bloody outrageous!' he snorted. 'What business have a couple of constables to ignore a direct order from a county inspector? That gobshite Mee was always a trouble-making weasel and Inspector O'Shea is a good man!' Willson was suddenly animated in his indignation. 'If you ask me the Shinners put Mee up to it. How else would an "eye-witness" account of his so-called mutiny appear in that Fenian rag, the *Irish Bulletin*, the next day, eh?'

'Rumour has it their divisional commissioner ordered them to shoot IRA suspects on sight,' Flynn said. 'Munster's a bad place these days, worse if the rumours are true.'

Willson snorted. 'Nonsense, just Fenian nonsense. Colonel Smyth was a good man and didn't deserve to be gunned down because of that oily git Mee's evil lies!' Willson was referring to the one-armed constabulary divisional commissioner for Munster, Lieutenant Colonel Gerald Smyth, an ex-Royal Engineer and Banbridge Ulsterman who was gunned down in the smoking room of the Cork Country Club on the strength of ex-constable Jeremiah Mee's account of the so-called 'Listowel Mutiny'.

'Well, sure, wasn't yer man a fool for going to an unguarded place like a country club in a place like Cork!' O'Neill said, as he banged through the door from the yard, making Flynn and Willson jump. 'You wouldn't get me wandering about on my own like that if I knew the Shinners were after me. Would you, Kevin?'

Willson gave O'Neill a cheeky look and Flynn reddened slightly, looking away, anxious to avoid being drawn into that conversation. 'I think I'll take a turn around the town,' Flynn said hurriedly as he buckled on his pistol belt and headed for the door.

Behind him he heard O'Neill's mocking voice call out: 'If you find yourself up on St Mary's Street say hello to Miss Moore for me, won't you now?' O'Neill and Willson both broke into raucous laughter.

'Sod off!' Flynn muttered as he banged the door behind him but they were right and Flynn knew that he would find himself on St Mary's Street and that he would probably bump into Kathleen.

Ever since that evening on Cairn Hill he had found himself thinking about her more and more and he knew that he would be disappointed if he didn't bump into her. It was a game they played in public. 'Good afternoon, Miss Moore,' he'd say and she'd reply, 'Good afternoon, Constable Flynn,' with mock formality.

'You know the Fenians won't be happy about you being seen with a peeler,' he'd said but she'd dismissed it.

'What do I care what the Fenians think?'

Everyone in the village knew that there was something going on between the two; that was the difference between Dublin and Drumlish. It was difficult to keep secrets in Drumlish, even from the police.

'Were you at Gallipoli?' Mr Moore had asked him when he first sat in the Moores' kitchen drinking a cup of tea. 'Do you know anyone who was?' he'd persisted. Flynn guessed that they were desperate to find out more of what had happened to their son.

'I'll ask around,' Flynn had said. He liked the Moores, they were honest folk, but he sometimes wondered if they approved of him being seen with their daughter. 'Do you mind?' he'd asked Mr Moore when they were alone.

'Mind what?' Dick Moore replied.

'Me walking out with your Kathleen?'

Moore had looked at him for a moment. 'Not at all. You remind me of my Davey, you know,' he said and that was the end of it. Kathleen had been fifteen when her brother disappeared and she constantly quizzed Flynn about the war. It was obvious that her brother's loss had left a big hole in her life and what made it worse was that his body had never been found, he was still missing.

'Do you know that except for going to Mass on Sundays I hardly speak to anyone else in the village, other than you and your folks,' he'd declared one afternoon as he chatted to Kathleen in her backyard.

'And do you mind that?' she'd asked, looking up at him with a smile.

'Not at all, it doesn't really bother me and it bothers me that it doesn't, if you get my drift?' Kathleen looked at him blankly. She didn't. 'Some folk are scared to be seen with the likes of me but you and your family, you've made me welcome and I like that.' He smiled.

She picked up his hand and held it on her lap. 'Then they're fools. You're a lovely man, Kevin Flynn, a lovely man,' she said, as she leant over and kissed his cheek.

No, I'm not, he'd thought. You wouldn't think that if you knew.

He was back in no man's land, the full moon bathing everything in a soulless silver light, his heart pounding in his chest. He pressed himself into the mud as stray bullets zipped low overhead. Quietly, he slipped into the trench, his boots thudding softly on the muddy fire step. The haft of the spade was hard in his hands and he tightened his grip, holding its razored blade before him as he slipped around the traverse. In the dark, a figure loomed from the shadows and he slashed at it with all his strength, feeling the shock shudder through his arms as the blade sank into flesh. It was so clear in his mind, like yesterday.

'Are you all right?' Kathleen had asked, and he realized that he had been squeezing her soft hand like a vice.

'I'm sorry,' he'd said and, making a show of glancing at his watch, he had made his excuses and left. As he rose to walk away he'd felt awkward, aware of the sweat soaking his shirt. 'I'll try and pop around tomorrow,' he'd said as he left.

A flapping paper caught Flynn's eye and he walked towards it. It was yet another rebel leaflet. He tore it from the tack that secured it and tossed it into a nearby bin before resuming his stroll. The sun was low in the sky as he walked towards the church at the end of St Mary's Street and his thoughts momentarily drifted to the book he was re-reading, *The Last Bow*, a collection of Sherlock Holmes stories he'd carried with him in the trenches.

He'd grown up on Conan Doyle and George Henty stories and reading had kept him sane amidst the insanity of war. Books were a place to hide from the horrors of everyday life. He stopped for a moment by the gates of the old cemetery and then turned on his heels to stroll back towards the barracks. Evening was drawing in and muffled voices drifted out into the street from behind drawn curtains and the usual repertoire of songs wafted from one of the pubs he passed.

Despite the troubles in the country, life went on in Drumlish. The singing faltered slightly as he poked his head into the smoky bar but picked up again when he turned to leave. Halfway down St Mary's Street, he paused.

'Good evening, Constable,' came a familiar voice from behind him. He turned.

'Good evening, Kathleen.' He smiled and took her hand.

CHAPTER 12

Balinalee, County Longford

THE MUSCLES IN Sean MacEoin's arms bulged as he sluiced cold water over his face. 'A *charaid*,' he said in Irish. 'Hot work,' he added, switching back to English and gesturing towards the two men watching him from the back of his forge. He wiped his blackened hands on an old rag. 'Best we go round the back,' he said as he led them through to a small back room where he usually took his lunch.

The room was bare with a plain wooden table and a few cupboards fixed to its walls. The windows were dusty and here and there hung the odd cobweb. A white enamelled lunch pail stood in the middle of the table and crumbs from a long-eaten sandwich lay nearby. 'Close up the shop for me will you, Paddy?' MacEoin said to Doyle and he sat down on a stool, pulling a battered leather-bound notebook from out of his back pocket.

As usual, the forge was neat and tidy, compact, orderly and organized, and each tool was in its place, close at hand and ready for use, arrayed with military precision. The forge told Doyle much about its owner, MacEoin: organized, methodical and ruthlessly efficient. It was just what he would expect from the man who was a living legend amongst the IRA and Doyle was in awe of him.

MacEoin had put the fear of God into him in the old cottage. The meeting had felt like an inquisition, which in reality it undoubtedly was, and Doyle was convinced that, despite his innocence, he was going to be blamed for the cock-up at Muldoon's farm and shot for treason. Suffice to say, it had come as a great relief to him that he had not. He'd sweated then as he did now in the stifling heat of the forge and felt like he was sealing himself into an oven when he heaved the workshop iron-bound doors shut and set up the closed sign in its grimy soot-stained window.

A couple of army trucks rumbled by, kicking up dust, and Doyle drew back into the shadows before withdrawing quietly to where

MacEoin and Connolly were poring over a tatty map. MacEoin looked up as he entered, smiled and, pushing his thick dark hair off his face, beckoned Doyle over. Doyle looked down at several scribbles near a small crossroads in the middle of a collection of houses on the Ballinamuck–Drumlish road.

'Paddy, you know this area, don't you?' It was part question, part statement, his tone amiable, a calculating glint in his eye.

Doyle nodded. 'I do,' he replied. 'I've people there.'

MacEoin nodded approvingly before turning once more to Connolly. 'Where would you think would be a good site for an ambush?' MacEoin looked up and smiled again at Doyle, a mischievous, boyish, winning smile. Doyle's open face reddened. He was flattered that MacEoin had asked his opinion but hesitant to answer through lack of real experience. After all, he was a follower not a leader.

'You done well when we hit the peelers at Ballinamuck, Paddy, my boy, and me and Sean here think you've got the makings of a decent section leader in you,' said Connolly, 'so tell us, Paddy, what would you do if it was your plan?' Doyle stared intently down at the map sprawled across the worn table. He was not very familiar with maps and like most people had no idea how to read the complex pattern of numbered and lettered grids.

MacEoin tapped the map with his index finger and Doyle leant forward, gazing intently, fascinated by the mass of small symbols scattered across the map and resolved to get someone to teach him how to read them. MacEoin's finger rested firmly next to the word 'Gaigue', a nothing of a village where the roads from Ballinamuck, Drumlish, Aghadowry and Tawnagh converged.

'Where will the enemy be coming from?' Doyle asked softly.

'Drumlish, this way,' Connolly replied as he dragged his index finger along the line of the road.

'Then if it was up to me, I'd put men here, here and here,' Doyle continued, trying to sound confident and soldierly, 'but shouldn't you be asking Commandant Maguire? It's his area after all and he's my boss.'

'Never you mind about Joe,' Connolly said reassuringly. 'Anyway, he works for me and besides he's away in Belfast on business for Sean here and won't be back in time for what we have in mind.'

'Besides,' MacEoin interrupted, 'I want to use the column for this job; you local boys can act as lookouts for us.' He looked at the locations pointed out by Doyle. 'Good, you've done well. I couldn't have chosen better myself!' MacEoin smiled at Doyle, who couldn't help smiling back as the blacksmith slapped him on the back. Doyle felt like he had passed some sort of test and was proud that MacEoin had endorsed his choice of fire positions.

'Be a good man,' MacEoin continued. 'Pop into the workshop and put the kettle on. I could murder a brew. You, Sean?' he said to Connolly, who nodded. 'All the makings are in yon box along with a tin of condensed milk.' Doyle picked up a slightly rusted tea caddy, half full of musty tea and an aging tin of Carnation evaporated milk before leaving the room. Behind him, he heard MacEoin saying, 'The big fella's told me he wants us to step up the pace in the county ...' Then his voice was muffled behind the closed door.

He dumped the tins next to the stove and picked up a tarnished copper kettle and headed out a side door to fill it at the pump in the back yard. Through the back window he could see MacEoin and Connolly talking and pointing at the map but he could not hear anything they were saying. Even when he returned to the workshop and plonked himself down next to the stove to watch the kettle boil, he could hear no more than a low murmur. He slumped in the chair, rummaging through his pockets for a battered packet of cigarettes and, with a sigh, he placed one in his mouth and lit it against the stove, then sat back to resume his vigil.

CHAPTER 13

Roath, Cardiff, South Wales

Jim O'Leary sighed wearily and flopped heavily onto the wrought-iron park bench, propping his crutches against the end with a clatter. The gentle breeze caressed his face as he raked his fingers through his unkempt blond hair and without thinking stretched his right leg out, flexing his ankle. His knee ached and sometimes he thought he could feel his other leg doing the same but that was impossible, it wasn't there, it had been incinerated months ago. He was just another amputee; the detritus of war, as far as most were concerned, whiling away the afternoon.

Stuffing his hands deep into his trouser pockets, O'Leary slumped back to watch leaden clouds scud across the slate-grey skies. It was going to rain later, he thought; he could feel it in his remaining joints. Wales was a bit like his homeland, in that respect; it was often raining and, considering he had never left Ireland before in his life, he was surprised how much he didn't miss it. In fact, he felt relieved that he didn't have to keep looking over his shoulder anymore.

No, despite his injuries life wasn't too bad really, once he'd resigned himself to his predicament. He had a generous pension from the constabulary, far better than its army equivalent, and his sister had made him welcome, finding space for him in the box room of her small red-brick terrace house off the busy Albany Road. It was just as well, really, as he didn't have anywhere else to go. Even his sister's husband, a swarthy short-tempered bucolic Welsh docker, had made him feel at home, although he suspected that that wouldn't last much longer.

McNamara quietly folded his newspaper and tucked it under his arm before walking slowly towards the one-legged man slumped on the park bench. He had waited until the park was deserted and a cruel smile played briefly on his normally sullen mouth as he caressed the handle of the small .22 calibre pistol that nestled in the depths of his jacket pocket. He felt a familiar tight ball of excitement begin to knot in the pit of his stomach as he closed in on his prey. He was going to enjoy this.

It was what he had been dreaming of during all those nights he spent in captivity, all that kept him going during the interminable beatings that laughingly masqueraded as interrogation. They'd called the wounded policeman O'Leary, and he'd held that name in his head, fantasizing about what he would do when he found him, biding his time. And when the opportunity finally presented itself, he had been surprised how easy it had been to give his captors the slip and escape. Living on the run had not been so easy, nor had getting across the water when he'd finally managed to track down where O'Leary had gone. But here at last was the murdering bastard who had shot his little brother Jerry in the back of the head.

It made no difference to McNamara that both he and his brother had already snuffed out several lives before that fateful day or that he had enjoyed putting a bullet into the brain of that snivelling traitor Muldoon. In fact, he'd rather enjoyed making the old farmer suffer for his crimes before he sent him on his way. No, what mattered was that his brother had been murdered by O'Leary and now, at last, was his chance to exact his revenge.

'Hello, Jim,' McNamara said quietly, as he stood in front of O'Leary. 'I bet you weren't expecting to see me, were you?' The County Longford accent almost took O'Leary by as much surprise as hearing a stranger use his Christian name in the middle of Roath Park and he desperately tried to place the angry-faced man who loomed ominously over him but, try as he did, he couldn't.

'Do I know you?' O'Leary spluttered.

'You should do, you bastard. You killed my brother,' McNamara hissed and O'Leary's eyes widened in fear at the muzzle of the gun that hovered in front of his face. Suddenly, he felt alone in the empty park. McNamara squeezed the trigger.

The bullet took O'Leary in the throat, shattering his larynx, although the small calibre and low velocity left him sitting on the bench as if nothing had happened. A trickle of blood ran from the entry wound and, unable to move, O'Leary began to choke, drowning in his own blood. His death would be slow and painful, just the way McNamara wanted it. Grinning, the gunman placed the pistol back into his pocket and stood back savouring the moment.

'Does it hurt, Constable O'Leary? Oh, I truly hope so.' O'Leary clawed feebly at his throat, his eyes wide in terrified disbelief. 'Not long now. Maybe another five, ten minutes and sadly it will all be over,' McNamara said quietly, before heading for the railway station and the first leg of his journey back to Ireland. All he had to do was find the other policeman and his mission would be complete.

CHAPTER 14

Moore's General Store, St Mary's Street, Drumlish

TINKLE! TINKLE! THE bell made Kathleen's father look up from the newspaper that he had long since stopped reading and watch the two men who entered his shop. As usual, business was pretty slow and he hadn't seen a single customer all day. Perhaps my luck has changed, he thought as the two young men let the door thud shut behind them. However, something inside the shopkeeper made him suspect that these men were not the sort of customers he wanted.

One of them whistled tunelessly as they made an exaggerated show of looking around the store, picking up the odd piece of merchandise and pretending to look at it before placing it carefully back on the shelves. Their heavy dark suits had seen better days, looking slightly worn around the knees and elbows, and their flat caps were pulled down low to shade their eyes, obscuring their features. He noticed that only one of them was wearing a collar and tie.

Moore licked his lips nervously before speaking. 'Good morning, gentlemen, and what would you be after on this fine morning?' He suddenly felt awkward and uncomfortable as they ignored him and carried on browsing aimlessly until the one with the tie and a pocket watch hanging from his lapel sauntered up to the counter and looked at Moore with cold, dark, angry eyes.

'Good morning, Mr Moore,' Fitzgerald said, in a soft, gentle tone. 'Business a bit slow of late, is it?' It sounded more a statement than a question, as if the man already either knew the answer or didn't really care. Moore's pulse increased as he noticed the other man turn the closed sign on the door and deftly slipped the bolt too.

'Look, I don't have much, but take what you want from the till,' Moore gabbled quickly, assuming that the two men were here to rob him. He could feel the sweat beginning to trickle from his balding temples down the side of his face. 'It's over there,' he pointed at the till at the end of the counter. The man with the tie shook his head and sighed in obvious disappointment.

'Don't you go worrying yourself, Mr Moore,' Fitzgerald continued. 'We're not here to rob you, just to have a little word.' Suddenly, Moore was frightened, very frightened. There was something vaguely familiar about Fitzgerald; as if he'd seen him somewhere before but, much as he tried, his fear-clouded mind couldn't place the man. To make matters worse his fear was rapidly degenerating into terror and he was rooted to the spot like a hare caught in a poacher's lamp.

''Tis a terrible business you losing your son to the Turks and all, terrible business and in the English army too. Still, if they'd caught him? I hear the Turks did terrible things to their prisoners, terrible things. It must be a fearful thing to lose a child, eh, Eunan?' Fitzgerald said, looking at the man by the door.

Eunan Hegarty replied with a casual nod of accord. 'Aye, a fearful thing.'

'Look, my boy is gone these five years past. Who are you? Did you know my Davey? Were you at Gallipoli with him?' Moore asked, grasping hopefully at a meagre straw. Perhaps the men had served with his son but the hope faded as quickly as it came.

'Oh no, Mr Moore, your boy and me, we never met. Me and my friend here, we're just a couple of patriots who happened to be passing and felt like a chat,' Fitzgerald said, in a casual, almost friendly tone, but despite the faux bon homie there was a rising air of menace, a barely suppressed violence about the man as he chatted casually to the shopkeeper. Fear's grip tightened its hold on Moore as he realized that the two men were IRA.

'W...what do you want of me?' he stammered, sweating.

'It would be such a shame after such a terrible loss to lose all this—' Fitzgerald gestured around the room '—or maybe something even more precious than just bricks and mortar, eh? After all, buildings can be put back up, stock rebought, but people?' He paused and smiled mockingly at Moore. 'Well, that's another matter, Mr Moore, another matter entirely, is it not?'

Behind him a large jar of pickled onions slid across the shelf and crashed onto the floor, shattering and discolouring the dusty floorboards with a lumpy pool of pungent vinegar. 'Oops! Butter fingers,' said Hegarty, with obvious insincerity.

'You're a married man yourself, Mr Moore?' Again, more of a statement than a question, Fitzgerald continued, ignoring the shattered jar. 'And young Davey had a sister, if I'm not mistaken. Pretty girl,' he said, exposing a feral row of twisted, nicotine-stained teeth, close enough for Moore to catch the stink of cheap tobacco and tea on his breath.

'Look! Be careful, will you,' Moore stammered pathetically. 'What is it you want with me?' he pleaded, dreading the answer as he miserably choked back his rising terror and fought to maintain his self-control.

'Oh, nothing.' Fitzgerald paused. 'Well, nothing yet anyways, Mr Moore.' The man's empty, soulless eyes made Moore shudder; they were cold and glinted hard as flint in the shop's lights. He flashed Moore another comfortless, mocking smile that dripped insincerity. 'Would you be a patriotic Irishman yourself, Mr Moore?' The question rang alarm bells in Moore's head and deep in the back of his mind he was desperately trying to convince himself that he was experiencing some sort of hallucination brought on by overwork or stress. This just could not be happening to him.

'Th ... that I am,' Moore stammered.

'Then you must be mighty disappointed, mighty disappointed, that your wee girl, young Kathleen, is carrying on with a traitor, a peeler from yonder barracks? It must grieve a man deeply to be let down by his loved ones, his own flesh and blood. That is unless you approve?' Fitzgerald leant over the counter and gazed intently at Moore's face, drawing so close that the stench of the man's breath was overpowering. Fitzgerald ran his eyes over the middle-aged shopkeeper's features, close enough to reach over and kiss him.

Despondently, Moore could feel himself being drawn into an abyss and the pressure on his bladder intensified as Fitzgerald frowned, a comic stage frown, and pulled back slightly. Moore struggled to look away but somehow he couldn't; it was almost as if he was losing control over his own actions, in some sort of deadly hypnotic trance. 'Now, don't you go trying to tell me that you didn't know about it, Mr Moore, because I know that would be a lie!' Fitzgerald's voice rose slightly, betraying a brittle edge of anger. 'That traitorous little bastard of a peeler has been seen with your daughter and he's even been here in your house,' he spat, barely able to contain his disgust.

Moore was now in a terrible state and felt the strength draining from his knees, pouring down his body like water, and he was terrified that he would start shaking. Another jar of preserves slid from a shelf and crashed to the floor, shattering, disgorging its contents on the floorboards.

'Oops!' said Hegarty. 'I always was so clumsy!'

Moore felt a churning feeling in his bowels and fought harder to control his bladder, cursing himself for having taken a cup of tea just before the two strangers had entered his shop. He was sure he was only seconds away from filling his trousers. 'Let me do you a very big favour, Mr Moore ...' Several more tins clattered across the floor. '... and give you some advice. Now listen very, very carefully because I will say this just the once, do you hear, just the once.' Fitzgerald stood up and pushed his hands deep into the pockets in the skirts of his jacket.

Behind him, Hegarty seemed to have lost interest in trashing the shop and strolled over to join his comrade by the counter, a cheery, boyish grin plastered across his craggy face. Moore watched, transfixed, as the collarless Hegarty stepped quickly around the counter, until he was standing by his side. Moore could see that Hegarty was stocky, powerful and desperately in need of a shave, his chin coated in a sheen of blue-black stubble. His dark blue eyes were fixed on Moore's sweating face as he stood close enough for him to smell him.

Moore suddenly yelped in pain as Hegarty twisted his right arm up his back until he thought that it was going to give way at the elbow and pop out at the shoulder. Excruciating daggers of pain shot through Moore as the IRA man used his other hand to drive his face hard into the counter top, shattering his nose with an audible crack against the polished wooden counter top. Coppery blood welled in his mouth and poured onto the wood in a bright crimson torrent. 'Now, I've already had a wee chat with that bitch of a daughter of yours, Mr Moore,' Fitzgerald said, softly dropping much of his polite facade, 'but it seems to me that we are still pissing about here. As long as she wants to whore for the enemy, then I cannot really guarantee your safety or your family's.'

Moore felt himself convulse with pain and fear. This was the first that he had ever heard of anyone threatening his daughter and he struggled to lift his head but as he squirmed Hegarty painfully ground his face further into the bloodied wood. 'Well, Moore, you seem a reasonable man to me and I like to think that I am too. So, I'll tell you one last time. That peeler-loving bitch of yours stops carrying on with the traitor. Do you understand what I'm about, Mr Moore?' Moore nodded as best he could in the circumstances, as the blood poured from his shattered nose. 'Because if the fornicating slut doesn't, I just can't be held responsible for what happens, do you hear?'

Again, Moore nodded. His shoulder felt like it was on fire as

Fitzgerald seized his wrist and flattened his hand violently against the counter. Bang! 'Aaaagh! Jaysus!' Moore screamed, his eyes misting in pain as he felt himself begin to faint. Fitzgerald wiped the blood from the butt of his pistol on Moore's shirt and popped the revolver back into his jacket pocket. Through tears of pain Moore gawped down in disbelief at his shattered little finger that was now splattered across the woodwork in a matted mass of gristle, bone and bloody flesh.

'Shit!' Moore hissed, as his captor released him and shoved him disdainfully to one side, like a piece of discarded garbage. The shopkeeper crumpled into a pitiful whimpering heap on the lino as pain shot through his hand. His nose throbbed as he felt the warmth spread across his trousers as his bladder gave way only moments before his bowels.

'I think that will be all. We're done here, Mr Moore, for now,' Fitzgerald added ominously, with studied pleasantness in his voice. 'Good day to you, and I wouldn't be thinking of squealing to the peelers, there's a good fellow. It would never do, so it wouldn't,' his voice receding. There was a final crash as Hegarty shoved yet another jar from the shelf, which fell and shattered before the door thudded shut, leaving the bell to tinkle like a soprano knell.

Tinkle! Tinkle!

In the back yard Kathleen was busily pegging up a bed sheet on the washing line when she heard a voice, harsh and menacing from behind her. 'Don't turn round, Kathleen, darling,' it said and she froze in mid peg, the sheet hanging half secured to the line. She began to turn. 'Don't!' the voice ordered again, cold as death, and she felt a hand shove her back towards the bed sheet. 'D'you know what's happening in your da's shop, Kathleen? Do you know what is happening because of you?' The voice continued without giving her time to answer. 'Some of the boys are having a wee chat with your da. And d'you know what about, Kathleen?' Again no real pause. 'No? Well, let me tell you, shall I? It's about you and that traitor you've been walking out with, to put it nicely.'

Kathleen desperately racked her brains to place the voice. It was very familiar, painfully so. 'You see, Kathleen, my wee darling,' the voice continued, insipid with false pleasantness and friendliness, 'it would be a terrible thing for anything to happen to your da, especially now your brother's gone too. Would your ma be coping? A traitor's bitch? There's folk hereabouts take poorly to traitors and their whelps.' Kathleen flinched, a tight knot of fear balling in her stomach.

'I'd wished it hadn't come to this, Kathleen, but you wouldn't listen,' the voice went on, 'but if you want to go whoring yourself to a traitor then …' She felt something hard press against the back of her head, followed by a metallic click. Her breath quickened, sharp, short, shallow breaths. 'Sure, you'll know what happens to traitors, don't you, Kathleen, darling?'

Fat tears welled in Kathleen's eyes as she screwed them shut; waiting for her brains to be pushed through her face and splattered across the hanging bed sheet. 'Say your prayers, ye fecking whore,' he said. 'Say your prayers! Say them!' he shouted.

'Er … Hail Mary …' she whispered, scarcely able to contain her panic, scrabbling for the words. '… full of grace, the Lord is with thee …' And then she was alone. It took a few seconds for the fact to sink in and a few more before she could move and when she did her knees buckled beneath her and she sank back against the yard wall, barely able to keep her feet, sobbing for breath. Her heart slammed against her ribs like a steam hammer as she sped off towards the back door. 'Da!' she wailed in terror.

Pots and pans clattered to the floor as she bulldozed through the kitchen and stockroom before bursting out into the shop, where the tang of urine and excrement battered her senses. She caught sight of her mother and father locked in a fearful embrace on the floor behind the counter. Her father's face was white as a sheet and she could see that he was shaking violently like a man who had seen the very devil himself.

'Da, are you all right?' she asked, and her father nodded weakly, trying to be brave in front of his daughter. 'There was a man in the yard, Ma,' she began, but her mother waved her hand to silence her.

'Kathy, dearest,' her mother said, 'I think it's best if you go away for a while.' And she took her daughter's hand and led her back out of the room towards the stairs.

CHAPTER 15

The Courthouse Inn, Drumlish, County Longford

'So that little gobshite McNamara's escaped, you say, sir?' Willson said, puffing out his cheeks in dismay.

The resident magistrate nodded. 'Yes, he has. Terrible business but still I'm sure that he'll be picked up sooner or later. These people rarely travel far and usually come back to the scene of their crimes. Can't help themselves, like a dog to his vomit, eh, Sergeant?' The RM smiled. It was the fourth Tuesday of the month, when Major Edmund Forbes – a distant relative of the Earl of Granard – heard cases brought before him at the Courthouse Inn, which served as a temporary Court of Petty Sessions. This was usually a busy day for policemen but business was a little slow these days.

Major Forbes was a dapper, compact, sharp-featured man in his fifties with bright, intelligent eyes, a neatly trimmed moustache and a well-made pin striped suit topped off by a crisply starched Imperial collar and tie, signalling that he was once a scion of one of the minor public schools dotted outside Dublin. His head was crowned by an immaculate dark Homburg and pale grey gloves clutching a polished blackthorn cane completed the ensemble. 'Well, Sergeant, let's hope you have more business for me next month, eh?' Forbes added. 'It's getting so it's hardly worth me bothering showing up for court these days.'

Willson nodded sombrely, barely concealing the worry. 'Trouble is, sir, that the blasted Fenians have put the frighteners on the folk hereabouts and now they are keeping away from the police or the courts. They make them use their own so. The cheeky buggers even claim to have their own police force!'

'Ah, yes, the Shinners and their blasted Sinn Féin courts. Kangaroo courts more like, if you ask me! The nerve of the blasted people, eh, what! Load of troublemakers the lot of them and the sooner we get them shipped off behind bars the better!' Forbes railed.

'I couldn't agree more, sir,' Willson added.

'Well, well, another quiet day ...' Forbes said cheerily, tapping his cane to his hat brim. 'And if I'm quick I'll be able to get to the golf club for a quick round and a spot of lunch. You play at all, Sergeant?' Forbes was an avid golfer and despite the risks seemed utterly unfazed by IRA attacks on RMs elsewhere in the country. He was the sort of thick-skinned individual who would have stood in front of a rioting mob and not only demanded but expected that they stopped when he told them to. Consequently, he was either too brave or too stupid to alter his usual routine – court in the morning, followed by lunch and a round of golf at his club outside Longford. It was such behaviour that had cost Colonel Smyth his life in Cork and it wouldn't have surprised Willson if the same thing happened to Forbes if he wasn't careful.

'No, sir,' Willson finally answered. 'I've never got round to it,' he added politely, recalling a quip he'd once heard that golf was an excellent way to ruin a good walk.

Forbes climbed into the back of his elegant silver-grey motor car and turned back to face Willson. 'Well, we'll have to see about that, old chap.' He beamed and then leant forward to tap his driver on the shoulder. 'On! On!' he ordered, before adding, 'See you next month, Sergeant.' The chauffer crunched the car noisily into gear, releasing the brake. The car lurched forward in a cloud of exhaust fumes and sped off down the street in the direction of the golf club, leaving the policemen in its smoky wake.

'Yes, we'll have to see about that, old chap!' the sergeant muttered under his breath, imitating the RM's crisp upper-class Anglo-Irish accent. Behind him, Constables Flynn and Mullan stepped out into the street, whilst Constable Reidy closed the courtroom door behind him. As usual, Constable O'Neill was back in the barracks' duty room. Sometimes Flynn thought that O'Neill deliberately avoided going out much and he was inclined to put it down to the Ulsterman's quietly perverse love of paperwork with its lack of risk. Alternatively, his time in the Irish Guards may well have given him a deep dislike of walking around. Either way, it spared the others the interminable monotony of the form filling or paperwork that seemed so dear to the RIC, so Flynn didn't feel he could complain.

'You'll be taking up golf then, Sarge?' Reidy quipped to his old friend with a cheeky grin, fully aware of Willson's view of the sport.

'Ach, away with you,' Willson replied, 'I've enough on my hands trying to look after you lot! Where would I be finding the time for golf!'

Flynn and Reidy laughed loudly at Willson's outburst but Mullan, still the outsider, remained silent, unable or unwilling to share the joke. The northerner felt he had nothing in common with the others in the barracks, even O'Neill, and he constantly pestered Willson for a transfer to a barracks back in Ulster. Suffice to say that Willson felt that he had enough on his plate and even putting up with the brooding Mullan was better than being shorthanded, so chose to ignore his persistent requests. Besides, Willson thought as he turned the key in the courthouse lock with a loud, satisfying click, the constabulary in its wisdom posted Mullan to Drumlish, so he better get used to it! He slipped the key into his trouser pocket and felt it bounce off his truncheon and rest amongst the tangle of handkerchief and small change in his pocket.

'What was that about McNamara?' Flynn asked. 'I thought I heard you and the major mention his name? Is the murdering bastard to swing yet?' he asked anxiously. Willson shook his head in obvious disappointment.

'No, he isn't, Flynn. I'm afraid it's bad news. The blackguard has escaped. Those bloody useless soldiers let him give them the slip! You know, I knew we should have kept the bugger here. I've never had a prisoner escape on me. It's a bloody disgrace!' he ranted. Flynn looked worried, very worried, his face pale and drawn. The other policemen looked at him, puzzled.

'Who's this McNamara then?' Mullan finally asked.

'Mick McNamara,' Willson said, 'is an evil little gobshite and it's him we think shot our Constable Jim O'Leary earlier this year, before yous two got sent here, and now he's out there, out there somewhere on the run. He's an evil, spiteful little shite from an evil, spiteful little family – so, boys, we'd best keep an eye out for him. He may come back looking to even the score or something, what with his brother being shot and all. His sort always do.'

'Don't worry,' Flynn replied unconvincingly, 'if he's got any sense, he'll not be coming back here any time soon.'

'Well, isn't that just the problem, Flynn, m'boy,' Willson said softly. 'If the likes of him had any sense in the first place, they'd not have joined the IRA! No, I'm fearful that we've not seen the last of young McNamara, so all we can do is make sure that we take better care of him than your bloody soldier pals!'

'Do you think that we should get in touch with Jim, let him know?' Flynn asked, but Willson shook his head.

'No need. Jim's well away from here and well out of it. He'll be safe enough.' Somehow, Flynn didn't feel reassured.

'Anyway,' Reidy chipped in inquisitively, 'never mind that, you and the good major were jawing for an awful long time, Sarge. So what did the pompous old bugger want then? C'mon, share.'

Willson frowned sternly at Reidy in mock severity. 'Like it's anything to do with you, Constable!' he said, before dropping the facade and breaking into a beaming grin, while running his tongue over his neatly clipped moustache in contemplation and saying to no one in particular, 'Do you know, I could murder a cup of tea.' He could feel curiosity consuming the others and was enjoying the moment, teasing them. 'The good major, as it happens,' Willson went on, 'has a wee job for us, a special mission!' He winked at Reidy and strode off towards the barracks.

A special mission! The words wafted pregnantly in the air behind him as he walked away and he felt like he was going to burst with excitement, waiting to hear which one would crack and ask what on earth he was on about. But to his chagrin they were playing him at his own game and walked in silence behind him until, after a few paces, he could contain himself no longer. 'Well, it would seem that you three culchie eejits will be going for a wee drive in the country.' The three policemen looked at Willson, who, smiling in triumph, walked on a few more steps further before speaking again. 'Next Friday there'll be a mail car coming from Longford and you three musketeers—' He looked at them '—will be helping escort it to Ballinamuck.'

'Oh, deep joy!' muttered Flynn. 'I've always been wanting to see the bright lights of Ballinamuck and now's my chance at last!'

Willson cast him a disapproving frown.

'So, Sarge, what's so important that it takes the three of us?' Mullan asked, but Willson just shrugged his shoulders dismissively.

'Damned if I know, Constable Mullan,' Willson lied. 'I just know that the good major is dead keen, so he is, that whatever it is gets from Longford to Ballinamuck. A gold-plated pair of golf clubs for all I know!' Reidy snorted and Willson continued, 'And besides, it's not just three of you. There'll be two of the lads from Longford coming with it – Constables King and Brogan. Any of you know them?'

Reidy nodded. 'Know them both, good fellas. I worked with them up in town. Proper peelers, not like yer men here,' he laughed, as he jerked his thumb at Flynn and Mullan.

'Excellent!' Willson chortled with genuine enthusiasm. 'It's about time we had some proper coppers around here!'

At the barracks, Willson hung back and let Reidy and Mullan go in before he called Flynn over, making sure that they were out of earshot of the others. 'Flynn, don't go telling the others but when you leave on Friday I will have a packet for you.' Flynn looked puzzled.

'What sort of packet?' asked Flynn, who despite his curiosity could hear alarm bells clanging in the back of his mind.

'I can't tell you and it's best you don't know,' Willson said quietly, 'but it's really important and I'm relying on you to guard it with your life. When you get to Ballinamuck barracks there will be a fella there, a District Inspector Philip Kelleher. He'll be expecting it and you are to give it to no one else, do you hear, no one, no matter what.' Flynn nodded, none the wiser. 'And tell no one either. I don't want the lads to know,' Willson added, tapping the side of his nose with his index finger in a gesture that was far from reassuring. 'Now, Flynn, I want you to take a turn around the outlying farms before sunset. It's always good to fly the flag on court days, just in case the local villains think they can have a free hand!' Willson announced loudly before wandering through the door to his quarters.

'OK, who fancies a little bike ride in the country before supper?' Flynn announced, from the middle of the duty room.

'Aye, all right then, I'll come with you.'

To Flynn's surprise it was O'Neill who had spoken. 'The sergeant wants us to do the rounds of the outlying area before sunset, so best we get going,' Flynn said, heading to the armoury to collect two carbines, whilst O'Neill headed into the back yard to fetch the bikes. 'You ever heard of a District Inspector Kelleher?' Flynn asked O'Neill as they pedalled along a quiet country lane.

'Aye, that I have,' O'Neill replied.

'And?' Flynn persisted.

O'Neill smiled. 'He's a new boy with Crimes Branch Special over in Longford. He fancies himself as a bit of a spy-catcher. He's like you, Kevin, a bit of a war hero,' O'Neill joked. 'Bit of a cowboy if you ask me.' O'Neill went quiet. 'Why do you ask? Not looking to transfer, are you?'

'Good God, no!' Flynn snorted derisively, 'I've enough on me plate with you lot in uniform without wanting to play cowboys and Indians with the Shinners to boot! I just heard someone mention his name, that's all.'

O'Neill gave him a quizzical sidelong glance and carried on pedalling. Flynn had the distinctly uncomfortable feeling that his companion was less than convinced but he was intrigued and decided to try and find out more about Kelleher, as Crimes Branch Special was the CID-cum-Special Branch of the RIC and its detectives operated in plain clothes. They were shadowy figures who lived, and died, in a shadowy world.

By the time the two policemen had completed their rounds the sun was low on the horizon and it was cold and damp. Flynn's knees ached as they cycled down St Mary's Street and he could see that the shutters were firmly closed on Moore's General Store. He gave his watch a cursory glance. It was still early. 'Will you be seeing Miss Moore tonight?' O'Neill asked.

Flynn knew that it was an open secret that he was seeing Kathleen but it still made him wince when O'Neill pulled his leg about his semi-clandestine trysts with his pretty young redhead. 'No,' he replied, resigning himself to the situation. 'It's getting late. I'll probably see her in the morning.'

When they reached the barracks, Flynn and O'Neill propped their bikes against the wall in the back yard and walked through the back door into the duty room. Willson was slumped in an old armchair and looked up from his copy of the *Police Gazette*. 'Ah, there you are, Flynn, my boy. I want you and young Reidy here to come with me and cycle over to Ballinalee in the morning. It's only neighbourly to visit now and then and besides the fresh air will do you good!' he laughed. 'I want to have a wee chat with their governor, Sergeant Hamilton, and see how things are for him and his lads over in Ballinalee these days. It's always good to compare notes,' he said, but Flynn was less enthusiastic.

Blast! Flynn thought. There goes visiting Kathleen tomorrow. O'Neill gave him a sympathetic knowing look and shrugged.

The next morning's cycle ride proved to be uneventful enough and in the end Flynn found himself hanging around impatiently, glancing at his watch, whilst Willson chatted with his old acquaintance Sergeant William Hamilton. It was obvious that the two of them went back several years, had history, and Flynn was beginning to think that there wasn't anyone that Willson didn't know in the RIC's socially dislocated extended family.

Flynn looked around. The street was deserted and he came to the conclusion that he didn't like Ballinalee but then it was fairly obvious that the locals didn't like his kind much either. Their hostility wasn't even thinly disguised behind the usual veil of forced politeness that seemed so common elsewhere. He became aware that he was being watched by a stocky, dark-haired man working in the smithy, with something that seemed to be more than casual interest, so he strolled slowly over to the forge, leaving Reidy to guard the bikes.

'Hot day to be working in a smithy,' Flynn said to the blacksmith, who slowly and deliberately put down his hammer and tongs and wiped his hands on an old cloth before muttering something in Irish.

'Sorry, I'm from Dublin!' Flynn said by way of explanation for his puzzled expression and the blacksmith smiled a warm, welcoming smile.

'Aye, so it is,' MacEoin replied. 'So what brings you fellas all the way out to Ballinalee the day?'

Flynn shrugged. 'Search me. My sergeant doesn't tell me a thing,' he laughed, changing the subject. 'Well, at least it's not raining!'

The blacksmith smiled. 'Give it time, Constable, give it time. You know what they say around here, Constable. If you can see the hills, it's going to rain and if you can't, it's already raining. Let's hope it doesn't pour, eh?'

There was something about the blacksmith that made Flynn feel uncomfortable. For all his charm and chit-chat, it was obvious from the look in his eyes that he was no more a fan of the constabulary than anyone else hereabouts and his quip about it pouring rang silent alarm bells in the back of the policeman's head. Yes, there was definitely something not quite right about the blacksmith but he couldn't quite put his finger on it, not just yet anyway. He resolved to ask Willson if he knew anything about him when they were heading home.

Flynn didn't notice the curtain twitch in the cottage next door or McNamara, fresh back from Cardiff, peering down from the recess of the cottage's upstairs gable window. McNamara couldn't believe his luck when he recognized the tall, dark-haired policeman chatting to MacEoin, and he licked his lips in anticipation of his coming revenge. 'It's him! It's him! It's the bastard who shot our Jerry!' McNamara squealed in violent agitation, his eyes smouldering with barely suppressed fury. 'By Christ I'll get you, you bastard, so help me, I will!'

'Get away from the bloody window, you fool! Do you want the peelers to see you?' Fitzgerald hissed angrily as he yanked McNamara back into the shadows of the bedroom. McNamara shot Fitzgerald a furious glance but the gunman wasn't afraid of McNamara. In fact, there seemed to be very little that Fitzgerald was afraid of and he laughed at the other man's attempt to intimidate him.

For a moment, Flynn thought that he heard something but the noise of the blacksmith resuming his work masked whatever it was that had caught his attention. It was obvious to Flynn that the blacksmith had done with small talk and after a few moments he strolled back towards the barracks. To his horror it was well gone three in the afternoon before Willson finished his business with Hamilton. As they reached Drumlish he noticed the village beginning to go into its predictable routine as life, already slow, began to slow down further for the evening.

Flynn had just finished putting his bike away in the shed when O'Neill came out clutching a steaming mug of tea. 'There you are, big man,' O'Neill quipped, before noisily slurping his tea. 'And how was the exciting metropolis that is Ballinalee today?' Flynn toyed with ignoring him but changed his mind and asked the Ulsterman what he knew of the blacksmith. O'Neill scratched his head and Flynn thought that he could almost see the man's brain working behind his dark eyes. 'Not a lot. I'm told that he fancies himself as a bit of a Shinner but I'm not sure that he's anything to worry about. Ballinalee's not my patch, Kevin.'

Flynn nodded, content to accept what he had heard from O'Neill, and after a short pause added, as casually as he could, 'You know, I think I'll pop up the street for a wee while.'

'If it's young Kathy Moore you're after, then I saw her with her da away in their dog cart whilst you were gallivanting out and about,' O'Neill said, through a barely suppressed smirk. 'Headed off to Newtonforbes, by the look of it.'

'Really?' Flynn replied casually, as he shut the shed door, sliding the bolt closed then strolling with O'Neill back into the barracks. 'Perhaps they're after picking something up off the train for the shop?' The nearest railway station was at Newtonforbes. 'I think I'll wander over and find out when she'll be back,' he said as he locked his carbine onto the rack and headed for the barracks' front door.

It was a short walk to Moore's General Store and the route was so ingrained in him that he didn't even recall walking it. The shop was quiet and the doorbell tinkled softly as he pushed the door open. The room was poorly lit, which surprised him, and the pungent stench of vinegar seemed out of place in the usually immaculate shop. At his feet, several dark stains discoloured the worn floorboards. He felt his eye twitch as the hairs prickled on the back of his neck. Something was wrong; something was very wrong. 'Hello!' he shouted. 'Is anyone in?'

A door creaked open and he heard light footfalls getting louder as, head down, Kathy's mother, Mrs Moore, shuffled into the shop, before letting out a deep, nervous sigh and looking up at Flynn.

'Good afternoon ... Oh, it's you, Constable Flynn,' she said nervously and Flynn could sense the fear in the usually bubbly woman's voice.

'Is everything all right, Mrs Moore?' Flynn asked, and she shifted her weight awkwardly, fidgeting with her apron, looking frightened and worried to see him. 'Is Miss Moore back from her travels?' he asked, but the woman just stood looking at him, her tired eyes red-rimmed from crying and sunken with stress. 'Is something wrong? Has something happened to Kathleen?' he asked anxiously.

She nodded. 'She's gone,' she said tonelessly.

'Gone? Gone where? When will she be back? What's happened?'

'There were some men ...' She faltered and then, collecting herself, pushing a stray strand of hair from her eyes, the way that Kathleen did, she continued, 'They hurt her father, broke his nose and fingers, they did. They said she had to stop seeing you or something terrible would happen.'

'Who? Who did?' he repeated.

'Who do you think?' she spluttered, looking at him as if he was a halfwit. Suddenly the penny dropped and fear mixed with anger welled up inside him at the very thought that the IRA had threatened his Kathleen or her family, just because of him.

'Where has she gone?' he repeated.

Mrs Moore looked at him and sighed, shaking her head. 'It's best you don't know. Best for everyone. They won't hurt her or my Dick if you don't know, if she doesn't see you anymore. I've nothing against you, Constable Flynn, you seem a decent man and you've been good to my girl but I won't let anything happen to my Kathy or her da, so help me I won't.'

Flynn's heart sank as his little world crashed down around his ears. Kathleen was all that had made life in Drumlish tolerable since the IRA had stepped up its efforts in the area. 'She's gone to Dublin, hasn't she? She's gone to stay with her aunt,' he asked, remembering what Kathleen had said about her holidays by the sea as a child and the way that Mrs Moore's eyes widened, as she struggled to hide her surprise, confirmed that he was right.

'No, she's not in Dublin,' Mrs Moore said, without lying too much, and he knew that there was no point in arguing the toss but did his best to hide that he knew she was not being completely honest with him. Kathy had to be in Dublin, he thought as he left the shop, and if she was, he'd find her, or he didn't deserve to call himself a Dubliner.

That night, Flynn couldn't sleep and it wasn't just Mullan and Reidy's snoring or the fear of what dreams may come that kept him awake. It was Kathleen, and he scoured his mind for anything she may have said about where her aunt lived in Dublin. There had to be something, a clue to where she had gone, and as he tossed and turned on his noisy bunk it struck him that she had talked about being by the sea. With a start he sat up in his bed. That had to be it! She wasn't in Dublin at all; her mother hadn't been lying. She was in one of the coastal suburbs that clung to Dublin Bay. The problem was, which one? It wasn't much, but it was a start. Eventually, after much tossing and turning, he drifted into a fitful sleep until the unwelcome ringing of the alarm clock shattered his dreams at six o'clock and he struggled out of his blankets to wash and shave.

Coughing, Reidy slumped out of bed and grunted as he opened the armoured shutters to let the first tentacles of daylight grope their way into the dormitory. From his bunk, Flynn couldn't help noticing that the room stank of stale humanity. At least they had three hours to get ready so there was no rush to get up.

Eventually, the mail car arrived, as expected, just after nine in the morning, and as Ballinamuck was only five or six miles away Flynn anticipated being there before ten. As Flynn looked from the dormitory window he could see that Reidy was already outside and the civilian post office driver seemed thoroughly pissed off, resisting any attempts by the others to strike up a conversation. Reidy, carbine in hand, was chatting to Constables Brogan and King.

'I know it's not far to Ballinamuck and there are five of you but take care, won't you,' Willson said to Flynn, as the Dubliner took his carbine from the rack in the armoury. Then Willson gave a quick furtive look around and discreetly slipped Flynn a small, tightly wrapped, flat brown package.

'Believe me, Sergeant, I will,' Flynn replied, as he slipped the package into his tunic pocket and secured the button.

Trying hard to look as if he hadn't noticed, O'Neill saw Willson pass Flynn something as they chatted in the armoury and wondered what it might be. O'Neill really hated being left out of the loop and mainly, as a result of his insistence upon running the barracks' administration, he had done his best to be at the centre of things ever since he had arrived back in 1919. He made a mental note to see if he could get anything out of Flynn later.

Click! Clack! Click! Clack! The duty room echoed with the sound of Flynn checking the working parts of his .303. The action was smooth, well oiled and clean, and he would make ready later. Old habits die hard, O'Neill thought, as he pretended to read the weekly situation report from Division before looking up at Flynn and smiling innocently. 'Enjoy your little outing and don't go doing anything foolish, my boy!' he quipped.

Ten minutes later the mail car was rumbling away down Main Street towards the post office and, unseen by its occupants, a mirror flashed from a cottage on the edge of the village. Up on Barragh Beg, one of the low hills to the east of the village, a lone figure lay in the scrub watching, waiting for the heliographic signal and nodded in approval as he saw the mirror flash once, twice, three times and then prised himself up off the ground, being careful to keep his silhouette from breaking the skyline.

The IRA scout crouched low and squelching through a shallow gruel of slurry and mud, using the cover of a low scraggy hedge to crest the hill behind him. Just about keeping his footing, he slipped and skidded down the reverse slope for fifty yards or so before stopping to gaze down at two trenchcoated men lounging against a dark Tin Lizzie automobile parked in the lane below. The scout raised both his arms above his head and waved them in wide sweeping arcs.

One of the men looked up and for a moment stared intently before tapping the other on the shoulder and climbing into the waiting Model T. The other raised both his hands and waved back in a series of sweeping arcs, copying the scout, before hoiking the starting handle out from the passenger side of the car and bending down to crank the car's engine into life. The engine spluttered into life on the third turn.

The man waved at the scout with the crank handle before leaping into the car. Even from where he was, the scout heard the gears crunch as the Ford lurched into motion and sped off down the lane in the direction of Gaigue. 'Well, that's me for the day,' the scout said to himself, as he headed back towards the village. 'I wonder what I'll be having for my tea later?'

CHAPTER 16

Friday, 27 August 1920, Gaigue Cross, County Longford

'KEEP YOUR WITS about you, lads,' Flynn said nervously, to himself as much as to the others, as the mail car trundled its way through the narrow country road leading to Gaigue Cross. It was ideal ambush country, rolling ground, low stone walls and stacks of cover and he really didn't feel happy with the situation.

'Where's this?' Mullan asked, as they rolled into a suspiciously silent scattering of low white-washed bungalows, clinging to the edge of the dirt road.

Flynn leant forward from the back and called into Mullan's ear, 'Bandra. Bit of a dump.' Mullan nodded. Flynn began to feel uneasy. The fields were empty, not even a cow to be seen. Where is everyone? Flynn thought, as he felt a nagging sense of anxiety begin to bubble to the surface, an old sixth sense coming back to life. Nervously, he laid his carbine across his knees, massaged the stock surreptitiously and made the weapon ready.

Beside him, Constables Reidy, King and Brogan were chatting quietly to each other in muted, barely audible whispers, drowned by the rumble of the mail car's engine and punctuated by the odd burst of laughter. Flynn felt no inclination to join in and made no attempt to broach their conversation. The driver ignored them all, locked in a miserable world of his own. 'John,' Flynn shouted across to Mullan, 'you know, something doesn't feel right. It is far too quiet!'

John Mullan half turned in the front passenger seat and shot Flynn one of his rare lopsided, leering smiles before speaking. 'Sure, Kevin, will you relax. What can the Shinners do? There are five of us, after all. We'd have to blunder into a pretty big flying column for them to take a crack at us!'

Flynn knew that the Ulsterman was an experienced soldier like himself and yet Mullan didn't seem to be perturbed by the stillness around them and had already turned back around before Flynn was able to reply. Somehow he didn't feel reassured. He couldn't put his finger on why he felt the way he did. Perhaps it was Kathleen's sudden disappearance that had unsettled him or the way that most of the general public tried to avoid eye contact or having anything to do with anyone in the police. It was obvious that the IRA-ordered boycott of the police was biting deep.

'Get a grip,' Flynn muttered to himself. He knew it was a cliché, but everything was quiet, too quiet, and it was obvious that the normal rhythm of life that you would expect to see in any rural community was missing. There were no children, no adults, not even dogs roaming the street. It was as if everyone had just disappeared. Nothing seemed normal and in a strange way it reminded him of that awkward moment of tranquillity that occurred between the end of a bombardment and the cacophony of whistles that heralded an attack. It was the quiet before the storm, he thought, praying that he was wrong.

Something off to the right caught his eye, a movement perhaps at the very periphery of his vision, and instinctively he tightened his grip on his carbine. A lone line of bed sheets on a washing line flapped in the breeze in the back yard of the last house and the hairs began to rise on the back of his neck, his pulse quickening, as if he sensed untold unseen eyes watching him, anticipating his destruction. Ahead, there was a dip in the road and as the mail car began its descent into Gaigue, towards the crossroads, he knew that he was entering a perfect killing zone, the perfect location for an ambush. His pulse raced and he felt his palms begin to slick with sweat.

Flynn couldn't see the young IRA scout hugging the shadows at the edge of the village, watching the mail car pass. The scout's mouth felt dry as anxiety and fear welled in the pit of his stomach and swirled through his abdomen. He slipped out of the back door into the yard and, grasping the long wooden prop, jerked the washing line, billowing off-white sheets like the sails of some long-lost galleon up into the air. A quarter of a mile further on, a lone figure crouching in the back garden of one of the now-empty cottages watched as the washing line innocently swept up and dropped, with the finality of the guillotine blade, back down.

The man was masked from the road as he turned and rose to his feet, waving his arms in the air like a human semaphore tower in the direction of Gaigue, and as he finally dropped his arms he saw something flash in the distance. The sun glinted briefly on the polished glass lenses of MacEoin's binoculars as he stood in silent contemplation of what he was about to unleash. 'This is it, boys! Get ready!' he called excitedly, anticipating the adrenalin rush to come. 'Remember, hold your fire until I say.' Then he doubled away to a low building, squatting on the crossroads, alert, his rifle at the trail.

MacEoin was glad that he had told the villagers to get out and stay out until the morning's business was concluded and relieved that they had packed up and left without a fuss. For the most part, the villagers were good republicans and those that weren't were no friends of the police anyway. Besides, the last thing he needed was a load of civilians getting in the way of a gun battle, getting themselves shot up. He knew the propaganda boys would make a meal of anyone getting caught in the crossfire, blaming the British for butchering innocent civilians, but that wasn't MacEoin's style. He saw himself as a soldier of Ireland and whilst he had no qualms about killing enemy soldiers, he was glad that the civilians were away. He would have got them away even if they'd been rabid Orangemen one and all.

Meanwhile, on the outskirts of Gaigue, the newly promoted section leader Paddy Doyle, stiff with tension, pressed himself down as far as he could behind the grey dry-stone wall that screened him from the road. He felt painfully responsible for the two young Volunteers, barely past their mid teens, who squatted wide-eyed and white-knuckled, clutching their rifles next to him, waiting for the trap to spring. 'Don't worry, boys,' Doyle whispered. 'Just do as I say.' He was in charge of the cut-off group at the Bandra end of Gaigue. 'Now hush,' he ordered, as he listened for the approaching mail car.

Clutching his brand new oil-smelling .303 rifle close to his chest, Doyle waited, hunched in cover, his heart hammering against his ribcage as if it were going to explode. He felt like he was about to have a heart attack as sharp pains lanced through his chest and sweat pooled in the armpits of his shirt and ran down his back. His stomach churned as if someone had plunged a whisk into it and was cranking it frantically, making him feel light-headed and sick, but he dared not show weakness in front of the others.

His mouth tasted bitter and he was desperate to remain calm. He tried to think what Maguire or MacEoin would do now; he couldn't imagine them falling apart under stress like he was. He needed to set an example to his new charges, it was what was expected of him, and it began to dawn on him that being in charge was all a charade and he was painfully aware that if he panicked the others would too. It was as simple as that.

'Hail Mary, full of grace ...' he began to mutter as he slipped the safety catch off on his rifle with a gentle click. It was funny, he thought, how fear made the mind zero in on trivial details and he found himself staring intently at the grass at his feet, watching myriad bugs scurrying about their business, oblivious of the affairs of men. From behind the wall he heard, and even felt, the mail car rumble past. It was so close he could smell its engine fumes. He trembled with fear and excitement. His time had come.

Suddenly, the quiet was ripped apart at the seams by a shrill, short whistle blast followed by the frantic crackle of gunfire. 'This is it, lads!' Doyle said to his boys, suddenly calm as he peeked over the wall to see a pall of gun smoke and muzzle flashes spitting from the cottage on the left-hand side of the crossroads.

The mail car windscreen shattered, showering Constable Mullan and the driver with razor shards of glass, making Mullan yelp in pain as one embedded itself in his nose. Another gouged a furrow in the driver's cheek, causing him to flinch, swerving the vehicle violently to the right as he flung his hands up across his face, exposing the rear of the vehicle to gunfire. 'Go! Go! Drive!' Mullan screamed frantically at the startled driver, as dark, venous blood oozed down his lacerated nose, dribbling onto his tunic.

Panicking, the driver missed the brake, stamping hard on the accelerator, over-revving the engine, which shrieked agonizingly as the vehicle lurched towards the corner of a low dry-stone wall. Crash! It smashed into the wall, grinding up onto three wheels as the engine squealed and coughed into silence. 'Get it moving!' Mullan shouted urgently at the driver and Flynn grunted in pain as he was thrown head first against the back of the cab with a dull thud.

Pale, wide-eyed and shaking, the driver stared in horror at the blood pooled in the palms of his cupped hands. 'Sod this!' he cried before diving out of his seat and huddling pathetically in the meagre dead ground behind the chassis, gulping for breath before leaping up and fleeing into the fields beyond before anyone could stop him. 'Get back here, ye gutless little bastard!' Mullan screamed but the driver wasn't listening, he was up and off over a low wall, running as fast as his fear-fuelled legs would take him whilst stray bullets clipped the wall.

★

'Leave him! Leave him!' MacEoin bellowed above the rising crackle of gunfire. 'Don't bother with the driver – concentrate on the peelers!' He raised his weapon to his shoulder and squeezed off another shot, which punched through Constable Brogan's chest, sending him tumbling backwards in a thick welter of dark spraying blood, as if struck by some invisible force.

'Shit!' Flynn yelped as bullets gouged chunks from the wooden facia of the mail car, showering him with splinters. The stink of blood and cordite was overpowering and Flynn felt light-headed and sick. He could see Brogan lying on his back, agonizingly grinding his feet into the bed of the vehicle, his hands snatching at the front of his tunic as dark blood oozed between his fingers, staining it black. Meanwhile King and Reidy squatted as low as they possibly could, trying to make the most of their scant cover, occasionally loosing off barely aimed shots in the rough direction of the cottage in a desperate attempt to keep their attackers' heads down. Flynn felt a hot brass cartridge case bounce off his shoulder as another bullet zipped overhead, close enough for the air to ruffle his hair on its way past.

Bizarrely, it felt like being back in the butts on a rifle range except this time he was the target! He screwed up his courage, bobbed up and snapped off a shot, inviting a flurry of bullets in reply. He saw Mullan fire off a hastily aimed shot before a hefty blow smacked him down hard into his seat. Mullan felt his shoulder go numb and warm blood flooded into his shirt and tunic, making them sticky as his strength ebbed from his fingers. He desperately fought against the rising tide of weakness and panic. He groaned as his carbine slipped from his knees and bounced, muzzle first, into the road.

Flynn watched Mullan tug at his holster, releasing a .38 revolver, and heard him grunt as he thumbed back its stiff hammer, shaking with pain before snapping off a shot at his assailants. Wood splintered from a flaking window frame and a shadowy figure ducked back into cover. Coppery blood filled Mullan's mouth and white lights began to dance before his eyes. 'Flynn! Reidy! King! Brogan! Get yourselves into cover!' Mullan grunted, as he snapped off a couple more rounds. 'Move when I say! I'll cover you!'

Bullets zipped past, flooding Flynn's mind with uncomfortable memories of khaki-clad men waiting to hop the bags into no man's land and stagger into the scything hail of gunfire. 'Ugh!' Mullan grunted, as a bullet tore through his knee, shattering the joint as he tried to shove open the passenger side door. He clutched the shattered joint and biting back his pain looked over to Flynn, his eyes burning with adrenalin-fuelled fury. 'Flynn, I'm done for! Get the others into the cottage! When I say move, go.'

Flynn shook his head. 'No! Hang on, John, I'll come and get you!' Another bullet ripped through the mail car near Flynn's head, showering him with debris, and he flinched back into cover.

'Flynn, just do it,' he pleaded and without a word Flynn nodded, knowing that Mullan wouldn't make it, accepting the inevitable as he had too many times before. The man may have been a bigot but he was a brave bigot nonetheless. It was a replay of a scene he had seen too many times before and had prayed that he would never see again. Straining against unconsciousness, Mullan banged off two more shots and then glanced back at Flynn. 'Give me your pistol, Flynn, I'm almost out!'

Flynn tossed his pistol onto the seat next to Mullan and then loosed off another shot from his carbine. Mullan dropped his empty revolver into the footwell and snatched up Flynn's loaded pistol, steadied it on the passenger door, took aim and fired, roaring like the dying Cúchulainn, his coarse Tyrone accent thick with pain.

Glancing over at the others huddled in the back of the mail car, Flynn shouted, straining to be heard over the cacophony. 'Reidy! King! Listen!' The two policemen looked at Flynn, a mixture of fear and anticipation in their eyes. 'If we stay here we're finished!'

'Tell me something I don't know!' Reidy snapped irritably.

'You two get into the cottage,' Flynn barked urgently, pointing at the nearest house, instantly taking charge of the situation. 'Me and Mullan'll cover you! When I say move, you and King get out and try and force your way into that cottage over there.' He pointed frantically with his right hand, palm extended. 'When you get there, cover me! Understand?' King and Reidy nodded anxiously and, after visibly steeling themselves, slid quickly over to the other side of the van into the dead ground behind, getting ready to move.

'Prepare to move!' Flynn bellowed, pausing briefly to fire. 'MOVE!' he shouted and they moved. Flynn rapidly palmed the bolt of his carbine, emptying the ten-round magazine in a flurry of unaimed shots, and saw one of the IRA gunmen jerk back into cover in a shower of brick dust and woodchip.

Constable King yelped as a bullet clipped his shoulder, spraying more blood high into the air as he rose to sprint for the cottage, and threw himself face first into the dirt. 'Blast!' King cursed as he forced himself back to his feet and trailing his damaged arm he bent low and doubled, weaving erratically towards the sanctuary of the cottage door. He hit it with a thud, winding himself, but it caved in easily under the full impact of his body weight and that of Reidy, who tumbled after him into the cool dark of the cottage.

From his vantage point opposite, MacEoin had a clear view of the crossroads. It should have been a perfect killing ground but things were already beginning to go badly wrong. The policemen had survived the initial salvoes and he feared that a protracted gun battle – something he was anxious to avoid – was unfolding before his eyes. That did not stop him feeling a degree of satisfaction, watching the policeman in the front passenger seat thrash in agony as he clutched his shattered knee. It was obvious that the man was finished and both MacEoin and the policeman knew it. MacEoin tapped Fitzgerald on the shoulder and pointed at Mullan.

'Brendan, finish him,' he ordered and Fitzgerald took up the pressure of the trigger but snatched it as he loosed off a round. 'Shit!' he muttered as he missed.

'Quick! The bastards are getting away!' MacEoin shouted when he saw two of the policemen slip out of the mail car into the dead ground behind. 'Brendan, Eunan, get round to the left and try and get a shot at those two!' He pointed where he wanted them to go and, without hesitation, Fitzgerald and Hegarty obeyed, keeping low to avoid the odd stray bullet that smashed into the room, to find a better fire position. MacEoin didn't watch them go and heard the side door bang open, letting him know that they were gone.

Mullan slid half out of the passenger door and snapped off another shot, shouting incoherently, but MacEoin ignored the man's cries and shifted his position slightly before squeezing off another shot. The rifle kicked back violently, fighting against his firm grip, and he saw another shard of wood spiral away into the air. The next bullet took Mullan in the head, just above the left eyebrow, sending fragments of bone and brains spewing across the back of the mail car cab.

The debris of Mullan's trauma splashed against Flynn's face in a shower of warm, sticky gobbets. 'Christ!' Flynn cursed, wiping his face with the back of his sleeve before glancing at Mullan's corpse, now hanging out of the cab door, a fist-size hole gaping in the back of his head. 'Sod this!' he hissed as another lump of razor-sharp wood tore itself from what was left of the facia, slicing his face as it passed. Blood ran down his cheek and trickled into the corner of his mouth. It was warm and bitter and he knew that if he did not move soon there would be a lot more of it – he would be finished. The sheer volume of adrenalin coursing through his body was making him queasy and he was trembling, wanting to puke. 'Deep breaths, deep breaths,' he repeated like some sort of holy mantra, steadying his nerves and trying to think.

'Flynn! Mullan! Can you hear me? Get ready to move! We'll cover you! Move!' Reidy shouted frantically from behind him as rounds zipped close over Flynn's head. He couldn't tell whether they were Reidy's or the IRA's; he just knew that he could not stay where he was any longer or he would die. With a grunting burst of fear-fuelled energy, Flynn seized the writhing Constable Brogan's tunic by the collar and hefted him off the crippled mail car.

Brogan let out a long despondent wail of agony and clawed at the front of his tunic. He was a dead weight but Flynn knew that he couldn't leave him lying out in the open, even if his bulk slowed him down. They floundered momentarily on the ground before Flynn finally rolled awkwardly onto his knees. Slinging his carbine across his back and grabbing Brogan as firmly as he could with his blood-slick hands, he hefted him towards the open cottage door.

Bullets zipped by, kicking up dirt around his feet, causing Flynn to skip slightly in a little dance as he made one last lung-bursting push to get the wounded man to safety. With a loud grunt he finally shoved Brogan through the door, stumbling and falling across the incapacitated man who cried out in agony. King slammed the battered door shut as it shook under the impact of several bullets smacking into its chipped planking.

Flynn felt himself shaking violently, sweat stinging his eyes as he levered himself off of Brogan and looked straight at King. He placed a nearby cushion under the badly wounded policeman's head and said wearily, 'Mullan's dead.' King gripped his wounded shoulder, his eyes dilated with shock as blood oozed between his fingers, dripping dark teardrops onto the tiled floor. Brogan moaned loudly and squeezed his chest in with both his gory fists, writhing on the floor amongst the empty cartridge cases and the heavy, rotten egg reek of cordite.

'He'll live,' Reidy said, nodding at King, 'but your man there ...' He didn't finish the sentence. Flynn knew that they had to act fast if they were going to keep Brogan alive and stop the IRA from overrunning the cottage and killing them all. He grasped Reidy by the shoulder, snapping him out of his stupor.

'Reidy,' Flynn panted, 'you keep an eye on the back. Get upstairs and make sure none of the bastards get near the back door! They'll try and flank us, you mark my words.' Reidy nodded and, snatching up his carbine, bounded up the cottage stairs. King was pale and stared wildly at Flynn as he pulled open his tunic, examining the gunshot wound. The bullet had gouged into King's shoulder, tearing out a jagged chunk of flesh, but thankfully it looked much worse than it was even if he was bleeding like a stuck pig. 'You'll be all right, it's only a scratch,' Flynn said reassuringly, smiling at King. 'You keep an eye on Brogan here and I'll keep an eye on the front for you.'

Flynn snatched an embroidered linen antimacassar from a nearby chair and stuffed it firmly into King's gunshot wound to soak up the blood and staunch the flow before pulling the man's tunic back over to keep the makeshift dressing in place. King seemed reassured and his face was beginning to pink again as he crawled over to where Brogan lay and began examining his wound. 'Shit! He's been shot in the chest,' King announced after pulling open the wounded man's tunic. 'Sure he's done for!'

'Not if I can help it,' Flynn shouted. Bright blood frothed and bubbled from the sucking chest wound every time Brogan wheezed out slurping breaths that were slowly inflating his chest cavity and collapsing his lungs. Without rapid action Brogan would die and both policemen knew it. Flynn looked frantically around the room for something to staunch the wound. 'Get into the pantry,' he shouted at King, 'and see if there is any greaseproof paper and some honey or jam!'

King frowned at him in obvious confusion. 'Are you after making a bloody sandwich or something? What about Brogan here?' he protested.

'Just do it! I know what I'm doing, trust me!' he shouted, galvanizing King into action as more bullets smacked into the cottage and smashed through already shattered windows, making the tattered curtains flap like shell-torn battle flags. King half crawled, half ran out of the pantry clutching a tatty roll of greaseproof paper and a battered jar of Henry Tate and Son black treacle, his eyes shining in triumph. 'You keep their heads down,' Flynn shouted and shoved a carbine into King's good hand before grabbing the paper and treacle. He knelt down next to Brogan and quickly examined the entry wound, wiping away the smear of blood before tearing a rough square of greaseproof paper from the roll.

Next he daubed thick lines of treacle on three of its four edges and as blood began to froth from the hole in Brogan's chest he slapped the patch down over the wound. Then he ripped a strip of cloth from a nearby tablecloth and wound it like a bandage around the wounded man's chest. Satisfied with his work, he looked up to see King staring at him in confusion. 'It's something I learnt in the war. The patch will stop air being sucked into his chest and collapsing his lungs. The open end will let the air out when he exhales and hopefully he'll still be alive when this is all over,' Flynn explained, as he tied off the bandage and checked to see if Brogan had any other injuries. Thankfully he did not.

McNamara slipped across the road in an attempt to work his way closer to the back of the cottage. He had seen the policemen retreat into the building and he was sure that the last one had been the object of his hatred, Constable Flynn. This was his chance to finish it once and for all. 'Christ almighty!' he yelped as a bullet clipped the wall by his head, showering him with masonry dust as he frantically looked around, trying to locate where the shot had come from, praying it wasn't from one of his own side.

Glancing up, he saw a shape in the cottage's upstairs window and ducked back behind the garden wall, trying to make himself as small as possible. Risking another look, the policeman's carbine barked again, chipping the mortar next to his cheek. He squealed and banged his temple against the wall in his rush to take cover. He was pinned down and he knew it. If he tried to go forward he would die so he did the only thing he could do in the circumstances and wormed his way back to the road.

'What are you doing?' MacEoin snapped after watching McNamara work his way back to the road and over to the command post.

He looked at his commander in frustration. 'It's no good. They've got the back covered. The bastards nearly blew my head off.' McNamara couldn't work out why MacEoin looked so angry and disappointed and the gunman hoped that it wasn't because they hadn't succeeded in killing him after all.

MacEoin was irate. One of the peelers was definitely dead, sprawled across the front seat of the van with his brains leaking out, but at least two more if not three were holed up in one of the cottages across the way. True, they were pinned down but MacEoin knew that the element of surprise had gone. The ambush had already dragged on too long and he knew that it would only be a matter of time before the noise of the fighting attracted attention and then the whole wrath of the British and their cursed Empire would begin to crash down on him.

He had wanted a quick kill and the last thing he needed was a real ruck; he simply didn't have enough men for a stand-up fight against a relief column. Bitterly he gave the mail car one long baleful look, his informant had been pretty adamant that it contained something important but he knew he would have to let it go. The policemen in the cottage had a clear line of fire to the vehicle and he knew it would be suicide to try and reach it as long as they were there.

'Damn!' he spat and both Fitzgerald and Hegarty gave him a brief sidelong glance before resuming their sporadic pot shots at the cottage. MacEoin leant against the wall, trying to think. His clothes stank of sweat and cordite and reluctantly he pulled his whistle from his pocket and slowly placed it in his mouth. He blew a long, loud blast and to his delight the firing stopped. 'Thank God,' MacEoin muttered, pleased that his men had enough discipline to cease fire and begin to withdraw in an orderly fashion. At least the Brits had been sent a clear message, which was something.

On the outskirts of the village Doyle heard the whistle blast and a tide of relief washed over him. It was over. 'Come on, let's go!' he said to his boys and led them to the north of the village, skirting the backs of the squat houses. In a way the ambush had been an anti-climax, albeit a welcome one. 'Maybe next time, lads,' he said in an attempt to cheer up his lads, who seemed genuinely disappointed at not firing a shot in anger, although he could tell that for all the huffing and puffing they were probably as relieved as he was that they hadn't been drawn into the shooting.

Doyle caught a glimpse of the bullet-riddled wreckage of the mail car, with its shattered windscreen, shredded wheels and rag-doll corpse hanging from the cab. Thick bloodstains slid down the side of the vehicle and discoloured the dirt road next to a discarded police carbine. Mesmerized, one of his boys slowed down, staring wide-eyed at the unfamiliar detritus of battle. It was the first time that the boy, Ed Riley, had ever seen a corpse and his eyes were drawn to it like a moth to a candle. Doyle hadn't got used to it either but he had a job to do and forced himself to look away as a bullet flew past his head. 'Jakers! Ed, keep moving! Keep moving or you'll get us all killed,' Doyle shouted, chivvying them on as another bullet zipped past – too close for comfort.

'Well done, lads!' MacEoin called as Doyle and his detachment trotted by. 'You done good!' Doyle could see that MacEoin looked exhausted, drained, his rifle hanging loosely at the trail in his hand. 'Keep going! Make for the rendezvous.' Doyle nodded, pleased with MacEoin's praise, pleased that he had been noticed by his hero as he stopped at the edge of the road to help his boys over the wall into the field beyond. The grass was wet on his boots and the sun had just slipped behind a long grey cloud as he led them away across the field to the rendezvous point in the distance.

Wearily MacEoin watched Doyle and his men go. They were the last and as he summoned up his last reserves of energy he poked his head back into the cottage that had acted as his command post. 'Brendan, give them a few more and then shift!' Without looking, Fitzgerald nodded and emptied the last rounds from his weapon into the side of the cottage before rising and running past his boss, off into the fields after Doyle. MacEoin took one last look around. His eyes fell on the mail car and he sighed before finally turning and following his men.

Squatting beneath a shattered window, Flynn heard the whistle blast as he held his carbine rifle across his chest. He fumbled through his pockets for another clip of ammunition and panted for breath, desperately trying to oxygenate his blood sufficiently to move. He felt drained, exhausted. A rapid succession of shots thudded into the front of the cottage and he cringed, trying to make himself as small as possible and melt into the floor. Then there was a ringing silence and he slowly raised his head to peer over the windowsill, half expecting to draw a flurry of shots. He could hear men moving and muffled shouting, then quiet. Then a lone figure emerged from the side of the cottage opposite, the one where most of the firing had come from, and dashed across the road followed seconds later by another man, stocky, clad in a brown suit and a flat cap clutching a .303 at the trail. The man stopped at the side of the road and looked back towards the crossroads.

The wreckage obscured Flynn's view but he was sure that the man was the blacksmith he'd talked to in Balinalee. It would seem that O'Neill had been wrong when he said that the blacksmith had been all talk and no action and Flynn shifted his position, trying ineffectually to line up his sights on the man. He stood up to get a better aim but the man had already gone.

It was painfully quiet and high-pitched tinnitus rang in Flynn's ears. He was conscious of the sweat soaking his armpits and a bead trickled down his temple. His ragged breathing was just about under control and he suddenly felt a savage craving for a cigarette. He glanced at his wristwatch, a souvenir of the trenches, but the adrenalin coursing through him blurred his vision. Blinking hard, he tried to focus on the watch face and then gave up as he waited below the window, straining to hear.

'I think they've gone,' he finally called to King as he walked towards the cottage door. His nerves were alive, half expecting a shot to cut short his efforts as he grasped the door handle and eased the bullet-scarred door open, letting in dusty talons of sunlight. Hesitantly his foot slid over the threshold.

'Be careful, Kevin,' King said, as he came down the stairs and slumped into a chair, exhausted, as the strength drained from his knees. Flynn could feel his eyes on his back and his hands began to shake slightly as he lifted his carbine into the ready position and, holding his breath, stepped into the street. The verdant hills were strangely quiet after the chaos of battle, disturbed only by the gentle rustling of leaves and the forlorn flap of laundry in the breeze.

Four miles away in Drumlish, Willson froze in mid step. It didn't register at first that the faint popping noise wafting on the breeze over the hills from the direction of Gaigue was the sound of distant gunfire. 'Jesus Christ!' he wailed as the penny dropped and he broke into an undignified sprint towards the post office and its telegraph office.

Drumlish's balding middle-aged postmaster, Peter O'Brien, was counting his stock of first-class postage stamps when Willson burst through the door, red faced and gulping for air. 'Mr O'Brien! The telegraph!' Willson spluttered incoherently. O'Brien looked confused and Willson jabbed a finger at the telegraph office door. 'I need you to send a cable to HQ in Longford! Tell them that it sounds like shooting up at Gaigue. I think the IRA has ambushed my boys!'

'Are you sure, Sergeant Willson?' O'Brien sputtered in disbelief.

Gasping like a landed fish, Willson bellowed, 'Just do it!'

O'Brien snapped out of his torpor and dashed into the telegraph office, leaving the sergeant contorted with fear as he listened to the incessant crackle of gunfire in the distance. He prayed that District HQ would respond quickly to his call. Half an hour later, the Auxiliaries arrived.

CHAPTER 17

M Company HQ, RIC Auxiliary Division, Longford

FLYNN WATCHED THE billowing blue-grey trail of tobacco smoke wisp from the ashtray as he cradled another chipped enamel mug of tea in both hands. The mug, as expected, was uncomfortably hot and as ever he toyed with putting it down or enduring the exquisite agony for a few moments more. The pain was comforting. It reminded him of nights when the bitter cold leeched through the studs of his hobnail boots. When it was so cold he'd stuffed his hands in the crotch of his trousers to keep warm. It reminded him of anything except Mullan's dead face staring at him like a landed fish. But every time he closed his eyes it was there.

'Is that everything?' the plain clothes detective asked, tapping Flynn's statement. He held out a pen. 'Sign here then and I'll take it to see the inspector.' Flynn signed and then, popping the papers in a brown card folder, the detective stood up and left the room, leaving him alone. From his seat Flynn looked out of the flaking iron-framed window and placed the mug on the table. The glass was cobwebbed and filthy and outside he could see RIC Auxiliaries checking their weapons and chatting without a care in the world. Some played cricket up against a wall whilst behind them men in overalls hosed down a row of dark blue RIC Crossley Tenders. The place looked more like a military barracks than the police station it was supposed to be.

He remembered the day he had been walking along Main Street with Reidy when he'd got his first sight of the Auxiliaries. They rolled into Drumlish at the regulation seven miles per hour, Lewis guns and .303s bristling from their Crossleys, exuding an air of menace. 'Who on earth are they? I didn't know the jocks had a regiment near here?' Flynn asked, confused by their khaki Balmoral bonnets and army surplus uniforms.

'They, Kevin, my boy, are the Auxies,' Reidy replied. 'They've set up camp in Longford. A rum bunch if you ask me.' Several Auxiliaries had waved at them as they rumbled by and Flynn had noticed that they were all wearing army officers' uniforms with medal ribbons splashed in abundance across their worn tunics. Some had pistols slung low, strapped to their thighs like Wild West gunslingers, all were armed to the teeth, ex-army officers recruited to take the fight to the IRA. 'They get a pound a day, all in,' Reidy continued and Flynn whistled in amazement.

'Sure, that's serious money!' Flynn said.

'Isn't it just. There isn't enough room in Phoenix Park to cope with the numbers so they train them in Gormanstown instead,' Reidy continued.

'They any good?' Flynn asked.

'As peelers they're lousy,' Reidy snorted, 'but at putting the fear of God up the Shinners they're second to none!'

'What brings them here? You would have thought that they'd have had enough of guns in the war?'

Reidy paused before he replied, 'I guess the war spoiled most of them for civilian life. Look at them, youngsters the lot of them, little more than boys really. Besides, there's not much call for gunmen when there isn't a war on.'

Flynn had the uncomfortable feeling that Reidy had meant him as well, a gunman looking for a war, when suddenly the crunch of hobnails on the gravel outside punctured his thoughts and he watched two Auxiliaries stroll past the window. 'Then he shouted, "I've lost my leg", and his mate turned round and said, "no you haven't Smithy, it's over here",' one of them said before they both burst into fits of raucous laughter. Like all of the Auxiliaries he'd seen, they had cigarettes hanging from their lips. They were a tough-looking bunch; 'Tudor's Toughs' they called themselves, in honour of their founder Major General Sir Henry Tudor.

A slight breeze came in through the open window, making sheets of green, pink and white paper flutter gently on the green baize noticeboard that filled the opposite wall. It was like any number of noticeboards in barracks all over the empire, ordering and regulating the Crown's minions across the globe. As he stubbed out his cigarette, pushing the now cold mug of tea away, the door burst open, making Flynn start. Jerking his head up, he started to rise when he saw a young RIC district inspector enter and stop in front of him. The man's eyes were deep, dark and strangely expressionless, like those of a man who had seen too much and at odds with his boyish, unaffected grin.

'Good afternoon, Constable Flynn,' he said, in a crisp Irish public-school accent. 'Please, don't get up, it's a pleasure to meet you at long last,' he added, waving Flynn back into his seat. Flynn felt a little alarmed that the officer seemed so pleased to meet him 'at long last'. He couldn't help but notice that the inspector's uniform was expensive, immaculately tailored and that he moved with the grace of a natural athlete. He had the look of a rugby player about him, Flynn thought.

'My name is DI Kelleher, Philip Kelleher,' the man said as he plonked a pair of black leather gloves, his Gieves and Hawkes cap and a blackthorn cane onto the table before flopping languidly into a chair opposite. He looked about twenty-three by Flynn's estimation, and he couldn't help notice the colourful line of ribbons for the Military Cross, War and Victory medals on his tunic. Like Flynn he was a child of the trenches. Like Flynn he had come of age in the trenches.

Kelleher grunted as he ferreted through his pocket and eventually pulled out an expensive-looking silver cigarette case engraved with the Prince of Wales feathers. He deftly flicked it open and offered Flynn a cigarette, exposing the crisp, fresh-laundered double cuff of his shirt and an enamelled Castleknock College cufflink. Flynn took a cigarette. Never turn down freebies, especially from an officer, he thought as he looked at Kelleher. 'Thank you, sir!' he said.

'You have something for me?' Kelleher said. It was more of a statement than a question and Flynn suddenly remembered the packet Willson had given him earlier that morning.

'Yes, sir, I believe I have,' Flynn replied, pulling the packet from his pocket and sliding it across the table. Kelleher looked at it and then, picking it up, he examined the seal. It was unopened. 'If you don't mind me asking, sir, what is it?' Flynn asked.

'Oh, nothing you need to concern yourself about, for the moment anyway,' Kelleher said as he casually popped the packet into his own tunic pocket, closing the matter before helping himself to a cigarette. There was a faint whiff of petrol as he flipped open a metal lighter and lit Flynn's cigarette. The smoke tasted pleasant, unlike the raw cheap ration-pack coffin nails he had got used to. It was obvious that even in his smokes the officer had expensive tastes.

'I read your report by the way,' the officer said, changing the subject as he blew out a long stream of smoke and tapped the beige folder he had tossed onto the table next to his cap. 'You know, you write well ...' He left 'for an enlisted man' unsaid but Flynn could sense him say it all the same. 'It really is good stuff, unlike most reports I read. Bad business, Constable Mullan buying the farm like that, eh, but fortunately the other chaps will pull through. That was quick thinking on your part, sorting Constable Brogan out like that. Constable Reidy has been singing your praises all afternoon!'

'It was nothing sir, just something I learnt in the army,' Flynn interjected.

'Come, come, Constable, you're far too modest. Most chaps would have gone to pieces but you kept your head. I like that.' He smiled. 'I want you to know that Mullan will probably get a posthumous Constabulary Medal on the strength of it. Not much, I know, for getting killed but better than nothing, eh? And it will help his family when it comes to pensions, et cetera.' He smiled cautiously.

'You may well get another one to go with that as well,' he said, pointing casually at Flynn's Military Medal ribbon. 'Dubs, wasn't it?' he said with the air of a man who already knew the answer. 'I was with the Leinsters myself, Ireland's finest!' he declared with a disarming smile.

'Hardly,' Flynn snorted. 'You must mean the Royal Dublin Fusiliers if you're on about Ireland's finest!'

Kelleher laughed. 'Old loyalties die hard, eh? I like that. Loyalty, that is.' His demeanour hardened. 'We were in the same division it would seem,' Kelleher said. 'Were you at Ginchy?' Flynn nodded. 'Me too. Now there's an experience I'm not keen to repeat. Is that where you got the gong?' he asked, too casually. Flynn had a feeling that he already knew the answer to that as well.

'It is,' he replied cautiously, wondering where this was going.

'Tell me about it,' Kelleher said, dripping with faux bonhomie.

'It was a real bugger's muddle,' Flynn began, 'and the battalion was all over the place, really in bits. My company commander was dead and this other officer dragged me off on a hare-brained counter attack. It was a miracle we weren't killed. He got an MC and I got this,' he said, tapping the MM ribbon.

Kelleher was watching him intently now, studying him almost. 'Do you remember the officer's name?' he asked suddenly.

'Yes, as a matter of fact I do, sir,' Flynn replied. Kelleher's gaze was fixed. 'Lieutenant Dalton.'

Kelleher took another drag on his cigarette. 'Emmet Dalton,' Kelleher said, tossing a photograph onto the table in front of Flynn. 'This him?'

Flynn looked closely at the picture. 'Aye, that's him,' he replied. 'Look, sir, you obviously know all about this, so why are you asking me these questions?' Flynn asked irritably.

Kelleher held up his hand. 'All in good time, Constable. Just indulge me for a wee while longer, please.'

Flynn glanced back at the picture. 'Mr Dalton ended up as a major, so I heard on the regimental rumour mill.'

'Oh, he did a bit more than that, Constable Flynn, a wee bit more than that. Major James Emmet Dalton MC, late of the Royal Dublin Fusiliers, is believed to be the commander of a particularly active IRA unit in Dublin and a very good friend of the big fella himself, Mick Collins!' Flynn's jaw dropped. 'And you—' Kelleher paused momentarily to add emphasis '—Constable Flynn, are the first member of the RIC I have met to admit to knowing him....'

Flynn spluttered. 'I wouldn't say I know him! We met once in the middle of a bloody battle!'

Kelleher smiled. 'And you impressed him enough for him to write you up for a medal. Now, I'm not saying that you're best pals or anything but he clearly liked you. You clearly impressed him.' Flynn looked worried. 'Don't look so pensive, Constable,' Kelleher continued. 'Like I said, old loyalties die hard and I think that you are still true to your oath as a soldier and a constable, eh?'

Flynn nodded. 'I know it sounds a bit trite, sir, but I gave my word to serve the crown,' he said, 'and I've been given no reason to go back on it.'

'Good man! The king's salt and all that!' Kelleher declared. 'Shame not everyone is so honest. There are those who have no qualms about betraying their trust and I have a feeling that you could be very useful yet for our cause.' Flynn felt uneasy at the phrase 'useful for our cause' and shifted uncomfortably in his chair.

'What do you mean, sir?' Flynn asked.

'There is a traitor in our ranks and I aim to flush him out,' Kelleher said. 'I can cope with the IRA – at least we have a good idea who they are – but the enemy within? Damn it! The gallows are too good for the treacherous little bastards!' he declared. 'You know, Flynn, I feel that I can trust you.' Flynn felt Kelleher's eyes on him, testing him. 'In your report you say you recognized one of the men who ambushed you,' Kelleher said, suddenly changing the subject.

Flynn nodded. 'I'd seen the man before at the blacksmiths in Balinalee.'

Kelleher pushed another grainy photograph across the table. 'This him?' Flynn nodded again and the inspector smiled.

'That, Constable Flynn, is Sean MacEoin. We've suspected for a while that he's been running IRA operations in the county but you are the first person to give a positive identification. I may well get uniform to pay him a visit, if he isn't already on the run. You know, Constable,' Kelleher continued, 'a man like you could be very useful to me. That packet Sergeant Willson gave you was a little test. Willson said you were a good man and I needed to see if I could trust you. You looked after my packet and didn't try to open it. If you had, you'd have found it stuffed with old newspaper, that's all. There are one or two hereabouts who wouldn't have been so honest.'

Flynn's eyes narrowed as he watched the inspector. 'Useful in what way?' he asked, his heart pounding.

'That, I'm afraid, I can't tell you just yet,' Kelleher said, flashing Flynn one of his disarming toothy smiles. 'How can I put it? Sometimes my duties require me to carry out special assignments of a politically delicate nature.'

Alarm bells clanged in Flynn's head. 'Please, sir, cut me some slack and spare me the "You're just the man for the job" speech and cut to the chase, will you? What do you really want?' Flynn blurted out and to his horror Kelleher burst out laughing.

'The look on your face!' Kelleher spluttered, trying not to choke as tears welled in his eyes. 'Please, don't look so worried, old chap, I'm not asking you to join some sort of loyalist death squad or anything. Lord no!' Flynn relaxed, obviously relieved. 'I'm not a big fan of the Shinners and the mess they've made of my … er … our country but I'm not a big fan of murdering them either. That sort of thing just adds fuel to the whole bloody bonfire. The rebels have a bizarre fascination with martyrdom after all. Personally I have no intention of supplying them with the stuff of yet another ballad. No, the powers that be want me to try and talk to them!'

The room was suddenly quiet and Flynn could hear himself breathe whilst the crunch of hobnails in the courtyard resonated in his ears. Outside, he could hear the birds twittering in the eaves and for the second time his jaw dropped. 'I need someone reliable to watch my back, someone who doesn't go to pieces in a crisis, someone who keeps his head in a fight and knows what to do in one, and if that man is also acquainted with someone in Collins' inner circle, so much the better!' Kelleher looked at Flynn. 'Well, Constable, what do you say?'

Flynn's mind raced. 'What about Sergeant Willson? He won't be happy, being left shorthanded again, what with Brogan and Reidy,' he said.

Kelleher smiled. 'Sergeant Willson is a bit of an old woman but he is a good man. He's been very useful these last couple of months but the heart's gone out of him. He's applied for a transfer to the Liverpool City Police, you know, so I'm not sure he'll be too worried. Besides, it was him who mentioned you to me in the first place.'

Suddenly, a small familiar voice in the back of Flynn's head was screaming, 'Don't do it! Never volunteer for anything!', but in all honesty he was already getting bored with ordinary police work – or more accurately the lack of it. IRA intimidation was widening the gap between the constabulary and the community and Flynn was increasingly worried about playing moving target to any would-be rebel with a gun. 'So, Sergeant Willson will not be minding?' Flynn asked as he looked at the grainy pictures of MacEoin and Dalton.

Dalton was in his British officer's uniform, a neat toothbrush moustache on his upper lip, looking proud and smug sporting his MC and for a fleeting moment he was back in that trench at Ginchy. Mullan was dead because of men like these. Kathleen was sent away because of men like these. Ireland was turning to shit because of men like these. It was then that Flynn realized that it wasn't the rebels' politics he despised, it was their methods, and that he couldn't care less whether Ireland was a republic or a monarchy as long as it was peaceful. 'All right, sir,' he finally said, 'I'll do it.'

Kelleher broke into a broad grin. 'Good man! I had a feeling that you'd say that. There's a patrol leaving in about half an hour. I want you to go with it. It'll wait in Drumlish whilst you collect your stuff then bring you back.'

Flynn nodded again and, as he sat wondering what he'd let himself in for, the inspector rose and strolled over to the door. His hand hovered over the handle and he turned to Flynn. 'Oh, yes, I nearly forgot but I think you'll be needing these,' he said, tossing something else towards Flynn, who was barely able to suppress his grin as he looked down at the new object. There on the table was a set of RIC sergeant's chevrons. It would seem that he had passed Kelleher's test with flying colours. 'From now on you're an acting sergeant.' Kelleher beamed. 'With immediate effect, so get them sewn on and get yourself over to Drumlish. We'll talk in the morning.'

Flynn picked up the stripes. Sergeant Flynn, he thought. Now there was something he thought he'd never hear again. The door thudded shut; the inspector was gone.

CHAPTER 18

Newtonforbes railway station, County Longford

IT WAS BLOODY obvious that Joe Maguire was not a happy man as he got off the train. 'MacEoin wants to see you,' Doyle said as they looked apprehensively at the plain clothes detective loitering by the station exit, obviously over-reading his paper, whilst another lounged, a little too nonchalantly, outside, eyeing up the passengers as they left. He was too well dressed to be anything else other than a detective. Only a complete halfwit would have been fooled and the policeman knew it; in fact, it was obvious that he counted on it.

'Jakers, keep it down,' Maguire hissed. 'The place is crawling with peelers.'

Doyle shrugged. 'Sure, everywhere is these days but I've lads watching over us.' Maguire pretended to ignore the detective as they left the station and the detective pretended to ignore Maguire as he secured his tatty brown cardboard suitcase to the luggage rack of his bike. It was a game they played.

'Aye, it's a grand game, is it not. They watch us and we watch them and we all pretend that we're not,' Maguire said bitterly. Doyle looked puzzled; it was all a bit too deep for him but then he was new to the game too.

'How was Belfast?' Doyle asked in a pathetic attempt to drum up a conversation but Maguire just shrugged.

'Shite as ever,' he replied irritably. 'Let's go. I've got words for the boss too.' Doyle lit a cigarette and puffed out a cloud of cheap blue-grey smoke whilst Maguire hopped onto his bike and pedalled off rapidly down the road, with Doyle cycling frantically to keep up. Behind them the detective folded his paper and walked into the railway station to join his companion.

'What do you know about this Gaigue Cross business?' Maguire asked when they were finally clear of the town.

'I was there, Joe, me and some of the boys. MacEoin ordered it,' Doyle replied. 'Commandant Connolly said it was all right,' he added nervously.

'Did he now?' Maguire replied, with obvious irritation. 'We'll see about that. They can do what they like with their flying column but I don't like my boys pulling an operation without me! So what did they have you doing then?' he asked Doyle.

'Nothing much,' Doyle responded. 'They got the boys to act as scouts and to cover the escape routes. It was the column who did the shooting. It was them that plugged the peeler.' Maguire nodded and Doyle could see that he was angry.

'That's not the fecking point!' Maguire spat, white with suppressed rage. Doyle knew that Maguire had a fearful temper when he got going. 'I'm sorry, Paddy, sure it's not your fault. You were only doing what you were told, like a soldier should,' he said quietly, aware that his anger was unnerving the boy. 'So what else has been going on in my absence?' Maguire asked.

'Mick McNamara escaped from the Brits! He's mighty bitter about his brother and none too pleased we left him,' Doyle said excitedly. 'They say that he did for one of the peelers who shot Jerry and now he's after the other one!'

'Well, it's good news that he escaped but this is war and he shouldn't take it personally. But then I would have expected no less from him,' Maguire sneered.

'The boss put me in charge of one of the cut-off groups,' Doyle said, instantly regretting referring to MacEoin as 'the boss' in front of Maguire. Maguire grinned at the boy, letting the comment pass.

'Well done, Paddy boy, your first command and in a real battle too! You'll be a commandant before you know it!' he teased and Doyle's face flushed with pride as the lazy summer sun beat down on them. As they pedalled Maguire went quiet, mulling over what he would say to MacEoin, and by the time they reached the smithy his temper had cooled a little. This worried Doyle; he'd been told that cool was when Maguire was at his most dangerous.

Outside the forge Maguire flung his bike against the wall and strode into the shadows of the forge. Dint! Dint! Dint! MacEoin's face was bathed in sparks as he rhythmically struck a red-hot iron bar. Even with the furnace, the forge was a welcome sanctuary from the summer sun. The blacksmith ignored him. 'Sean!' Maguire shouted. The hammer paused in mid stroke and MacEoin turned his head, looking across the workshop at the figure framing the doorway.

'Joe, you're back!' MacEoin beamed as he put his tools down and wiped his hands on his apron. 'Come on in!'

'Who said you could use my boys?' Maguire asked angrily, ignoring MacEoin's outstretched hand.

'What?' he finally said.

'You heard me! Who said you could use my men!' he demanded and MacEoin's smile slipped.

'Keep the noise down! Do you want everyone to know our business?' he said. Doyle could hear their raised voices and looked anxiously towards the RIC barracks, expecting it to disgorge gun-toting policemen at any moment but instead a bored constable looked out of the window and Doyle felt his stomach turn. Shortly afterwards the policeman disappeared and after a few moments he heard the crackly tones of a gramophone record coming from the direction of the barracks.

MacEoin pulled the workshop door shut, cutting out the street, before turning to face Maguire. 'How many times do I have to tell you, Joe, they're not your boys, they belong to the army, and I command in this county, so that makes them mine!' he said slowly, deliberately, with a hard, threatening edge to his tone. Everyone knew that MacEoin was a bad man to cross, but then so was Maguire.

'I don't care what you or GHQ thinks – they are my boys! You know how it works; they picked me, not you. Your precious GHQ didn't give me the job and without me most of them would give up and go home and you know it! So spare me the GHQ bollocks! No one around here gives a toss what Mulcahy or Collins think!'

The blacksmith remained quiet. He was all too familiar with the pseudo-democratic quirks and vagaries of the Volunteers' command structure but he could not allow anyone, even Maguire, to defy his authority too openly. 'Anyway, Joe, it was too good an opportunity to miss, you understand. My sources told me that it was a good target and a good opportunity to put pressure on the police.' He decided not to tell Maguire the real reason for his decision to attack the mail car. 'Besides, there was no way of getting word to you away in Belfast before the attack so I decided to get on with it. Sean agreed with me and, besides, it doesn't do the boys any good to be idle for too long.' MacEoin added, 'Your boys done good, and we got one of the bastards to boot!'

Maguire looked far from placated. 'I don't bloody care, Sean. You used my boys without me knowing! So what was so flaming important about the post that you had to attack it?' He could tell that there was something MacEoin wasn't telling him and he couldn't care less whether Sean Connolly approved of the plan or not. As far as he was concerned Connolly was so far up MacEoin's arse that he might as well wear him as a hat. 'I don't give a shit what you do with your column boys but keep away from my lads, unless I say so!' MacEoin stood stock still and silent. 'Did you plan this pantomime before you asked me to go to Belfast? Is that why you asked me to go, to get me out of the way?' Maguire squared up to MacEoin and for a moment the blacksmith thought that he was going to take a swing at him.

'Joe, Joe.' MacEoin raised his hands, attempting to ease the tension. 'It was an opportunity too good to miss, that's all.' Maguire relaxed. The moment had passed and he felt the rage ebb from him. There was a noise behind him and he spun around, tensing once more, ready for action, and only relaxed slightly when he saw it was McNamara standing in the back doorway.

'You left me, you bastard!' McNamara spat accusingly.

Maguire's hand slipped into his pocket and grasped the butt of his pistol. 'There's no need for that,' MacEoin said as he placed his hand on Maguire's forearm.

'It's a fecking war, you eejit,' Maguire hissed at McNamara. 'If I'd stayed then we all would have been in the bag or worse. Look, I'm truly sorry about Jerry but there was nothing I could do about it.' McNamara looked unconvinced.

'Precisely,' MacEoin interrupted. 'It's a war and people die. Sadly, that is the nature of the business. Look, Mick, Jerry's sacrifice will not go unremembered. He died for Ireland, for the cause, and it's a price all of us here are prepared to pay. We all knew that when we volunteered, so let's just hope that it wasn't for nothing. It's hard enough to be fighting the Brits; let's not fight amongst ourselves. Isn't that what the bastards want? That's how they've always beaten us, by divide and rule!'

McNamara stared at Maguire in silence. 'Happen you're right,' McNamara said eventually, 'though I want those bastards in Drumlish to pay.'

MacEoin sighed. 'There will be time enough for killing, Mick. Time enough, *tiocfaidh ár lá.*'

Maguire had always had his doubts about McNamara. He loved guns and killing too much and he was convinced that Mick wasn't quite all there.

'Oh, Joe, by the way, in the circumstances I thought that it was best that Mick joined the column,' MacEoin said, referring to the County Longford Flying Column, the band of full-time IRA men who acted directly under MacEoin's orders.

McNamara smiled and Maguire sighed with relief. 'You're not wrong. I don't need to be watching my back on a job.'

MacEoin nodded and turned to McNamara. 'Now, Mick, be a good fella and get yourself back next door. If the peelers were to see you, then there'd be no end of trouble.' McNamara stared angrily at Maguire in naked hostility before nodding his head and leaving the room. 'Now we've got that sorted, can we get back to the business in hand?' MacEoin asked Maguire. 'Don't worry about Mick – he's a wee bit of a wild one but he has a fearful hatred of the Brits and we need that. Now, we've been through a lot, you and me,' MacEoin continued, 'what with the rising and all, but times are changing, so they are. The war is hotting up and I think that I might be going on the run, after our little stunt at Gaigue. I'm going to need good men around me. We need to work together, Joe. If we don't pull together, the Brits will have won.'

Maguire nodded. He knew that what MacEoin was saying made sense. 'All right, but next time I want to know.' MacEoin didn't like Maguire's tone but he would let it pass for now. Things had not gone well with Maguire's battalion since he was elected its leader and MacEoin made a mental note to speak to Connolly about finding a replacement.

Be very careful, Joe, MacEoin thought to himself, very careful.

Maguire let go of the gun in his pocket, knowing that shooting either McNamara or MacEoin would be suicidal. He realized that despite their history he really didn't like MacEoin, with his false charm, but not enough to throw everything away shooting him. The blacksmith put his arm around him and directed him towards the back office. 'Well, Joe, how was Belfast?'

CHAPTER 19

Greville Arms Hotel, Granard, County Longford

'BLOODY RAIN!' CURSED the drayman hunched under an old oilskin rain cape, puffing on his pipe. Puddles of rainwater filled the potholes and the wheels of the dray sent up gouts of water every time it bounced through one. Water was pooling on the driver's bench and he felt it soak through the seat of his trousers. 'Bloody rain!' he muttered again as the dray lurched heavily through another pothole, soaking the two policemen walking down the pavement. 'Sorry, Constable!' the drayman called before muttering quietly, 'Bloody peelers! Bloody rain!'

'Bloody eejit!' cursed a sodden young constable as the rainwater began to broach his defences and seep down the neck of his greatcoat, causing his mind to wander to fantasies about firesides and hot drinks.

'Sure, it's always quiet on a Wednesday afternoon, what with the shops taking stock and all,' the other constable said.

'You just have to keep an eye out for the traffic. Out here in the sticks these culchie beggars seem to make the rules up as they go along.' The young policeman looked menacingly after the retreating dray before turning and resuming his stroll back to Barrack Street and the end of his shift. As they passed the Greville Arms, the older constable, Peter Cooney, gave the front door a furtive sidelong glance and then said quietly to his companion in a broad Sligo accent, 'You'll not want to be going in there.'

'Why's that?' the younger man asked.

'Because it's crawling with Shinners and they'll shoot you as soon as look at you. Best be giving it a wide berth,' Cooney replied. 'Old Sergeant Campion used to pop his head in every now and then, just to let the Fenians know he had his eye on them.'

'Wasn't he the fella who shot himself?' his young companion asked.

'Aye, that he did, but 'twas a terrible accident, so it was. Terrible!

He'd put his blasted gun in his tunic pocket to pump up his bicycle tyres and the stupid thing fell out and went off. Poor man bled to death before we could do anything about it. Sure 'twas a terrible business. Some here about say it was just deserts, curse them. He was a hard man was Sergeant Campion.'

Kitty Kiernan walked past the two policemen without a word. She had no intention of swapping pleasantries with traitors like them and she got the impression that the feeling was mutual. 'That's Kitty Kiernan,' she heard one of the policemen say from behind her. 'They say she's Mick Collins' squeeze. Right vipers' nest of Fenians the Kiernan family. You'd do well to stay well away, especially if she really is mixed up with Collins,' she heard, as their voices grew faint and they headed towards the barracks.

It had never really crossed Kitty's mind that the police knew about her family's involvement with Sinn Féin and the IRA or even Mick Collins. Collins, MacEoin and her brother did their best to shield her from what was going on but she wasn't stupid. She could see the risks that men like MacEoin ran every day for Ireland, which is why she was so pleased that her brother was not an activist. She'd heard MacEoin refer to it as a game once or twice and that they were all players, which had puzzled her at the time but it somehow made sense.

As she pushed open the pub's front door, the stink of tobacco smoke, beer and stale people slapped her in the face. She paused as she furled her dripping umbrella. 'Afternoon, Miss Kitty,' a gruff voice called from the lounge bar as she unbuttoned her raincoat and headed for the door marked 'Private' besides the dark, drink-stained bar.

Despite the early hour the bar was already beginning to fill with the 'usual suspects', mostly workmen popping in for a swift pint on the way home or, in some cases, instead of going home. McNamara, Fitzgerald and Hegarty sat in the corner, nursing dark pints of stout. McNamara took another mouthful of the dark liquid before getting up and following Kitty towards the door.

'How was Dublin?' a familiar voice asked as she entered the back room behind the bar. MacEoin put down the mug of tea that he was nursing and rose from his chair. 'It is always a pleasure to see you, Kitty, especially when you've been away to see the big fella!' he said with a smile, referring to his friend and military superior, Michael Collins. 'Now, tell me, did Mick give you anything for me?'

Kitty glanced behind her as she heard the door open and saw

McNamara step into the room. She looked nervously at McNamara; she didn't like him much.

'Don't go minding Mick there, he's a good lad. So what did Mick give you for me?' he asked again, his hand outstretched, the very incarnation of charm itself. Kitty drew out a long hat-pin and removed her hat before plonking it down on the table and pulling a small envelope from its lining.

'I'll be reading that later,' MacEoin said as he popped the envelope into his waistcoat pocket. MacEoin found Kitty an extremely useful direct line to Collins in GHQ.

'Sean, is it safe for you to be here?' Kitty asked.

'Sure it is,' he said confidently. 'Why do you ask?'

She told him what she'd overheard the policeman say and MacEoin laughed.

'They're a bunch of old women without their sergeant and they won't be setting a foot in here. Don't worry yourself about it Kitty, darling. The local plods know better than to stir up trouble here. Isn't that so, Mick?' he said to McNamara, who nodded in agreement.

'That they do,' McNamara said.

'You look worried, Kitty, darling,' MacEoin said reassuringly. 'Was there anything that happened in Dublin?' He looked concerned. 'Is Mick all right?' he asked, meaning Collins not McNamara.

'Mick's fine,' Kitty said. 'It's not that ... it's ...' she stuttered.

'It's what?' MacEoin asked. 'Take your time, Kitty, tell me what's happened. If someone has done anything to you, just give me their names and I can get the boys to have a word with them.'

'Oh, I don't think that that will be necessary,' she replied. 'I'm not sure whether it is trouble but it was the strangest thing. There was a man at the station ...' Kitty paused. She was a pretty girl and MacEoin watched her closely. If someone had taken a fancy to her, he could understand that but he also knew that the mere mention of Collins' name would have been enough to send any would-be suitor scuttling for cover. But Kitty wasn't stupid and MacEoin knew she wouldn't have mentioned Collins to a total stranger.

'So, what did this man want?' MacEoin asked, flashing Kitty a reassuring smile as he gestured for her to sit. 'Was it some fella trying to get you to walk out with him?' he asked.

She shook her head. 'No, it was not,' she replied. 'He said that he was a policeman and that he wanted to talk to Mick!'

MacEoin's eyes narrowed as he churned this information around in his mind. 'Well, Kitty, my girl, tell me all about what this shoneen wanted with you.' He paused and asked finally, 'Tell me, was he alone? In fact, tell me everything that he said.' Kitty sat down and began to speak.

The platform had been thick with billowing grey smoke mixing with the damp air, filling the empty platform with a fine smog, as the train hissed to a halt at Newtonforbes station and a lone porter, clad in the green livery of the Midlands and Great Western Railway, reluctantly emerged from the snug warmth of the ticket office to assist any alighting passengers with their baggage.

The stationmaster had glanced at his fob-watch. The train was more or less on time and Kitty stepped lightly from the dark crimson second-class carriage onto the platform and placed her floral carpet portmanteau at her feet. She noticed that she was the only passenger on the platform. 'Afternoon, miss,' the porter said politely, in his thick Longford accent, and he tapped the peak of his cap subserviently, anticipating a tip. 'Take your bag for you, miss?' Kitty smiled.

'Yes, please,' she said and the porter picked up her bag and turned towards the station exit and the bus stop outside. The shops were already shut or closing and two young men lounged in an open-topped car, chatting. She didn't recognize either of them but they were obviously waiting for someone. The porter placed her bag down at the bus stop and she gave him some money. 'Thank you, miss,' he repeated, touching his cap again before scurrying back to the comfort of the ticket office and a warming cup of tea no doubt.

She noticed the men stop talking and the nearest, a dark-haired man in his early twenties, got out of the car and began to walk across the street. She was rooted to the spot when she realized that the man was walking towards her with steady purposeful strides. Maybe MacEoin had sent someone to collect her from the train, she thought, but somehow she had a niggling feeling that that was not the case and that the man was not a friend. She tried hard to bite back on the fear that was welling up inside her; besides, she knew that she would never outrun the men and so she watched his approach like a cornered gazelle watches a ravenous lion.

Then the man was in front of her and with a boyish grin he doffed his hat, exposing a mop of dark, wavy hair. 'Good afternoon, Miss Kiernan. It is Miss Kiernan, isn't it?' he said. It was obviously a rhetorical question for he gave no indication that he didn't already know the answer, and his crisp Irish public-school accent told Kitty that he was unlikely to be one of MacEoin's boys.

'My name is Philip Kelleher, District Inspector Kelleher of His Majesty's Royal Irish Constabulary, and if you don't mind, miss, I'd like to have a little chat with you if I may,' he said, with forced civility. Kitty knew that it was an order, not a request, and despite his cheery tone there was an edge to his voice that told her she had no choice in the matter.

'What do you want?' she spat contemptuously. 'I doubt that I have anything of interest to say to the likes of you!'

Kelleher smiled warmly, unfazed by her spleen. 'Au contraire, Miss Kiernan, au contraire,' he teased, his dark eyes sparkling mischievously. 'I believe that you could tell me quite a bit that would be of interest, especially as you have just been visiting a certain Mr Collins over in Dublin, eh, what? I'm sure I'd be fascinated by that.' He smiled when he saw her visibly blanch at the mention of Collins' name.

How much did they know? she thought. How did he know that she had just been to visit Collins? Did the Brits know where he was? Had she endangered him? She could feel the panic rising once more like the tide.

'Oh, please don't worry, Miss Kiernan, your secret is safe with me,' he chirped as he gestured towards the waiting car. 'Please, allow me to give you a lift home to Granard.' And placing his arm around her shoulder, looking to all the world like he was greeting his girlfriend, he steered her gently towards the waiting car. She was trapped and she knew it. The driver sat silently behind the wheel and only spared her a cursory glance. She noticed how pale his grey eyes were before he resumed scanning the street. His scarred face was blank and emotionless. Kitty shivered involuntarily.

'After you, miss,' Kelleher said politely as he helped her into the car and the driver started the engine. She thought again about running but her body language must have been obvious and Kelleher placed a firm hand in a vice-like grip on her shoulder. 'I wouldn't if I were you, miss,' Kelleher said with a smile and helped her into her seat.

'You'll get nothing from me,' she said defiantly and to her intense irritation Kelleher just smiled.

'That depends,' he said, running his eye over her body and leaving the sentence unqualified, as she looked nervously at the inspector. There was a hint of menace in his charming voice and now she really did feel afraid. 'Let's go,' he said to the driver and the car crunched into gear and lurched off down the road. For a few minutes Kitty and Kelleher sat in silence. She tried desperately not to look at the inspector but, uncomfortably, she felt inexorably drawn to him. 'Well, Miss Kiernan, don't look so worried, it's not like I'm going to shoot you or anything!' he finally said. 'Believe me, if that was what I wanted you'd already be dead and, besides, I don't shoot women. Not unless I have to,' he quipped in a tone that was hard for Kitty to tell whether he was joking or not.

'What do you want?' she finally said through gritted teeth. 'Am I under arrest then?'

'Oh no, far from it, so please, just sit back, enjoy the ride, as they say, and listen to what I have to tell you. I have a message for you that I want you to pass on to Collins, and please don't insult my intelligence by claiming that you don't know him. I know you do and I know that you have just been with him in Dublin.'

Kitty stared at Kelleher; she was trying to work out who this Kelleher was or even if it was his real name and what he was after. She knew that there were policemen out there who sympathized with the cause; even Mick had told her that he had contacts in the army, the police and the civil service, so why couldn't this policeman be a potential recruit? Surely, if he meant her or Collins harm, he wouldn't have just walked up to her, bold as brass, and said hello the way he did? The man began to intrigue her and she had to admit that she found him attractive to look at, even if he was probably a traitor to Ireland.

'Go on, then,' she said, trying to sound calm, in control, 'be about your business and then be on your way, Judas.'

'Charming,' he laughed before continuing. 'It's quite simple really, Miss Kiernan. I have powerful friends in the Castle and over the water in London too and they want me to make contact with Collins. Now I know, and you know, that you are in regular contact with the man, so to speak, so let him know what I have just said.'

Kitty looked at him, aghast. 'And you think that even if I did know Michael Collins that he'd risk meeting you just because I asked him to?'

'You know, Miss Kiernan—' He smiled again, like a shark '—you'll never know unless you ask him, will you?' Suddenly the car lurched to a stop and Kelleher leant across her, slightly too close, and slipped open her door. 'I think this is your stop, Miss Kiernan,' he said, 'and believe me when I say it's been my pleasure.'

She stepped onto the pavement and the grey-eyed driver handed down her portmanteau. Neither spoke. 'Remember, Miss Kiernan, please pass on my message. It's very important and don't worry about getting in touch. I'll find you.' He doffed his hat once more and hopped back into the passenger seat of the car, then it spluttered off into the dampening evening.

'And that, Sean, is what happened on my way home,' Kitty said as she finished her tale and turned back to face MacEoin who was still gulping down the last of his tepid tea. 'Do you know anything about this Inspector Kelleher?' she asked him.

MacEoin shook his head and shrugged. 'Never heard of him,' he lied. 'Don't you worry yourself, Kitty, darling, I have a few contacts in the constabulary and I'm sure I can find out who he is. Mick—' He turned to McNamara '—get on to it for me, will you? Get the lads to ask around. I want to know everything there is to know about District Inspector Kelleher.'

'Will do, Sean,' McNamara said, and left the room.

MacEoin looked back at Kitty and smiled reassuringly. 'He said he'd be in touch?' She nodded. 'Good,' he continued. 'There might be some mileage in this. Best we let the big fella know about it. See what he has to say. He'll not be pleased that the peelers have been bothering you, so he won't. You done good, Kitty, my girl. You let me know as soon as you hear from this Kelleher fella again. As soon as, mind you, as soon as. Until I know what this peeler is up to, I think that we should tread very carefully around this Mr Kelleher of yours, very careful indeed.' He patted the envelope in his pocket and touched the peak of his flat cap with his thumb and index finger. 'Be very careful, Kitty. If this fella is up to no good, then he's a dead man, is young Inspector Kelleher, so he is.' And he was gone.

Kitty sat back in her chair, thinking about the handsome young policeman with his dark eyes and boyish grin. It really worried her that Kelleher seemed to know so much about her and that she knew almost nothing about him – but maybe that would change in time. What worried her even more was that she did not really know whether she was looking forward to meeting him again or not.

CHAPTER 20

Longford Town

FLYNN HAD BEEN unnaturally impressed at how easily Willson had accepted the news of his transfer to special duties. 'Sergeant already and the ink not dry on your enlistment forms? God save Ireland, what has become of the constabulary?' Willson had joked.

'Well, now, I'll miss you, Kevin, my boy, for you've the makings of a decent copper about you,' O'Neill had said, barely able to hide his disappointment that Flynn was going. 'Don't do anything stupid,' he added quietly. Flynn knew that he'd miss Willson with his puffing and panting and O'Neill's sardonic wit, but without Kathleen, Drumlish held few attractions for him. Maybe, if he played his cards right, he'd get a transfer to the relative safety of the depot in Dublin. Until then he was stuck with Kelleher and his harebrained scheme to make contact with the IRA leadership and all the cloak and dagger sneaking about.

Longford town centre was busy despite the Troubles and as Flynn leant at the corner of Richmond and Main Street, watching the shadows lengthen, he forced himself to gaze once more at his tatty copy of the *Irish Times* for the umpteenth time and realized that he had long stopped even pretending to read it. There were too many long words and even the crossword was beyond him. Kathleen was good at crosswords, he thought, as his mind drifted to more pleasant distractions.

'Stay focused,' he muttered to himself as he scanned the shoppers for any signs of anything suspicious, although he wasn't really that sure what suspicious behaviour looked like in the first place, especially as he'd received no real training in detective work. It felt really strange to be in civvies again after so long. He'd got used to uniforms of one sort or other and sometimes it almost felt like he'd never been out of one since he was eighteen. It made him even more conscious than usual of the dead weight of his .38 Webley revolver in the bottom of his overcoat pocket. 'Wouldn't it be good if policemen didn't have to carry guns?' he'd once said to Willson.

'Aye, there was a time,' the sergeant had replied dolefully. 'I guess you've heard I'm off to Liverpool then? At least there are no guns there,' the sergeant had said. 'Let's hope not, eh?' Flynn had added. 'Aye, let's hope not,' Willson had agreed. It would be a few weeks yet before he left.

From his vantage point Flynn could see Kelleher and Kitty strolling arm in arm down Main Street, chatting and looking casually into shop windows like an intimate couple. He could see them laughing and rolled his eyes. 'Are you sure that this is a good idea?' he'd asked Kelleher about his meetings with Kitty. 'Where is all this going?' Flynn persisted.

'Slowly slowly catchy monkey,' Kelleher had replied in good spirits but Flynn didn't really have a clue what he was on about.

'You know, sir,' he'd said to Kelleher, 'I haven't really been trained for this cloak and dagger malarkey.'

Kelleher had just looked at him and said, 'Just stay calm and keep your wits about you. It's a bit like going on a trench raid. Piece of cake really.'

Sounds like *Boy's Own* bollocks to me, Flynn had thought and now he was beginning to regret volunteering to work with Kelleher. Never volunteer for anything, Flynn rued. Didn't the army teach you anything?

He shivered as a cold wind picked up and with a quick flick of his wrist snapped the collar of his coat up against the chill before tucking the newspaper under his arm. Then, as casually as possible, he relocated to a shop doorway some fifty feet away whilst further down the street two constables walked through the crowd, scanning the shoppers suspiciously as they approached him. One of them even looked directly at Flynn but without a glimmer of recognition. Thank God for that, Flynn thought. The last thing he needed was to be recognized by some local policeman. He felt conspicuous enough as it was.

'Is that the bastard?' Fitzgerald asked Maguire as they watched Flynn move from his street corner observation post.

'Aye, that's the beggar,' Maguire replied quietly.

'Shall I cap him now?' Fitzgerald asked, without emotion. Maguire shook his head. Further down the street Maguire could see Paddy Doyle following Kelleher and Kitty and he was worried that

McNamara was out there somewhere, well out of sight. He was the wild card and Maguire hoped that he wouldn't do something stupid, like gunning down Flynn in the street.

'You seen Mick anywhere?' Maguire asked Fitzgerald.

'Eunan's with him – he'll make sure he doesn't do nothing stupid,' Fitzgerald said as he glanced up and down the street.

'Yous in the Rah, mister?' Flynn suddenly looked round to find a flea-bitten, barefoot urchin of about ten years of age standing beside him. 'Yous in the Rah, mister?' he pestered again, meaning the IRA. It never ceased to amaze him how the street kids seemed to be able to sniff out suspicious characters like a bloodhound.

'Piss off!' Flynn hissed, shoving the boy to one side.

'Yous a peeler then, mister?'

'Piss off!' Flynn repeated.

'So, mister,' the boy persisted, oblivious of Flynn's remarks. 'Yous after yer man over there then?' Flynn assumed that he meant Kelleher and cursed silently. Was it that obvious? But then it dawned on him that assumption was the mother of all cock-ups and he realized the boy was looking somewhere else. It was then that Flynn saw him, a young man, pretending to look in a shop window a few yards behind Kelleher, his right hand firmly in his trenchcoat pocket. Flynn cursed himself for being shown up by a ten-year-old. 'Anyone else?' Flynn asked. The boy grinned, a grubby gap-toothed grin.

'It'll cost yer, mister,' he said and Flynn flicked a shiny silver sixpence in the boy's direction. He was quick and caught it easily in his grubby paw before nodding off in another direction. Flynn looked around at a tall blond man standing on his own, about thirty yards back. 'Now, be a good fella and piss off!' Flynn hissed, and the boy darted away into the crowd.

'Shit!' hissed Maguire. 'That little brat has fingered Doyle.' Fitzgerald went to move but Maguire caught his arm. 'Wait,' he ordered.

Fitzgerald looked up and noticed Flynn looking at him, so he quickly turned to look in the shop window. 'Me and you are going to have words, you little beggar,' Fitzgerald muttered, making a mental note to speak to the boy.

Flynn was worried and blood pounded in his ears, reminding him of the sea breaking on the shore. He felt incredibly conspicuous and vulnerable and felt a sudden urge to run after the two uniformed policemen and tell them everything. He fumbled in his pocket for a cigarette, grazing his knuckles on his pistol.

'Can I get you a light?' Flynn jumped.

A man stood next to him, casually gazing off down the street, looking at nothing in particular. Flynn cursed himself for letting someone creep up on him like that and allowing the boy to distract him. It was a schoolboy error. Maybe the boy had done it deliberately? He tried to stay calm and looked down at the man who was lean and dark, a few inches shorter than Flynn and about ten years older. His flat cap was pulled very low over his eyes – his cold, hard, empty eyes – and the collar of his worn trenchcoat was flipped up against the elements. The man smiled at Flynn with an utter lack of warmth, dripping insincerity, showing his teeth like a circling shark.

The man struck a match against a matchbox and held the flaring piece of wood up in his cupped hands for Flynn, who leant forward, placing the tip of his cigarette into the flame and drew in. It was then that he noticed, as the man shook out the match and tossed it away, that there was something wrong with his left hand – the thumb was missing. Probably a war wound from the man's age. There were plenty of men about with bits missing after all.

'Thanks,' Flynn said.

'Don't mention it,' Maguire replied, completing the ritual, and for a moment there was silence. 'You be careful now,' he said with a smile whilst patting Flynn on the arm before melting expertly into the crowd. Flynn stood still, the smouldering cigarette hanging from his lips as he tried to work out whether what had happened was something or nothing.

'Where have I heard that voice before?' he thought and he racked his brains trying to remember whether he had met anyone with a missing thumb. Then the penny dropped, dropped like a stone. The man he had shot in February outside the barracks, the bloody thumb in the dirt. He shuddered and then panic gripped him as he desperately scanned the crowd. He could no longer see the two men the boy had pointed out. Galvanized into action, he sped off down the street, barging his way noisily through the crowd until he saw Kelleher and Kitty ahead of him, strolling along, oblivious. He skidded to a halt behind them.

'Yes?' said Kelleher, with obvious irritation, giving Flynn a hostile look.

★

Maguire finally met up with Doyle and Fitzgerald on the corner of Great Water Street and climbed into the black Austin Tourer that was waiting for them there. 'Any sign of Mick and Eunan?' Maguire asked but Fitzgerald shook his head and, much to his irritation, after ten minutes there was still no sign of them. Two policemen strolled around the corner and headed in their direction.

'All right, let's be off then,' Maguire said and without a word the driver pulled away as Doyle slumped back in his seat and muttered, 'I don't know why we don't just shoot the bastards and be done with it?'

Maguire gave Doyle a sidelong glance. 'Because, Pat, m'boy, the boss, he don't want it yet. That, m'boy, is why.'

'Jesus, Joe, I nearly had a heart attack when I saw you give that peeler a light!' Doyle spluttered and Maguire flashed him a toothy smile. 'Why did you have to go and talk to him?' Doyle asked.

'Because I was after getting a good look at the fella, just so I know what he looks like. After all, I wouldn't want to be shooting the wrong man!' Maguire laughed. It was a hollow laugh, like a man making an effort to laugh at a joke that wasn't really funny. Fitzgerald laughed too. Doyle nodded again and shifted in his seat as the car bumped over a pothole, wondering whether it was all just talk or whether Maguire really was that cold about killing.

'I really wish that we would just get on with this bloody business and take the bastards out. Isn't that where all this is leading anyway?' Doyle asked, without really expecting an answer.

'Arra, you're probably not wrong, Pat, but it's up to yer man MacEoin, not us, when we do it. Orders is orders and we have ours, so we do, isn't that so, Brendan,' Maguire said, glancing sidelong at Fitzgerald.

'That's what soldiers do, Pat, what they are told, and until we get told otherwise we just keep an eye on those two fellas. There'll be time enough for killing, so there will. There is always time for killing.'

Maguire snorted.

'Well?' Kelleher repeated imperiously and Flynn looked nervously at Kitty.

'This place is crawling with Shinners,' Flynn said, noticing Kitty shoot him a dirty look when he said Shinner.

'Of course it is,' Kelleher said, unsurprised. 'I'd've expected nothing less,' he added. Kitty interrupted the two men.

'My lift is here,' she said. Kelleher looked surprised as she pointed at an Austin Tourer parked at the end of the street. Four men were sitting in it.

'I thought you were taking the bus?' Kelleher asked.

'My brother arranged a lift,' Kitty said. Flynn looked at the car and straight into Maguire's eyes. Maguire smiled and nodded.

'That's the bastard!' Flynn hissed but Kitty ignored him and turned to Kelleher.

'Until next time,' she said and walked off across the street whilst Kelleher watched her retreating backside closely.

'Who's the *bastard* in the motor?' Kelleher asked as the car pulled away.

'Those men were IRA – they were following us!' Flynn said.

'Of course they are,' Kelleher said. 'I'd have been surprised if they hadn't. That's why you tag along, to keep an eye on me. After all, it's not like I'm trying to hide the fact that I'm trying to make contact with the local republicans.'

'That's all well and good, sir, but I'm sure that one of the little shites had the nerve to come up and talk to me,' Flynn replied.

Kelleher looked at him and shrugged. 'Well, what makes you think that it was one of the other side, eh?'

Flynn's brow furrowed as he thought about his response. 'Because, sir, he was sitting in that bloody car!' Flynn shuddered at the memory. 'He was an evil-looking bastard. His eyes were empty; you'd know the type, sir. There were loads in the trenches: blank, cold, almost beyond caring.'

'Just a few,' Kelleher replied with a smile. 'Always found them useful in a fight, but bloody scary to be around otherwise.' Flynn shrugged and the two men turned and started walking back towards the Auxiliary barracks.

'He was one of the men who attacked Drumlish barracks last January,' Flynn said to Kelleher.

'How do you know?' Kelleher asked.

'Because he'd lost his thumb,' Flynn replied.

'And?' Kelleher interrupted, intrigued.

'And when the IRA attacked the barracks last February we found a thumb out on the street after they buggered off in the morning. And I have got an awful feeling that I have just met the man whose thumb it was, the man I shot.'

'You know, Sergeant, I really didn't take you for the windy type. That's why I recruited you, because you've shown that you have some guts, so please don't tell me that your nerves are going?' he said deliberately, pricking Flynn's pride.

'No, I'm fine, sir, I just think we need to be careful,' Flynn said. 'I don't trust that flaming Kiernan woman.'

'Anyway, Miss Kiernan tells me that the rebels are willing to meet with me next week …' Flynn looked intently at the young DI as he spoke, suddenly listening intently to his every word. 'She has arranged for me to meet the local IRA's top man in her family's hotel in Granard.'

'And you trust her?' he spluttered incredulously.

'I don't see why not….'

'With all respect, sir, she's a Shinner too, so how do you know that it isn't a trap, a set-up?'

'Because, Sergeant, I think that I've seen enough of Miss Kiernan to know whether she's spinning me a line or not.'

Flynn almost spoke but stopped himself; after all, he knew it was useless to argue the toss with the DI when he got an idea in his head. He'd also spent long enough in the army and the RIC to learn when to speak and when to shut up and now was definitely a time to shut up. He had come across similar situations in the army, when some officer had decided to do something that seemed more like a slow-motion train crash in the making rather than a cunning plan, but he also knew that for the moment he had little choice but to go along with it.

'So who will you be meeting, sir?' Flynn asked.

'She couldn't say …' Wouldn't, more like, Flynn thought. 'But she said they would be prepared to deal with me.'

The words rang crashing alarm bells in Flynn's head. 'So, sir, will we be getting the boys from M Company to provide back-up?'

'Good God, no,' Kelleher said, 'they'll only frighten them off. No, we keep this under our hats for the time being.' Flynn had had an awful feeling that Kelleher was going to say that.

'The local lads from Granard barracks then, sir? Head Constable Carroll's a good man. Surely if we get him on board it won't raise any suspicions?' Kelleher shook his head again.

'No. Definitely not, the local plods are scared witless of the local IRA, especially since that oaf of a sergeant managed to shoot himself, and it really wouldn't surprise me if they managed to bollocks it up. No, we can do without them as well, for the time being.'

'So, sir,' Flynn began, with a sinking feeling in the pit of his stomach, 'who will be providing back-up then?'

Kelleher stopped, looked at him and smiled. 'You will, old chap, you will! I think as things stand, we won't need anyone else.'

Flynn suddenly felt very sick as he stuffed his hands deep into his overcoat pockets.

'You know, sir, I had an awful feeling that you were going to say that.' It was then that he felt the matchbox in his pocket.

Behind them, two shapes hugged the shadows, hanging back as they followed the two policemen. 'We should be getting back,' Hegarty said but McNamara simply gave him a look filled with hatred and resentment.

'Not yet. I want to know where these bastards are going,' McNamara said before following them down the street.

CHAPTER 21

Parnell Square, Dublin

MICHAEL COLLINS STOOD wreathed in cigarette smoke looking down at the street below and the quiet of another lazy Dublin Sunday morning. 'You know, Emmet, it was on a Sunday just like this that we followed Paddy Pearse to the GPO back in sixteen, full of bullshit and bluster, ready to die for the republic,' he said wistfully, without turning around.

'I know, I read all about it in *The Times* and a right bunch of eejits I thought you were too!'

Collins laughed as he turned around. 'I'd forgot, Emmet, my boy, that you were one of them, back then – an officer and a gentleman in the English king's army!'

Emmet Dalton smiled and sipped his tea. 'I'd rather I thought I was being sensible at the time. But Christ, was my old man fuming when he saw I'd taken the king's shilling, so he was. "My son, a redcoat!" he ranted. A marriage of convenience, pure and simple. I like to think that I was fighting for the rights of small nations like ours. I didn't have a problem fighting for Ireland with the British, as long as they played fair by us, and now I have no difficulty fighting for Ireland against them. I'd've been happy if they'd kept their promises but ...'

'But you've learnt the golden rule of being an Irishman – never trust what the English say. I would have thought you yanks would know that, what with your revolution and all,' Collins teased. Dalton had been born in America but had moved to Ireland when he was two years old and had grown used to his friend Collins' ribbing.

'I'm as Irish as the next man!' Dalton said, smiling mischievously, putting on a broad country brogue instead of his usual middle-class Dublin tones.

'For sure you are,' Collins replied with a boyish grin, playing up his Cork accent. 'Especially if the next man is Dev!' he joked, having a dig at de Valera, the political leader of the rebellion who was another Irish-American. Collins slapped Dalton firmly on the shoulder and both men laughed loudly.

'When you two have quite finished?' Frank Thornton, Collins' intelligence chief, said, rolling his eyes. He knew that Collins was always one for loud jokes and boisterous horseplay but Thornton didn't have much time for it. It was all a bit childish as far as he was concerned but the lads seemed to like it.

'All right, all right, Frankie, what have you got for me today?' Collins asked his intelligence chief.

'Well, to start with, Brugha is getting pissed off that the lads seem to listen to you more than him!' Thornton said, referring to Cathal Brugha, the rebels' minister of defence and nominally in charge of the IRA, who resented the fact that most of its members looked to his subordinate, Collins, for leadership. No one doubted that Collins was the real brains behind the IRA.

'Aw, bugger Brugha!' Collins declared.

'I'd rather not, old chap,' Dalton reposted and the two men burst out laughing.

Thornton coughed. 'When you two have finished your music hall act, perhaps we could get on.'

'What else then?' Collins asked. 'I've to be at the Dáil this afternoon, so I suppose we must get on.'

Thornton nodded. 'I've something interesting from Sean MacEoin over in Longford,' he said.

'Sure, how is Sean?' Collins beamed at the mention of his old friend.

'There is a peeler sniffing around your Kitty,' Thornton said and Collins' face darkened.

'What do you mean, sniffing around?' Collins asked.

'It would seem that a certain District Inspector Kelleher has got in contact with Kitty. He wants her to set up some sort of meeting with you!' Thornton said.

'Does he now?' Collins snorted. 'And who does he work for, do we know?'

Thornton shook his head. 'No idea. I've got some lads looking into it, but I don't think it's that snake, Winter, up in the Castle.' Collins glanced down at the street once more and watched a couple of army lorries clatter by, loaded with bored Tommies off on a raid somewhere, and all because some traitor sold his country for a few measly quid, no doubt.

'So what shall we do with him?' Collins asked. 'I've contacts enough with the Brits and the Castle – why should I be wanting another?'

'He's one of you culchie bastards from Cork,' Thornton added.

'Well, there you are then,' Dalton laughed. 'He must be a grand fella?'

'Jaysus, ye cheeky feckin' jackeen, you,' Collins chortled, in a broad Cork accent, and turned to Thornton. 'So, Frankie, what do we know about this District Inspector Kelleher then? Son of English planters gone native, I'll bet, eh?'

'Like Emmet says, he's a Corkonian like you, Mick, but a Castle Catholic if there ever was one. His people hail from Macroom where his old fella's the local GP.' Thornton flicked through his notebook, looking like a policeman giving evidence at a court hearing. 'The family live at number eleven, South Square, Macroom. It's a big family. Good Catholic fella is Doctor Kelleher; he's bred a load of little west Brits.'

'Someone's been doing his homework,' Collins quipped.

'It's what you pay me for, Mick, when you pay me at all!'

'Ach, away with you, Frankie, you'll get your rewards in heaven!' Collins joked.

'In that case, I'll be happy to wait to draw my wages,' Thornton replied with a wry smile.

'Go on then, Frankie, what else have you for me?' Collins asked. Thornton flicked through another couple of pages in his notebook.

'He's a bit like Emmet here,' he said. 'He got a Military Cross in the war, touched by the king's very hand no doubt!' He glanced at Dalton, who had received his MC from the king at Buckingham Palace. 'Public schoolboy is our Kelleher, Castleknock College old boy and plays rugby for Leinster. Rumour has it he's tipped to play for Ireland next season, if he's still about.'

'You seem well up on bloody English garrison sports all of a sudden, Frankie,' interrupted Collins, lightheartedly. 'Shame, though, this Kelleher fella sounds like someone we could use....'

Thornton pressed on, determined to finish making his report. 'Not much hope of that – the man's a loyalist through and through.'

'So, Emmet, what do you think?' Collins asked his friend.

Dalton sighed and bridged his fingers in front of his face before giving his opinion. 'I know the type, met plenty in the British army. In his mind he's as Irish as the next man but that makes his sort more of an enemy than the fellas from over the water, if you ask me. At least the Brits are foreigners, but this one – he's one of our own gone bad.'

'Tell me, Ginchy,' Collins said, using Dalton's old army nickname, 'what do you think?'

Dalton looked at his friend. 'I think he's dangerous. What does Sean think?'

Collins nodded. 'Tell me, Frankie, what does the good blacksmith of Balinalee think of all this?'

Thornton paused for a moment in thought. 'Difficult to tell, Mick. He thinks that Kelleher might be useful but he doesn't like Kitty being involved.'

'Aye, I'm not best pleased either,' Collins replied. 'How did he know about Kitty and me, eh? I'd like to know who?'

'Come on, Mick, it's hardly a secret, is it? All of us know about you and Kitty,' Dalton said.

Collins nodded. 'Yes, you're not wrong there but there are lots of things that we know about each other that are a closed book to the Brits. No, someone's informed and I want to know who. Frankie, sort it for me, please.' Thornton wrote a note in his book. 'Now, back to this Kelleher business,' Collins continued.

'Could we turn him?' Thornton asked.

'I can't be doing with that just yet,' Collins said. 'I've a big job brewing in the city so the last think I'm wanting is to muck about with a schoolboy spy who's read Childers' book and thinks this whole business is some sort of adventure. No, I'll have nothing to do with him.' The atmosphere was suddenly leaden.

'It's a shame,' Dalton said quietly. 'The army can always use experienced soldiers.' Collins looked at Dalton.

'All right Emmet, I'll leave it up to Sean to deal with. If he thinks that he can turn him, then all well and good. If he can use him, fine. If he can't, then he has my authority to shoot him.' Thornton nodded and scribbled another pencil note in his book before putting both in his jacket inside pocket, then stood up and walked to the door. His hand hovered on the handle.

'There's another fella working with Kelleher called Flynn. Do I get Sean to deal with him too?' Collins nodded, giving the death sentence he was passing only a moment's thought. 'Maybe you know him, Emmet,' Thornton said. Dalton's brow furrowed. 'I'm told that he was in your old regiment, the Dublin Fusiliers. He was given a gong for killing Jerries.'

Dalton frantically trawled his memory. 'Ach, you know, Frankie, loads of fellas got gongs in the war and Flynn's not exactly a rare name in Dublin! There was a Sergeant Kevin Flynn with me when I got my MC,' Dalton said. 'I wrote him up for a Military Medal. Surely it can't be the same fella?' Thornton pulled out his notebook again.

'This fella is called Kevin too,' he said.

'Well, if it's the same man then it really is a shame. I quite liked the man, until you told me he was a copper,' Dalton said.

'Can't be helped, Emmet,' Collins interrupted. 'He's made his bed now. It's up to Sean how he deals with him.' Dalton nodded and Thornton plonked his grey fedora on his head and walked out of the room, banging the door shut behind him.

'You know, I've got a sniff that old bastard Winter has brought in some professionals from over the water to give our lads a rough time,' Collins said, referring to the British intelligence chief in Dublin Castle, Brigadier-General Sir Ormonde de l'Épée Winter, known by his men as 'The Holy Terror' because of his boundless energy and enthusiasm for cloak and dagger espionage. 'My sources tell me that Winter calls them his Cairo gang. Buggered if I know why, but they're real operators who've cut their teeth keeping the Brits' bloody colonies in order, not like the local boys. Paddy Daly and the squad will have their work cut out dealing with them, so they will, and I'll need your boys to lend a hand.'

Dalton nodded. 'No problem, Mick.'

'We can't let the Brits get the better of us in the city, Emmet, so when I find out who these people are, and where they are hiding, I'm going to kill them all, every last one. It's about time the Brits realized that we are serious and eliminating this so-called Cairo gang would send a fearful message to the suits in Whitehall!'

'Aren't you worried about reprisals?' Dalton asked.

Collins looked at him. There was a fire in his eyes that Dalton rarely saw. 'If they overreact they'll just be throwing petrol on the fire,' Collins said. 'If they kill or burn, sure, even their own newspapers will damn them, let alone the Irish and American press!' Dalton knew he was right. Collins took another drag on his cigarette before stubbing it out in a stamped tin Guinness ashtray on the desk in front of him.

Outside, tyres screeched on the cobbles below, whistles shrilled, 'Move! Move!' voices barked and Collins glanced out of the window. Below, two military lorries disgorged a gang of heavily armed soldiers and they heard the front door splintering under sledgehammer blows. 'Best be going,' Collins said calmly, before grabbing his hat and heading for the door, followed closely by Dalton. The house was suddenly alive with shouting, doors crashing and boots clattering on the stairs.

'Break it down!' came a barked command in a rolling Wiltshire burr and the doors burst inwards as several Tommies surged through it into the deserted room, upending chairs, refilling the empty room with noise. A column of smoke coiled lazily towards the ceiling from a crushed cigarette in an old tin Guinness ashtray and three empty teacups sat abandoned on the table in the middle of the room.

The soldiers looked suddenly at a loss as to what to do as they stood self-consciously in the empty room, like naughty schoolboys, when a well-dressed man in smart civilian clothes, a detective from the Dublin Metropolitan Police's G Division, strolled briskly to the table. He looked down at the table and picked up the cigarette butt, examining it closely with obvious disgust. 'They've gone, sir,' ventured a corporal. The detective dropped the stub back in the ashtray and looked at the soldier in disdain.

'You don't say?' he said, before turning on his heel and storming out.

CHAPTER 22

M Company HQ, Auxiliary Division RIC, Longford

IT WAS AN ordinary box of matches and he had thought nothing of it when he had found it in his coat pocket. It was only when he got back to his room and saw the box on his bedside cabinet that he realized that it was not his and it was only when he slid open the box that he found the note. 'Tell Kelleher to back off or he's a dead man,' the note said in a bold, spiky scrawl and Flynn suddenly knew that it must have been the thumbless IRA man who had slipped it in his pocket when he patted him on the shoulder and wished him luck. Classic pickpocket's diversion, Flynn thought. Cocky blighter, aren't you, but why would you give me a written warning?

Popping the note in his pocket, Flynn set off for the officers' mess to tell Kelleher about the message. It was a short walk to what passed for the officers' mess, which was in reality a large detached house in the corner of the barracks. At the front door the mess orderly had given Flynn a disdainful look before insisting that he wait on the step whilst he went inside to fetch Kelleher from his afternoon tea in the mess anteroom. 'Yes? What is it?' Kelleher asked, brushing toasty crumbs from his lapel with ill-disguised irritation at being interrupted.

'I found this in my pocket, sir,' Flynn said, handing the inspector the note, and he watched him flick his eyes over it.

'Brief and to the point, I'd say,' Kelleher observed. 'Where did you get this?'

'That fella in the car, the one who lit my fag, he must have slipped it in my pocket when he was talking to me. The thing that worries me, sir, is why would he do it?'

'Who knows,' Kelleher replied. 'We've probably walked into the middle of some sort of IRA power struggle. They're always stitching each other up. You know how it is – if two Fenians enter a room, one is bound to form a splinter group! This chap probably doesn't want

MacEoin to get all the glory for setting up my meeting with Collins.' He laughed at his own joke but Flynn didn't find it funny.

'So, what are we going to do about it, sir?' Flynn asked.

'What do you mean?' Kelleher replied.

'I mean, sir, that if the Shinners are squabbling amongst themselves then perhaps it's best we back off, like the man said. It's pretty explicit, sir. It says you're a dead man if you go ahead,' Flynn said.

'Nonsense,' Kelleher replied. 'If this chap is going against MacEoin then I'm sure he'll sort him out for us, and if there is a split in the IRA in Longford, then perhaps this is an opportunity to exploit it!' Flynn went to speak but could see from the look on Kelleher's face that it would be useless to argue with him. 'Anyway, this is *der Tag*, as the Hun would say, the big day. My meeting is tonight at nine o'clock. If I don't show up then we may as well kiss goodbye to Collins or anyone else taking me seriously again and, besides, my orders are pretty clear. I've been told to make contact with Collins and Kitty is the best chance that we've got.' Flynn still didn't look convinced. 'Don't tell me you're losing your nerve on me, Sergeant?' Kelleher smiled but Flynn was still not reassured. 'Go get something to eat. I'll meet you in the orderly room at six,' he said as he turned to re-enter the mess.

'It's still not too late to arrange back-up from M Company,' Flynn said and Kelleher just looked at him and walked away. 'Bugger!' Flynn muttered as he walked off towards the sergeants' mess for something to eat. After all, you should never go into battle on an empty stomach.

Later, Flynn sat impatiently in the Orderly Room staring at the clock. It was twenty past seven. He fiddled with a silver florin coin trying to see if he could run it along his hand, twisting it from finger to finger like he'd seen one of his soldiers do during the war, but he failed miserably, conscious that the Auxiliary on orderly duty was watching his pathetic efforts. As usual, Kelleher was late.

'Doing anything interesting?' asked a bored young Auxiliary seated at the duty desk who'd been awarded a DSO and Mentioned in Despatches during the war.

'Nope,' Flynn replied noncommittally to the duty officer who had once been a temporary lieutenant colonel in the Royal Artillery and it made him laugh that they were now the same rank. But despite their equivalent status as sergeants, the Auxiliaries were better paid and called Cadet, which was the title used by RIC officers under training – Flynn supposed that went a little way to make the ex-officer Auxiliaries feel superior to mere NCOs. 'Do you miss the army?' Flynn finally asked the Auxiliary, who paused and put down his pen, looking at him for a moment.

'I suppose so, but it's a regular army mafia and there isn't much room in it for temporary officers like me when the shooting stops,' he said. 'Besides, I commanded an artillery brigade but if I'd stayed I'd've dropped back to lieutenant and been lucky to get a troop! No thanks.'

'So how did you end up here?' Flynn asked.

'Problem is there isn't much work for ex-officers and I sort of missed the excitement.' He looked at Flynn. 'And you? Were you in the army?'

Flynn nodded. 'Royal Dublin Fusiliers. I was a sergeant. Found it hard to fit back in when I came home so I joined the constabulary. It's a bit like the army.'

The Auxiliary smiled. 'Quite,' he said, and went back to his paperwork. Flynn looked out of the window; it was dark and he glanced at his watch. It was a German watch, a souvenir of an encounter with a Saxon *Unteroffizier*. They had blundered into each other in an old trench and Flynn had taken the man's face and his life with a sharpened spade. He'd also taken the man's watch and it had served well ever since. It was half past seven. The door flew open and the duty officer jumped in his seat. 'Do you mind!' he muttered, neglecting to call Kelleher sir.

Kelleher ignored the Auxiliary and spoke to Flynn, rubbing his hands together, exuding boyish enthusiasm for his coming tryst in Granard. 'Well, are you ready to go?'

'Yes, sir,' Flynn replied, suddenly feeling very old as he stood up and reluctantly trailed after Kelleher out of the room. Outside, the courtyard was bathed in the amber glow of half a dozen electric street lamps and across the way a Lancia armoured car squatted in the corner. An Auxiliary sat astride its turret whistling tunelessly as he polished a long belt of .303 ammunition, which he fed into the vehicle's open hatch, and looked up indifferently as the two policemen strolled past before returning to his task. 'You know, sir, I really do have a bad feeling about this,' Flynn said, fingering the note in his pocket.

'Sergeant, I know you do, but everything is arranged,' Kelleher replied, his tone brittle with irritation.

'We could still get these lads—' Flynn indicated towards M Company's HQ '—to provide back-up. It's not too late. I mean, if things go pear-shaped, I'm not sure how much help one man will be?'

'Better than none, in theory, but I am beginning to wonder! Now stop being such an old woman and be quiet! I don't want everyone knowing our business. We need to be extremely discreet,' Kelleher snapped and Flynn sensed that the pressure was getting to the inspector more than he was letting on. He still didn't know who was pulling the inspector's strings but it was obviously someone important, someone with clout, someone who didn't like being disappointed.

Flynn climbed into the driving seat of their car. Kelleher got into the front passenger seat next to him and pulled out a service revolver, checked it was loaded, then shoved it into his coat pocket. Flynn checked his own revolver and popped it back into his shoulder holster when he noticed Kelleher sliding a small automatic pistol into a holster strapped to his shin. 'Insurance,' the inspector said with a grin. 'Look, Sergeant, I'm not stupid. I know that these people would kill you or me without any hesitation but there are bigger things at stake than you and me ...' Not in my book, Flynn thought. 'And if we have to take a few risks, well so be it.'

Flynn started the car and slipped it into gear. The gate sentry lifted the barrier and waved their car through, the Auxiliaries had got used to Kelleher's comings and goings and knew better than to ask questions, mostly because they knew that they wouldn't get a straight answer. 'So, sir, what makes you think that this isn't a set-up then?' Flynn asked. He couldn't see the inspector's face in the dark but he could tell that he was smiling again.

'Curiosity, Sergeant, simple curiosity, that's why. Don't you think that they haven't been sitting around trying to work out what I'm up to, who I work for, why I want to talk to Collins? Of course they have and I'm willing to stake my life that they will go through with this meeting,' Kelleher said confidently. 'And besides, I think young Miss Kiernan has taken a shine to me. She'll not let them shoot me!' he joked.

'For all our sakes I hope that you're right, sir, I really hope so,' Flynn muttered quietly.

'Who knows,' Kelleher said suddenly, 'we may be able to stir up some trouble amongst the Shinners. The sooner our country is shot of people who think that they can build a better country by killing people, the better. You know, I came home thinking that life would be better after the war. I thought that people had had enough of killing. How wrong I was.'

Flynn had never heard his boss speak like that before. Suddenly he thought he caught a glimpse of car headlights in the rear-view mirror. 'Hang on a minute, sir, but I think we are being followed,' he said.

'Shall I try and give them the slip?' Flynn asked but Kelleher shook his head, his eyes shining in the moonlight.

'Ah, the game's afoot,' Kelleher said, quoting straight from a Sherlock Holmes novel. 'No, let them keep on us. If they are part of this, they'll know where we are going anyway.'

'They're still behind us, sir,' Flynn told Kelleher as their car passed through the outskirts of Granard, heading for Main Street and the Greville Arms Hotel. It was quarter to nine and the streets were almost deserted. Flynn shrank into the depth of his overcoat. It started to rain.

McNamara sat in the passenger seat nursing a Mauser automatic pistol. 'Keep up with them,' he hissed at Hegarty, who was doing his best to follow the tail lights of Kelleher's car through the winding lanes to Granard, and snapped the wooden holster onto the weapon before pushing a clip of bullets into its magazine. Hegarty watched him from the corner of his eye. He didn't like McNamara much, the man seemed a little unhinged to him, but MacEoin had been adamant.

'Stick with him and make sure he doesn't do anything stupid,' MacEoin had ordered.

'Jesus, boss, don't I get the lunatic to babysit!' he'd declared and MacEoin had flashed him a winning smile.

'He's a good fella,' Fitzgerald added, 'just a little excitable, that's all.'

'Grand!' Hegarty muttered. 'Just grand!'

CHAPTER 23

Sunday, 31 October 1920, Greville Arms Hotel, Granard, County Longford

MAGUIRE LOOKED AT his watch; it was almost nine in the evening. Everything was quiet and the room was dark. Doyle eased his fingers into the gap between the curtains and glanced nervously at the Greville Arms Hotel opposite. He hated waiting; he hated it almost as much as what almost inevitably followed the wait.

'May we come in, sir?' Maguire had politely asked the bewildered balding householder fifteen minutes before who, well into his sixties, was obviously terrified of the gunmen. 'Don't go worrying yourself, you'll come to no harm,' Maguire had reassured as he pushed past without waiting for a response, followed by Doyle. A scared-looking old woman peered down the hall from the kitchen. 'Good evening to you, ma'am,' Maguire said, 'sure I could murder a cup of tea. Would you be a love and put the kettle on?' He smiled again and the old woman nodded. Maguire looked back at the old man. 'My friend and I will be making use of your front room for a wee while,' he said. 'This is army business. Now, I know you won't do anything foolish, so why don't you get yourself into the kitchen and stay quiet.'

The man's eyes widened with fear and he scurried away to the kitchen and, once inside, Doyle switched off the gas lamp and the room went dark. He looked over at Maguire; cool as a cucumber settling into a comfy chair, the black shadow of a gun just visible in his lap. He still couldn't get over how calm Maguire always seemed to be just before they went into action. 'Ah, will you stop your fidgeting and sit down,' Maguire said gently.

In the back room of the Greville Arms, MacEoin and Fitzgerald sat quietly, waiting. MacEoin had just checked his weapon for the third time and Fitzgerald slid a loaded magazine into his Colt 1911 .45 pistol. 'Are you ready?' MacEoin asked Fitzgerald as he tucked the loaded gun into the waistband of his trousers. 'Jeez, but you'll be careful doing that unless you go shooting your arse off!' MacEoin quipped.

Fitzgerald laughed. 'Don't go worrying about me!'

Lawrence Kiernan poked his head in through the door. 'There's still no sign of them,' he said nervously as the rain rattled noisily off the window pane like a crazed, ragged tattoo of drums.

'Will you stop fussing. My boys have got every angle covered. It will run like clockwork.' MacEoin flashed him a beamy smile but Kiernan wasn't reassured as he retreated into the lounge bar where Kitty sat in the corner sipping a glass of ginger ale, looking worried, really worried. It had all seemed so straightforward when MacEoin had told her to cultivate her contact with Kelleher but now that MacEoin and the inspector were due to meet, she felt sick and petrified. Kiernan walked over to his sister.

'You look worried, Kitty,' Kiernan said.

'Says you!' she exclaimed. 'You look like you've drunk a bottle of castor oil yourself!' She smiled weakly and Kiernan sat down next to her and looked at his watch.

'Did you say yer man Kelleher would be here at nine?' he asked.

'I did,' she replied, looking out the window.

'Sean has everything under control, he said not to be worrying,' her brother replied, more to himself than Kitty. She tensed as the lume of a car's headlamps groped their way through the squall outside.

'They're here,' she said to her brother, who nodded and walked to the door behind the bar, poking his head through. Kitty couldn't hear what her brother said but she guessed he was warning MacEoin that Kelleher had arrived.

'It's still not too late,' Flynn said hopefully to Kelleher as he watched the windscreen wipers fighting a losing battle against the torrent of rain. His heart was pounding.

'Ours is not to reason why!' Kelleher said with a nervous grin, his eyes hidden.

'You know, sir, I've never really liked the next line!' Flynn replied and his boss shot him a disapproving look as he made to get out of the car.

'No, you stay here,' Kelleher said. 'I'll go in, make contact and if I need help, I'll call. If you hear anything unusual, come in!'

Anything unusual! Flynn thought. The whole bloody set-up is

unusual. But he'd learnt to keep his opinions to himself. 'Are you sure? I don't think this is a good idea, you going in there on your own,' Flynn pleaded.

'Sergeant, you have your orders. Stay here. I'll call if I need help,' Kelleher said sternly as he climbed out of the car into the sheeting rain. His eyes glinted in the pale streetlight with a mixture of fear and excitement. Flynn had seen that look dozens of times in the eyes of men about to go on a raid. Some men fell in love with the buzz it gave them and he wondered if Kelleher was such a man.

Kelleher pushed open the front door of the Greville Arms and walked boldly into the middle of the lounge bar where several men sat drinking, ignoring him. He took off his hat, shook the water from it and undid his dripping wet trenchcoat, then he walked across the room to where Kitty was sitting. Behind the bar, Kiernan mechanically towelled a glass and watched the policeman cross the room, like an extra from a bad western. One of the drinkers nodded at Kiernan, got up and crept over to the front door, where he quietly slid the bolt shut before sitting back down.

'Good evening, Miss Kiernan,' Kelleher said, the very personification of charm. He smiled and she looked nervous and played with her glass. 'Is everything ready?' he asked. Kitty nodded.

'Lawrence,' she said, calling over to her brother, 'could you fetch the gentleman a drink?'

Kiernan nodded. 'Sure, and what will you be having?'

'Another of whatever Miss Kiernan is having and a dry sherry,' Kelleher said and there was a slight stir in the room. Not many of Kiernan's regulars asked for sherry. The Greville wasn't a sherry kind of bar.

'Very good,' Kiernan said as he popped open another bottle of ginger ale and poured out a schooner of sherry then placed them on the table before withdrawing back to the bar. Kelleher looked at Kitty and didn't notice Kiernan slip through the door to the back room.

As Maguire watched Kelleher from the shadows he slowly screwed a silencer onto the muzzle of his pistol. 'Best get ready, Pat,' he said to Doyle, matter-of-factly. 'It's show time.' Doyle nodded and massaged the grip of his pistol in nervous anticipation, his stomach churning and his skin tingling with excitement.

Out of sight, around the corner from the pub, Hegarty pulled up and applied the car's handbrake. 'Well, this is it. We wait here until we get a signal to move.' McNamara looked at Hegarty with a mixture of frustration, anger and disappointment. There was an unnerving glint in his eye.

'I want to be in at the kill!' McNamara declared with an unsettling leer. 'One of those bastards was there when they killed my brother and I want the shite to pay!'

'All in good time,' Hegarty said quietly, trying to keep McNamara calm, resenting MacEoin's orders to babysit a madman.

'Sod this!' McNamara hissed as he jumped out of the car and splashed off towards the pub.

'Shit!' Hegarty spluttered and jumped out in pursuit but McNamara had already reached the corner before he caught up with him and, grabbing his sleeve, yanked him back from the corner – but not before Flynn thought he saw a shape poke around the corner then jerk back out of sight.

'I really have a bad feeling about this,' Flynn muttered as he went to open the car door but stopped when he felt something cold and hard press against the back of his head.

'And so you should, peeler! So you should!' a familiar voice said from behind. He recognized the voice; it was the man with the missing thumb. He cursed for allowing himself to be distracted and failing to notice Maguire and Doyle as they came out into the street behind his car and crept up on him. 'Now, don't move,' Maguire continued, 'or you are a dead man.'

Flynn thought that he saw a movement by the front door and felt confused and angry. You stupid fool, he thought. How on earth did they creep up on me! The pressure against the back of his head increased and he momentarily thought about trying to escape. A bag went over his head and it went dark.

'Lie across the front seat and put your hands behind your back!' Maguire hissed and Flynn meekly complied, as he lay down and felt them tie his hands. 'Now come with me and if you try anything I will kill you! Is that clear?' Maguire said as he punched Flynn hard in the kidneys and dragged him from the car.

Hegarty stood on the corner and watched Maguire and Doyle drag the policeman into the street. 'Maguire's got one of them,' Hegarty said and McNamara smiled cruelly, his face menacing in the shadow of the gaslight.

'Grand. I just hope that the boss lets me shoot the bastard! I want to hear him beg for his miserable feckin' life!' He beamed as he strode off towards Maguire. Hegarty rolled his eyes.

'Get up, you shit, and move!' a venomous voice spat in Flynn's ear and he felt a boot thud into his back as he fell to his knees. The ground was awash and water soaked through his trousers while someone grabbed his collar and wrenched him to his feet. Every time he stumbled a rain of blows brought him back to his feet. Suddenly, he was jerked to a halt and a hard blow drove deep into his groin, plunging him to his knees, fighting back the urge to vomit as more blows thudded into his head, legs and body.

'Easy!' Maguire barked at McNamara. 'The boss doesn't want him dead, yet! Get him in the car and let's get out of here.' Flynn felt himself being thrown into the back of a car and, as he lay there dazed, the engine spluttered into life and he felt the car begin to move.

'Just sit there quietly,' a voice said. 'You may get to live a little bit longer.' Flynn felt miserable, alone and very, very afraid, then he felt a blow on the back of his head and then nothing.

Kelleher heard a car engine start outside. 'What was that?' he asked Kitty.

'Nothing,' came a voice from behind him, making Kelleher look up suddenly and turn to see MacEoin and Fitzgerald standing at the end of the table, looking down at him. He recognized MacEoin from his picture in the intelligence file but not the other man. Kitty blanched. 'Would you give us a minute, please, Kitty,' MacEoin said quietly and Kelleher half rose politely as she stood up to leave.

'Until next time, Miss Kiernan,' Kelleher said as she walked away but she couldn't bring herself to look at him – she knew there wouldn't be a next time. Fitzgerald slipped his hand around the butt of his pistol, sliding it slowly from the back of his trouser waistband.

'So you wanted to meet with me?' MacEoin said flatly.

Kelleher looked up at him and took another sip of his sherry, his heart racing. 'I had rather hoped that your people would have sent someone more ... er ... how can I put it, senior?' he said. MacEoin smiled noncommittally.

'Don't worry yourself, Inspector Kelleher,' MacEoin said, 'the big fella himself has authorized me to deal with you on his behalf.'

'Has he now?' Kelleher looked sceptical as MacEoin sat down opposite the inspector.

'Please, Inspector, before we get down to business, do finish your drink,' he said and Kelleher narrowed his eyes whilst he studied MacEoin's face, trying to fathom out what sort of man he was dealing with. Kelleher finished his drink with a flourish as the rain battered against the window. The street outside was still.

'It's a foul night,' Kelleher said, placing his glass back onto the table. 'Now down to business,' he added with a smile.

'Aye, down to business,' MacEoin sighed. Fitzgerald pulled the Colt .45 from behind his back and pointed it at the policeman, whose eyes widened in surprise.

'Now just one minute ...' Kelleher faltered as he stared down the barrel of MacEoin's pistol.

'I think our meeting is just about over,' he said, pulling the trigger, shattering Kelleher's face and splattering his blood and brains on the wall behind him. The inspector's body slumped heavily onto the floor and then Fitzgerald pumped a further couple of rounds into him just to make sure. 'I'm sorry about the mess,' MacEoin said casually to Kiernan as he walked towards the door. Within minutes, the bar was empty.

Upstairs, Kitty sat rocking in an armchair, hugging a cushion, tears welling in her eyes and streaming down her face as the volley of shots made her jump. She felt sick as she looked out of the window. Lights were coming on up and down the street and she knew that it would only be a matter of minutes before the police arrived.

CHAPTER 24

Monday, 1 November 1920, an abandoned croft,
County Longford

IT WAS VERY dark. Flynn was in no man's land. A machine gun jabbed glowing red and green tracer rounds, lancing into the night, searching for a kill. He pressed himself flat against the ground, deep into Mother Earth, but it was cold and unyielding and his heart thudded erratically against his ribs whilst blood rushed, like a breaking tide, in his ears. He eased himself forward and slid quietly into the trench, landing softly on the firing step with a gentle crunch. He shifted his grip on the sharpened entrenching tool in his hands, his eyes shining in the pale moonlight. A shadow moved and he raised the spade, ready to strike.

Suddenly, the heavy impact of a work boot thudded into his side. 'Wakey! Wakey!' brayed a harsh, unfriendly voice followed by another blow that crashed painfully into his ribs, making him groan in pain, wrenching him away from his nightmare and forcing him into a sitting position. The bag was torn from his head, exposing his eyes to stabbing needles of light. He hurt all over, his mouth tasted of stale blood and the room stank of damp and disuse mixed with excrement. As his head cleared he could see grainy fingers of sunlight groping through cracks in the boards that shielded the room's one window, obliterating the view.

McNamara landed another hefty kick to his ribs and Flynn doubled over once more in a fit of painful coughing. His face throbbed and he could barely open one eye and as he ran his tongue around his mouth he could feel that it was cut and swollen. At least they haven't broken my teeth, Flynn thought.

'Enough!' another voice commanded and Flynn squinted the second figure into focus. It was the man without a thumb. He was smoking, and from his tone and manner obviously in charge, if only just. Flynn gazed at him for a moment, weighing him up as the stench of stale sweat mixed with tobacco played in his nostrils. Behind him a third man, much younger than the others, stood anxiously by the door, nursing an obsolete Mauser rifle. 'Give him a drink,' Maguire ordered.

'Piss off!' McNamara hissed. 'Why bother? Let's just shoot him!' McNamara flashed Flynn an evil smile as he pulled out a Mauser C96 automatic pistol from under his jacket. Click! He cocked the weapon and pointed it at Flynn's head. 'This is one of the bastards who killed Jerry,' he snapped, looking at Maguire, his face contorted with pure malice. 'Are you going to squeal, peeler? Like your friend did when I shot him?' Flynn's eyes widened in shock; this was the first he had heard of O'Leary's death. 'That's right, pig! I put the little swine out of his misery over in Cardiff. Squealed like the filthy piglet he was. How he begged before he pissed himself,' McNamara gloated pitilessly.

Flynn looked up at the gunman in horror and felt the rage build inside him as he strained against his bonds. McNamara laughed loudly and pressed the pistol against Flynn's forehead. 'Let's just get on with it.' Flynn screwed his eyes closed, waiting for death, for release, but Maguire shoved McNamara's arm upwards, angry at the gunman's spiteful behaviour.

'When the time comes, you can do it, but 'til then, Sean's orders are clear. He lives! You'll have to wait. The boss wants me to have a wee word with him.' Flynn felt sick listening to the two men discussing his death as if he wasn't in the room and eventually McNamara glared at Maguire then slid the gun back into his jacket.

'I'll wait for now, Joe, but I won't wait long!' A thrill of almost sexual anticipation rippled through McNamara as he looked down at Flynn and savoured the thought of putting a bullet through the policeman's head, of shredding his brains and snuffing out his existence. He knew that he would really enjoy killing Flynn, just like he had enjoyed killing O'Leary or the traitor Muldoon or, indeed, any of his other victims. He loved the control, the power of life and death, the ability to take away everything from someone with the gentle flexing of a finger, as simple as switching off a light.

McNamara smiled to himself as he recalled how Muldoon had begged for his life as he knelt, trussed like a lamb in an abattoir awaiting slaughter. How his brother Jerry had laughed at the look in the old man's rheumy eyes; that look of disbelief they all had just before he pulled the trigger. It was that look that he enjoyed most – the realization that it was all over and that there was nothing they could do, nothing except accept death. Yes, he would look forward to seeing the same look in the policeman's eyes; he would enjoy killing Flynn, for his brother's sake, as well as his own. Then he would settle his account with Maguire – he would enjoy that too.

Maguire threw McNamara a hostile sidelong glance as he took down an old army water bottle from a makeshift hook – a rusty nail hammered into the wall – and pulled out the cork stopper before kneeling down next to Flynn, studying him closely. 'Here, drink this.' He smiled. 'You're going to need your strength.' He poured some water down Flynn's throat and the policeman sputtered before being able to swallow a little. The tepid liquid cooled his throat, washing away some of the blood. It was his first drink in hours and his throat was dry with fear.

'I don't suppose you've some poteen?' Flynn croaked with a cracked smile and in a shriek of outrage McNamara kicked him hard in the side, causing him to convulse in a spasm of pain and coughing before he managed to look back up at his assailant. He could see McNamara's face contorted in pure hate, his eyes burning with fury.

'Leave him!' Maguire barked.

Biting back his pain and fear, Flynn thought of what he'd just heard about O'Leary and forced himself to calmly look up at McNamara and smile humourlessly. 'Touch me again and I will kill you,' Flynn said tonelessly as he stared at McNamara. Maguire smiled but McNamara snarled with rage and snatched his gun back out of his pocket, levelling it at Flynn. The policeman's eyes were cold, grey and empty as he fixed McNamara with a hard pitiless stare that did little to hide what he had planned for the gunman. McNamara's hand began to tremble.

'Steady, Mick,' Maguire chortled, 'I do believe Mr Peeler here means it!' Then the IRA man laughed a harsh, forced bray before turning to the furious gunman. 'Come on, we've things to be going on with, so leave him for now. His time will come soon enough.' He took hold of McNamara's sleeve and pulled him towards the door.

Doyle shifted uncomfortably in the doorway. He knew that the policeman was an enemy, a traitor, and accepted that he had to die but he just wished that they would get on with it and execute the man rather than string it all out. Hegarty had laughingly said something about getting the peeler to dig his own grave to save them the effort but Doyle wasn't looking forward to that either.

Then, as suddenly as it had all started, the door thudded shut, leaving Flynn alone in the room with his fears. He knew that he had to do something soon or he was a dead man. Biting back his pain he wrestled with the heavy hemp rope that bound his wrists but his struggles simply tore his skin, achieving little. 'Bugger,' he cursed and frantically looked around the room for something sharp to part the cords. There was nothing. He urged himself to calm down and then, wriggling furiously, tried to slip his arms under his legs but they were bound too tight. He was stuck with his hands tied behind his back, trussed and helpless, unless something changed soon.

Wobbling, he finally lurched unsteadily to his feet and staggered towards the boarded-up window. He may as well try and find out where it was he was going to die. His knees trembled beneath him and he felt sick as he leant against the wall, his bladder straining as he fought against the urge to pee, determined not to give them the satisfaction of seeing him piss himself.

He was beginning to recover his senses now that the initial shock of capture had passed and his fear was also slowly subsiding. He was becoming irritated rather than afraid that he had been so lax as to let himself be captured and, deep inside, the determination to escape was beginning to grow. He needed a plan, if only to keep his mind occupied.

Racked with pain and frustration, he pressed his battered face against a crack in the board and strained to see what was outside through his one good eye but could see very little. He sniffed; the air was dank, laced with decay, and it felt like early morning to him. He drew back slightly from the crack when he heard muffled voices outside and a car engine coughed into life. 'Eunan, go tell the boss that we've got the prisoner secure and find out what he wants us to do next? Take Mick with you,' Maguire said as Hegarty and McNamara climbed into the car. Flynn recognized the same dark Austin Tourer he'd seen pick up Kitty as it drove past his vantage point carrying two men. He wondered how many more of them were out there and began to make a mental appreciation of his situation. He wondered where Kelleher was. He must be around here somewhere too, he thought.

Suddenly, the door swung open, shattering Flynn's thoughts, and he span around. Maguire leant against the door frame, relaxed, confident, dangerous, eyeing his helpless prisoner. He pointed a pistol at Flynn and flashed him a charmless smile. 'It's a beautiful view, is it not?' he said conversationally, as Flynn wobbled slightly, fighting to stay upright and not wet himself. 'Come over here, peeler, and don't try anything stupid.' He flicked the pistol almost casually, beckoning Flynn towards him. The man dripped confidence and capability.

'Or what?' Flynn said softly. 'You'll kill me sooner than you planned to anyway?' Maguire's face was blank, betraying nothing of his thoughts. Flynn watched him, studying him; he felt strange, almost peaceful. It was as if he had come to terms with the fact that he was already a dead man and suddenly he felt calm for the first time in ages, almost as if a great weight had been lifted from his shoulders.

Maguire shrugged indifferently. 'Who knows what fate holds for us,' he said and Flynn stepped slowly towards him. His mind focused on the building pressure in his bladder as he followed Maguire into the front room of the croft. The room was cold and he blinked rapidly as he adjusted to the light and quickly drank in his surroundings. The sour smell of unwashed bodies and neglect slapped him across the face like a duellist's challenge and he noticed the ash from a long-dead fire tumbling from the blackened grate whilst feeble shards of light fumbled through the caked-on grime of two cracked, cobwebbed windows, pooling in the room and deepening the shadows. The place was thick with dust and rat droppings and before him a musty, woodwormy table teetered precariously in the middle of the room.

The damp air made Flynn's joints ache like they had in the trenches, a legacy of too many nights sleeping rough, and only the throbbing pain in the rest of his body distracted him from it. His bladder was beginning to hurt now, spurred on by the cold, and he desperately needed to pee.

'Sit!' Maguire ordered as he pointed at a tatty chair by the table, which Flynn seriously suspected would collapse under his weight. A pitted, bone-scarred knife stood skewered in the centre of the table and the youth with the rifle stood nervously by the door, chewing his lower lip, giving Flynn the occasional furtive glance. Flynn gently tried working his bonds again as he eased himself onto the chair, his eyes fixed on Maguire.

'What now?' Flynn asked defiantly. He was determined not to give these men the satisfaction of seeing him break. Every fibre of his body was now focusing on his bloated bladder.

'You know,' Maguire said wearily, 'I really tried to warn you off this nonsense with young Kitty Kiernan but you wouldn't listen.' Doyle glanced out of the door and then back at Maguire, his face shadowed by his tatty cap. 'And look where it's got you now. Your boss Kelleher is dead …' Flynn looked up suddenly. 'And you are here, a dead man walking. I really had hoped that it wouldn't have come to this.'

Maguire sighed wearily and palmed back the hammer of his revolver to half-cock. Click! Flynn prayed his bladder wouldn't give out. 'Pat,' he said over his shoulder to Doyle, 'take a look outside, would you now? Is there any sign of the others?' Doyle felt a mixture of fear and excitement balling in his stomach as he quickly scanned the farmyard before looking back at Maguire and shaking his head.

'Shouldn't we wait for the others, Joe? You said that the boss wanted to talk to this one.' Doyle sounded anxious, dreading seeing the policeman shot.

'Not this time, Pat,' Maguire said, hanging his head wearily, as if suddenly the whole world was pushing down on his shoulders. 'There has been a slight change of plan.' He looked at Flynn; his eyes were full of sorrow as if he'd struggled with some dilemma and come to some unfortunate but inevitable conclusion. 'I'm truly sorry that I have to do this but you really haven't left me with much choice.' Maguire's voice was soft, almost soothing, as he raised his revolver.

Flynn tensed, forcing himself to stare straight at Maguire to meet his gaze and his fate head on. This is it! he thought as his breathing became erratic and he felt his whole body begin to tense. He fought to control himself. Maguire suddenly swung his arm round in a swift motion and pulled the trigger.

The bullet tore through Doyle's throat, slamming the lad against the door with a loud thud. His rifle fell as he slid down the door onto his backside, leaving a dark smear of blood behind him. Bright blood frothed from the wound as he wheezed for breath and welled through his fingers as he clawed at his neck, eyes wide, in stunned disbelief. Flynn was rooted to his chair in stunned silence as Maguire sighed and walked slowly over to Doyle, his arms hanging loosely by his sides. The boy looked up, confused, at his killer.

'I'm sorry, Pat,' Maguire said gently before he pointed his gun at Doyle's head and, after a brief pause to aim, loosed off two more rounds into the young man's head. Doyle's body shuddered violently under the impacts and his right leg twitched for a second or two before he finally lay still. Dark blood trickled down the flaking door, snaking around gobbets of brain as it dripped.

'It's truly a bloody pity,' Maguire muttered to himself as he looked ruefully down at Doyle's body and poked it with the toe of his boot. 'He wasn't a bad lad, you know. Just in the wrong place at the wrong time, that's all. Shit happens in war, I guess,' he added as he turned to Flynn and put his pistol on the table. 'Now let's get you untied.' He yanked the knife from the table as if nothing had happened whilst Flynn stared at Doyle's shattered skull, the boy's lifeless eyes wide in surprise. Flynn's ears were ringing in the silence. 'We don't have much time before the others get back,' Maguire said, as he reached behind Flynn and sawed through his bonds.

'Who the hell are you?' Flynn asked in astonishment, turning to face Maguire.

'Never mind who I am,' Maguire muttered. 'Suffice to say, I'm on your side. You're lucky to still be alive; McNamara has really taken a serious dislike to you. As for that fool Kelleher, he has gone and got himself killed so the least I can do is try and get you out of here.' He pulled Flynn's hands free. His wrists were rope-burned and sore.

'What happened to Kelleher?' he asked.

Maguire glanced out of the filthy window, scanning the horizon.

'MacEoin shot him,' he said, with all the emotion of someone inured to death, as if discussing the weather. Both men had seen enough killing not to get too teary about it. Flynn nodded. After all, he'd half expected to hear that he was dead anyway. The policeman glanced down at Maguire's hand and as he looked up he caught Maguire's eye and Flynn realized that he knew it was him who had shot his thumb off.

Flynn shifted uncomfortably; his wrists burned. 'Let's go then,' he said, but Maguire shook his head.

'No, it's best that I stay here.'

Flynn gestured towards Doyle's corpse. 'But what about him?' he said. 'You can't stay.' Maguire picked up a piece of the cut rope and held it towards Flynn.

'Tie me up and gag me, then give me one hell of a crack on the head. I'll tell them that you got free and gave me a good kicking. It's not like you don't look like you could. Doyle must have disturbed you whilst you were tying me up so you shot him with my gun,' he said, putting together a plausible version of events. 'That's why I got him to stand by the door, so that it would look like he was walking in when you shot him.'

Jesus, what a cold bastard, Flynn thought as he looked at Maguire and shivered, but despite everything he felt a twinge of admiration for the calm, calculating way he'd disposed of Doyle. It was obvious that Maguire had not enjoyed killing the boy but Flynn had met plenty of men like him in the trenches and was realistic enough to know that they were good men to have with you in a fight. 'It seems plausible,' Flynn said. After all, there were no witnesses to contradict Maguire's version of events. 'Are you sure you'll be all right?' Flynn asked.

Maguire shrugged. 'I reckon,' he said as he sat on the rickety chair. 'After all, why shouldn't they believe me? I'm the OC of the local IRA battalion.' Maguire couldn't help laughing when he saw the look of shock on Flynn's face.

Suddenly, the urge to urinate pushed itself back into his mind and Maguire watched curiously as Flynn walked to the corner of the room and fumbled with his flies. The sound of running water echoed around the room and Flynn sighed with obvious relief. 'Sorry about this, but I've been dying to go for ages. It took everything I've got to hold it in and stop you bastards thinking you'd made me wet myself!' he said over his shoulder and Maguire laughed. 'So where are we?' Flynn finally asked, as he buttoned up his flies.

'We're in an old abandoned farm and if you head off that way—' He pointed off into the distance '—you should reach Drumlish. It's about four and a half miles away.' Carefully avoiding treading on Doyle's corpse, Flynn looked out of the door and held his watch up to the sun.

'You can use it to find north,' Flynn said, when he saw Maguire's puzzled look.

'Aren't we the Boy Scout!' snorted Maguire from the chair. 'Now stop farting about and tie my hands and be on your way. McNamara and Hegarty could be back any time and if you're still here I may not be able to help you!' Flynn squatted down behind the chair and tightly bound Maguire's hands. 'Now gag me and fetch me a hell of a knock on the head. I want them to think that you put me out. Punch me in the face first!'

'If you insist.' Flynn shrugged before slamming a haymaker into Maguire's jaw. The man's head snapped back and his lip split in a welter of blood. 'Shit!' Flynn hissed as he clutched his fist in his left hand. Maguire shook his head and spat out another gobbet of spittled blood. His skin was already beginning to discolour.

'Now hit me with the pistol, hard on the back of the head.'

'Are you sure?' Flynn asked and Maguire nodded again.

'Just get on with it!' Without a word Flynn picked up the pistol from the table and smacked it into the seated man's head. 'Jaysus!' Maguire yelped.

'Sorry,' Flynn muttered apologetically, 'but I've only ever killed people with these things before.' He forced a makeshift gag into Maguire's mouth. Blood leaked from the gash in the back of the man's head into the cloth then onto Flynn's hands and he wiped them on an old cloth before stuffing the gun into his jacket pocket. 'Whoever you are, thanks,' he said, patting Maguire on the shoulder before picking up Doyle's discarded rifle. He rummaged through the boy's pockets and pulled out a couple of rounds, which he slipped into his own before taking a good look at the rifle. It was an antique single-shot Mauser, like the ones smuggled into Howth by the Irish Volunteers in 1914. He worked the stiff mechanism and a bullet bounced onto the ground. He picked it up and replaced it in breech, cocking the weapon and twisting the safety catch to the on position.

'I'll need these if they come after me,' he muttered, rising painfully to his feet and, without a backward glance, walked out into the farmyard. He knew that he really was a dead man if the IRA caught up with him again, especially as it looked like he had gunned down the young lad. He checked the direction again and after one last rapid all-round look, loped off into the fields. It would have been much quicker to get to Drumlish by road but that way would also increase his chances of recapture, so he kept to the fields and moved slowly behind walls and hedgerows, trying not to spook the sheep or break cover.

An hour or so later the landscape began to look more familiar and he headed towards a piece of high ground ahead of him. To his left, he caught the sound of a car engine about a hundred yards away on the road and he tucked himself into the cover of a hedge. Gently, he eased off the safety catch and took a few deep breaths. His body ached from his exertions and it had taken him just over two hours to cover four and a half miles. He had to assume that the others had found Maguire and the boy by now. The car passed.

A movement in the corner of his eye caught his attention and he froze. The undergrowth was moving. He shifted his weight and eased his rifle into his shoulder, holding his breath, straining to listen. A hare burst from its cover and dashed across the field. Somewhere a dog barked. Scared but relieved, he lay still and waited for what seemed like an eternity before cautiously levering himself onto his knees. He sighed in relief. Drumlish nestled below in the hollow between the hills and he carefully rose to his feet. Around him, birds twittered and a gentle breeze caressed his cheek as he stepped off down the hill towards the village.

It took longer than he had expected to work his way around the edge of the houses, sticking to dead ground until he was close to the barracks, then he cautiously eased himself into the alleyway that led to the back gate and, keeping close to the wall, crept towards it. He fought to stay alert as the black wooden gate drew nearer. During the war, too many men died because they got sloppy at the end of a patrol, assuming they were safe before they really were, and he was determined not to make the same fatal mistake.

Exhausted, he finally leant against the gatepost and looked up and down the alleyway. He was knackered and starving as he listened to the sound of movement on the other side of the wall. He placed his hand on the gate and pushed. It was locked. 'Oi! Open this bloody gate!' he shouted whilst looking fearfully up and down the alley and hammering on the gate with his fist.

'Who is it?' a voice shouted from the barracks yard. It was O'Neill.

'It's me, Kevin!' Flynn shouted. 'Open up, quick!'

'All right! All right!' O'Neill called as the bolt rasped from its socket and the Ulsterman peered out. Flynn threw his weight against it and barged past O'Neill, slamming the gate shut behind him.

'Bolt it quick!' Flynn barked and slumped against the wall, safe at last.

O'Neill stared in wide-eyed disbelief at Flynn as he bundled in through the gate and stood for a second or two before galvanizing himself into action. 'Jesus, Kevin, is that yourself? You look like shit!' he said, staring at Flynn's battered face and filthy clothes. Reaching over, he gently took the rifle from Flynn's hands and casually flicked open the breech, ejecting the round. 'There, that's better,' he added as he picked up the discarded bullet and slipped the rifle sling over his shoulder. He helped his exhausted friend towards the back door. 'We heard about the business over in Granard this morning. Christ, will Willson have a flaming heart attack when he sees you, so he will! We thought that you'd copped it!'

Flynn grinned at O'Neill and licked his lips. 'So did I,' he said wearily, utterly drained, 'so did I.'

O'Neill slapped him firmly on the back and laughed. 'Get yourself inside.'

'They've killed Jim,' Flynn said wearily. 'One of the Fenians told me they'd killed Jim.'

O'Neill went white, shocked by the news as he put his arm comfortingly around Flynn's shoulder. 'Jesus, I could murder a drink …' O'Neill muttered, as he pushed Flynn gently towards the back door. 'Now let's get inside.'

CHAPTER 25

Monday, 1 November 1920, Drumlish RIC Barracks

THE ROOM WAS thick with the greasy stench of fried bacon mixed with stale sweat and tea. Mrs Willson bustled around the room juggling chipped willow pattern plates of sandwiches oozing thick brown sauce and looking much older than her forty years. She plonked them down onto a table littered with dog-eared files and tatty papers. Her face was etched with strain; life in the barracks was taking its toll on the sergeant's wife. 'You'll feel better with this inside you,' she said, handing Flynn a plate of sandwiches.

'Thank you very much, Mrs Willson,' Flynn said as he took the plate. He picked up one of the wedges of bread and bacon and took a massive bite. There was something strangely comforting about bacon sandwiches and after the first swallow he began to feel better. He sank into the depths of the barracks' only decent armchair outside of Willson's family quarters. Everything seemed just the way he remembered it, yet already it had changed. He didn't belong anymore, it wasn't his barracks and, as he stared at the floor chewing mechanically, he knew that yet again he was an outsider. Just like when he'd come home from the war.

Flynn took a generous sip of tea, liberally laced with whiskey. It caught in his throat; the fiery cocktail flared in his gut, tingling through his limbs. He felt light-headed; alcohol, even small quantities, always did that to him when he was knackered and he yearned for sleep but knew he couldn't. He needed to get back to Longford; he needed to find out what had happened to Kelleher; he needed to find out what happened next.

O'Neill splashed some more whiskey into Flynn's mug. 'Bit like old times, eh?' he soothed with a warming smile but Flynn's befuddled brain couldn't quite grasp what he meant. 'We always got rum in our tea after a patrol. A bit of gunfire on a cold morning – can't beat it, eh,

Kevin, my boy?' Flynn nodded and attempted to smile as he remembered divvying up rum to his own boys, numbed and exhausted amongst the squalor of the trenches.

'I've telephoned County HQ,' Willson said, referring to the barracks' new telephone, whilst he perched on the edge of the table, a mug of tea in one hand, a half-eaten sandwich in the other. 'They'll be sending some people to collect you later today. I also had a chat with Paddy Carroll, the head constable over in Granard, just to let him know that you'd turned up. He seemed happy with that anyway.'

He really isn't up to this, Flynn thought as he looked at Willson's drawn features and the fear in his eyes. Willson's cheeks were sallow and, like his wife, he was coping poorly with the strain; after all, his little world had been turned upside-down. It was almost as if someone had taken a jigsaw and thrown all the pieces in the air and he didn't like it one bit. He could see that the sergeant was counting down the days until he could pack his bags and leave for a new life as a bobby over the water in Liverpool. Indeed, Mrs Willson made no secret of the fact that she was counting the days too.

'So, what the hell happened?' O'Neill asked.

Flynn sighed, sat back and told them what had transpired in Granard before he was captured. 'You know, I still don't have a clue who was giving Inspector Kelleher his orders,' Flynn said, 'but whoever they are, they really aren't going to be happy with the Shinners doing him in.'

Willson took another mechanical bite of his sandwich and O'Neill shifted his weight, watching Flynn closely. 'How do you know that Kelleher's dead?' O'Neill asked, aware that neither he nor Willson had mentioned the inspector's fate. Flynn rubbed his face and ran his fingers through his matted hair, then rasped his hand across his stubbly chin.

'It's funny, but one of the Shinners told me. He said that Kelleher had been killed. Shot. Do you know what happened? There hadn't been any shooting before the bastards jumped me!'

'Not really,' Willson said. 'When I telephoned Head Constable Carroll, he told me that they've arrested one of the Kiernan girls.' He paused for a moment to gather his thoughts. 'Kitty,' he added. Everyone in the area had heard of the Kiernans because of their business interests but everyone in the constabulary also knew that the entire family were up to their necks in republican politics.

'That's her, she was Kelleher's contact,' Flynn muttered angrily. 'He told me that she was pretty well connected. As far as we could tell, she's Mick Collins' girl. I told him she was trouble, that we couldn't trust her, but the bloody fool wouldn't have it and look where it's got him now. Jesus, I told him!' he said as he slumped in the chair.

'Easy now, Kevin,' Willson said, trying to calm Flynn down. 'The head constable said something about there being no witnesses, so it's unlikely that they will be able to hold this Kiernan woman for long. Unless you saw anything, then it looks like Kelleher's killers will get away with it. Gunned down in a public bar and no one to see? Christ, I'm sick to death of this country and that's a terrible thing to say about your own. I'll be glad to see the back of it, Kevin, my lad!'

'So, Kevin, what happened to you?' O'Neill interrupted as he liberally splashed more whiskey into Flynn's tea. Already it was beginning to make his head spin. ''Twas a rare stroke of luck to get away from the Shinners then?'

'It was the damnedest thing,' Flynn began whilst Willson wiped a smear of bacon grease from his chin with the back of his hand. 'I must look like shit?' Flynn muttered.

'You do that, Kevin, my boy, but you were saying?' O'Neill laughed as he put down the whiskey bottle and swung backwards onto a nearby chair, resting his forearms across its back and watching the Dubliner.

'Like I said, it was the damnedest thing. They took me to an old croft, a right dump, about four miles over thataways—' He waved off the way he'd come '—up in the hills.' Willson muttered something about thinking he knew where he meant but O'Neill said nothing. 'I thought that they were going to kill me. Mick McNamara was there—'

'That little shite,' Willson interrupted but Flynn pressed on regardless.

'For sure, it was him who said he'd shot Jim and if he'd had his way he would have shot me but the fella in charge wouldn't let him. I don't know who he was but he seemed to be in charge and the others did what he told them. By Christ, McNamara was put out by it and I don't think that there is any love lost between the two. You know, I think that he was involved in the attack last January. You know, when we found that thumb in the road. I think it was him, the fella I shot.'

Willson was nodding along as Flynn spoke but the Dubliner noticed that O'Neill had gone very quiet, his dark, intelligent eyes fixed on Flynn's face, searching his every gesture, measuring his every expression, studying him intently. 'Why do you say that?' O'Neill asked.

'Because, Gary, he didn't have a thumb on his left hand, just a stump. It was the same fella who tried to scare me and Kelleher off the Kiernan girl in Longford.' Suddenly, the telephone jangled into life and Willson picked up the handset. Willson seemed to brace up and Flynn could tell that whoever was on the other end of the line outranked him.

'Sergeant Willson ... speaking ... uh hum ... aye ... really ... very good, sir ... I'll let Sergeant Flynn know.' Flynn watched him nodding. Willson put the handset down and took a deep breath. 'That was Head Constable Carroll; he says that they've had to let the Kiernan girl go. No evidence, he said. No bloody witnesses. No bloody point.'

Flynn had never seen Willson so depressed but what struck Flynn was how calmly O'Neill took the news, almost as if he was expecting it. 'You don't seem terribly surprised that they let Kitty Kiernan go, Gary,' he said to O'Neill and he thought that he saw something flicker deep in the Ulsterman's eyes.

'Not really,' O'Neill replied dismissively. 'If, like they say, she's Mick Collins' girl, then the frockcoats in the Castle won't be after provoking the big fella, will they? What would be more likely to get the man to do something drastic than locking up his girl?'

Flynn nodded. After all, it made sense that the politicians – the frockcoats as they called them – would bend over backwards to placate senior rebels. The police and the army called it the revolving door: the security forces would arrest a known republican and the politicians would order them released in the bizarre belief that it would encourage the rebels to be reasonable and negotiate a deal. Sadly, Flynn thought, the rebels didn't really reciprocate in kind and, whilst it was true some IRA officers let prisoners go, most of the time the only way out for captured soldiers or policemen was a bullet in the back of the head.

'You reckon it was the frockcoats that did it?' Flynn asked O'Neill.

'Aye, that I do, Kevin, that I do. Who else, eh?'

'Blasted politicians!' Willson muttered. 'That's what is wrong with this country, too many bloody politicians! The boys over in Granard won't like it, so they won't!' O'Neill laughed and Flynn would have too if it wasn't for the fact that he was too tired and apathetic to be bothered.

O'Neill looked back at Flynn. 'So Kevin, you didn't say what happened?'

'Like I said, this fella with the one thumb, he seemed in charge. There were four of them: this fella, McNamara and another two. He sent McNamara and one of the others off to get further instructions, so he said. I heard them through a crack in the boards over the window of the room they were keeping me in.' Flynn massaged his temples. He felt shattered and he was surprised at how hard it was becoming to speak. 'Then this fella came and told me to follow him and I saw there was just him and this young lad and I thought that my time had come.'

Flynn paused again and sipped his tea. It was growing cold but the whiskey was still good. He sat back and put the mug on the table next to the empty plate littered with crumbs and grease. 'It was then that it happened,' he continued. 'It was then that he shot the other fella.'

There was a pause. 'Who shot the other fella? What other fella?' Willson looked confused.

'I don't know who the hell he really is,' Flynn said, 'but he saved my life. Said he was on our side but who he works for, buggered if I know! It's like a bloody great monster with too many bloody heads!'

'What the hell are you on about now?' Willson asked, confused.

'All this bloody cloak and dagger bollocks!' Flynn cursed. 'Who knows who the hell is working for who! For all I know, the bloody man was probably working for Kelleher. Buggered if he told me anything about where he got his information from.'

'And this fella said he was on our side?' O'Neill asked in astonishment.

'Aye, he did. He also said he was an IRA battalion OC,' Flynn announced and an awkward silence settled on the room.

'And you don't know who he is?' Willson asked.

'Not a clue,' was all Flynn managed.

O'Neill jumped as the front door banged open and Flynn didn't recognize the two constables who stepped into the room. Replacements, Flynn thought as he sank back into his chair. The new arrivals muttered something that Flynn didn't quite catch as they made their way to the gun room to shed their weapons and get a cup of tea.

'Do you mind if I go and get my head down?' Flynn asked and Willson helped him up and led him up the stairs to the constables' dormitory. His limbs felt like lead and his mind was beginning to wander as the adrenalin ebbed from his body. If he'd had the energy he was sure that his hands would have been shaking but even his nerves couldn't be bothered.

As Willson plodded back down the stairs he saw his two new constables debriefing O'Neill about their bicycle patrol out to the outlying farms whilst the Ulsterman scribbled notes as usual into the barracks' occurrence book. Willson knew that he could rely on O'Neill to write it all up and make sure that the paperwork was all up to speed and had already written to HQ recommending that O'Neill be made an acting sergeant and given control of Drumlish barracks when he moved over the water to Liverpool. Willson knew he would be leaving his little fiefdom in safe hands.

He looked at the clock on the wall and picked up the key from the mantelpiece, opened the glass and wound the mechanism with a gentle grinding noise. As he popped the key back onto the mantelpiece he noticed O'Neill putting his cap on and slipping on his overcoat. 'And where are you off?' he asked O'Neill.

The Ulsterman shrugged. 'I thought that someone should take a turn around the village and the boys have just got in, so I thought that I'd do it.'

'Aye, off you go then,' Willson said as he shuffled off to his private quarters at the back of the barracks. O'Neill watched him go then quietly closed the barracks' front door and, turning up his collar against the cold, walked off towards the post office. He still hadn't returned when the Auxiliary patrol arrived to take Flynn back to Longford.

CHAPTER 26

Monday, 1 November 1920, Kilshrewley, County Longford

IT WAS DARK by the time Fitzgerald reached Kilshrewley and the stress of the day was beginning to catch up with him. He felt light-headed, his water-logged brogues squelching as he limped up the path towards the flickering lights, and his stomach rumbled loudly as he rapped upon the cottage's flaking wooden door. The latch rattled and a shard of light slashed the darkness as the door creaked open. A shadowy face peered out and Fitzgerald pushed his way past into the room.

MacEoin sat quietly by the fire, nursing a glass of whiskey and he looked shattered as he watched Fitzgerald walk towards him. He had a lot on his mind, it had been a hard few days and tomorrow didn't look like it would be any easier. 'We got that peeler up by Breaghy,' Fitzgerald said as he flopped down in a fireside armchair. MacEoin responded with an almost imperceptible, indifferent nod. His face was pale and if Fitzgerald didn't know any better he'd say he was in shock, his manner distracted.

'Eh, what was that, Brendan?' he eventually said.

'The peeler, the one visiting his wife in Balinalee, we got him up by Breaghy, me and Frank and his boys.' He tossed Constable Peter Cooney's warrant card onto the table. 'You know, Sean, I think that the Granard plods may be taking it badly having a DI shot on their patch and one of their own too.' MacEoin glanced at the warrant card and then, almost absent-mindedly, flipped it onto the smouldering turf in the grate. It began to curl and blacken at the edges before flaring into oblivion. MacEoin sighed and looked wearily at Fitzgerald with sad eyes, his spirits weighed down by something.

'You know, Brendan, right now the peelers are the least of my problems. I've got a much bigger problem to sort out and I'm really sorry as hell to drag you into this but I've got a job for you. Pat Doyle is dead,' MacEoin said. Fitzgerald hardly knew the lad but he'd heard good things about him all the same. 'You know the peeler who was with Kelleher, the one that Joe and Mick caught outside the Greville? He escaped. Pat got shot. Like I said, the local peelers are the least of our troubles.' Fitzgerald looked confused. 'I've just got some news that worries me and I need to get over to Granard.' MacEoin looked straight at Fitzgerald. He looked tired, yet his eyes burned with a cold fury. 'Like I said, I've got a wee job for you.'

CHAPTER 27

Monday, 1 November 1920, An abandoned croft,
County Longford

MAGUIRE'S HEAD HURT like hell. Flynn's blow had been clumsy, inexpertly delivered and he thought that he'd blacked out once or twice as he watched Doyle's greying corpse stiffen in the mildewed air. Even the silence hurt. He heard a car and the crunch of boots then muffled shouts. As he opened his eyes, Hegarty was halfway across the room and McNamara was kneeling next to Doyle checking for a pulse, muttering. The boy's flesh was cold like rubber sheeting. 'Joe, what the be-Jaysus happened here?' Hegarty asked as Maguire lolled, fighting back a wave of nausea.

'He screwed up, that's what happened!' McNamara snapped angrily at Maguire.

Hegarty shot McNamara an angry glance. 'Shut up and do something useful. Get Pat out of here – put him in one of the sheds and cover him over. We'll get someone to come and fetch him later.' McNamara opened his mouth to speak. 'So get on with it!' Seething, McNamara hefted Doyle onto his shoulder. The shed was dark and he placed Doyle away from the door in the shadows and covered him with a pile of mouldering hessian potato sacks that had definitely seen better days.

What a bloody waste! he thought to himself, adding another reason for hating Maguire to his mental list. 'I'll do right by you,' he said quietly before heading back to the others.

Maguire vomited, his head spinning; his legs felt like jelly. 'So what happened then, Joe?' he heard McNamara hiss. 'How did that bloody peeler get from being tied up in the back room to Pat dead, you tied up and him off and away, eh?'

Maguire squinted at McNamara and shook his head to clear his vision. 'What are you suggesting, eh, Mick?' he managed to say.

'Easy, Joe, he isn't trying to say anything. Are you, Mick?' Hegarty said as he helped Maguire into the waiting car. 'So, Joe, what happened here? Take your time.'

'I'm afraid that I can't remember much. I remember me and Pat standing out here talking, then it's all … all … gone. He must have got free somehow—'

'No shit!' McNamara interrupted.

'… and smacked me on the head.' Maguire put his hand to the back of his head and felt the lump and crust of blood matted in his hair.

'Pat must have walked in on you and the bastard shot him with your gun by the look of it. Pat's rifle's gone too so the shit's armed,' Hegarty speculated and Maguire nodded, relieved that his alibi seemed to be holding up for now but McNamara's attitude worried him.

'For God's sake, don't puke in the car!' Hegarty cried as Maguire slumped into the back of the car. His nausea was ebbing now and he allowed himself a brief smile from the shadows as it started to rain. He'd made it.

'Looks like the bastard shot Pat in the throat and then finished him off when he was down. If I get my hands on him, I'll make him sorry for the day he was born!' McNamara shouted above the noise of the engine. Maguire fought back the urge to laugh at McNamara's outburst. The sheer hypocrisy of it all was one of the reasons he had lost faith in the cause in the first place and he knew that if Pat had been a Brit then McNamara would have been waxing lyrical about how he'd deserved it.

'We'd best get you over to Dr Kenny in Granard,' Hegarty said and it only seemed a few moments later that Maguire was watching Hegarty knock loudly on the doctor's back door. There was movement from inside and a girl in her mid teens opened the door a crack and peered out.

'Hello, Marcy,' Hegarty said quietly. 'Is your dad in?'

'Who is it, Marcy?' a voice called and Maguire recognized Joe Kenny the moment he walked into the kitchen, as ever swathed in bluish pipe smoke, cleaning his glasses with a corner of his handkerchief before perching them back on his snub nose. 'Away with you now, girl,' he said softly to his daughter before turning to Maguire. 'Well, well, Joe, what on earth have you been up to? Better still, don't tell me. I don't really want to know.' He smiled, reaching for his Gladstone bag and pulling out a small bottle of iodine. 'Well, let me take a look at you,' he said as he dabbed the antiseptic on the back of Maguire's head. 'Is there somewhere you can take him?' he asked Hegarty. 'He needs to rest.'

Hegarty nodded but said nothing. It was another short car ride to a safe house at the edge of the town and once inside Maguire felt tired, bone weary, and it was almost as if someone had hit the 'off' switch when his head finally hit the pillow. Within seconds he was snoring loudly. 'No wonder he's not married!' Hegarty joked as he covered him with a few old blankets but McNamara just cursed under his breath as he went to leave.

'Keep an eye on him,' Hegarty told the young IRA Volunteer who lived in the house with his parents. 'Don't let him leave until I get back. He's had a rough day. Best we find Sean and let him know what has happened.'

'Best we send someone to fetch Pat too,' McNamara said as they reached the car.

Hegarty paused, the door half open in his hand. 'Tell you what, Mick, you take the car and find the boss. Tell him what happened to Pat and Joe. I'll go to the Greville and organize someone to fetch Pat home.' Words couldn't describe the depth of relief he felt as he watched McNamara drive away.

On the corner of Main Street, Hegarty froze in the shadows. There were armed policemen outside the Greville Arms and he ducked back into a shop doorway, watching them as he revised his plans. He was wet, it was late and he needed somewhere to stay so he decided to make his way over to McGovern's office. If anyone knew what was happening then it would be MacEoin's pet solicitor so, turning up his collar, he set off to find the lawyer.

McGovern looked flustered and worn, like a man with too many problems and too little sleep. 'This Kelleher business has really set some hares running,' he told Hegarty as he ushered him nervously into his office. In the distance the RIC barracks was alive with activity; lights flickered in its yard. 'The peelers aren't happy. They arrested Kitty after the shooting and I've only just managed to persuade them to let her go.'

Hegarty smiled. 'That's something at least. Look, do you mind if I crash here tonight?'

CHAPTER 28

Tuesday, 2 November 1920, Granard, County Longford

'QUICK, MR MAGUIRE! Wake up!' The pile of musty old blankets moved slightly and Maguire shoved his head out of the jumble, cautiously opening an eye and wincing as the light skewered his brain. He was snug and warm and he knew that the moment he moved his head the pain would return, throbbing in waves around his skull. The dressing lashed to his head had shifted in the night and most of it was in a tangled bloody mess on the pillow whilst around him the room smelt of sweat and old socks. He felt sick. 'For Christ's sake, what?' He winced as a needle of pain lunged into his brain. 'What the hell are you shouting for?'

'It's the Greville!' the shrill voice continued excitedly and Maguire pulled himself painfully out of the blankets and sat up. Instantly, pain rippled through him, followed by a wave of nausea; it felt almost as if he'd ruptured some invisible membrane above his bed and unleashed a torrent of suffering that was pouring down on him. He'd had better hangovers.

'Jaysus, will you keep the noise down, boy? Now calm down and talk to me. What about the Greville?' he said, rubbing his eyes and looking at the adolescent boy panting with excitement, his eyes wide and his face pallid with fear. The lad looked vaguely familiar but his name escaped him.

Christ, he thought, the boys are getting younger every year. Dust danced in the shards of light seeping through the gap in the cheap curtains and Maguire could tell from the tendrils that it was mid morning. He peeled back the heap of blankets and forced himself to smile reassuringly at the lad. 'Try breathing and then tell me what on earth you are blathering on about,' Maguire said.

'It's the Tans!' the adolescent shrieked, referring to the nickname given to the temporary constables recruited by the RIC to top up its manpower. 'It's the Tans! They're going to burn the Greville down! The peelers are slopping it with petrol and trying to torch it!'

'Jaysus!' Maguire cried and sprang off the bed, instantly regretting it.

Swaying slightly, he snatched up his jacket and, feeling light-headed, his vision momentarily faded into a haze of white and shooting stars before crashing back to reality. 'Have you a gun?' he barked urgently and the boy nodded. 'Give it here then!' he demanded, holding out his hand impatiently. The lad's hand darted behind his back as he rummaged for something in the waistband of his trousers. He produced an old black .38 revolver and plonked it in Maguire's outstretched hand. Dumb place to keep a gun, he mused silently as he watched the boy, unless you want to give yourself another arsehole!

Bang! Outside a shot rang out and the boy's eyes widened in fright. Maguire broke open the revolver and checked that it was loaded then snapped it shut with a practised flick of the wrist. 'Is there anything else?' Maguire asked but the boy shook his head. 'Best you stay here,' he ordered and the boy looked relieved to be let off the hook by a superior officer.

'But Mr Hegarty said to stay here and keep an eye on you ...' the lad began but Maguire cut him short.

'Did he now? Well, I can look after myself,' he said and headed for the door while the boy struggled to work out whose instructions to obey. Seeing as Hegarty was only a squad commander and Maguire was a commandant, the boy knew who would win in a game of 'rank trumps'.

Outside, shouting came from the direction of Main Street followed by the staccato rattle of gunfire. The cocktail of fresh air and a surge of adrenalin quickly cleared his head. He was suddenly very alert, his agues forgotten. He heard the sound of breaking glass and several more shots punctuated the morning air, not enough to make him think a gun battle was taking place but more like someone letting off rounds into the air.

A woman scurried past, head down, shawl clasped tight to her body and he blocked her way, demanding, 'What's going on?' She stared at the gun hanging from his right hand and looked around in panic. 'It's all right, I'm not going to hurt you,' he reassured. 'What's happening?'

'It's the peelers; they're trying to burn out the Greville!' Her words tumbled out and before Maguire could stop her she was off down the street, keen to be away. She was not alone; there were others trying to put as much space as possible between themselves and the ruckus on

Main Street, as net curtains twitched, and he could have sworn that he could hear door bolts being drawn shut as he ran past.

He stopped for breath on the corner of Main Street and Church Street to get a better view of the commotion further down the road and to the barracks beyond. Several shop windows had already been smashed and a small knot of five or six men in the rifle-green, almost black, RIC uniforms were beating on the front door of the Greville Arms. One was splashing liquid from what looked like a petrol can against the front of the building whilst another waved a carbine in the air and loosed off rounds randomly. Yet another fumbled with something, then flicked his hand towards the Greville. Whoosh! The petrol exploded into flames and cascaded up the front door, belching oily black smoke into the street.

A policeman hurled the empty can through the Greville's plate-glass window whilst the others laughed and one fumbled with the cap of a second petrol can. More glass shattered as policemen fired into the front of the pub and one of them cried, 'Not so brave now, you Fenian bastards!'

To Maguire's horror the fire was beginning to take hold and he knew there was a real danger of the street going up if no one did anything soon. He straightened his arm and, squinting along the barrel of his revolver, took aim at the knot of men. Bang! The shot startled the policemen, who froze. It took training for a man to instinctively dive for cover when shot at and Maguire knew that these men lacked any meaningful combat training. He loosed off a second shot and they scattered like cockroaches exposed to a sudden light.

Zip! A bullet flew low over his head and he ducked back behind the angle of the brickwork. A movement in the corner of his eye distracted him; it was Hegarty who sprinted over to where he was firing blindly down the street. He looked like he'd just woken up as well. 'So you're back with us then?' He smiled.

Maguire rolled his eyes before shaking his head and risking another quick glance up the street. The policemen were in full flight back towards the barracks so he let off another couple of rounds just to keep them moving. Wood crackled and sparks drifted through the air as the hotel blazed. There were a couple more shots from somewhere and he guessed that the furore had attracted the attention of a couple of other Volunteers in the vicinity. 'I guess they torched the Greville in revenge for Kelleher getting shot,' Maguire said to Hegarty, who nodded.

'I guess so,' Hegarty added while scratching his chin. He needed a shave but then so did Maguire.

'They'll be back. Them and the Auxies too, I bet,' Maguire said.

'Don't I know it,' Hegarty replied as they headed off towards the Greville. They kept close to the walls, ducking in and out of doorways just in case some peeler decided to take a pot shot at them. Broken glass crunched beneath their feet from put-in windows and a petrol can lay discarded in the street, a stain of liquid pooling around it. The air was thick with the acrid stench of petrol fumes. Maguire looked nervously at the upended can.

'For God's sake, don't strike a bloody match!' he called to Hegarty, who was squinting against the glare and heat. They ducked back as the bar exploded, showering glass and sparks into the street, igniting a pool of petrol, making the two men cringe back further from the flames as others emerged into the street looking dazed.

'Quick! Get some water!' Maguire cried in a desperate bid to organize some sort of attempt to fight the fire. Slowly buckets of water began to appear as a chain of people formed but it would be pointless without proper fire-fighting equipment. Wearily, Maguire wiped oily soot from his eyes and thanked God when he heard the clatter of bells and hoofs as the fire engine careered into view and skidded to a halt.

Professional as ever, the firemen took charge of the chaos just as Maguire slipped into the background. He looked towards the barracks and saw Head Constable Carroll standing smugly on its front steps. For a moment he felt like he had caught his eye and Carroll waved a mocking salute before turning and closing the door behind him as he vanished inside. 'You bloody fool,' Maguire muttered bitterly.

'Don't worry, we'll get even with them,' Hegarty said, disturbing Maguire's thoughts, distracting him from the throbbing pain in his skull. 'We'd better get out of here. Let's get over to McGovern's office, until the fire's out.' A broad grin split Hegarty's face. 'Sure, will he be pleased to be seeing me again so soon!'

The fire burned all day but at least most of the damage was confined to the Greville's ground floor. The place was a blackened, smouldering, waterlogged, steaming, smoking mess as Maguire picked over the debris. Lawrence Kiernan stood despondently in the middle of it all, trying to comprehend what had happened to his precious hotel. He was visibly shaken.

'We'll make them pay for this,' McGovern said quietly as he placed a reassuring hand on Kiernan's shoulder.

'By Christ, we'll make them pay,' Hegarty butted in.

Kiernan stared blankly into some unseen middle distance, as if he was not really aware that they were there. Maguire looked around and shook his head. 'What a flaming mess.' A gentle breeze ruffled his hair and caressed his cheek and the damp stench of the gutted bar filled his nostrils.

'Am I glad to see you,' Kiernan finally stuttered, looking at the three men and staring at his partially burned bar where, miraculously, a lone bottle of Jameson whiskey stood on a shelf, its label singed but otherwise intact.

'So there is a God,' Maguire said as he stepped briskly past and plucked it from its sanctuary before pulling out the cork and taking a long swig from the bottle. The fiery liquid coursed through his stomach and sent ripples of warmth through his tired limbs, giving him a new lease of life. Looking around he said, 'Bit of paint and a new carpet and it'll be good as new!' Kiernan gave Maguire a look that showed that he was far from convinced. Maguire offered Hegarty the bottle.

'Don't mind if I do!' Hegarty declared then raised it to his lips and took a long pull before smacking his lips with satisfaction.

'Why the hell did they torch my bar?' Kiernan asked, looking at the two bedraggled gunmen.

'Why do you think?' Maguire said. 'Maybe because we shot one of their inspectors in this bar and the bastards have had enough! I told Sean it was a stupid idea!'

Hegarty smacked his lips appreciatively. 'At least Kitty is free.' Maguire looked at him, puzzled. 'The peelers lifted her after Kelleher was shot but Mr McGovern here got them to let her go.' Maguire looked at McGovern, who nodded slightly, confirming Hegarty's information.

'No wonder they're pissed off and I don't think that we've seen the end of it. I think we need to get you out of here before the lynch mob comes back,' Maguire said, looking out of the broken window towards the barracks. 'Christ knows what that bastard Carroll will do next if he is prepared for his lads to burn down the bloody town. So we've got to get out of here. Larry, where's Kitty now?'

Kiernan blinked a few times as he struggled to think; his face was streaked with dirt and soot. 'She's … she's over at the house,' he finally stuttered.

'The pair of you need to stay clear of here,' McGovern said. 'I'm going to lodge a formal complaint as soon as I get back to my office.'

Hegarty took another pull of whiskey. 'What good will that do?'

McGovern sighed and looked at Hegarty as if he was talking to a small child. 'It will make the Brits embarrassed, it will make them pay compensation and it will make them look bad in the papers. The last thing the great British public want to read about is their beloved bobbies going on the bloody rampage! That's why. If you'll excuse me, I've got a few phone calls to make.' McGovern crunched back off out of the front door and was off down the street to his office.

Maguire turned to Hegarty and said, 'Look, go see if you can find any of the local boys and get a perimeter set up around the barracks. That way if any of the bastards come out, we can get them, just in case they decide to try and encore. Make sure you get someone to get out to the Longford road. That way we can see if the Auxies are coming. We also need to let Sean know what's going on. When you've done all that, get over to the house. I'll be there with Larry.'

'I don't think so!' came a voice from the back of the bar and Hegarty and Maguire spun around, levelling their revolvers as they did so. Maguire let out a breath and relaxed, releasing the pressure from the trigger. There in the shadows Fitzgerald stood impassively blocking the blackened doorway that led to the office behind the bar.

'Jaysus, Brendan, we could have bloody shot you, creeping up on us like that!' Hegarty said, lowering his gun. Kiernan just stood there, rooted to the spot like a frightened rabbit.

'You don't think what, Brendan?' Maguire asked. The foresight of his pistol hovered momentarily over the middle of Fitzgerald's face before he lowered it, blinking to clear his vision.

'The boss wants to see you,' he stated, looking indifferently at the devastation around him.

'For Christ's sake, Brendan, can't you see that we're in the middle of something here?' Maguire snapped.

Fitzgerald stepped closer, a brief, cold smile flickering across his lips. He looked unnaturally clean amongst the grime. 'Don't you go worrying, Joe, Sean sent me to fetch you. He needs to speak to you.'

Maguire stretched out his arms and looked around in askance. 'And what about all this mess?'

Fitzgerald glanced disinterestedly around the room and then looked back at Maguire. 'Like I said, don't you go worrying yourself. Sean sent some back-up.' Fitzgerald smiled a cold, comfortless smile. Even his normally yellowed teeth seemed white against the darkness of the room, like some sort of oversized rodent, Maguire couldn't help thinking.

'Eunan here can take charge. He's good for it. I've already sent some of the lads to make sure the peelers stay bottled up in their little bunker. Best Larry here gets himself home,' Maguire said.

Fitzgerald turned to Hegarty. 'Joe here is right, Eunan. Get someone up onto the Longford road to keep an eye out for the Auxies.' Then he reached over and gently took the whiskey bottle from Hegarty's hand and placed it carefully on the ruined bar. 'I don't think that the peelers will be making a fuss for a wee while yet. Things may be different later if the Auxies arrive. Besides, Joe, it's only a fifteen-minute ride over to see Sean, so we can be back before the hour,' he added reassuringly. 'Anyway, Sean needs to know what's going on here and I'm sure that he'll want to have a say in how we play this, once we've worked out what the hell is going on.'

Hegarty nodded briefly before slipping past Fitzgerald. He deftly picked up the whiskey bottle and was gone before Kiernan could make any comment about him pilfering his stock.

'Think of it as a contribution to the cause,' Maguire quipped, almost reading Kiernan's thoughts as he shot Hegarty an angry glance before scurrying away through the ruins of his prize business.

'Have you got a clue why the local plods have got it into their heads to torch the Greville and put in a few windows?' Maguire asked Fitzgerald.

The gunman shrugged noncommittally. Maguire watched him carefully; there was something about Fitzgerald's manner he didn't like but then there was no change there, he thought. 'Come on, best be off – the car is out back,' Fitzgerald said and turned towards the door without looking back to see if Maguire was following, his tone more like an order than a request, and Maguire felt that he had little option but to comply. After all, MacEoin was Maguire's superior officer so it made perfect sense that he would want to speak to him. It was bound to happen sooner or later so he may as well get it over with.

'You really do look like shit,' Fitzgerald laughed, lightening the atmosphere as he led Maguire through the hotel. They stepped into the back yard where an idling car was parked next to a scorched stack of empty beer barrels. Dirty water mixed with stale soiled beer pooled amongst the cobbles and everything stank to Maguire like a bad hangover.

One of MacEoin's flying column lounged in the driver's seat cradling a pristine .303 rifle, wearing a stained, rumpled trenchcoat, his battered slouch hat casting a deep shadow over his unshaven face, hiding his eyes, although Maguire could tell he was watching him. His chest was criss-crossed by two beige cotton ammunition bandoliers that gave him the look of a Mexican bandito from one of those Wild West films and all the man needed was a droopy moustache to complete the ensemble.

'In you hop, Joe,' Fitzgerald chirped, holding open the back door and Maguire climbed up into the car. Its canvas soft top did little to keep out the wet and the seat was already damp beneath his backside as water seeped through the seat of his trousers. The 'bandito' gave him a silent sidelong glance as Fitzgerald climbed into the front passenger seat and then turned away as he crunched the car into gear and it jolted into motion.

A fine drizzle began to fall, bouncing amongst the puddles, and Maguire suddenly remembered how hungry he was. 'Not long now,' Fitzgerald said and after ten minutes or so Maguire could tell that they weren't actually heading to Balinalee but one of the hamlets outside it. Ever since the Gaigue Cross operation, MacEoin had more or less been on the run and Maguire guessed that they were probably heading to Kilshrewley, one of the blacksmith's favourite little hidey-holes.

Eventually the car lurched to a halt outside a rundown cottage nestled in a fold in the ground and the motion made Maguire feel mildly nauseous. The rain was closing in and Maguire couldn't see more than a hundred yards or so in any direction. Raindrops rattled noisily off the car's canvas soft top and sounded like a ragged drum roll. 'Shit!' Fitzgerald muttered as the bandito applied the handbrake and he turned up his collar against the wet.

Maguire felt the mud and water squelch over the tops of his shoes as he stepped out of the car and ran over to the front door. It was only a few yards but by the time he got there he felt like a drowned rat. Fitzgerald looked at Maguire and barely managed to suppress a smile; the man was as wet as he was despite his raincoat and hat. Inside was empty, the air smelt damp and Maguire could hear the rain bouncing off the slate roof, the watery tattoo aggravating the throbbing at the back of his head. A turf fire smouldered in the grate and he made his way over to it. Steam rose from his clothes as he rubbed the warmth into his hands.

'So where is Sean?' he asked. Fitzgerald silently shut the door and peeled off his sopping coat. His hat had already lost its shape and draped over his face like a scarecrow's. Maguire began to feel nervous. 'So where is he?' he asked again.

'He'll be along soon enough,' Fitzgerald replied as he tossed his hat onto a peg on the back of the door. Droplets dripped on the floor making a growing stain on the dirt floor, dark like blood.

'Perhaps we should get back to Granard?' Maguire asked.

'He'll be along,' Fitzgerald said again and reluctantly Maguire plonked himself down in a seat by the fire and felt his clothes drying out as he sat there, whilst Fitzgerald sat at a table at the other end of the room, looking at his watch. The morbid silence hung heavily in the air. The door at the back of the cottage suddenly swung open and MacEoin strode briskly into the room. He looked tired, like he hadn't slept properly in days, which he hadn't. He shook his hat, scattering droplets around the room.

'Jaysus, what a day!' MacEoin declared to no one in particular as he tossed his coat over the back of a chair and sat down in the chair opposite Maguire. He smiled.

'So, Joe, what happened?' he finally asked, leaning back in his chair.

'The peelers have burnt out the Greville ...' Maguire started.

'Not in Granard, Joe. I mean when Pat Doyle got shot.'

So Maguire told him and MacEoin listened patiently as he recounted his tale, every now and again nodding quietly. 'And that is what happened, is it?' he asked after Maguire had finished speaking.

'To be honest, Sean, I don't really remember that much.'

MacEoin's face hardened slightly as the firelight reflected in his eyes and he bridged his hands in front of his face, deep in thought. 'You know, Joe, I had a feeling that you would say that. There's nothing more you want to tell me? Nothing you've forgotten, eh?'

'Shit, Sean! There is a load I can't remember. The bastard fetched me a hell of a blow on the head. Jaysus, I've got the mother of all headaches and you are asking me all these bloody questions!'

'So it would seem. But you know, Joe, I've got a wee problem.'

Maguire's brain raced as he watched MacEoin impassively doing his best to mask his emotions. He had an awful feeling that the blacksmith was fencing with him, playing a game of poker, and despite his headache, poker-faced Maguire fought to keep his wits about him. Where was this going? he thought.

'My problem, Joe, is that I've been given a very different version of events, very different indeed.'

'I don't follow you, Sean,' Maguire said, looking puzzled.

'I've been told that you helped the peeler escape and it was you who killed Pat.' MacEoin's words felt like a slap across Maguire's face.

'Who says?' he demanded angrily. 'I bet it was that wee gobshite

McNamara. He'd say anything to try and get me in the shit since his brother was shot. It was tough luck Jerry copping it like that, but that's war, Sean, and the bastard has decided that it's my fault. You've seen him – he's a bloody basket case!'

'No, it wasn't Mick,' MacEoin said sadly, shaking his head as the door creaked quietly open behind them. Maguire turned and saw a shadowy figure enter the room and the blood drained from his face as he recognized the man who he knew was his accuser.

'I told him,' said Constable Gary O'Neill, as he stepped into the light.

CHAPTER 29

Kingstown, County Dublin

Fᴿᴏᴍ ᴡʜᴇʀᴇ Kᴀᴛʜʟᴇᴇɴ stood on the West Pier, Kingstown harbour was quiet and she could see the myriad little yachts and fishing boats bucking up and down at their moorings on the choppy brown waters whilst down by the lifeboat shed a couple of lifeboat men busied themselves cheesing down lines, making the place ship-shape, idling away the time before their next call-out.

Around her lines sang and timbers creaked as the salt-laden breeze whistled through rigging shrouds and sent unsecured canvas flapping. If she'd known anything about the sea she'd have known that there was a storm rising and from the slate-grey skies Kathleen knew that she had best get undercover before the rain came.

The smell of fish, mixed with the tang of salt in the air, made her hungry and she was acutely conscious that she had not eaten for several hours. The bitter wind ruffled her hair, sending curly red streaks across her face as she looked out onto Dublin Bay at the tattered wisps of smoke belching from the funnel of a distant Royal Navy gunboat, battling against the tide towards Dublin. For a brief moment she felt sorry for the men trapped in the pitching grey steel box and thanked her lucky stars she wasn't with them. She loved looking at the sea but had no real urge to go on it.

The truth be told, Kathleen badly missed Drumlish with its green hills, its fields and twee cottages, not like Kingstown with its harbour, its parks, church spires and big Georgian houses and so many people. Whilst the train journey had, as ever, been a bit of an adventure of sorts, mostly because she had never really been anywhere but Drumlish and her aunt's house in Kingstown in her entire life, she could have done without it. In her dreams she had always wanted to travel but whenever she saw the crowded, filthy streets of Dublin she wasn't so sure – yet Flynn had told her it was a beautiful city. 'It's a grand place,' he'd said. 'You just haven't looked at it properly.' She remembered his smile and how much she missed it.

Maybe he was right. 'In Dublin's fair city, where the girls are so pretty,' the song declared but from what little she'd seen of the place she was decidedly unimpressed. In fact, she had become distinctly unimpressed with Kingstown, sea views and all, and her aunt's boarding house was beginning to feel more like a prison than a sanctuary.

'Remember that for the time being no one must know that you are staying with your aunt,' her father had instructed, waving his bandaged and splinted hand at her and for the first time she had noticed how old and worn he looked. There was a haunted, fearful look in his once-laughing eyes as he slouched under some invisible weight. She had never seen him look this way, not even when he got the telegram telling him that Davey was gone.

'But why?' she'd asked. 'Surely I'll be safe, all the way away at Aunt Rebecca's. I may as well have emigrated, it's so far from here!'

Her mother looked older too and she pushed a strand of lank, lifeless red hair from her eyes as she spoke to her daughter. 'These people aren't mucking about, Kathleen, and after what they did to your father's hand, sweet Jesus knows what they might be doing to you, if we don't get you away from here.'

'But what about my Kevin?' she pleaded.

Her mother gave her a baleful glance and sighed. 'Child, that is why we must get you away, because of Kevin. They threatened you, Kathy, and ...' She trailed off, her eyes reddened with tears and in her head Kathleen could still hear the voice of the man who pressed the gun to her head in the back yard, the familiar voice that she still couldn't quite place.

'You see, Kathleen, my darling,' the voice had said, 'it would be a terrible thing for anything to happen to your da, especially now your brother's gone too ... sure, you'll know what happens to traitors.'

'Mick Early is one of them,' she blurted, 'and there was a man with a gun out back when they broke da's hand.'

Her mother's face blanched paler and her father groaned as he buried his face in his good hand. 'All the more reason to get you away, Kathy,' Mrs Moore had gabbled, her face flushed with fear. 'Remember, whatever you do, no one must know where you are,' her father had said as he helped her on to the train. 'I'll let you know when it is safe to come home.' She was haunted by the look on her father's face as he waved her off. 'I'll make them pay for this,' he'd told her, as he'd hugged her one last time, but deep down they both knew there was nothing he could do, absolutely nothing. He thrust an envelope into her hand and said, 'Give this to Aunt Rebecca. It will explain everything.'

She had stuffed the envelope into her bag and watched her father disappear in a cloud of smoke as the train pulled away from the platform. For the entire journey she was convinced that everyone was watching her but despite her paranoia she knew that none of them were really interested in her. That is, except for the young man on the other side of the compartment who kept smiling at her from over the top of his book but she had a feeling that his motives were far from political. By the time she reached Dublin she had avoided saying a word to anyone, except the conductor when he checked her ticket.

From Dublin, the trip to Kingstown was a nightmare of cabs, trams and strange accents but eventually she had found herself outside the familiar if somewhat faded facade of her aunt's once-grand Georgian house, towering four floors over Mellifont Avenue off Upper George Street. When she rang the doorbell a short woman of indeterminate middle age answered the front door and smiled welcomingly. She had the same washed-out red hair as Kathleen's mother and a friendly face that was reminiscent of her too.

'Aunt Rebecca?' Kathleen asked.

The woman looked at her for a moment then replied, 'Kathleen? Is that really you? And what brings you all the way to Kingstown? Are your parents with you?' Kathleen shook her head and handed her aunt the envelope, who rapidly scanned the scrawled note then popped it into a pocket on the apron that she wore. 'Come on in, Kathleen, come in,' she said and ushered her into the house.

The house had clearly seen better days and the stairwell smelt faintly of damp and mildew as she climbed to the attic room at the back of the house that was to be her new home until the holiday season ended and she was able to occupy one of the larger guestrooms overlooking the street. The rooms were light and airy with high ceilings and would make a pleasant change from the cramped attic.

Mrs Rebecca Finnegan was an enigma to Kathleen. She was kind enough, respectable and long-since widowed but she said little about her life and nothing about how she came to be running a boarding house in Kingstown. Kathleen assumed that it all had something to do with Mr Finnegan but Aunt Rebecca never talked about him. It was almost as if he had never existed.

Kathleen's thoughts were snatched back to the present by the shrieking gulls swirling inland, escaping the brewing storm and dismissing her memories along with her indecision. It was time to act. When all was said and done, she was thoroughly sick of Kingstown, and missed home with its fields and cottages. More keenly, she missed Flynn, she missed him more than she had missed anyone in her life, especially as the forced seclusion of Kingstown was slowly killing her.

Chewing her lower lip nervously, the shifting wind ruffling her hair, tossing coppery strands across her face, she stared intently at the envelope clutched in her gloved hand and then headed off the pier towards the imposing Royal Irish Yacht Club building on Harbour Road and the nearest pillar box. In the distance two dark blue uniformed Dublin Metropolitan Police constables strolled along, their helmeted heads bent as the wind whipped up the edges of their oilskin rain capes, reminding her of her own policeman.

It was an old hexagonal pillar box with VR embossed boldly in flowing script on its red-painted iron carcass and she began gently placing the letter into the gaping mouth of the box when something made her pause once more and glance quickly about at the boats bobbing in the marina, straining against their mooring lines and at the gulls circling above her head. She thought that she heard a distant gunshot on the wind but the policemen carried on strolling and she shrugged it off as nothing as a raindrop struck her cheek, cascading like a fat tear down her cheek.

The downpour was heavy and if she didn't get on with it she'd soon be soaked. A hefty raindrop struck the surface of the envelope, scouring a thin blue stream across the address. She flicked the gobbet of water off her precious letter and glanced at the address – Constable K Flynn, c/o The RIC Barracks, Drumlish, County Longford. It was still legible and she blotted the envelope on her sleeve before dropping it into the pillar box. 'There, it's done,' she whispered softly before hurrying off towards her aunt's house, and by the time she reached the top of Queens Street she was a bedraggled, sodden mess.

'Quick! Come on in and warm yourself by the fire, Kathy darling,' her aunt said when she saw her come in. 'I'll fetch us some tea,' she added before shouting down to the scullery for a tray of tea as Kathleen settled by the fire, feeling the warmth seep into her arms and legs.

'Thank you, Aunt Rebecca,' she said as she took a cup of tea and looked out of the window at the rain lashing against the glass. At least he'll know where I am, she thought, and a slight smile crossed her face as the thought of him warmed her as much as the fire. He'll come for me, I know he will.

CHAPTER 30

Wednesday, 3 November 1920, Kilshrewley near Ballinalee, County Longford

M AGUIRE LOOKED UP as Fitzgerald pulled back the hammer of his revolver and pointed it at him. Click! The sound reverberated around the room and Maguire flinched involuntarily, convinced that the sound would be the last thing he would ever hear. He bit back on his welling panic and thought carefully about what to say next. Sweat trickled down his back and his armpits were soaked and he knew that beads would soon be running incriminatingly down his temples. If he didn't think of something fast he was finished.

The sandy-haired policeman stepped from the shadows, his hands thrust casually into his pockets and the front of his civilian overcoat pulled open, exposing the dark green uniform beneath. Even in the gloom his medal ribbons provided a splash of colour and Maguire couldn't help letting his eyes linger on them for a moment too long. The policeman's dark eyes glinted in the firelight, casting deep shadows across his angular features, and Maguire stifled the urge to get up and smack the sickening self-satisfied smirk off the Ulsterman's smug face. 'And who the hell is this?' Maguire snapped indignantly. 'Why is this bastard peeler here anyway?' he said, attempting to bluster his way out of the corner he had been so deftly backed into.

'Gary here is one of my men in the constabulary,' MacEoin said quietly, 'and he's been telling me some disturbing things about you, Joe. Terrible things, if they're true. Terrible.' Maguire could see that the hurt in MacEoin's eyes was real and as he glanced at O'Neill, his eye sockets felt like they were lined with sandpaper. He knew that MacEoin had several sources inside the RIC but he had never in his wildest dreams imagined that this Protestant Ulsterman, the very antithesis of the republican stereotype, was MacEoin's man. More importantly, neither would anyone else, which was why O'Neill was just about as perfect a choice of spy that there could be. Bugger! Maguire thought.

'Flynn told me everything about how you done for Paddy Doyle. Everything, Maguire, everything, do ye hear, Joey boy?' O'Neill's voice disturbed his thoughts as his mind groped for an escape route, a lifeline. He looked at O'Neill and then at MacEoin and felt sick.

'What is this? Is this some kind of bloody joke, Sean? Is it April first already? Because I'm missing something here! Some bloody English janissary, a bastard planter to boot, comes swanning in here accusing me of treason and what makes it worse, Sean, is you seem happy to take this Orangeman's word for it!'

MacEoin threw back his head and laughed a forceful, humourless, discordant laugh, before shaking his head. 'Orangeman, is it? Joe, how wrong you are. Gary here is a good republican boy. His people were out in '98 and paid the price at the end of an English rope. Sure Wolf Tone himself was a Prod and a descendant of one of that cursed Cromwell's men, Joe. You know that? What care I if a man is a good Catholic boy or a Protestant, as long as he's loyal to the republic?'

It was Maguire's turn to laugh, despite his sore head. 'You know, Sean,' he finally said, 'it's a wonder you can keep a straight face and say it when everything about the politics of this bloody country is riddled with sectarianism! We talk of an Ireland of Protestant, Catholic and dissenter but so far no one has done anything to make it happen. Christ, the Brits have always kept us down by dividing us and that's all this bloody planter is doing now – driving a wedge between us!'

'You know, Joe, I trust Gary. He's one of us, an Irishman through and through, and by Christ, aren't the O'Neills as Irish as they come, so why shouldn't I trust a man who has turned his back on his own community for the sake of the republic, for the sake of his people, for the sake of Ireland! Besides, Joe, Gary here isn't the one on trial; you are, so give me one reason, Joe. Just one reason why Gary here has got it wrong and all the things he's heard are wrong.'

'Maybe this Flynn character is lying, stirring up trouble. Maybe your man here—' He pointed at O'Neill '—is working with him to stir up trouble. Maybe he heard wrong, maybe I have no bloody idea why he's saying it but think, Sean, I'm not the one here who swore an oath of allegiance to their bloody king-emperor, am I?' he blustered.

'You know, Joe, I would love to believe you, after everything we've been through, I truly would, but what I'm wanting to know is, if it is true, what did the Brits do to make you turn traitor, to sell us all out?

Did they offer you money to prostitute yourself? Tell me it wasn't money, Joe, not thirty pieces of silver they gave you to sell your friends with a kiss? Please tell me it wasn't money? Well, this is Kilshrewley not Gethsemane and if you're playing Judas I'll make you pay! By Christ, I'll make you pay!' he shouted angrily, banging his hand hard down on the table.

Maguire shifted uncomfortably in his chair, desperately trying to think of a plan as MacEoin, suddenly calm, leant forward and rested his chin on his hands and stared intently, studying Maguire's face as if he was trying to probe the man's soul. As he opened his mouth to speak, his words were cut short by the crash of the door flying open and Hegarty tumbling into the room, barely missing Fitzgerald, who only just managed not to snatch the trigger of his half-cocked pistol, gasping for breath.

'Jaysus! What the hell are you about, Eunan?' Fitzgerald shouted, visibly shaken by his friend's arrival. 'Aren't you supposed to be in Granard?'

MacEoin looked up, obviously irritated. 'Yes, Eunan, what do you want? Can't you see that we're in the middle of something here?'

Hegarty took several more deep breaths and blurted out, 'It's the Brits! It's the bloody Brits!'

MacEoin looked suitably puzzled. 'What about the Brits?' he asked slowly before adding testily, 'For God's sake, will you bloody well calm down and tell me what the hell is going on?'

Hegarty gulped down a few more breaths and began again. 'It's the Brits. They're on their way to Ballinalee to burn it down....'

'Now hold on! Hold on!' MacEoin interrupted. 'What do you mean the Brits are going to burn down Ballinalee? What Brits?'

'Their army,' Hegarty managed to splutter. 'The whole bloody British army is on its way to burn it down, I tell you, hundreds of the bastards!'

MacEoin was visibly shaken. 'How many?' he asked.

'I don't know, hundreds,' Hegarty stammered.

'Oh shit!' O'Neill muttered. 'I've got to go!'

'Why the bloody hell didn't you tell me about this?' MacEoin shouted.

The Ulsterman shrugged lamely as MacEoin shot him a hard stare. 'I didn't know ...' The Ulsterman's voice trailed away into an embarrassed silence.

'Go!' MacEoin shouted and O'Neill quickly ducked out the door and was away. Maguire slid his right hand slowly into the skirt pocket of his jacket but MacEoin rounded on him. 'Don't you go doing anything stupid, Joe. I've not done with you.' He paused and held out his hand. 'The gun, please!'

Fitzgerald's gun still pointed at his head; it was disturbingly close and fleeting fantasies of drawing and shooting his way out quickly evaporated. He knew he'd be dead before the weapon cleared his pocket and sighed, 'All right.' He slid the pistol from his pocket and placed it in MacEoin's hand, who tossed it over to Fitzgerald, who caught it easily and stuffed it into his own coat pocket.

Maguire could see the naked hatred in MacEoin's eyes as he snapped at Fitzgerald, 'Get the boys together, as many as you can and quick. I think that we've got a bastard of a fight on our hands.' Fitzgerald dithered briefly then dashed out of the door, shouting as he went. A car engine spluttered into life and Maguire heard Fitzgerald shouting frantically, as doors banged and the sound of footsteps reverberated outside.

He noticed Hegarty standing like a jilted bridegroom by the door, looking at MacEoin like a bemused puppy. 'Will someone tell me what's going on?' Hegarty demanded.

MacEoin jabbed a finger in Maguire's direction. 'Keep an eye on him and don't let him out of your sight or you'll be answering to me! The bastard's under arrest, do you hear? Keep him here.' None the wiser, Hegarty nodded and cradled a rifle in the crook of his arms as MacEoin left, banging the door behind him. Maguire knew that Hegarty was the weak link, his best chance of escape. Suddenly they were alone.

All hell had broken loose outside and the popping of distant gunfire echoed across the fields, whilst nearby a Lewis gun rattled out its staccato tattoo. 'What the hell's going on, Joe?' Hegarty blurted. 'Why was Brendan pointing his gun at you? Why did Sean take your gun? Why does he want me to keep an eye on you? Why are you under arrest?'

Maguire shrugged and settled back in his chair. 'You tell me, Eunan. I haven't got a bloody clue what is going on anymore. Not a bloody clue.' The pain in his head was beginning to subside again and for the first time since he woke up, Maguire felt calm. He was beginning to see a way out but it would take time.

The hours passed slowly and the fire became a pile of glowing embers in the hearth. The morning was increasingly punctuated by the sound of gunshots and Hegarty kept glancing nervously into the lane and then back at Maguire, who was still slumped in his chair. Maguire's eyes were sore and the pain in his head had subsided to a gentle throbbing pain but he tried not to make it too obvious that he was watching Hegarty's every move, biding his time. He stood up suddenly and winced.

'What are you doing?' Hegarty asked nervously.

'I need a leak!' Maguire announced and began striding towards the back door.

'Stay where you are, Joe! Stand still or I'll shoot you, God help me I will,' Hegarty spluttered.

Maguire stopped by the table. 'Would you have me piss myself, Eunan?' he asked. 'I'm fair bursting to go!' Hegarty hesitated, racked with indecision until he saw Maguire shift from one foot to the other and cross his legs.

Hegarty nodded. 'All right, Joe, but don't do anything stupid or I'll shoot you myself.'

'I would expect nothing less,' Maguire replied with a reassuring, comradely smile as he stepped out into the yard, followed by Hegarty. The sunlight jabbed sharply at his eyes, resurrecting the pain in his head, and momentarily cocking his head to one side, he listened to the distant gunfire before strolling towards the outhouse. Think! Think! Think! he thought frantically as he opened the door of the outside toilet. A biplane circled above Ballinalee in the distance.

'Don't shut the door,' Hegarty said.

Maguire looked at him and shrugged. 'I'll be wanting a crap as well. You can watch if you like,' he said, as he slipped off his jacket and hung it on the back of the door before beginning to unhook his braces. The buzzing of the aeroplane was getting closer and he smiled at Hegarty. 'Well? Are you afraid that I'm going to flush myself down the bog or something?'

Hegarty grimaced at the prospect of watching Maguire straining away on the toilet. 'All right, shut the door if you must, Joe, but I'll be waiting for you out here.' Maguire shut the door and bolted it before looking around the small brick outhouse.

'Shit!' he muttered quietly, as he looked around at the little room. 'Am I in the shit or what?' There was no way out as he sat on the stained toilet and buried his head in his hands. 'Bugger!' Maguire hissed.

'What was that, Joe?' Hegarty asked.

'Nothing!' Maguire called, grunting to make it sound as if he was having difficulties evacuating his bowels. Somewhere a machine gun rattled out another staccato tattoo and as Maguire peered through a chink in the battered door, he saw Hegarty pacing impatiently up and down.

'Come on, Joe!' Hegarty shouted. 'Get a spurt on, will you!'

'All right! All right, I'm done,' Maguire called back, resigning himself to the futility of trying to escape, and took one more look through the chink in the door to see a muddy British army lorry skid to a halt in front of the cottage. Maguire dived onto the grubby toilet floor, curling up into a tight ball.

CHAPTER 31

Wednesday, 3 November 1920, outside Ballinalee,
County Longford

NEWLY PROMOTED LANCE Corporal Purton was not happy with being woken up at such a god-awful hour and dragged out of bed to bomb up so that, according to his platoon commander, Mr Crawford, they could 'stick it to the Shinners and give them a pasting!' He liked his scratcher and really didn't relish that he had survived Jerry's best efforts to blow his brains out only to risk copping it in some rural backwater of his own bloody country. To make matters worse, it was raining as usual; it was always bloody raining. If he'd wanted to spend so much time in close proximity to water he would have joined the navy! No wonder they called it the Emerald Isles.

The winter sun had been struggling its way across the hills when the convoy reached the outskirts of Ballinalee and Purton noticed that the line of dark brown vehicles seemed to stretch back forever. As far as he could tell, most of the battalion were here; this was the biggest operation he had taken part in since he'd come to this bloody country and he just hoped that it would be worth the rushed breakfast and the lack of sleep.

He could see policemen and Auxiliaries in their strange rakish bonnets and khaki uniforms mixed in with the soldiers. This was a combined operation, Mr Crawford said; part of the army's mission to provide what was grandly called 'Military Aid to the Civil Power'. Another bloody wild goose chase out in the cuds, more like!

Purton didn't really know what the hell was going on but Mr Crawford had told the platoon that because the IRA had recently murdered two policemen, one an ex-officer, and kidnapped another in as many days, they were off to arrest the ringleader of the murder gang, a blacksmith from Ballinalee called Sean MacEoin and, as Mr Crawford said, 'Put the bloody Shinners back in their box!'

Crack! Thump! Purton instinctively ducked as a shot zipped overhead and cursed long-sufferingly, 'Bugger! What now!'

Zip! Zip! 'Debus! Debus! Deploy left! Go left! Move! Move!' a voice shouted, punctuating the shrill blasts of officers' whistles. Old instincts kicked in and Purton felt deeply ingrained drills begin to kick in. The time for thinking had passed. He cursed as he lurched heavily into the drainage ditch at the side of the road in a clatter of brass and iron as his boots skidded in the slime.

The sump was cold and wet as he squatted down in it and that once-familiar bitter taste stung his mouth, drying his throat, as he scanned his front desperately for signs of the enemy. Zip! Another round sped close overhead. Purton's tin hat was giving him a headache. God knows who invented the bloody things, he thought, but the git obviously never had to wear one!

The drizzle stopped as quickly as it began and Purton felt pressure beginning to build in his groin. He desperately needed a pee and as liquid mud seeped over the top of his boots, caking his puttees, he suddenly felt like he was back at Wipers. The thought did not please him one bit. 'Did I get through the flaming war for this?'

'Shut up, Corporal Purton!' the company sergeant major snapped, as he trotted briskly past. He hated attracting the CSM's attention. More bullets zipped overhead but, despite his best efforts, he couldn't see where they were coming from. 'Where the bloody hell are they?' Purton snapped as his section straggled alongside him, staring wide-eyed, awaiting inspiration. The novelty of command was already beginning to wear off and Purton suddenly remembered exactly why he had avoided promotion like the plague during the last show.

Much to Purton's disgust and astonishment, he couldn't help noticing that Sergeant Eastbury looked relaxed, ever the consummate professional, an 'Old Contemptible' who had been all the way through the Great War from the very beginning and yet the chaos and carnage of battle never seemed to faze him. Men like Eastbury unnerved Purton.

'Get a brew on, Buscott! Looks like we're going to be here a while,' Eastbury snapped at one of Purton's soldiers, a fresh-faced lad who had missed the war and who was quite obviously bricking himself. Trembling, Buscott rummaged frantically through his haversack, snagging his cold fingers until they bled on the buckles and damp webbing, yanking out a brew kit wrapped in a brown cloth pouch, along with a small stove. The stink of petroleum spirit wafted towards

Purton as Buscott fumbled with a match, lighting the stove, before filling a mess tin with water from his canteen and balancing it precariously on top.

Brewing up was one of those timeless rituals as old as the British army, a rite enacted by generations of soldiers across the empire. It was good for morale; it steadied the nerves; whatever you do, when in doubt make tea! Without tea the British army would be finished, everyone knew that.

Zip! Zip! A few more stray rounds passed overhead and Sergeant Eastbury absentmindedly pulled a hard-tack 'dog' biscuit from his pocket. He gave it a cursory glance before grunting as he bit off a corner with a crunch. Crumbs, like fragments of baked shrapnel, cascaded down his tunic and he equally absentmindedly brushed them away with his left hand. 'You know, Corporal Purton, old chap, I think that we've just been given a great big, crusty, steaming shit sandwich and I am afraid that we are all about to take a great big bite!' he said with a toothy, humourless smile.

'Thanks for that, Sar'nt,' Purton said, giving Eastbury a sidelong glance. 'That's made me feel so much better!' Sergeant Eastbury looked at Purton for a moment before sniffing disdainfully and gazing off into the middle distance once more. Purton couldn't help but notice how hard and empty the sergeant's eyes were, glinting in the morning sunlight like beads of jet, his thousand-yard stare always searching. Eastbury gave Buscott a grin and a wink. 'Two sugars and a splash of condensed milk, lad. *Guram chai, jaldi! Jaldi!*' He turned back to Purton. 'It's just like the old days!' he declared, looking genuinely pleased before picking up his rifle and heading towards the platoon command post further up the road. Purton had an awful sinking feeling that Sergeant Eastbury was one of those worrying people who actually enjoyed the war and missed it now it was over.

Lieutenant Crawford gave Sergeant Eastbury a slight nod of recognition and, clutching a badly folded map, looked anxiously back at the houses a hundred yards or so to their front.

'What seems to be the problem, sir?' Eastbury asked Crawford as they squatted in the lee of one of the lorries.

'Bloody Shinners have felled a telegraph pole across the road. It looks like we will have to go in on foot.' Eastbury said nothing but eyed the young officer nervously.

'Yes, Sergeant? Is there a problem?' Crawford asked.

'Could be messy, sir. Street fighting can be hard work.'

Lieutenant Crawford smiled at his sergeant and stuffed the map back into his leather map case; he knew that men like Eastbury were the glue that held his platoon together, the backbone of the entire army. 'Well, I don't suppose the lads are afraid of a bit of hard work, eh?'

'Suppose not, sir.' Eastbury sniffed. 'But this'll be the first time for most of the lads, sir. First proper fight, I mean. It might be a bit of a shock for them. Close quarter stuff is always messy.' Crawford shifted his weight slightly, acutely aware that his sergeant's comment was probably aimed as much at him as most of his soldiers. Zip! Zip! More stray rounds passed overhead and Crawford did his best to act as if nothing was happening.

Eastbury noticed a trace of concern on the lieutenant's face and gave him a reassuring smile. 'Don't worry, sir. The lads will be fine once they get going. It's the waiting that does for you, not the doing. You could see it when we were hanging around on the fire step, time to think, but once you've hopped the bags, you're too scared, too busy or just too knackered to think.'

Crawford watched his sergeant carefully. Major Calvert, his company commander, had said something similar. 'Keep 'em busy, keep 'em moving!'

'Well, carry on, Sergeant. Get the lads standing by. We go on my command,' Crawford said softly.

Eastbury nodded and turned to face the line of helmeted Tommies huddled in the ditch. He slid his bayonet from its scabbard with a soft shush and held it high above his head.

'SEVEN PLATOON, LISTEN IN!' he bellowed in a clear parade-ground voice that rolled down the line like a summer storm. 'SEVEN PLATOON! SEVEN PLATOON WILL FIX BAYONETS! FIX ... BAYONETS!' Suddenly, the ditch was alive with the sound of bayonets rasping from scabbards and clicking menacingly into place. Purton fixed his own bayonet. He never liked it when they fixed bayonets in earnest; it always meant that the enemy were going to be getting far too close for comfort!

Eastbury felt a deep well of satisfaction as he looked up and down the line; there was something about this moment, the moment before the chaos that always gave him a buzz, a warm, tingling feeling. To his right and left, the rest of the company were doing likewise and soon a line of bayonets was glittering in the sun like a silver cornfield swaying in the wind. When he was satisfied, he turned back to the lieutenant. 'On your command, sir.'

Crawford licked his lips. His mouth was gritty and his stomach churned as he slipped his revolver from its polished holster. 'Thank you, Sar'nt. The OC wants Seven Platoon to clear the area to the left of the road and secure that cottage there—' He pointed at a croft next to the road '—and then clear the roadblock so that the rest of the company can resume the advance.'

Eastbury nodded. 'Piece of piss, sir.'

The buzzing of an aero engine disturbed Purton's private misery and he looked up at a Bristol Fighter that was now circling overhead. Close air support had been invaluable during the final battles of the war and Purton took some comfort from the aeroplane overhead. 'Shame we've got no artillery support,' he said to Buscott, who laughed nervously.

'We can do without the bloody drop shorts!' Buscott muttered. Purton glanced back at the command post. His platoon commander and Sergeant Eastbury were engrossed in conversation. Lieutenant Crawford pointed up the road and he followed the direction he was pointing in, towards a cluster of cottages squatting by the road.

Another bullet passed close overhead and as Purton sunk deeper into the ditch, he turned to Buscott. 'You'd best put that away, lad. I think it'll be a while before we get a brew.' Buscott rolled his eyes and, muttering long-sufferingly, quietly but expertly stuffed his brew kit back into his haversack before putting out the stove and emptying his mess tin of its lukewarm contents.

Purton watched Major Calvert kneel next to Lieutenant Crawford. They were too far away for him to hear what was said but he had a sinking feeling when he saw Sergeant Eastbury nod and bent low double towards where he was crouching. 'Corporal Purton, it's your lucky day, Major Calvert has got a little job for you!' he announced smugly and pointed at the waiting lorry.

It only took a few minutes to get to Kilshrewley and Purton rather hoped that setting up the company's command post in some old cottage would be a bit of skive but that misapprehension was shattered along with the lorry's windscreen when the driver pulled up next to the nearest cottage. Purton was showered with glass and as he tumbled from the cab, with warm blood running down his cheek, he saw the lone rifleman standing next to a shabby outhouse desperately re-cocking his rifle.

Squatting in the lee of the lorry's cab, Purton touched his face and then looked at his fingertips. They were bright with blood. 'Bugger,' Purton cursed again and after two deep breaths shouted, 'Section!

Right side debus! Debus! MOVE! GO! GO! GO!' Behind him his lads tumbled out of the lorry and huddled nearby as he cocked his rifle and poked his head around the side of the front wheel. He saw the rifleman running towards the scrub behind the outhouse and threw his rifle up into a firing position.

'Not so fast, Paddy!' he shouted and snapped off a shot at the fleeing gunman. He cursed as the bullet ripped into the branches above Hegarty's head. 'Bugger!' Purton spat. 'After him! MOVE! MOVE!' he shouted as he re-cocked his rifle and stood to get a better bead on the fleeing gunman.

Hegarty's back filled his sight picture as he steadied his breath and took up the pressure on the trigger. His rifle barked and he saw his target drop in a gout of dark blood, like a broken rag doll as his legs collapsed beneath him, his momentum carrying him forward a few paces before the ground leapt up to punch him in the face. He tried to crawl towards the bushes but his body refused to respond and he writhed on the ground.

Purton cautiously crept forward until he could see the fallen IRA man lying in the grass, then he raised his rifle. He fired again, and the body twitched under the impact. He re-cocked his rifle and moved closer, his heart pounding, blood thundering in his ears, his mouth dry. A familiar voice was screaming at him from deep within his skull as adrenalin flooded his body. He knew men like Eastbury who loved this feeling but he hated it.

He kept one eye on the distant fields as he stood over Hegarty's body lying on the crushed grass and cautiously shoved it with his foot. It rocked slightly and he thought he saw it move and fired a third shot into the man's head, shattering his skull, speckling the grass with fragments of skull, hair and brain. Purton squatted down and tossed Hegarty's discarded rifle to one side, out of the man's reach – just in case – before seizing hold of his jacket, rolling the body over. Blood welled from two fist-sized holes torn in the man's chest and splashed onto the wet dark stain beneath him.

He wrinkled his nose. He had never got used to the sight of dead people, even at Wipers, and his headache was much worse now as he felt his hands trembling. He stood up shakily. 'Steady, Jake, steady,' he said to himself. He struggled to steady his breathing, sucking in air through his nose as he watched Privates Buscott and Fenton scanning the horizon, their bayonets glinting in the sunlight. Purton pointed, open handed, at the cottage.

'Buscott! Fenton! On me! We need to clear that cottage,' he ordered. He looked at the body. 'Williams, get that thing on the wagon,' he called to a young private, no more than eighteen years old, who was standing by the lorry looking suitably worried. The soldier nodded.

'Right-oh, Corp!' the boy called as he slung his rifle and doubled towards Purton, who with Buscott and Fenton strode briskly towards the cottage in an open arrowhead formation, weapons at the ready. It was then that Purton heard something move in the outhouse and, raising his right hand, he signalled the others to stop. All three froze. Purton levelled his rifle at the outhouse door and stepped forward on the balls of his feet, mouth dry.

'All right, Paddy, come out with your hands up! Do anything stupid and you're dead!'

Maguire peered through a crack in the door at the wiry British soldier, pointing his rifle straight at the door. At that distance a .303 round would punch through the door easily and the brick behind most likely. 'For God's sake, don't shoot! Don't shoot!' Maguire shouted as he gingerly drew back the bolt and opened the door. 'I'm coming out with my hands up! I'm on your side!' he shouted and stepped out into the light with his hands held high above his head.

Purton's bayonet hovered inches from his nose and he was acutely aware of the gaping maw of the muzzle waving around in front of him. 'I'm on your side!' Maguire said again. 'I'm a British intelligence agent and unless you want to find yourself up to your neck in shit, I suggest you take me to whoever is in charge here!'

Purton looked at him sceptically for a moment, weighing up what he'd just heard and shrugged. 'Of course you are, Paddy! Of course you are. Now come with me!' he snapped, as he grabbed Maguire's lapel and dragged him towards the waiting lorry. 'Just shut up and move or I'll shoot you myself!' he added menacingly.

CHAPTER 32

M Company HQ, Auxiliary Division RIC, Longford

T HE WATER WAS refreshingly cold as Flynn held his face beneath its
surface, feeling his nerves tingle. It invaded his mouth, his nose,
his ears, and a stream of bubbles snorted from his nostrils as he
splashed water across his neck. Shaking his head like a wet dog, he
picked up a towel and blotted his unshaven face dry as he looked at
himself in the mirror, his wavy hair sticking up in unruly tufts.

His mouth tasted foul, as if something had crapped in it, and he
struggled to remember the exact details of the night before when the
Auxiliary patrol had deposited him back at HQ. However, the half-
empty glass of brandy and the discarded bottle lying empty on the worn
floorboards helped him guess. He toyed with the idea of going back to
bed but the uninviting tangle of rough grey blankets helped him easily
dismiss the thought. The air was fetid, reeking of stale booze, and his
shirt was stiff with dry sweat. He opened the window with a grunt and
grimaced slightly as he caught the odour of his armpits. He wrinkled
his nose in disgust and peeled off his soiled shirt, tossing it in a ball
onto the bed.

'What the hell has happened to you, Kevin, my boy?' he muttered as
he picked up the empty bottle and tossed it, clattering, into the bin by
the door. He looked at the glass on the dresser; it had been the only way
that he had been able to get to sleep, the only way to blot out the
dreams, his only path to oblivion, and it worried him that drink was
becoming an old friend ever since the Somme. He picked up his towel
and wash bag and headed for the ablutions.

Shaved and showered, he felt baptised, resurrected, revived and
slightly less nauseous as he buttoned up a fresh shirt and gazed at the
courtyard below. It was a bright November day, crisp and fresh, and the
cold air caressed his face as he whistled tunelessly to himself. The
sunlight pricked at the dull ache behind his eyes but it was worth it to

get some fresh air. He was suddenly gripped with an overpowering craving for caffeine and bacon sandwiches.

It was then it struck him. Where was everybody? The motor pool was empty and, except for the obviously bored Auxiliary guarding the main gate, lounging against the sandbags as he smoked, not a soul stirred. The guardroom door swung open and a second Auxiliary emerged clutching two mugs of what Flynn assumed was tea, a cigarette hanging from his lips.

Flynn smiled; he couldn't work out whether the Auxiliaries deliberately flouted the basic mores of police or even military etiquette by smoking and drinking in public in uniform, although he seriously doubted whether they even cared. The Auxiliaries were, for the most part, the detritus of the war, staving off unemployment in a society that neither wanted them nor knew what to do with them – a law unto themselves.

One of the Auxiliaries laughed; a harsh bray that disturbed Flynn's musings. The sentry drained the last dregs from his mug and flicked it two or three times to make sure it was empty before handing it to the other man, who headed back towards the guardroom, shaking his head and laughing quietly. Then, out of the corner of his eye, he saw a battered, mud-bespattered army lorry drawing up to the main gate. Its canvas awning gaped in places as if something had punched through it and he saw that the windscreen had a fist-sized hole in it, radiating a web of lines across its shattered surface. As it got closer, it became obvious to Flynn that it had been shot out.

The sentry frantically took one last drag on his cigarette before grinding it out with his boot and picking up his .303. He strolled over to the right-hand side of the cab to speak to the driver whilst, behind him, the other Auxiliary stepped out onto the guardroom veranda cradling a pump-action shotgun – just in case. A helmeted Tommy leant down from the cab but Flynn was too far away to make out what they were saying.

The sentry nodded and hefted up the barrier whilst the man with the shotgun slipped quietly back into the guardroom and the warmth of the stove that was belching contented puffs of dark smoke into the morning air. The lorry pulled into the courtyard and stopped directly below Flynn's window. He finished buttoning up his tunic as he watched a helmeted soldier leap out of the passenger side of the cab and walk to the back of the lorry.

The soldier's face was obscured by his helmet but from his vantage point Flynn could see the man was a lance corporal and, by his shouting, obviously in charge of the men who were disgorging, bayonets fixed, from the back of the lorry. Two of the squaddies reached into the back of the lorry and heaved out a handcuffed civilian, who landed heavily and fell to his knees. 'Up you get, Paddy!' one of the soldiers announced as he lifted the man back to his feet.

'Don't go giving me any grief, Mick,' the lance corporal added wearily. Then Flynn recognized the lance corporal: it was the squaddie he'd chatted to on the army truck the day his friend Jim O'Leary had been wounded over at old Tom Muldoon's farm. The stripes were still bright and clean on the soldier's worn khaki sleeves and Flynn guessed that the lance-jack was only newly minted. The prisoner looked up at the sky and as he surveyed his surroundings caught Flynn's eye and gave him a broad, toothy grin. It was Maguire.

'What the ...' Flynn muttered.

'Good morning to you, Sergeant Flynn!' Maguire called out with a grin and a cheery wave of his cuffed hands.

'Corporal!' Flynn shouted and Purton looked up, a bemused expression plastered across his tired, harassed, thin face. 'Stay where you are!' he ordered, before ducking back in the window, grabbing his cap and making a dash for the stair.

'What now?' Purton muttered, rolling his eyes as Flynn burst dramatically out of the mess front door and strode towards him.

'What is going on here, Corporal?' Flynn demanded sternly, in his best brusque senior NCO tone. Flynn knew that it was the best way to handle soldiers: take charge, don't give them time to think and baffle them with bullshit! Purton and the others instinctively braced up in response to the barked command and as the badly bruised policeman approached he noticed the medal ribbons and realized that he had met the man before.

Like him, Purton also noticed the policeman had been promoted recently and said, 'Good morning, Sar'nt, I thought you were based over in Drumlish?'

Flynn looked him up and down as impassively as possible. 'Never mind where I'm supposed to be, Corporal. Would you mind telling me what on earth is going on here? This man ...' He pointed at Maguire. 'Why is he in handcuffs? Why is he a prisoner?'

Purton gave Flynn a puzzled look, like he'd been asked an obviously ridiculous no-brainer of a question. The chief clerk had once told him that everything that they say about the Irish was true and he almost made a comment about how thick Irish policemen were but the look in the sergeant's eyes made him stop and think better of it. 'Cos he's under arrest, Sar'nt,' Purton eventually said, with a shrug and a sigh. He reminded Maquire of someone patiently trying to explain something to a dim-witted small child. It was Flynn's turn to roll his eyes.

'I can see that, Corporal, but why is he under arrest?'

He was beginning to see why, despite obviously surviving the war it had taken Purton so long to make lance corporal, when he'd made sergeant in a matter of months. Maguire shrugged and gave Flynn a sympathetic look. Flynn shot Purton an impatient stare.

'Well, Sergeant,' Purton began, 'there is a bit of a big show going on over at some place called Bal … er … Ballya … er …'

'Ballinalee, Corporal,' one of the Tommies chipped in.

'Aye, that's it, Ballinalee. Most of the battalion are involved anyway and our company was sent to cordon off one of the roads into the place when an almighty scrap broke out, sodding bullets everywhere. By the sound of it we must have trapped half the bloody Shinners in the county in the place. Anyroad, it was like being back at bloody Wipers! I'm glad to be away from it, to be honest.'

The other Tommies nodded in enthusiastic agreement but then Purton noticed the dangerous glint in Flynn's grey eyes and quickly resumed telling his story. 'The OC, Major Calvert, proper gent is Major Calvert, well, he sent us to clear some houses outside the town to use as a command post and clearing station for any casualties. That's where we found this little bastard …' He pointed at Maguire. 'His mate took a pot shot at me and then scarpered. I dropped the little bugger with a few rounds and then we found him hiding in the shithouse. Your mucker tried to leave you in the lurch, didn't he, Paddy?'

'In the shit, more like,' one of the soldiers quipped and the others laughed. Maguire rolled his eyes. 'Didn't get far, though? Did he?'

'And?' Flynn asked. There was a brittle edge to the policeman's voice.

'Major Calvert kept him for questioning overnight—' Flynn noticed Maguire's black eye '—and decided to send him back here and lock him up until the lads from intelligence can have a wee chat with him, didn't he, Paddy? No offence, Sar'nt,' he added hastily, as he nudged Maguire in the ribs with his rifle butt. 'Mind you, he's a necky bastard this one, Sar'nt. Real cheeky. Keeps saying he's a British agent, that the Shinners were holding him prisoner. As if! He's got IRA written all the way through him like a stick of bloody Blackpool rock!' Purton said, smiling proudly at his own astuteness.

'That, Corporal, is because he is one of our bloody agents!' Flynn barked. 'This man saved my life!'

Purton's face froze as the penny dropped.

'Oh!' he said slowly.

Maguire held up his hands in front of himself and smiled meekly. 'Now, Corporal, me auld fella, would you mind unlocking these?' he said with a grin, in his thickest culchie accent, as Purton rummaged in his pockets, producing a small bunch of keys. After fumbling with the handcuffs, they fell to the floor with a quiet clink. Maguire massaged his sore, reddened wrists, rubbing them vigorously as Purton and his men stood like guilty schoolboys, shifting their weight awkwardly as they lapsed self-consciously into silence. Maguire held out his hand to Flynn and announced with an infectious grin, 'We meet again, Sergeant. Joe Maguire, currently in the employ of His Majesty, late commandant of the Irish Republican Army.'

'Sergeant Kevin Flynn, Royal Irish Constabulary. I didn't expect to see you again in a hurry,' Flynn replied, shaking his hand firmly.

Maguire looked around. 'A bit bloody quiet round here, isn't it?' he sniffed before turning to Purton and saying, 'Be a good fella, Corporal, and ask that chap over there—' He waved vaguely at the sentry '—and find out where everybody's gone.'

Purton looked at Flynn. 'Just do it, Corporal!' he snapped and the harassed NCO doubled over to the gate.

'They're all over at Ballinalee,' Purton shouted from the gate.

'Bugger!' Maguire muttered.

'What's the problem?' Flynn asked Maguire, who bit his lower lip thoughtfully.

'Is there a telephone nearby?' Maguire finally asked.

Flynn nodded. 'There's one in the guardroom I think or over in the orderly office. Why?'

'I need to make a couple of calls,' was all Maguire said before running off towards the guardroom, where he exchanged a few words with the sentry then disappeared inside. He emerged five minutes later and ran back to Flynn. 'I've just had a word with my boss. When this is all over you and me are going on a trip to Dublin, but first—' Maguire said.

'When what is all over?' Flynn interrupted.

'But first you, me and this lot,' he persisted, gesturing at Purton and his men, 'need to get over to the barracks in Drumlish.'

Flynn was still puzzled and asked, 'Why do we need to go to Drumlish?'

'Because I've just tried calling Sergeant Willson and the telephone line is dead and, if I'm right, the reason why I was hiding in a bloody shithouse will be there and unless we do something about the bastard, people are going to die! The gobshite knew that I'd helped you escape.'

'But that's impossible. I haven't even had a chance to write a report yet,' Flynn said.

'Really, is that so? Well, you bloody well told this bastard!' Maguire snapped.

'Look, I've only talked about what happened since I escaped and they are both coppers. You can't be seriously suggesting that Sergeant Willson is an IRA spy?'

Maguire shook his head. 'No, I'm not suggesting that Willson's an IRA spy at all but that two-faced bastard O'Neill is!'

'Bollocks he is! O'Neill was in the Irish Guards, he's an Ulster Prod through and through ...' But then some of O'Neill's comments to Mullan began to make sense. 'You're bloody serious, aren't you?' Flynn said, as he stared at Maguire in horror. 'Please tell me you're joking,' he blurted in disbelief.

'Do I look like I'm bloody laughing? Do I look like a flaming comedian?' Maguire snapped. 'There are plenty of ex-soldiers in the IRA; some are even Protestants like O'Neill.' Flynn looked at the glint in his eyes and knew that he was serious, deathly serious.

'Shit!' Flynn hissed, as he pulled himself into the lorry. 'Let's go.'

When they finally reached Drumlish and burst into the barracks, Willson nearly spilt his tea in surprise. 'What the ... I wasn't expecting to see you back so soon!' Willson declared.

'I didn't expect to be here either,' Flynn replied. 'Is Gary here?'

Willson shook his head. 'It's funny you should ask but I haven't seen him since before you left yesterday ...' He looked at the gun in Flynn's hand and the soldiers behind him. 'Is there a problem? I'm beginning to worry about him.'

'I wouldn't bother if I was you. He's well enough for now at least,' Maguire interjected.

Willson looked Maguire up and down with an air of professional disdain.

'Who's he?' Willson sniffed. He didn't like the look of the scruffy man in the grubby civilian clothes. Some sort of corner-boy by the looks of him.

'This is Mr Joseph Maguire. He's the man I told you about, the one who saved my skin the other day. He's one of our agents.' He leant towards Willson. 'He works for Special Branch, all very hush-hush, I'm sure,' Flynn added, tapping the side of his nose with his index finger.

Willson's eyes widened slightly. 'Is he now? And why is he interested in our Gary then or aren't I allowed to ask?'

So Flynn told him.

CHAPTER 33

Drumlish, County Longford

IT WAS A crisp, brittle morning and the damp seeped into every fibre of O'Neill's being as he wheezed his way down off the hills. You've gone soft, Gary, me boy – too much bloody tea and paperwork, he thought, lamenting his lack of fitness since leaving the Guards. His feet were killing him and from the pains shooting up his legs he knew that once he peeled off his sodden socks his feet would be a mess of torn blisters.

'If only I had a car, I'd've been back ages ago,' he muttered but he knew that if he had, he would almost certainly have been stopped at an army checkpoint. In the circumstances it was safer, albeit infinitely slower, to walk. Unfortunately, he had only got a few hundred yards or so from the croft when he was forced to take cover in a slimy waterlogged ditch to avoid the British and, huddled there, it was easy for him to imagine that he was back in the trenches, whilst the ripple of gunfire from the direction of Ballinalee only added to the illusion.

He decided that his best hope was to wait until sunset before he struck out for Drumlish and hunkered down to kill the remaining hours before dark closed in. More gunshots echoed across the fields from where he'd come from, whilst more lorries passed in both directions, along the track. He didn't have a clue what was going on but from the sheer volume of gunfire all around him he concluded that the British had launched a major operation and that MacEoin had one hell of a fight on his hands.

By the time it was dark and he felt that it was safe to get going he was soaked through, cramped and cold and he could barely feel his fingertips. He rubbed his hands vigorously to get the blood flowing. 'You really are too old for this shit,' he muttered as he peered fruitlessly at his wristwatch. It wasn't luminous and the thick clouds made it impossible for him to see a thing. When he looked up there were neither moon nor stars to be seen, only the darkness, and it didn't really take him long to get hopelessly lost as he stumbled amongst the gorse and moon-grass. It didn't help that the gunfire had faded away with the sunlight and although sporadic shots did slice through the silence he couldn't tell which direction they came from. It was like trying to get back across no man's land after a raid.

Fear and darkness had a terrible knack for disorientating and he wandered in circles for what felt like a couple of hours before he got his bearings. The sun was creeping over the eastern horizon before he recognized Drumlish nestling down in the glen. 'Christ knows what I'll tell Willson,' he muttered, trying to think how he could excuse his overnight absence when he'd only gone out to take a turn around the village. He knew he was lucky to have escaped Kilshrewley at all; the place was crawling with soldiers and, from the noise of gunfire, it sounded like the entire British army had swept through the area.

The sun was well up in the morning sky by the time he reached Cairn Hill and beyond it the familiar shape of St Mary's Church and Drumlish's main crossroads; he could make out the barracks and the Longford road in the distance. As he caught his breath he saw the black shape of an army truck approaching the village. He expected to see it pass below him on the way to Ballinalee but it did not. He shrugged and began his descent into the village, no longer caring whether the soldiers saw him or not. He would feed Willson some cock and bull story about being kidnapped and escaping.

As O'Neill got closer to St Mary's Roman Catholic Church, he could see the parish priest, Father John Keville, and the sexton, engrossed in conversation as they stood by the churchyard's lichgate. The sexton nudged Father Keville and pointed at O'Neill as he limped past in the direction of the barracks. Both men stopped talking and stared. 'Good morning, Constable O'Neill,' Father Keville called out but O'Neill barely spared him a glance as he grunted and carried on his way.

'Bloody ignorant Protestant bastard,' the sexton muttered quietly as he leant on his shovel.

'Now, now, my son,' Keville reproved and the two men resumed their conversation, strolling off in the direction of the parochial house.

The village was quiet and O'Neill assumed that the fighting over in Ballinalee had kept most people safely indoors, especially as it was now into its second day. No doubt wild rumours were flying across the county, terrifying people into believing that between them, the Brits and the IRA were turning their quiet county into bandit country like Cork and the rest of the wild south-west.

As O'Neill drew level with the post office, its front door swung open and the postmaster, Peter O'Brien, stepped out and took a few deep breaths of morning air, his thumbs hooked into his waistcoat pockets. He watched O'Neill approach, fully aware that the policeman knew his secret – he was one of MacEoin's men too. Few people, especially the British, had a clue how completely infiltrated the Irish postal service was by republican sympathizers. Consequently, nothing passed through the mails to or from Drumlish RIC barracks or any other barracks, for that matter, without the IRA knowing about it, thanks to O'Brien and men like him all over the country.

O'Brien beckoned the bedraggled O'Neill over with a few rapid sweeps of his arm and, after a furtive look up and down the street, the Ulsterman rapidly joined him in the doorway. 'Did you get to see Sean?' O'Brien asked, as he polished his glasses on a piece of rag. O'Neill nodded, without taking his eyes off the barracks down the street.

'Aye, I did that,' he replied.

An army truck with a shattered windscreen was parked outside the barracks and a lone soldier stood in front of the cab stamping his feet to fend off the cold. The postmaster pushed his glasses back up his nose. 'Jesus, Gary, you look like you slept in a flaming hedge. What the hell is going on yonder? There have been soldiers passing through all the time.'

O'Neill kept his eyes on the lorry. 'Ballinalee is crawling with the enemy, Auxies, soldiers, the flaming lot. It's overrun with them. Last time I saw Sean he was trying to get as many of the boys together as he could. Sure, there's one hell of an almighty scrap broken out. Do you know what they are up to?' he asked, nodding towards the truck.

'I know as much as you do, Gary. Probably passing through, if what you say is right,' O'Brien replied. 'Marching to the sound of the guns, eh?' O'Neill couldn't make up his mind whether to carry on down to the barracks or to stay put and watch what was going on. Something told him to stay put, so he did. Behind him, O'Brien loitered, looking over O'Neill's shoulder at the truck.

'Did Sean send any orders?' O'Brien asked.

'I think that he's got his hands full at the moment, don't you? It was all I could do to get away as it was,' O'Neill said. O'Brien had been genuinely shocked and surprised when he had discovered that O'Neill was one of MacEoin's contacts but since then he had regularly passed information between the policeman and the blacksmith. He also knew that he would be expected to help O'Neill disappear if there was an emergency but O'Brien was wary of the Ulsterman, unsure whether to trust him or not. After all, he had betrayed his own kind but then who would suspect a Belfast Protestant of being a Fenian!

A flurry of activity in the barracks caused O'Neill to duck back into the doorway, dragging O'Brien with him. As he watched, a group of about half a dozen Tommies trooped out of the front door and mounted the waiting lorry. He stared in morbid fascination as its engine spluttered into life, briefly drowning out the pounding of the blood in his ears. Hopefully, they would soon be on their way. Three more figures emerged from the barracks and walked towards the parked vehicle. O'Neill could see that one was Sergeant Willson but it took a second or two for it to sink in that the others were Flynn and Maguire.

'Damn!' he hissed.

'Gary! Is that you?' he heard from behind him and as O'Neill swung around he saw two policemen on bicycles pedalling slowly down the street, rifles strapped across their backs, returning from an early-morning patrol. The words rolled down the quiet, empty street like a tsunami, catching the attention of the trio, Willson, Flynn and Maguire, who stood like three startled meerkats, staring towards the source of the shouting. Suddenly, everything stopped; time seemed to stand still until Willson shattered the silence.

'Look! It's O'Neill!' the sergeant cried and pointed up the street towards the post office.

'Jesus Christ!' O'Neill blurted. 'Peter, get me out of here!'

The Ulsterman snatched out his revolver and hastily snapped off a couple of unaimed shots in Willson's direction, scattering the soldiers and policemen as they dived for cover. 'Shit!' O'Brien cried. He was an intelligence agent, not a soldier, and he was unused to gunfire. The close proximity of the shots stabbed at his eardrums, causing him to flinch, but he only hesitated for a split second before he grabbed O'Neil's sleeve. 'Come with me, quick!' He dragged O'Neill by the arm into the post office, shouting, 'For God's sake, Constable O'Neill, what on earth are you doing!' loudly enough for half the village to hear. Still shouting, 'Help! He's got a gun!', he pulled O'Neill into the kitchen behind the post office and shoved open a cupboard. 'In there,' he ordered.

'Oh, great! You want me to hide under the sink.'

'Shut up and get in!' O'Brien hissed as he shoved O'Neill into the small space. Thud! O'Neill banged his head on the way in and cursed as the back of the cupboard gave way. Before he knew it, he had plunged into a cramped, dark hidey-hole. The hatch squeaked shut as he landed with a soft thud on a pile of hessian sacking and wriggled into a roughly upright position.

His nostrils were full of the smell of burnt cordite, gun oil and slightly rotted potatoes. His heart was in his mouth as he crouched in the darkness, waiting, and he heard the kitchen door bang open and the sound of several pairs of boots stamping around. There was shouting and an English voice shouted, 'Where did he go?' He heard O'Brien say, 'That way! Be careful, he's got a gun, I think he must be out of his mind!', and then the sound of the hobnailed boots receded until he was left all alone in the silence, the silence and darkness. Time lost all meaning in the darkness, with only tinnitus and the pounding of blood in his ears for company. He was afraid, like a cornered fox waiting to be torn apart by the hounds, but worse, much worse than that he felt claustrophobic in the dark, the stifling dark, as he fought the urge to burst out of the cupboard and gulp in the fresh air.

He had been buried by a shell at Loos and as he lay entombed in the wet clay he had felt the same terror welling up in him that he felt now. He was buried alive, entombed, forgotten, left to drown in the earth. He could even feel the sticky clay filling into his nose and mouth, drowning him, sucking him slowly, inexorably down to hell. He was soaked in sweat. He felt like screaming but even now he was paralyzed with fear.

Flynn stood outside the post office as Purton and his men emerged from the front door. 'Well, any sign?' Flynn asked.

The corporal looked dejected. 'He's gone. The postmaster said he saw him legging it off into the fields. With just the eight of us, we don't have a hope in hell of catching him. It's like he vanished into thin air!'

A look of bitter disappointment flashed briefly across Flynn's face. 'Thanks, Corporal Purton, you and your boys did your best. It can't be helped that he's given us the slip. Me and Mr Maguire here need to get back to Longford pretty bloody pronto, so I'd appreciate it if you could give us a lift back to HQ. After that you'd better get back to your unit. I should imagine that your OC will be wondering what has become of you.'

Purton smiled. 'Don't worry, we'll get you back to Longford, Sar'nt, and if it keeps me and my boys out of the fight for a bit longer, then so much the better.' He grinned.

Flynn turned to Willson. 'O'Neill is a slippery little bastard and dangerous to boot. You keep an eye out for him and if you see him be bloody careful, do you hear? I'm not so sure about O'Brien either, come to think of it. It seems strange that he could get out the back of the post office and get away scot free. Disappeared into thin air? I wonder. I think you need to keep an eye on him as well.'

'But O'Brien seems a decent enough sort,' Willson replied.

'So did O'Neill and look at him,' Flynn retorted.

'Good point!' Willson said, before adding, 'I'll be keeping an eye out for both of them. Don't you worry about me.'

As Flynn climbed onto the waiting lorry, he could see people beginning to poke their heads out of doorways to see what the commotion was. He banged on the back of the driver's cab as Maguire flopped down beside him and offered him a cigarette. 'All right, Corporal, let's go,' Flynn shouted and the lorry lurched off in a flurry of crunching of gears, towards Longford.

Suddenly, O'Neill's world was flooded with light that lanced at his eyes like needles and his hand instinctively groped for the pistol at his waist as a head thrust its way through the hatchway. It took a few seconds for him to realize it was O'Brien.

'They've gone!' the postmaster announced and O'Neill relaxed slightly before barging his way past, out of the confines of his hiding place. Predictably, he banged his head on the way out, collapsing onto the kitchen floor in a rumpled heap. He rubbed his sore head and gulped for air. The knot of fear inside him was beginning to unravel and it took several minutes before he felt composed enough to speak. 'Now get me out of here!' he eventually said.

CHAPTER 34

Gaigue, County Longford

'I REALLY CAN'T BELIEVE that the British don't know that we do this,' O'Brien said, shaking his head while steaming open yet another brown OHMS envelope. 'Bugger!' he cursed as the steam scolded his fingertips. It was an unglamorous job but a vital one. He hated steaming open envelopes but he knew that MacEoin counted on him to intercept anything that the RIC, civil service or British army were dumb enough to put into the local postal system.

The faintest hint of a smile cut across McNamara's face and he chuckled to himself quietly, like some sort of malignant leprechaun. O'Neill paused and looked up from what he was reading. 'And what are you chuckling about?' O'Neill rasped. God knows, he didn't feel like smiling, he could hardly believe that it was only just over a week since Kelleher had been shot and his entire world had imploded as a result. He was a wanted man on the run; worse still MacEoin had him riffling through the post until things quietened down.

'This!' McNamara said triumphantly, tossing a letter across the table at O'Neill. The Ulsterman put down the piece of paper he was holding and looked down at the unfolded piece of notepaper covered in neat, round, girlish handwritten script.

'It's a letter ... and?' he said, none the wiser, and McNamara rolled his eyes irritably; he was finding it hard to contain his anger and impatience.

'It's from that Moore bitch, the whore who's been shagging your mucker Flynn.'

O'Neill shrugged. 'And?'

'This could be what we need to flush the bastard out and pay him back for everything he's done to both of us, him and that traitor Maguire. Bastards killed my brother Jerry and kiboshed your cover between them!' Everything that McNamara said was true but O'Neill still looked blank. 'Read it then!' McNamara said tersely, stabbing the letter with his index finger impatiently.

O'Neill picked up the letter and ran his eye over it. 'So? I still don't get it ...' O'Neill said, looking in askance at McNamara. 'It just says how much she misses Flynn and that she still loves him, the usual wet love-letter bollocks! Besides being stupid enough to persist with her stupid flirtations, what earthly use is this to us?'

'Jaysus, if everyone in Ulster is as thick as you, then how the bloody hell did you planters get us off our land?' McNamara said bitterly and O'Neill felt his cheeks momentarily flush with anger. He'd turned his back on his own community to fight for the republic and was getting sick of sectarian jibes, the bane of Irish unity.

'Probably because the culchie croppy eejits up nort' were t'icker!' he snapped, in a thick stage-Irish accent. For a moment O'Brien was afraid that the two men would come to blows but McNamara seemed content to let O'Neill's barbed quip pass, for the time being anyway.

'I'll tell you what earthly use it is to us, Gary, my boy. It'll flush Flynn out from whichever stone he's hiding under, that's why,' McNamara said triumphantly, his eyes flushed with excitement and a look that made O'Neill think that he was expecting a round of applause and a fanfare as well.

'But she still thinks he's in Drumlish. Look, she's even addressed it to him at the barracks,' O'Neill replied, still obviously puzzled by McNamara's drift.

McNamara sighed heavily: 'We don't need to know where Flynn is, do we? All we need to do is make sure that he gets this letter and then he'll be off to Kingstown to see his bit of skirt, then we've got him. All we have to do is get down there and wait for the shite to show up, then we cap him and his shagabout! He may even let us know where Maguire has gone before we send him on his way.'

O'Neill felt uncomfortable looking at the manic gleam in McNamara's eyes. 'Christ, do you pick your moments, Mick! Haven't you noticed that ever since Kelleher and Cooney were shot, the Brits have been on the rampage round here? Didn't it take Sean three days to get the bloody army out of Ballinalee and since they hanged Kevin Barry, the rest of the country is like a bloody tinder box. If Mulcahy and Collins wanted a frigging war, then they've bloody well got one and you seriously think that right now Sean will give a toss about where Flynn and his girlfriend, or even Maguire, are? Besides, Kingstown is in the Dublin Brigade area. If he's down there, then dealing with him will be their business, not ours.'

'Give it here!' McNamara snapped testily as he snatched back Kathleen's letter and scribbled down the Kingstown address on a scrap of paper, which he stuffed in his jacket pocket. 'Here, O'Brien,' he called imperiously, waving the letter in O'Brien's general direction, 'put this back in its envelope and make sure it gets delivered. The bloody peelers will make sure that it gets where it's going.' Without a word, O'Brien took the letter and popped it back into its envelope before gumming down the flap. He really didn't like McNamara much and was becoming convinced that the man was mad and silently prayed that he would be off soon.

'You leave Sean to me,' McNamara said knowingly, breaking into a broad, disconcerting grin. O'Neill ignored him, pretending to read the letter that he had been looking at before McNamara interrupted him. It was addressed to a place called Scotland House, a false address used by British intelligence for informers to anonymously send information about republicans. O'Neill shook his head and sighed; the fool who'd written the letter had signed his name and even written his address. McNamara stood up abruptly and picked up his coat from over the back of a chair. 'I'm off to see Sean with this,' he announced and pulled on his coat, fishing his cap from its pocket.

'You'd best take this,' O'Neill said as he handed McNamara the informer's letter. As the door slammed shut behind McNamara, O'Neill felt a twinge of guilt. He knew that he had just sentenced its author to death and that as soon as MacEoin saw the letter there would be another grieving widow, fatherless children even, in the county – but war was war, and if there was another empty bed in the county that night, then so be it.

On the outskirts of Ballinalee a burnt-out police Crossley Tender partially blocked the Longford Road and an eerie silence hung over the town. Empty cartridge cases lay scattered in the street and broken glass crunched beneath McNamara's feet as he strode towards Rose Cottage, MacEoin's home and temporary HQ during the gunfight that was already being fêted by republican propagandists as the Battle of Ballinalee. No doubt it would make a cracking ballad, McNamara thought.

Despite the lull, no one really had a clue what was going on – battles were like that. The IRA attack on the RIC barracks had locked the place down behind its steel shutters but MacEoin had no idea whether he had inflicted any casualties. His boys had also forced the British troops to pull back out of the village but, deep down, he knew it was only a temporary respite. They would be back; it was only a matter of time.

McNamara pushed open the front door of Rose Cottage and was shocked at how drawn, pale and just plain exhausted MacEoin looked. 'It's all quiet in the town,' McNamara said with a smile but MacEoin barely looked up from the half-written report that he held in his trembling hand. An un-drunk cup of tea stood cold on the table next to an equally untouched sandwich and the exhausted MacEoin's eyes were red and rheumy, his face dark with stubble. 'You look like you could use some sleep, boss,' he added.

'Me and everyone else,' MacEoin replied, before picking up his pen and adding a few words to the report. 'The final casualty reports haven't come in yet, we've a few missing still, but it looks like none of the boys were killed. That's something anyway, but I don't know what damage we've done to the bloody Brits either.' MacEoin paused for a moment. 'What are you doing here anyway? I thought you were helping O'Neill and O'Brien censor the mail.'

'That I was, Sean,' McNamara replied, 'but something has come up.' He tossed the informer's letter onto the desk and waited for MacEoin to read it. The blacksmith gave it a quick once-over and handed it over to his deputy, Sean Connolly, who was sat across the table from him.

'Deal with it, Sean, please,' he said and Connolly quickly glanced at the letter before folding it up and putting it in his pocket. He rose and left the room without a word. 'Is there anything else?' MacEoin asked McNamara, who was still hovering in the room expectantly.

'It's Maguire and Flynn. I think I know where to find them,' McNamara said.

MacEoin looked up and, rubbing his reddened eyes, replied, 'It will have to wait – there is too much going on and I need every man here to keep the bloody Tans under control, Mick!' McNamara felt a surge of disappointment course through him and MacEoin began to question whether he really needed such a hothead around in the next couple of days. 'Where are they?' MacEoin finally asked.

'Dublin,' McNamara replied.

The blacksmith rubbed his chin for a moment. 'Tell you what, Mick, it may well be your lucky day. When I sent word to GHQ about all the shenanigans going on over here, Frankie Thornton sent word that he would like to have a wee chat with my man Gary O'Neill and see if there is anything more we can get out of him. Tell you what, Mick. You take Gary down to Dublin – there's a train out of Mullingar tomorrow. Take him to Vaughan's hotel; they'll know where to find Frankie. Hand him over, tell the Dublin boys what you know about Maguire and Flynn and get your arse back here PDQ, understand?'

'Would I be doing anything I wasn't meant to,' McNamara replied as a broad, evil grin slashed across his face. 'I'll get your man O'Neill to GHQ for you and be back before you even begin to miss me!' MacEoin was too tired to talk further and picked up his pen to add a few more words to his report. When he looked up next, McNamara was already gone.

CHAPTER 35

Dublin

'AND YOU REALLY have no idea where they have got to?' Emmet Dalton asked Frank Thornton as he took a deep breath of damp evening Dublin air through the open window. Thornton stubbed out his cigarette in a battered tin ashtray.

'Nope, not a clue,' he replied.

Dalton turned and gave him a quizzical look. 'Hmm, should I be worried that no one knows where he is?'

'To be honest, Ginchy,' Thornton said, using Dalton's nickname, 'I don't really know. When I spoke to Sean last he said he'd sent Mick McNamara to Vaughan's a few days ago. He should have shown up a few days ago, but the thing is, there's been no sign of him. No sign of O'Neill either.'

'Have the Brits got them, do you know?' Dalton asked.

'I don't think so,' Thornton said. 'If the Brits had got them, I'd've heard something. My people are all over the place.'

'So where are they? Should I be worried? Should we be worried?'

Thornton raised his hand to calm Dalton. 'To be honest, Ginchy, I don't really know. According to Sean, this McNamara fella's been going off the rails since his brother was killed by the Brits ...' Thornton paused. 'He blames Maguire and some peeler called Flynn and Sean seems to think that he might be looking for them.' Dalton gave him a quizzical look. 'Joe Maguire, Commandant Joe Maguire, the treacherous shite from Longford who turned out to be a Brit spy.'

'Ah, that Maguire,' Dalton said slowly.

'Aye, that Maguire, and this Flynn fella, the one who was working with the fella that Sean shot at the Kiernan pub, you know, Inspector Kelleher. Anyway, McNamara has got it into his head that these two did for his brother and Sean thinks that he might be going after them.'

'Do we know where Maguire and Flynn are?' Dalton asked.

'Haven't a clue,' Thornton said, 'but when Sean last saw McNamara, he was babbling on that he knew where they were, or at least, he seemed to think he knew how to find them and my guess is that they are somewhere in the city.'

'Blast!' Dalton muttered. 'The last thing we need is someone out of control on some sort of bloody vendetta, not now.'

'Do we tell Mick?' Thornton asked.

Dalton stared back out of the window and massaged his temples as he wrestled with his decision. 'No, we don't tell Mick, he's got enough on his plate as it is. Tell you what, Frankie, keep an ear to the ground and try and find this McNamara chappie and, when you do, make sure that he doesn't get a chance to do anything stupid.'

Gary O'Neill was distinctly unimpressed with his surroundings: a dingy room deep in the heart of one of Dublin's notorious insanitary slums as far as he could tell. He felt dirty just sitting there and McNamara insisted that he keep away from the equally tarnished windows, just in case he was seen. He could hear children playing in the street and the ceiling groaned and thudded under the constant squeaking of rusty bedsprings and forced squeals of passion in the prostitute's room above that had kept him awake half the night. Worse still, the entire crumbling edifice stank of damp and decay, like a pile of rotting cabbage mixed with urine and stewed.

'Are you sure Sean said to wait here?' O'Neill asked McNamara, who was sprawled out on the sagging flea-bitten mattress of the decrepit bed. For a moment O'Neill thought that McNamara was asleep but then the man stirred and pulled the cap from over his eyes.

'Aye, he did that,' McNamara grunted before slumping back onto the bed, resuming his nap. O'Neill risked a look out of the dirt-encrusted window at the street below and watched the filthy urchins splashing gleefully in the suspiciously brown liquid that overflowed in the gutter at the side of the road. Further up the street a couple of older boys were hoofing an old tin can back and forth in an approximation of football. Suddenly, the boys scattered to the roadside as a couple of army lorries careered around the corner into the street.

'Brit bastards!' a falsetto voice screamed as a whistle shrilled and the lorries crunched to a halt, disgorging soldiers who swiftly formed a cordon across either end of the street, bayonets glinting menacingly in the sunlight.

'It's the Brits! How the hell did they know we were here?' O'Neill called back to McNamara, who was already swinging his legs over the side, his boots thudding down on the ageing floorboards. As he stood up he pulled a Luger automatic pistol from his pocket, checked that it was loaded and then cocked it with a deft flick of his hands. 'You have got to be bloody kidding me!' O'Neill said in disbelief as he watched his companion make ready. 'There's half the bloody British army out there and you think that you can shoot your way out with that?'

'Here, take this.' McNamara shot him a cold glance before pulling a revolver from his other pocket and tossing it to O'Neill, who caught it and instinctively checked the cylinder to make sure that it was loaded. 'It's got five rounds in it. I left one empty so you don't shoot your bloody foot off!' Too many people had managed to shoot themselves by mistake over the last couple of years and McNamara was referring to the fact that he had only put five bullets in the cylinder, leaving the sixth chamber empty, making it safe so that it could not go off accidentally.

'And what if I need more than five bullets?' O'Neill asked.

McNamara rolled his eyes and plucked an unopened box of .38 bullets from his jacket pocket and tossed it over to O'Neill. The box rattled as he caught it and he stuffed it into his pocket, patting it reassuringly. Just like in most trouble spots around the world, ammunition was freely available in Ireland, if you knew where to look, and McNamara couldn't remember where he got this particular box from. For that matter he couldn't remember where the pistol had come from either, he just got it from somewhere. Someone had once quipped that if you dug up all the arms caches in Dublin there wouldn't be a single building left standing and McNamara was sure that it wasn't too much of an exaggeration.

Quietly, the two men slipped out onto the tenement landing. It smelt of stale urine and unwashed bodies and a shabbily dressed sallow woman clutched a grubby ring-wormed baby to her flat chest, watched them with empty, disinterested dark eyes. They reminded O'Neill of the blank unintelligent gaze of a dairy cow standing in a meadow waiting for milking. McNamara raised his finger to his lips, gesturing her to be quiet.

They froze as they heard the noise of a door shatter under the blows of a sledgehammer, drowning the shouts and whistles in the street. O'Neill thumbed back the hammer of his pistol to half-cock. His heart was hammering in his chest and he could feel his hands beginning to tremble as adrenalin flooded his system. He forced himself to steady his breathing and peered down the gap in the middle of the stairwell, expecting to see khaki-clad figures doubling up the stairs.

Nothing moved, blood pounded in his ears and his vision began to tunnel, making him light-headed. Somewhere, a woman was keening, shrieking abuse as others joined in, and he could hear dustbin lids being slammed into pavements like galvanized jungle drums, sending a warning to the streets around that a British raid was underway. McNamara stole another glance out of the cobwebbed window at the end of the landing.

'They're raiding the house over the road!' McNamara said as he watched the soldiers dragging a couple of men out of the house opposite and bundled them into a waiting lorry. A crowd had gathered, jostling the soldiers. A cobble-stone bounced off the bonnet of the lead lorry, ricocheting through the windscreen and narrowly missing the driver.

O'Neill felt a wave of relief pulse through him and he eased the hammer of his pistol forward with a soft click. They were off the hook. The dull-eyed woman looked at him indifferently. She could have been pretty once, O'Neill thought, as he ran his eyes over her, but life in the slums had put paid to that, condemning her to a subsistence of squalor, disease and death. He hoped to God things would be different after the British had gone. 'Is there another way out?' O'Neill asked.

She stared at him blankly, as if weighing up what to say, rocking the sniffling bundle of rags in her arms. 'That way,' she said in an abrasive north Dublin slum accent and gestured, with a slight flick of her head, towards the rear of the building. 'There's a back stair.'

O'Neill nodded and called to McNamara. 'Come on, let's get out of here!' The gunman spared one last glance into the street in time to see the wet lumpy brown contents of a chamber pot plunge from an upstairs window onto an unfortunate squaddie below, to a ripple of jeering laughter. McNamara could see the officers and NCOs trying to restrain their men. 'You think this is funny!' the effluent-coated soldier barked at the crowd. 'You think this is bloody funny!' He jerked up his rifle, smashing the butt into the nearest face. 'Now that's funny, you Mick shit!' the soldier shouted as he slammed the weapon down on the prone figure writhing at his feet, clutching its face. A moan of horror, like a wave, rippled through the crowd and more cobble-stones thudded into the knot of soldiers, bouncing indiscriminately off lorries and tin hats.

'C'mon!' O'Neill called again.

'Bastard!' McNamara hissed through gritted teeth, as he raised his

Luger into a firing position, took a brief aim and squeezed the trigger. The window exploded in a shower of glass and the effluent-soaked soldier was thrown to his knees as the 9mm round tore into his dorsal muscle before lodging in his shoulder blade. For a fraction of a second it was as if time stood still. You could have heard a pin drop in the stunned silence and then all hell broke loose.

'Shit!' O'Neill cried. 'Shit! Shit! Shit! Shit! Shit! What the hell have you done?' McNamara snapped off another couple of rounds into the rapidly dispersing tangle of soldiers. The crowd had already taken to its heels. Officers and NCOs tried to restore order, barking orders, punctuated by harsh, rasping whistle blasts as their men dove for cover. A bullet thudded into the ceiling above McNamara's head, peppering him with fragments of a dilapidated plaster motif and the floodgates of adrenalin reopened as O'Neill realized that it hadn't taken them long to work out where the shot had come from.

'Mick, you eejit, let's go!' O'Neill shouted again as he began to edge his way towards the back stairs. He noticed that the woman had gone, her woodwormed door wedged firmly shut. 'We've got to get out, now!' He could hear the battering on the front door below and knew that they only had seconds left to get out. With an ominous crash, the door splintered inwards and through the banister O'Neill could see greatcoated soldiers tumble inwards, brandishing bayonets that seemed huge in the confines of the tenement's foyer.

'Damn!' The word flashed in his head like one of those enormous neon signs he had once seen in Paris during the war. 'Damn! Damn! Damn!' The sign seemed to expand its vocabulary and flash on and off as he watched and then the shadow of the gallows began to loom large as blood roared in a raging torrent inside his head. McNamara pulled a Mills bomb from his pocket, jerked the pin free with his index finger and then, letting the spring-loaded lever fly across the landing, dropped the grenade into the hall below.

BANG! Razor-sharp slivers of cast iron slashed through the foyer, turning it into an abattoir, and O'Neill staggered as the floor shook under his feet, his ears searing with pain. The shockwave of the blast tore through him as it was vented up the stairway, showering plaster dust, and a high-pitched ringing pulsed through his head. He ran his tongue over his top lip, feeling the bitter coppery taste of blood dripping from his nose, and he felt off-balance. McNamara grabbed O'Neill's arm and, mouthing something, dragged him towards the stairwell and the floor above.

Slowly, the ringing and nausea began to recede. 'Quick! Up! The roof, now! MOVE!' O'Neill began to make out McNamara's words as he dragged him by the arm up to the next floor. Down in the foyer the dust began to settle on the writhing, gore-bespattered carnage just as the second wave of soldiers cautiously probed their way into the building. O'Neill heard one of the soldiers curse as his boot skidded in a pool of bloody slime. Even in his confused state, O'Neill knew that it would only be a matter of moments before they would be up and after them. As his head began to clear, O'Neill could hear children crying behind flimsy, flaking, Georgian plasterboard walls of the decaying tenement. They were taking the stairs two at a time now in their haste to get away.

'Where the bloody hell did you get that from?' O'Neill gasped. Ignoring his questions, McNamara lengthened his stride. O'Neill could hear the heavy thud of boots on the stairs behind him and through gritted teeth forced himself to keep pace with his fleeing companion. Below, doors crashed open to the cry of women and children as soldiers began clearing the first floor and, for a brief moment, O'Neill felt a glimmer of hope that the soldiers' caution could maybe give them just enough time to get away.

Moments later the two fleeing men burst onto the top landing and McNamara began looking frantically around. Then he stopped dead before making a rapid beeline for an inauspiciously shabby cupboard door tucked away in the corner. 'We're stuffed!' O'Neill wheezed despondently and re-cocked his revolver, resigning himself to being gunned down at the top of the stairs of some squalid Dublin fleapit. Behind him he heard McNamara wrench open the door. Below him the sound of boots was getting louder.

'Over here!' McNamara panted and O'Neill looked around in time to see McNamara vanishing up an even smaller flight of stairs. Gasping for breath, O'Neill followed, pausing briefly to shut the door behind him before bounding up into the attic. Although it was dark, dusty and full of cobwebs, it was occupied by a family that was huddled in the corner, watching the two gunmen with large, fearful eyes. 'You haven't seen anything!' McNamara said to them as he prised open a skylight window. 'C'mon!' he barked at O'Neill as he climbed out onto the roof.

O'Neill hated heights. His palms begin to sweat uncontrollably as he stepped out onto the narrow ledge that ran along the bottom of the roof and he felt unsteady on his feet. He glanced down and saw the back yards below, criss-crossed with grubby washing and filth. Shots were still ringing out and he could hear shouting in the street below and his head began to spin. He tore his eyes away from the squalor below in time to see McNamara vanishing into a skylight several doors further down the street. Moving as quickly as he dare, he shuffled along the ledge until he reached the window and climbed in. McNamara was leaning against the wall, panting, a broad grin slashed across his face. 'Now let's get out of here!' he panted.

They kept to the back alleyways and O'Neill didn't feel safe until they were several blocks away from their hideout. He didn't know Dublin at all and didn't have a clue where they were. 'So who informed on us?' he asked McNamara. The gunman gave him a characteristic sidelong glance without breaking his stride.

'No one, we were just in the wrong place at the wrong time. They weren't after us.'

'So why the hell did you shoot at them?' O'Neill demanded.

'Because they are the bloody enemy and we are at war, that's why!'

Shit! He really is as barking mad as they say, O'Neill thought as he slipped into silence and began to question the wisdom of accompanying McNamara to Dublin. 'So, what now?' he asked after a while but McNamara seemed reluctant to answer.

'Shush, I'm thinking!' he eventually muttered before resuming his sullen silence.

'Shouldn't we make contact with someone?' O'Neill persisted.

'We will,' McNamara replied as they emerged from a side street into Sackville Street and O'Neill realized that they had been hiding in the bowels of Dublin's infamous red-light district, known as the Monto, after its main thoroughfare Montgomery Street. The Monto was reputably the largest red-light district in the British Isles, if not Europe, and its alleyways and backstreets had provided many a rebel on the run with a place to hide, where no one asked questions or, indeed, wanted to know in the first place.

Sackville Street seemed like another world to O'Neill. Once the widest street in Europe, it teemed with life, bustling with pedestrians, shoppers and businessmen going about their affairs. In front of the shattered cadaver of the GPO building, the epicentre of the 1916 Easter Rising, the street was dominated by the towering edifice of Nelson's Pillar and much to McNamara's obvious disgust, a British flag fluttered defiantly over the post office's bullet-scarred portico. All around, O'Neill could see the tell-tale signs of battle.

They walked in silence past the statue of Daniel O'Connell, 'The

Liberator' who had campaigned fiercely for Catholic emancipation during the first years of the previous century, and onto the O'Connell Bridge beyond. The stink of the River Liffey assaulted O'Neill's nostrils and mixed with the saline tang of sea air wafting up the estuary, reminding him of his long-past childhood bank holiday sojourns to Portrush or Benone Strand.

O'Neill almost bumped into McNamara's back as he drew up suddenly and looked back the way they'd just come through the bustling crowds towards the shell of the GPO. 'Bastards!' McNamara muttered, more to himself than to O'Neill, his face taut with barely suppressed rage. The Ulsterman gazed momentarily at McNamara's face, trying to discern what was going on behind the man's empty eyes.

'I was here, back in sixteen,' McNamara sniffed, referring to the Easter Rising. 'There in the GPO. I was with the O'Rahilly on Moore Street when he died. We ran straight into a bloody ambush, mown down like ripened corn by a bloody machine gun somewhere on the edge of Great Britain Street. He bled out, you know, the O'Rahilly, in a godforsaken bloody doorway in Sackville Lane. Now there was a patriot, God bless him. What a waste, what a bloody waste.' McNamara looked genuinely moved, uncharacteristically so, and as suddenly as he had begun he lapsed back into silence.

'So where to now?' O'Neill asked.

McNamara shot him a grin – cold and humourless – and a flinty glint flared for a moment in his fathomless eyes. 'How do you fancy a trip to the seaside?' McNamara finally answered. 'We've got a wee bit of business to attend to, down in Kingstown.'

CHAPTER 36

Dublin Castle

D UBLIN CASTLE WAS under siege. There were no trenches dug around its walls cutting it off from the outside world, no soldiers encircling it preparing for a final bloody assault across a ragged, rubble-strewn breech, yet the Castle, the arrhythmic heart of His Majesty's government, the seat of royal power in Ireland for almost 800 years, was under siege nonetheless.

Fear hung oppressively in the air, like humidity on a hot day, and Flynn could almost taste it as he strolled through the Castle precinct. He had seen it etched on almost all the civil servants' pinched faces since he had arrived. Every crevice, every nook, every cranny had become home to some pale, drawn clerk or typist who was too afraid to go home at night. The government was in meltdown.

And yet life in the Castle was surreal, a seemingly endless round of parties to boost the inmates' morale, but the more they tried to obscure the shadow that hung over the place the larger it loomed, like an insatiable monster. There had been a dance on the night they arrived but neither Flynn nor Maguire could face it. 'Jesus, I really can't wait to get out of this place,' Flynn said to Maguire as he watched sundry clerks and typists dancing around the main ballroom. 'You know in the trenches we used to go out of our way to pretend everything was normal but it never was, not really.' Maguire had shaken his head and said, 'Fools are fiddling whilst Rome burns,' and then added, 'I'm off to bed,' before striding impatiently towards their billet. Flynn had only hung around for a few moments longer before following him.

The next morning began with a rushed greasy breakfast in the crowded refectory before Maguire looked at his pocket watch and announced, 'C'mon then, we've got to report in,' and shoving back his plate, rose from the table.

'Where to now?' Flynn asked Maguire as he picked up his plate and headed to the drop-off point for dirty dishes.

'You'll see,' Maguire replied and led Flynn out into the Castle's Lower Yard with its old grey tower, one of the last vestiges of its medieval past and just about the only indication that the place had actually been, once upon a time, a castle. Across the yard an engine spluttered into life, rupturing the quiet, and Flynn turned to see a touring car full of heavily armed Auxiliaries pull off towards the gate and the city beyond. Maguire nodded towards the tower. 'There. That's where we're off to, Kevin, my boy!'

Outside the tower door a bullet-headed man stood puffing furiously on a cigarette. His clothes were immaculate, obviously bespoke, and even through the haze of rich nicotine smoke, the man exuded the relaxed confidence that came with power. He had to be someone of consequence, Flynn surmised. The man looked at Flynn and Maguire and broke into a broad smile, briefly interrupting his incessant shifting from one foot to the other. He was one of those men who bristled with energy, the 'action this day' sort Flynn'd come across far too often in the army.

The man took one last frantic drag on his cigarette, like a man about to go over the top any moment, and then with a cheery wave bounded enthusiastically towards them, the sun glinting off his monocle. As he drew closer Flynn could see that the man was in his mid forties. His eyes were dark and quick, drinking in his surroundings, and they reminded Flynn of a snake – dark, fathomless, deadly, poised to strike. 'Good morning! Good morning!' he called in the sort of crisp, self-confident, self-important public school accent that made Flynn suspect that the man was an army officer of some description, a man used to having his own way.

'Joe! How the devil are you, old chap? Bloody marvellous to see you, bloody marvellous!' he gushed a little too ebulliently to ring true as he vigorously pumped Maguire's hand before turning and looking at Flynn, making him feel like he was under a microscope before he thrust his hand towards him. 'And you must be Constable Flynn! Splendid! I've heard so much about you!' Flynn's heart sank; he hated it when people he'd never met before said that they had 'heard so much about him,' especially the ones who acted like they were in charge, and a familiar alarm bell began to clang inside his head as the man pumped his hand too. Flynn had no idea who the man was but he had a feeling that he was going to be trouble – trouble with a capital 'T'.

'Where are my manners?' the Englishman declared suddenly, his dark, expressionless eyes glinting. 'Please, please, come this way,' he added, turning towards the tower as somewhere in the distance the muffled sound of gunfire rolled into the courtyard and reverberated off its walls and all three looked up for a moment like men studying the weather. 'Let's hope that it's our lads sticking it to the blasted Shinners for a change, eh?' The man clapped Maguire on the back, all bon homie. 'On! On! There's work to be done,' he said, before speeding off back towards the tower.

'Who is he?' Flynn mouthed quietly to Maguire as he gestured towards the man's receding back.

'You'll see soon enough.' Maguire smiled. 'But as it happens, he's my boss! Now come on!'

'You know, Joe, I had a feeling you were going to say that!' Flynn muttered as Maguire sped off after the Englishman in the direction of the tower. Flynn shook his head and followed as another series of distant gunshots echoed across the yard.

He was met at the door by a tall middle-aged man with a neat moustache and wavy fair hair who eyed Flynn suspiciously, as if he was weighing him up, much as the Englishman had a few minutes earlier, his hard eyes betraying nothing of what was behind them. He exuded the dangerous confidence of a man who knew how to look after himself. 'This way, Constable,' he said in a pronounced Mayo accent.

Flynn gave him a polite smile and squeezed past into the confines of the tower. The man gestured up a flight of stairs and waited for Flynn to climb and on the third floor landing Flynn reached an impressive albeit somewhat spartan office that smelt of wax furniture polish and expensive tobacco. The Englishman stood behind a large leather-topped desk piled with thick beige and scarlet card-covered files and a crystal glass ashtray overflowing with the detritus of a serious nicotine habit. He was already lighting another cigarette when Flynn entered the room. Maguire had already made himself at home in a dark wood leather upholstered chair by a triplet of windows that overlooked the Lower Castle Yard.

'Ah, so I see you've already met Head Constable Igoe,' the Englishman announced and Head Constable Eugene Igoe gave Flynn a cursory nod before swinging the office door shut with a soft click. Igoe folded his arms and leant against it and Flynn couldn't quite work out whether he was keeping people out or them in. 'Please, please, take a seat, my dear chap,' the Englishman said chummily, as he gestured towards an empty chair. 'Take a seat, Kevin. You don't mind if I call you Kevin, do you?' The man didn't wait for a response, safe in the knowledge that Flynn was unlikely to say no and even if he did, Flynn had a feeling that the man would call him Kevin anyway.

Flynn dropped into a chair and tried, unsuccessfully, to look relaxed. It was then that he noticed the name etched in brass on the tally sitting on the man's desk – Brigadier General Ormonde de l'Épée Winter CB CMG DSO (Late RA) – and blanched. So this was Maguire's boss, the man they called the 'Holy Terror' himself; in short, the man responsible for running British intelligence operations in Ireland, the man who revelled in the codename 'O'.

Offering Flynn a cigarette, Winter was obviously relishing the theatricality of the moment and shot Flynn a cold smile, whilst sifting deftly through the pile of folders on his desk. He plucked one free and thumbed through it. Flynn felt distinctly uncomfortable and shifted uneasily in his seat as Winter shifted his gaze to Maguire. 'Well, let's get down to business, shall we, eh what? I've read your report, Joe. Damn rum business this O'Neill chappie blowing your cover and all. Worse still, he was one of our own, eh, Eugene?' he said, looking over to Igoe. 'Sends all the wrong blasted signals, having a Protestant republican, don't you know.'

'Bloody bad business, sir,' Igoe concurred.

'Well, Joe, Eugene here tells me that a little bird has told him that your man O'Neill is out and about in these parts. Apparently, he was seen getting off the Mullingar train with another fellow, his minder no doubt. We don't have a positive ID of the minder yet, do we, Eugene?' he asked Igoe.

'Not yet, sir, but I'm sure we'll get one soon.' Igoe pulled a folded sheet of paper from his pocket and placed it on Winter's desk. It was a police artist's sketch of a man's face.

'Is this the best we've got?' Winter asked, as he tossed the sketch onto his desk. Maguire leant forward.

'May I?' he asked, pointedly omitting to say 'sir'. Winter handed him the sketch and Maguire studied it closely. He held it up for Flynn and turned to the brigadier. 'I could be wrong but it looks like a fella called Mick McNamara to me, eh, Kevin?' Flynn nodded.

'You know him?' Winter asked.

'You could say that,' Maguire said slowly. 'I was his commanding officer!' Winter effervesced ebulliently, snorting a harsh, sharp laugh that grated on Flynn's nerves.

'Excuse me, but that is absolutely bloody marvellous. What a stroke of luck, eh, Eugene?' Winter gushed at Igoe, who nodded again, keeping his thoughts to himself. The man was a closed book, his eyes cold and calculating. 'Head Constable Igoe here has a bit of a knack of finding people, don't you, Eugene, old chap? A gift some would say, eh?'

'If you say so, sir,' Igoe replied noncommittally.

'If I say so! If I say so! You're like a bloodhound, Eugene!' He turned to the others. 'Head Constable Igoe here has made quite a name for himself over in Galway, didn't you, Eugene, catching Shinners? So good, in fact, I've invited the good head constable to come and work for me here in Dublin. We've got the rebels on the ropes here in Dublin and I want him to set up a new unit for me; a special operations unit to winkle out Shinners from whatever stone they are hiding under, finish them off, what! It's still a work in progress but I'm minded to call this unit the Identification Branch of the Combined Intelligence Service, or something like that, anyway. I gather you've done a bit of intelligence work yourself, Kevin, old chap?'

Flynn felt his stomach knotting and he tensed slightly as the brigadier addressed him. He didn't know where the man was taking this conversation but Flynn already had an inkling that it wasn't anywhere he wanted to go. 'I'd hardly call it that, sir,' he replied.

'Now, now, Constable, you're far too modest. Nasty business with Kelleher but Joe here speaks very highly of you in his report. Cool head under pressure, what! No more than I'd expect from a man with a Military Medal, eh?' It struck Flynn that Winter had been doing his homework. 'You know, Joe, I was thinking of spiriting you away over the water but I think in the circumstances I have a better idea. Yes, a much better idea. I don't like what this O'Neill chap has done and I think that the Shinners need to be sent a message that it's just not on. I'm getting sick to death of malcontent bloody policemen. Seeing as you know O'Neill and this McNamara chappie, how do you fancy having a go at bringing the treacherous little bastards to justice?' It wasn't really a question.

'Eugene here will give you your instructions and you'll report to him. I want those bastards off the streets and I want it done ASAP, understand? Oh, and by the way, you are not to mention this meeting to anyone. Is that clear?'

Without waiting for Flynn and Maguire to respond, without even looking up, Winter plucked another folder from the pile of files and flipped it open as Igoe opened the office door. 'There's transport downstairs. They'll take you over to the depot in Phoenix Park. I'll meet you there at the guardroom at 9 a.m. on Monday,' Igoe said dismissively. It was obvious that the meeting was over.

CHAPTER 37

RIC HQ, Phoenix Park, Dublin

'So why did you do it?' Flynn asked.

'Do what?' Maguire replied, as he nursed his mug of strong, sweet tea.

'Change sides, of course.'

'I didn't. Change sides, that is.' He slurped another mouthful of tea and looked casually around the depot canteen. Flynn looked at him, unconvinced. 'I'm on Ireland's side. I still am.'

'So how come you were IRA and now you're not?'

Maguire flashed Flynn a smile and placed his mug down with a gentle thud. 'Ah, now there's a tale,' he said before picking up his tea once more and holding the mug in his cupped hands, feeling the warmth leech into his palms. He felt a perverse pleasure in making Flynn wait for him to tell his story. 'Call it an epiphany if you like. When you were a lad, I bet your da read you bedtime stories about the three little pigs. Mine? I got stories of how the English pitch-capped my great-grandfather back in '98, how they stole my country and murdered my people. Jaysus, did my folks teach me to hate the English, the devil and all his works or what?' He laughed dryly. 'Every generation needs its revolution, they say, to keep the torch burning until the next generation comes along. How ironically "British" of us – it's not the winning or losing that matters, it's the taking part, eh?'

Maguire slid his mug of tea further away and looked Flynn in the eye. 'Why did I change sides, as you put it? Why did you? You're as Irish as me, yet you joined their army. You became a peeler. Why?'

'Because I don't agree with what the Shinners are doing.'

'Exactly, and neither do I. I just didn't realize it until that bloody pointless Rising. What a bloody farce that was. Pearse told us that Ireland was ready for revolution, like hell! I had plenty of time to think when I was rotting in Frongoch internment camp. You tell me what sort of country can we build if we keep thinking that the gun is the answer? People didn't vote for this bloody mess. No one said back in 1918 "vote for us and we'll cause anarchy". They talk about democracy but mean agree with me or get lost. Very bloody democratic! No wonder the Prods up north are so afraid of us. Now don't get me wrong, Kevin, I'm still on Ireland's side. I still want the British to leave my country alone but if it's all right for us to kill anyone who disagrees with us then what's to stop any malcontent with a gun doing the same? It's a recipe for anarchy. You mark my words, Kevin. The moment the Brits leave, and they will, the first thing the rebels will do is turn on each other, so unless we learn to get what we want peacefully, there'll be civil war. You mark my words.'

'And that's why you switched side,' Flynn said.

'I changed methods, not sides, that's all. Besides, where do you fit in? Where do any of you fit in, in their new Ireland?' Maguire swept his arm across the room at the other policemen idling away their time in the canteen. 'You're worse than the Prods, you're one of "us", a Catholic Irishman who dances to John Bull's tune. You're a traitor, Kevin, like all of the rest, like me even. Isn't that why you joined the RIC, because you don't agree with the Shinners? I was recruited by British intelligence to help stop these people wrecking my bloody country any further. God, if we had peace, then maybe the Brits really would piss off and leave us alone to sort our differences out without resorting to bloody murder.'

Flynn laughed. 'Now, just for a moment there, I thought that you were just another Irish romantic!'

Maguire gave him a sharp look and then burst out laughing. 'Sure, aren't we all romantics at heart! It's our curse!'

'Ain't it just!'

Several heads turned in their direction, doubtless trying to work out what the joke was before turning back to their own muffled conversations. 'So what do you think of this Igoe fella?' Flynn asked but before Maguire could answer, the canteen door banged open and a great-coated constable stepped in out of the rain. He doffed his cap and shook the excess water from it before closing the door behind him. Pulling a crumpled piece of paper out of his coat pocket, the constable glanced at it and then, looking up, called out loudly. 'Has anyone seen a Constable Kevin Flynn?'

'What now?' Flynn sighed, before raising his hand. 'Over here!' The constable wove his way through the tables until he stood next to Flynn and Maguire. The constable, Stephen Fallon, was a passing acquaintance of Flynn's, having gone through training together. Fallon smiled as he approached Flynn's table.

'The orderly sergeant said I might find you here. This turned up in the mail room and he said I should make sure that you got it.' He held out a crumpled envelope. Flynn took it.

'Who's on duty tonight?' Flynn asked.

'Sergeant McLain. He sounded like he knows you.'

'Bugger me! He was my old gaffer back in Drumlish. I'll have to swing by the orderly office and say hello. I didn't realize he was here.'

'I'll give him your regards.'

'There's a right old reunion going on here,' Maguire quipped as Fallon walked back towards the door. 'That old duffer, McLain, O'Neill, McNamara. Jaysus, it's just like being back in Longford. Perhaps we should throw a party!'

Flynn ignored him and looked down at the envelope, toying with it, turning it around in his hands. The postmark was two weeks old, stamped with Kingstown and Drumlish. Rain had smudged the neat feminine script that flowed across the paper. Kingstown. Kingstown. Who did he know in Kingstown? He snagged open the envelope and flicked open the letter.

'And what has got you grinning like a Cheshire cat?'

'Nothing,' he lied, as his cheeks flushed deep red.

'Nothing, my arse, it'll be some colleen writing to you.'

'So what do you think of this Igoe fella?' Flynn asked desperately, changing the subject as he folded the letter and popped it in his jacket pocket.

Maguire shrugged. 'It looks like Winter has us painted into a corner. There isn't a lot we can do but go along with him, but never mind that nonsense; we don't have to worry about Igoe until Monday. So tell me who the letter is from. I don't see no wedding ring so who's the young lady?'

'If it's any of your business, it's from a girl I used to know in Drumlish, Kathleen Moore. It would seem that she has been staying with her aunt in Kingstown and she's trying to get in touch with me. She's asked me to write her or drop by if I happen to be in the area.'

'Ah, so she's still keen on you, is she, this Kathleen?' Maguire asked with a knowing smile.

'I reckon,' Flynn replied.

'She's taking a bit of a risk, isn't she?'

'What do you mean?'

'You do realize that the post office is full of rebel sympathizers.' Flynn looked at him blankly, none the wiser. 'I'd be gobsmacked if you are the only one who has read that letter. If it's not their people reading people's mail then it's ours. Christ, the IRA's Directorate of Military Intelligence has an entire section dedicated to reading the mail.'

'Away with you,' Flynn said. 'Who'd be interested in this?'

'Anyone with eyes, Kevin. Just look at the envelope.'

Flynn pulled the paper back out of his pocket and looked at the address, looking up at Maguire with a puzzled expression. 'So?'

'Jaysus, you're not the sharpest pencil in the box, are ye? Look at the address. Who is it addressed to?'

'Constable Kevin Flynn, care of the RIC Barracks, Drumlish ...' Flynn's voice trailed away into silence.

'Exactly! It's addressed to a peeler. Who wouldn't be interested? It's addressed to one of England's janissaries! Do you think that one of our people wouldn't be interested if they found a letter addressed to one of the enemy?' Flynn leapt up, sending his chair clattering against the table behind, attracting further curiosity. Maguire grabbed the sleeve of his jacket, holding him in place. 'What are you doing?'

'Going to Kingstown, of course. Kathleen may be in danger.'

'Just calm down. That letter must be over a week old. If the IRA were going to do anything to your girl, then you're already too late, believe me. They'd also make sure you knew about it. No, she's still all right and besides, the last thing you want to do is charge across Dublin at night, what with the curfew. If the rebels don't shoot us, some bloody trigger-happy squaddie probably will.' Flynn didn't look convinced. 'Look, it's Sunday tomorrow. Why don't we ...'

'We?'

'We. You don't think I'm going to let you go running off on your own? Like I said, why don't we blag a car from the motor pool and then go over to see Kingstown. Don't worry, I won't play gooseberry but at least you'll get there in one piece. And besides, it's pissing down – we'll get soaked, you Jackeen eejit!'

'All right, I'll wait, but you better be right,' Flynn replied sceptically.

'Look, if you are that worried, why don't you telephone the local DMP station in Kingstown and get them to take a look in on your girl? You've got the address. Let's get over to the orderly office and say hello to your old mucker Sergeant McLain. I'm sure he'll let you use the phone. After all, what else are old friends for?'

CHAPTER 38

Saturday, 20 November 1920, Kingstown, County Dublin

T HE TWO MEN hopped off the tram into the early evening's long shadows and walked slowly down the road, trying to attract as little attention as possible. O'Neill couldn't help noticing that the air was saltier here than in the middle of Dublin, making him feel tired, and the gentle breeze reminded him that he had not eaten all day. His stomach grumbled loudly. 'I could murder a brew and a piece,' O'Neill said to McNamara, who did an excellent impression of ignoring him as he fantasized about a mountainous greasy Ulster fry.

It was almost as if their close shave in the Monto and the GPO had pushed McNamara deeper into himself, becoming more taciturn than ever. He'd said hardly two words to O'Neill since they'd got on the tram and the Ulsterman was beginning to appreciate why so many people gave McNamara a wide berth and why so many people thought that he was dangerous.

'So why are we going to Kingstown?' O'Neill had asked but McNamara hadn't deigned to answer; he simply gave him a sidelong glance and then returned to staring out of the tram window. O'Neill had the uncomfortable feeling that McNamara was keeping something back from him, until it was too late for him to do anything about it. 'Shouldn't we have checked in by now?' O'Neill began but McNamara cut him off.

'Not here, not now. I'll fill you in when we get there. Jakers, will you just have a little faith. Trust me.' O'Neill felt far from reassured; the last thing he felt like doing was trusting his companion but in the circumstances he didn't feel like he had much choice either. He gave a deep sigh and glanced out of the window, trying to conceal his nervousness; he had never really looked at Dublin before.

It's funny, he thought, how people never really stop and look around them. Even when he'd been a recruit at the RIC depot in Phoenix Park he'd never really bothered to explore the Empire's second city. After all, where he came from Dublin was the nearest thing to Sodom and Gomorrah a Limavady boy could come across. Despite being his nation's capital, O'Neill never really felt at home in Dublin, with its strange accents and its grand Georgian streets that contrasted starkly with the red-brick industrial linen towns that he called home. Whilst Belfast looked more like Manchester, with its linen mills and shipyards, than with any other town in Ireland, O'Neill was an Antrim country boy at heart.

The Empire had brought prosperity to the north but it had not brought peace, far from it. There was a dark side to his homeland; beneath the prosperity was a land fractured by sectarian hatreds that all too often flared into self-destructive violence and O'Neill prayed for the day that his people would see beyond how they worshipped their God and saw that they were all Irishmen and women who were being exploited by the British state.

'Don't look so guilty and stop drawing attention to yourself,' McNamara said quietly. 'If you sit there looking like you expect to be arrested then it will only be a matter of time before you are, you should know that.' O'Neill knew that he was right; after all, his experience in the RIC had taught him that.

'Won't they be looking for us?' O'Neill asked.

McNamara shook his head. 'Why should they be? It's not like what happened doesn't happen every day,' McNamara said matter-of-factly. 'Besides, they haven't got a clue who we are, so who will they look for? We're not local boys so the G Men won't be looking for us,' he said, referring to the plain clothes detectives of the Dublin Metropolitan Police's G Division, its detective branch. 'The G Men'll be too busy keeping an eye on the local players anyway.'

He'd often heard policemen refer to active rebels as 'players' but it was strange to hear an IRA man use the term. It was as if the Troubles were some sort of game and, somehow, sadly, it seemed to make sense – after all, regardless of side, unless you were in the game you did your damnedest to get on with life as best you could. Trust the British, O'Neill thought, to treat the destiny of Ireland like some sort of glorified cricket match! If indeed it wasn't the winning or losing but the taking part that mattered to the Brits, then it puzzled him how on earth they had managed to build their bloody Empire in the first place!

'You still haven't told me why we are going to Kingstown?' O'Neill asked as they stepped off the tram.

'Settling an overdue account.' McNamara scanned the street, alert, his hands thrust deep into his raincoat pockets.

'I must say, Mick, my boy, you've cleared everything up nicely. Now I know exactly what we are doing, I'm much happier indeed.' O'Neill paused momentarily, trying to contain his anger and frustration. 'Now, if you don't give me a straight bloody answer, I'm going to get back on the bloody tram!'

'All right, O'Neill, I'll tell you why we are here. Commandant MacEoin—' O'Neill had never heard McNamara use Sean MacEoin's Volunteer rank before and it made him suspicious '— wants us to take care of some unfinished business for him,' he lied. 'You see, that loyalist tart of your former comrade-in-arms, Constable Flynn, is hiding out around here and the boss wants us to use her to flush him out from under whatever stone he's hiding under and take care of him.'

'Are you sure? Sean didn't mention any of this to me,' O'Neill began suspiciously but McNamara cut him short.

'Why would he? You're only along for the ride because the boss couldn't spare anyone else; if he had, then I could have offloaded you on GHQ ages ago.'

'So how do you intend to "flush Flynn out" then?' O'Neill asked, feeling distinctly uncomfortable with the situation. He vaguely remembered McNamara waving a letter around and shrieking like a banshee when he had been censoring the mail with O'Brien back in Gaigue. He rolled his eyes. 'Please don't tell me this has got something to do with that blasted letter you were blathering on about?'

'And what if it is? I put it back in the post and Flynn will have got it by now, so I expect that he'll be winging his way to the seaside to see his slapper any time now. All we have to do is find her and then wait and if we're lucky that shite Maguire will be with him, and we'll kill two birds with one stone.'

'I'm not so sure.'

O'Neill had got along well with the young Dubliner back in Drumlish and he wasn't keen on seeing Flynn dead; to be honest, he wasn't keen on doing anything until he'd spoken to someone in GHQ. He didn't trust McNamara one bit. 'First things first, we need to find somewhere to stay and get some scoff. Shouldn't be too difficult. It's not like its high season or anything – there are bound to be loads of places with space. Then we have to find Mellifont Avenue. That's where we'll find the loyalist bitch,' McNamara announced as he strode off towards the seafront, with its myriad guest houses and hotels. 'You still got your warrant card?' he asked nonchalantly.

O'Neill nodded, confirming that he still had his RIC identity card with him and asked, 'Why do you want to know?'

'Because it will come in useful!' McNamara replied.

By the time they reached the seafront the wind had picked up and a slight spray was whipping in from Dublin Bay. O'Neill didn't like the seaside at the best of times and although his family dragged him up to wind-blown Portrush as a child he'd avoided the sea like the plague whenever he could. He had too many bad memories of vomiting over the side of troopships to be taken in by the 'romance' of the sea.

It was then that O'Neill noticed the rows of salt-rimed Georgian houses sporting 'Vacancies' signs in their neat bay windows and doily-lace curtains. McNamara drew short in front of one of the less ostentatious hotels, the very originally named 'Sea View'. 'This will do,' he said, and climbed the steps without waiting for O'Neill to acquiesce.

It was dark by the time they had finished eating greasy egg and chips, washed down with strong orange tea. 'Drink up, O'Neill,' McNamara said, through a mouthful of egg-sodden bread. 'There's work to be done!' He pushed back his chair and stood waiting by the door of the deserted dining room for O'Neill to put down his tea and join him.

'Is everything to your liking, gentlemen?' the landlady asked as she emerged smiling from the kitchen to collect their dirty plates.

'It's grand, Mrs Doyle, just grand!' McNamara beamed, as O'Neill pushed past him into the hall.

'I'll be locking up at ten, gentlemen,' Mrs Doyle said. 'So make sure that you're back by then, please. Besides, it's not good to be out and about at night these days. You'll not want to be out after curfew, gentlemen,' Mrs Doyle added.

'Sure, we'll be back long before then. We just thought that we'd take a wee turn along the prom before turning in,' McNamara said, trying to avoid being drawn into conversation with Mrs Doyle. Ever since they had arrived at her boarding house she had been trying to fathom out who they were and what they were doing in Kingstown, not because she was being exceptionally nosey but because that was just the way people were in these parts.

She smiled sweetly, accepting that her latest probe had been neatly parried, and proceeded to clear the table with feigned disregard for what the two men were up to. She consoled herself with the thought that they'd crack soon enough and let slip, especially if their 'turn along the seafront' took them past a pub or two. She'd not met an Irish man yet who hadn't kissed the blarney stone after being in his cups.

'Nosey bitch!' McNamara declared out in the street, flipping up the collar of his overcoat against the evening chill. 'Come on, it's this way.' McNamara's shoes crunched on the cold ground and as O'Neill followed, he felt his joints aching arthritically, a memento, like Flynn's, of his time in the trenches. He found it hard to match his companion's rangy gait. He could sense McNamara's impatience as he bowled on down Queen's Road past the yacht clubs and the marina with its bobbing boats chafing at their moorings in the breeze. If he'd been in the mood, which was unlikely, O'Neill would probably have found the whistling of the wind through the boats' shrouds musical, magical even.

It was cold and the backing offshore wind cut through O'Neill like a razor as it whipped spray across the street and made a sterling attempt to wrench his hat from his head. 'We're here,' McNamara suddenly announced when they stood on the corner of Mellifont Avenue and Victoria Terrace. He leant against the wall and nodded in the direction of a row of Georgian townhouses. 'The bitch is over there.' The heavens opened and it started tipping down with rain.

'Great! So what now, big fella, eh?' O'Neill declared.

'Get back!' McNamara snapped and shoved O'Neill into the shadows. 'Peelers!' he hissed as he saw two blue uniformed Dublin Metropolitan Police constables strolling down the street towards them. Instinctively his hand pawed the gun nestling in his coat pocket. The policemen stopped outside a house halfway up the street and, after a brief discussion, knocked on the door. A shaft of light lunged out into the night, silhouetting what looked like a middle-aged woman. O'Neill could feel the tension in McNamara as he watched. The woman said something inaudible and the policemen stepped into the light.

'Shit!' McNamara cursed. 'That's the house. That's the flaming house.' He was angry, frustrated even. 'Blast, we'll have to come back tomorrow. I want a wee word with young Miss Moore. Come on, let's get back and get some sleep. We have a long and busy day ahead.'

CHAPTER 39

Sunday, 21 November 1920, Phoenix Park, Dublin

IT WAS STILL dark and the RIC depot was deserted, on the cusp of waking, when Flynn and Maguire made their way through the morning chill to the MT office at the south-western corner of the parade ground. Their shoes crunched loudly on the gravel and Maguire was sulking because when he'd told Flynn they would go to Kingstown in the morning, he had hoped it would be after breakfast.

'I thought that we'd get an early start,' Flynn had said cheerily but Maguire just blew noisily on his hands, in an exaggerated attempt to keep warm, and muttered darkly. Unsurprisingly, the MT office was closed. It was quiet, the lights off, and through the window Flynn could see a figure slumped in an armchair nestled up to a pot-bellied stove. It was the MT department's duty driver, napping. Flynn rapped loudly on the flaking green-painted door. A hacking cough punctuated the stillness of the office and a muffled voice cursed as the door scraped open, revealing the freshly woken incumbent. He had all the dishevelled charm of a man robbed of his sleep.

'What?' the man said irritably in a thick English west country accent that betrayed his anger, suspicion and foreignness.

'We've come to collect our car,' Flynn said, flashing his warrant card.

The constable looked in disbelief at the clock – it said 6.32 a.m., and then back at the two men. 'What bloody car. It's half six! This is the first I've heard of this, so go away and come back later when the MT officer gets in. Now piss off.' He went to close the door but Maguire gently shoved Flynn aside and wedged his foot in the door, forcing it open. His face was deathly pale, his eyes dark and dangerous, and as he smiled at the Englishman, his face reminded Flynn of a skull.

'Excuse me, Constable, what is your name and number?' Maguire smiled sweetly, his head cocked to one side.

'Why do you want to know?' the constable asked nervously, looking at Maguire's empty eyes with renewed suspicion.

'Well, my friend, I need to be able to tell Brigadier General Winter, the director of intelligence operations in Ireland, who countermanded his orders and refused to give us the transport he authorized. That is why, my friend.' The constable visibly paled. 'Look, I've got the director's personal phone number here ...' Maguire began rummaging in his pocket. 'Why don't you give him a call and discuss it with him? I'm sure that he'll appreciate the early-morning alarm call; after all, he's usually up and about at this hour. Who are you again, old chap?' Maguire gave the constable a sickly sweet rictus smile and held out a folded piece of writing paper between the first two fingers of his right hand. The constable stared at it for a few moments and licked his lips as Maguire waved the paper gently under his nose.

'All right, all right, that really won't be necessary. You can have that one over there ...' He pointed at a brown touring car parked in the corner of the MT yard. Maguire beamed as he took the vehicle's paperwork from the constable, who was obviously glad to be shot of them.

'Thank you ever so much, old chap, that'll do nicely. It's been a pleasure doing business with you. I'll be sure to tell the director how helpful you've been.'

Despite the cold and damp, the car started smoothly enough and the bored sentry showed no curiosity whatsoever as they pulled out of the camp – people came and went at all sorts of strange hours anyway.

The depot approach road was lined with tall trees and Flynn turned left at the junction, opposite the civil service cricket ground onto Chesterfield Avenue, the wide, straight boulevard that slashed straight across the middle of Phoenix Park, like a knife wound leading out of the park into the heart of the capital. He reckoned that it would take about half an hour to drive the twelve or so miles to Kingstown and he didn't expect any traffic.

Weak tendrils of autumn sunlight had begun to creep through the city's streets by the time they had reached the banks of the Liffey and they drove along the north bank, past the grey stone edifice of Royal Barracks. It was early and Dublin was having a lie-in, like the lazy city always did every Sunday. 'For a moment, back there, I thought that we'd be walking!' Flynn said.

'Always ask an officious twat for their name and they start flapping.

It works every time!' Maguire joked, as he slouched back in his seat, pulling his hat over his eyes. 'Now be a good chappie, would you? Shut up and drive. Wake me when we get there.'

CHAPTER 40

Sunday, 21 November 1920, Kingstown, County Dublin

'I'M COMING! I'M coming!' Kathleen's Aunt Rebecca called, as she scurried down the hall to the front door, doing up her housecoat. It was early, 6.47 by the hall clock, and she wondered who on earth would be knocking on her door at such an ungodly hour on a Sunday morning. She didn't go to Mass that often so she rarely rose early on Sundays outside the holiday season, and hoped that it wasn't some priest coming to berate her.

Through the front door's frosted glass she could see the outline of two men on the doorstep and keeping the door on the chain secured she opened the door a little and peered through the gap. One of the men held up an RIC warrant card and smiled reassuringly. 'Good morning, ma'am, I'm sorry to disturb you at this early hour on a Sunday,' he said ingratiatingly, in a soft Northern Irish accent. 'My name is Detective Constable O'Neill and this is my colleague Detective Constable McNamara. May we come in, please?' McNamara flashed Aunt Rebecca a warm, friendly smile as she took the door off the chain and swung it open.

'Is there something wrong, Constable? It's just two of your colleagues called around last night. They said it was just a routine check but nothing seems to be routine these days.'

'It's nothing to be alarmed about, ma'am. Please, could you tell me if there is a Miss Kathleen Moore from Drumlish living at this address?'

Aunt Rebecca looked worried. 'She's not in any trouble, is she?'

McNamara smiled pleasantly. 'No, not at all, we just need a wee chat with her, that's all. She's not in any trouble. Could you go fetch her for us, please?'

Aunt Rebecca directed the two men into the guests' parlour at the front of the house and invited them to sit before leaving to fetch

Kathleen. McNamara plonked himself on a gaudily coloured chaise longue and looked around the over-stuffed room full of pot plants and photographs whilst O'Neill stood at the large Georgian window, looking up and down the street. It was still quiet and the leaden sky promised more rain to come. He felt nervous. McNamara still hadn't explained his plan to him and he wasn't convinced that they really were acting on orders from MacEoin. 'Look, I think that we should go. I've got a bad feeling about this.' The look on McNamara's face told O'Neill that he had no intention of leaving without seeing Kathleen and with a deep sigh of resignation the Ulsterman went back to looking out of the window. He could hear the cries of the gulls coming in from the sea as they wheeled overhead.

Kathleen followed her aunt into the parlour and looked at the two men waiting for her. The man by the window looked vaguely familiar, as if she had seen him before somewhere, but she couldn't quite place him. He turned and smiled and then the penny dropped. 'Constable O'Neill! I didn't recognize you without your uniform.' She smiled. 'So what brings you all the way from Drumlish?'

'The same thing that brought you here in the first place, Miss Moore. Kevin Flynn.'

'Kevin? What about Kevin? Has anything happened to him?' She looked afraid.

'Has he been in touch?' McNamara asked.

Kathleen looked blankly at him and then back at O'Neill. 'What's the matter?' she asked again.

'Nothing to worry about – we just need to talk to Kevin. Has he been in touch since you wrote to him?' McNamara asked. Suddenly Kathleen felt a knot in her stomach. How did they know that she'd written to Flynn? She tried to stay calm but she could already feel her head begin to spin. O'Neill was speaking again in his soft Ulster accent, dripping with forced concern and sincerity … just like the voice of the man who had threatened her when her father had been beaten up.

'I know you!' she blurted, suddenly afraid.

O'Neill smiled reassuringly. 'Of course you do, Kathleen. I worked with Kevin over in Drumlish.'

'No! I know you. I know you. It was you … it was you …' Her voice trailed away. Aunt Rebecca looked confused as she glanced from Kathleen to the two policemen. 'You threatened to kill me!' Kathleen said quietly.

'Don't be ridiculous,' O'Neill said. 'Why would I do that, eh?'

'I think you gentlemen should leave,' Aunt Rebecca interjected, placing herself between the policemen and the girl. 'I think that my niece has answered enough questions for now.' She turned her back on the men and placed a comforting hand on Kathleen's shoulder.

'Aw, sod this!' McNamara snapped, pulling a stiletto from his coat pocket and seizing a fistful of Aunt Rebecca's red hair, jerking her head back so that her chin pointed towards the ceiling. The woman's green eyes widened in terror and surprise as she felt the point of the knife dig into the flesh at the side of her neck. Its rubbery surface resisted momentarily before giving way under the pressure with a quiet ripping sound. McNamara smiled as he felt the blade grate against the woman's spine as it burrowed into the gap between it and her windpipe before he wrenched his arm forward, tearing through it in a welter of spraying blood that splashed across the girl's face. Kathleen screamed.

O'Neill was rooted to the spot as the full horror of what had just happened crashed down on him like a hammer blow. 'What the hell did you do that for?' O'Neill shouted in disbelief. McNamara let Aunt Rebecca's twitching body fall to the floor like a discarded rag. A grotesque gargling noise rasped from her severed trachea as she rapidly exsanguinated onto the parlour carpet, convulsing momentarily before lying quietly in the spreading incardine puddle.

'Where's Flynn?' McNamara asked coldly, his normally dead eyes shining with near orgasmic excitement as he waved the gore-stained blade at Kathleen. Terror crashed through her body, momentarily paralyzing her, her eyes transfixed by her aunt's bloody corpse and instincts of fear, fight or flight sent a surge of adrenalin coursing through her body. Kathleen ran.

'What the hell did you do that for?' O'Neill shouted again and McNamara lunged forward, seizing a handful of Kathleen's hair just as she reached the parlour door. She screamed as her head wrenched backwards and he yanked her off her feet back into the room, where she landed on her back with a thud, leaving her winded and gasping for breath. Something warm and sticky soaked through the back of her dress and her hands were wet. She screamed again. 'Shut it, bitch!' McNamara hissed and he kicked her violently in the side.

'Jesus, what did you do that for?' O'Neill repeated. He could already feel the noose tightening around his neck. McNamara straddled Kathleen, pinning her to the floor as he grasped one of her breasts and squeezed it in his left hand, holding the gore-gobbeted knife blade millimetres from her right eye, hovering over the pupil. She blinked involuntarily as something dripped into her eye and sobbed, mesmerized by the razor tip, as it trickled like a scarlet tear down her face.

'Mmm … well, I can see what that shite Flynn sees in you,' he muttered, as he groped her. 'Now, let's start again, shall we? Where is Flynn?'

'I don't know.'

'Wrong answer, bitch! I wonder how much he'll fancy you after I've taken your eye, eh?' He pushed his weight down on her, pushing his groin against her stomach. Kathleen keened pathetically as the blade began to descend towards her right eye. Sickened, O'Neill turned his back on the nightmare that was unfolding in the guesthouse parlour.

He didn't want this but short of shooting McNamara he couldn't see any way of making it stop. He dragged his old police revolver from his coat pocket and cocked it with a gentle click. He knew that he had no choice if he was to end the insanity. The hairs rose on the back of his neck and he steadied his trembling hands as he gave one last look up the street, just as a brown touring car swung around the corner and glided to a halt in the street outside. The driver glanced across the street and up at the ground parlour window and straight into O'Neill's eyes. It was Flynn. O'Neill was suddenly afraid, very, very afraid. 'Jesus Christ, it's them!'

McNamara paused, looking up, his eyes shining in excitement, the blade almost touching Kathleen's eye. 'What?' he asked, looking at O'Neill.

'It's Flynn … shit … Maguire is with him!'

McNamara grinned like a Cheshire cat. 'It must be Christmas!' He twisted his hand into Kathleen's hair and tugged her to her feet. 'I'm going to enjoy this.'

CHAPTER 41

Sunday, 21 November 1920, Kingstown, County Dublin

WHAT THE ... IT can't be, Flynn thought, doing a double take as he climbed out of the car and looked straight into O'Neill's eyes. 'Joe, it's that bastard O'Neill!' he shouted and ran across the road towards the front door. Maguire was about to speak when the parlour window exploded and a bullet ricocheted off the cobbled street, punching a hole through one of the car's rear doors.

'Now, the MTO won't be liking that!' Maguire shouted as he ducked back down behind the car, pulling out his gun and cocking it. 'Are you all right, Kevin?' he shouted across the street to Flynn, who was now huddled in the doorway. He ducked down as two more shots rang out, shattering the frosted glass above Flynn's head. Flynn gave Maguire a 'thumbs up' and despite feeling like crying inside, he forced himself to smile.

'O'Neill! Come out with your hands up!' Flynn shouted.

Bang! Another chunk of wood flew from the door frame, causing Flynn to squirm before snatching a quick glance through the tattered remains of the frosted window. Kathleen was streaked in blood, her wavy hair matted with gore, struggling, her head forced back by a forearm locked around her neck whilst McNamara stood behind her, shielding himself with her body, his arm straight out, pointing his gun at the door.

Wide-eyed, she jerked when she saw Flynn's head poke over the broken glass, throwing McNamara's aim as he snatched a shot. The bullet went wide, ploughing into the coving in a shower of plaster dust. Flynn ducked down again, panting to control his breath. 'Shit!' he muttered before shouting, 'If you harm her, McNamara, I swear ...'

Bang! A bullet smashed through one of the lower panels of the door, missing his head by inches as he huddled lower, wrapping his arms around his head. Blood pounded in his ears and he fought to overcome the paralysis that was creeping through him. 'If you don't move, you die,' he heard a voice shouting inside his head, the same voice that had kept him alive during the war. Move or die!

Maguire cursed under his breath and glanced up and down the street, steeling himself to move, feeling the tension building in his leg muscles, feeling his heart hammering on his ribcage. Heads were poking out of doors and windows as people were drawn by the ruckus they were causing. 'Call the police!' he shouted frantically, hoping that someone in middle-class Kingstown was still willing to cooperate with the authorities. Then, he was up and running, head down, to join Flynn on the front steps, as fast as his legs would carry him. He let out a guttural growl as he flung himself down heavily besides his cringing companion. 'So, what's the plan?' he said, flashing Flynn a toothy grin.

For a fleeting moment O'Neill had to remind himself that he wasn't back in the trenches. The house had become an abattoir, the walls daubed with blood and as everything spiralled horribly out of control he felt his life slipping through his fingers like fine sand. He had to do something and he knew that if it wasn't soon, he'd be dead. McNamara stood in the hallway grappling with Kathleen, who he was trying to use as a shield. O'Neill looked down at the bloody footprints on the carpet and then back at the mess in the middle of the parlour floor that had once been Kathleen's Aunt Rebecca. O'Neill wasn't a squeamish man but the sheer pointlessness of it all made him feel sick.

'Sean never ordered this!' he shouted at McNamara. 'Sean would never have ordered this, you fecking lunatic! Christ, you're on your own, you sick bastard!' O'Neill made a break for the back of the house.

'Come back, you gutless shit!' McNamara shouted and struggled around to snap a shot off at O'Neill as he vanished through the door at the end of the hall. Seeing her chance, Kathleen managed to wrench herself free and sank her teeth into McNamara's wrist, tearing the flesh and drawing dark blood. 'Bitch!' he shrieked as she broke free and sprinted up the stairs, screaming in blind terrified panic. Frantically, McNamara snapped off another two shots at the front door before dashing up the stairs after Kathleen.

'I'm going to kill you, you loyalist bitch!' he shouted, clearing the stairs two at a time whilst, ahead, Kathleen rushed blindly on without a thought of where she was going or what she would do. She spat several times to try and get the fragments and taste of McNamara's blood from her mouth and felt herself heave as she fought off the urge to vomit.

Flynn heard McNamara scream and raised his head again just in time to see the gunman's heels disappearing up the stairs. He grabbed Maguire by the collar and heaved him to his feet. 'C'mon, the bastard is getting away!' He shoved the shattered doorway open and the two men stepped cautiously into the hallway, weapons at the ready. Every nerve, every fibre of Flynn's body screamed at him as he walked the razor's edge between life and death.

Thud! Thud! Thud! The hand grenade bounced down the stairs into the hallway. Instinct kicked in. 'GRENADE!' Flynn screamed, diving through the parlour door, luging across the bloodstained carpet and thudding into the body that sprawled in the middle of the room. Maguire was slower and the blast caught him just as he tumbled down the front steps. The grenade shredded the hallway, wrecking the clock and shattering what was left of the windows before tearing the remnant of the front door from its hinges with a loud crash.

Flynn coughed violently, clearing the blood that was pouring from his nose. His ears were ringing painfully and as his vision cleared, he found himself staring into Aunt Rebecca's dead-fish eyes. 'Jesus.' He grimaced and pushed himself up onto his knees. Blood was everywhere. 'Joe, are you all right?' he shouted. There was a grunt from the hallway. Flynn gave a quick look up the stairs before dashing back to the front door where Maguire was slumped. 'Joe!' he shouted again, ears ringing, oblivious of the volume of his voice.

Maguire's face was a bloody mess. His left eye socket oozed dark blood and a fragment of shrapnel had gouged a deep trough along his left cheek, leaving a small flap of skin that exposed the muscle and bone below. He was staring, fascinated, at his left hand – the index and middle fingers were missing. 'Bugger!' Maguire muttered repeatedly as he turned his hand around, mesmerized by the blood that dripped from the shattered stump of his hand. 'I've lost my fingers!' he finally declared and Flynn resisted the compulsive urge to point at the severed digits in the street and say, 'No you haven't, they're over there!' Somehow, he didn't think that Maguire would appreciate the joke.

He quickly ran his hands over Maguire but thankfully couldn't find any other injuries. The dark oozing blood told him that the grenade fragments hadn't cut an artery, so at least Maguire wouldn't bleed out on the steps. Flynn saw a floral embroidered cloth lying crumpled on the hall floor and, keeping one eye on the stairs, snatched it up and tore it in half lengthways, wrapping it around Maguire's shattered hand. He used the other half to bandage his comrade's head. 'I'll not lie to you, Joe, you look a mess but you'll live. Now, you sit here a while and rest. I'm going to get McNamara.' Maguire's head lolled slightly and Flynn shook him violently. 'Stay awake! Don't go to sleep, Joe!' Maguire looked at him with his good eye and nodded, giving him a weak smile, exposing his bloodstained teeth.

McNamara hadn't bothered to see if the grenade had taken care of Flynn and Maguire; he had just dropped it and run. If Flynn was still alive he could deal with him later; right now, he was more interested in catching Kathleen and taking care of her. Even better if Flynn was only wounded by the blast, then he could watch Kathleen die before he finished him off too.

By the time Kathleen reached the third floor she realized that there was nowhere to go and, as there were no guests, was no one to help her either. She darted through one of the bedroom doors and slammed it closed behind her, fumbling with the flimsy lock before rushing to the window. She wrenched the window open, looking frantically for the fire escape. 'No!' she wailed. She was in the wrong room; the fire escape was next door. She looked down for a fleeting moment, contemplating jumping before she accepted that the drop would probably kill her. She paused for a moment to watch O'Neill throw away his coat and dash for the back gate, before she turned and ran back to the door.

Although it seemed like longer, it only took a second or two to unlock the door and swing it open. She froze. McNamara was standing at the top of the stairs, his back to her. He heard the door click open and turned slowly. He smiled. 'Hello, Kathleen.'

She tried to slam the door but McNamara threw his full weight against the door, forcing it inwards and hurling Kathleen across the bedroom, where she crashed into the washstand in a flurry of splintered wood and broken porcelain. Her landing drove the air from her lungs and before she could get up she felt a savage blow crash into her ribs. Sobbing, she crumpled to the floor and McNamara kicked her again.

'Get up, bitch!' he ordered as he wound his hand into her hair again and heaved her to her feet. McNamara held her face close to his own. He was so close she could smell him. He smiled, all teeth, like a shark, and gazed into her eyes, basking in her fear. He was enjoying himself.

Flynn heard a crash and a scream on the floor above and made a lunge for the last flight of stairs. Unthinking, he cleared them two or three at a time in his haste to get to Kathleen, oblivious of the possibility that McNamara could be waiting for him at the top. When he reached the top landing he frantically looked around, his weapon held cocked, ready, in front of him. One of the bedroom doors was stoved in, hanging on its hinges, and he heard a piercing scream and a loud thud. 'You bitch!' He heard McNamara's voice from the direction of the room and walked towards it.

Flynn saw Kathleen's swollen cheek and black eye above McNamara's forearm clamped firmly around her throat, shielding his body, his chin level with the girl's right ear. His pistol was pressed upwards, deep into the soft part of her throat, threatening to splatter her brains over the ceiling. His eyes were wide, shining with manic excitement and he smiled when he saw Flynn in the doorway.

'Take another step and I'll k ...' McNamara began to say. The bullet smashed through his front teeth, gouged along his tongue and tore through his spine at the base of the skull, severing his spinal cord and sending his quadriplegic body crashing against the wall. The Luger tumbled from his nerveless fingers and went off as it bounced on the floor, drilling a hole in the skirting board near the door. Kathleen fell to the floor and sat in a puddle of urine as her bladder gave out and, wide-eyed in stunned silence, she watched Flynn walk slowly, deliberately, across the room towards McNamara's limp body. Flynn thought that he saw McNamara's eyes move slightly as if they were following him.

'I didn't come here for a chat,' he muttered before firing three more shots into the gunman's head in rapid succession, ruining what was left of his face and shattering his skull. 'That's for Jim.' Flynn stood looking down at McNamara for what seemed like an age, as if he were trying to fathom what he had just done. He looked stunned and the pistol dropped from his hand with a dull thud as he fell to his knees next to Kathleen. She fell into his arms and it was only then that she noticed that he was trembling, even more than she was. 'You're safe now,' he muttered, and then, sobbing with relief, she kissed him passionately.

'Shit! Where's the key? Where's the bloody key?' O'Neill cursed, as he frantically scrabbled around for the back door key. The grenade blast was contained in the front hall but he flinched all the same before pulling his revolver from his coat pocket and firing twice at the lock. The noise was deafening in the confines of the kitchen and hurt his ears but the lock fell apart as he hoped.

After several fierce kicks the door finally moved and O'Neill was through it and into the back garden. He looked down at his bloodstained overcoat and discarded it by the back steps before looking around quickly for an escape route. He ran off down the path, through the gate and off into the lane that ran behind the houses and he didn't stop until he reached the corner at the end of the row. Steadying his breathing, O'Neill tried to blot out the receding ringing in his hears and pounding blood rushing through his head.

Cautiously, he edged along the alleyway towards the street, every nerve straining. At least he was alive, not just breathing, but alive, alive in the way that you can only be when death is possibly a heartbeat away. He squatted down low and peered around the corner into Mellifont Avenue. The brown touring car was parked on the other side of the street, about fifty feet away, and if he could only make it there and get it started before Flynn and O'Neill came out of the house he'd be away, scot free.

Slowly, O'Neill rose to his feet and stepped lightly into the road, his weapon held low, out of sight but ready at his side. As he crossed the street he saw someone slumped in the doorway, his face obscured by a bloody swathe of cloth. O'Neill continued walking cautiously towards the driver's side door, pointing his gun at the man.

Maguire opened his eye. It took him a second or two to register that there was a man in the street by the car and it took a second longer again to register that the man was armed and maybe a fraction longer for it to sink in that it was O'Neill. He didn't move.

O'Neill turned away from Maguire and fumbled with the driver's side door. Maguire carefully picked up the gun in his lap and slowly lifted it so that it was pointing at O'Neill. His hand was trembling as he took up the pressure on the trigger. O'Neill felt something slam into his shoulder, hurling him into the side of the car, catching his face on the edge of the door as he fell to his knees. He put his hand up to his left shoulder and grunted and felt the blood seeping through his torn jacket. He could move his arm so the bullet hadn't shattered his shoulder. O'Neill looked around to see Maguire levering himself to his feet and staggering down the steps towards him, his gun held out threateningly. O'Neill slowly began to raise his own weapon.

'Go on, just try it!' Maguire barked. 'I won't miss next time.' O'Neill sighed and let the pistol drop to the cobbles with a thud and slumped against the car, just as a khaki armoured lorry swung around the corner. Thank God, Maguire thought. The army had arrived.

Sitting anxiously in the front passenger seat of the armoured lorry, Sergeant Grey didn't have a clue what the hell was going on, only that there was some garbled message about a shooting on the seafront. 'Stop!' Grey barked at the driver as the vehicle skidded across Mellifont Avenue's cobbles, slewing to a halt in the middle of the street. He could see two men, one sat with his back to a parked brown car and another standing over him, his head wrapped in a bloody bandage, pointing a gun at the sitting man's head. Grey jumped out of the cab, his hobnails crunching on the cobbles. 'Debus! Enemy front!' he shouted and several more soldiers tumbled out of the back, in a well-rehearsed drill, clutching rifles with bayonets fixed, glittering in the morning sun. They swiftly formed a skirmish line across the street, pointing their rifles at Maguire and O'Neill like a firing squad. Maguire looked at the sergeant and was about to speak.

'Help!' O'Neill shrieked. 'I'm a policeman and this man is trying to kill me!'

'Don't move or I fire!' Sergeant Grey shouted firmly. 'Put down the weapon. Put it down now!' Maguire hesitated momentarily and then let the gun fall to the ground. 'Put your hands up!' the NCO ordered and Maguire slowly raised his arms above his head. It was only then that Grey noticed the swathe of bandages on the man's left hand.

'Thank God you've got here. I thought he was going to kill me, so I did!' O'Neill said, as he began to struggle to his feet.

'Stay down!' Grey barked at O'Neill, who slumped back down. 'Herriot! Garbut! Get their weapons!' the sergeant commanded and two soldiers, weapons ready, cautiously approached O'Neill and Maguire, kicking the discarded handguns away from the two men.

'Don't listen to him …' Maguire began.

'Shut it, Paddy!' Grey barked.

'I'm a policeman. Constable Gary O'Neill, RIC special operations. Look …' He began to reach into his jacket.

'Stay still!' Grey barked again, his bayonet a foot or so from O'Neill's face. O'Neill froze and moved his hand gently away from his body. 'Garbut.' The sergeant looked at one of the soldiers and then nodded at O'Neill. Private Garbut groped inside O'Neill's jacket and tugged his warrant card from his inside pocket and flipped it open.

'Look, Sarge,' Garbut said, showing the card to Grey. 'He is a copper.'

Grey pointed at another soldier with a Red Cross satchel slung over his shoulder and beckoned the man over. 'Davies, take care of Constable

O'Neill.' He turned to Maguire and drove his rifle butt into his side, sending him crashing on to the floor. Fresh blood wept through his bandages. 'Get this piece of Shinner shit over by the wagon.' Maguire lay panting, weighing up his options, but he knew had none.

O'Neill was on his feet, wiggling his fingers, testing his arm; it hurt like hell but at least he could move it. He smiled as one of the soldiers handed him his .38 police revolver and when Sergeant Grey asked him what was going on he tucked it into the waistband of his trousers and began to explain.

Maguire stood by the lorry staring at him with barely disguised hatred. O'Neill groaned and clutched his shoulder. 'There's an IRA gunman in there. This one shot me as he was making a break for it. If you hadn't got here, well ...' His voice trailed off.

'He's a bit of a mess,' Grey said, looking at Maguire.

'Dead on. He tried to get me with a grenade but cocked it up. I think my partner is still in there.' O'Neill sagged against the car and groaned, exaggerating his weakened state.

'Quick, Davies, you can drive. Take this car and get the constable to hospital. Move it!' Grey shouted as he bundled O'Neill into the back of the car. Davies started the engine and the vehicle, the touring car, lurched off down the road and seconds later it was around the corner and away. Grey was unsure what to do next.

Bang! Bang! Bang! Bang! Four shots rang out in rapid succession from inside the house and Grey and his soldiers instinctively scattered for cover in the doorways and gates of the neighbouring houses. Maguire didn't move. He shook his head slowly and Grey thought he could see a trace of a smile, causing him to angrily sprint over to Maguire and backhand him across the face. A tear of blood trickled down the Irishman's cheek. 'What's so funny, you Fenian shit? Who's inside? Tell me now!'

'Ask him!' Maguire said, flicking his head towards the front door of the house, and as Grey looked around he saw a bloodied man standing in the doorway holding a blood-soaked young woman in his arms. He was holding something out in front of him at arm's length.

'Don't shoot!' the man called. 'I'm a policeman!'

'Stand still!' Grey ordered, nervously pointing his rifle at the couple in the doorway.

Flynn pulled Kathleen up short and raised his hands slowly above his head as unthreateningly as possible. 'My name is Constable Kevin Flynn. I'm RIC! Special operations! Don't shoot!'

'Come down slowly and keep your hands where I can see them,' Grey ordered and Flynn walked slowly down the steps, followed by Kathleen, holding out his warrant card for the sergeant to see. Grey scanned it quickly and relaxed. Flynn dropped his arms and gathered Kathleen, trembling, back into them, comforting her quietly, stroking her hair.

Flynn looked at Maguire and where the car should be and then back at Grey. 'What's going on here?'

'We stopped this one from shooting your oppo. It's all right, one of my men has taken him to hospital. I hope you don't mind us using your car?'

'That *is* my oppo, as you put it, Sergeant,' Flynn snapped and Maguire smiled, waving his bloody hand at Sergeant Grey. 'The man you've sent to hospital is a bloody IRA spy!' Sergeant Grey's face went ashen as the awful truth of what he had done sank in.

O'Neill placed the pistol against the back of Davies's head. 'Pull over here, sonny.' Davies stopped the car. 'Now get out and leave the engine running. Face the wall and keep your hands above your head.' Davies's knees felt weak as he climbed out of the car and stood facing a brick wall. His mind's eye kept seeing his brains dripping down it and he felt sick. 'Now run!' O'Neill ordered coldly and the soldier ran back the way they had come. O'Neill climbed into the driver's seat and, tucking his gun underneath his right thigh, he drove back towards the middle of Dublin.

CHAPTER 42

Sunday, 21 November 1920, Dublin Castle

'JESUS CHRIST, THIRTEEN flaming dead that we know of and another six wounded! What a bloody mess.' Head Constable Eugene Igoe slumped back in his chair and looked at Flynn. The city was in chaos. It had been a bad day. 'How the hell did the Shinners know where our men were?'

Flynn looked down at the head constable in confusion. 'What's happened?'

'The IRA found out where several of our people were staying and about nine o'clock this morning they shot seventeen of them. Like I said, at least thirteen are dead, so far. God knows how many of the wounded won't make it through the night. Thankfully, most of the people they shot weren't doing intelligence work, but too many for comfort were!'

'How did they find them?' Flynn asked again.

'Because they were sloppy, because they underestimated the flaming enemy, because there are too many little shites like O'Neill and McElligott feeding information to the bloody enemy, that's why. I tell you what; things will be bloody different when I get this new unit of Winter's up and running.' Flynn's jaw dropped with genuine shock. 'For Christ's sake, Constable Flynn, you don't think this is the end of it, do you? Two Auxiliaries were gunned down in Northumberland Street and, as you can imagine, the bloody Auxies are none too pleased, I can tell you. Worse still, a load of them and some of our boys—' he meant members of the regular RIC '—went over to the GAA game at Croke Park this afternoon. The last I heard, there were fourteen dead and Christ knows how many wounded there. One report puts it up at over eighty.'

'I guess that explains all the fuss out on the streets,' Flynn said.

'Oh, it gets better! Our lads caught one of the IRA bastards in Lower

Mount Street, shot him through the ankle. Would have been better if it'd been the head, but that's life, eh? We did have Dick McKee and Peadar Clancy, the so-called brigadier and vice brigadier of the Dublin Brigade and some fella called Conor Clune in custody as well.'

'Did have?'

Igoe looked up, his face drawn and weary as he spoke. 'Aye, did have. All three were shot whilst trying to escape earlier this evening in the Castle guardroom. Mary mother of God, the newspapers are going to have a field day over this. I can see it now ...' He spread out his hands above his head. 'You don't have to be the sharpest pencil in the box to work out they'll be calling it "Bloody Sunday" before the blasted day is out!'

'I suppose that explains all the soldiers and Auxies racing about when I got back from Kingstown,' Flynn said.

'Ah, yes, Kingstown.' Igoe looked up at Flynn. 'I gather that O'Neill got away?' Flynn nodded. 'At least, I hear that you got one of the murdering bastards. What was his name ...' He picked up a sheet of typed paper. 'McNamara. Michael McNamara. Nasty piece of work, so I hear. Well, he'll be up to no mischief anymore. Well done for that. How is the girl, Miss Moore? I gather it was her aunt that this McNamara murdered?'

'She's downstairs with a policewoman. McNamara turned the bloody house into an abattoir. Christ, it was like being back in the trenches. She's pretty shaken but hopefully she'll pull through. Jesus, I hope so.' Igoe gave him one of those concerned looks that all policemen learned to give to members of the public when discussing upsetting events but Flynn saw straight through it, understanding exactly why Igoe was doing it.

'Where's the brigadier?' Flynn asked, looking around.

'Where do you think? He's in a meeting with the rest of the grown-ups to try and work out what we do next to get out of this flaming mess. Rather him than me or you, eh? That's why he gets paid what he does. Let's hope all of this doesn't spook the frock coats in Whitehall into doing something bloody stupid and selling out to the murdering Fenian bastards, eh?' Igoe looked out of the window into the Lower Castle Yard where another couple of army lorries loaded with soldiers were getting ready to set off on another sweep of central Dublin.

'How is Maguire? I hear that he got cut up pretty bad.'

'The doctors are looking at him now. He caught some shrapnel from a grenade and, well, let's say he'll not be winning any beauty competitions but at least he'll live.'

'That's good news, at least. Now that the IRA have managed to knacker the brigadier's intelligence network for the time being we need to be pretty bloody quick-smart setting up a new one. This time will be different, by Christ it will – we need to use Irishmen not bloody English army officers who've read too much bloody Kipling. This isn't some bloody great game, it's a war, a nasty, brutal, shitty little war and it will take men like me, you and Maguire to win it – in short, people who know how the Fenians think. I want you and Maguire to join my new intelligence unit. What do you say?'

It was getting dark when Flynn entered the Lower Castle Yard and the dull orange lamps cast deep shadows around its perimeter. The courtyard was empty and Kathleen sat alone on a low wall near the gate with a voluminous overcoat draped over her shoulders, her wavy red hair blowing gently in the evening breeze as she stared at her feet. She looked deep in thought. Turning up the collar of his coat, Flynn walked towards her, his feet crunching on the gravel. She looked up as he approached and pushed a wayward curl from her face, forcing a smile. He couldn't help but notice how pretty she was. He noticed that they had found her some clean clothes and thanked God that the blood was gone from her face and hands.

'Let's get you out of here,' Flynn said. 'You can stay with my parents.'

'What then?' Kathleen asked.

She stood up and, taking his hands in her own, pressed her head against his chest, her damp red hair ruffling in the breeze. She smelt of soap.

'You know, Kathleen Moore, I love you,' he said quietly.

She smiled and kissed him.

EPILOGUE

Monday, 5 December 1921, Cadogan Gardens, Kensington, London

SPECIAL BRANCH DETECTIVE Sergeant Kevin Flynn had a clear view of the front door of 15 Cadogan Gardens as he leant against the black iron railings on the corner with Cadogan Street and fiddled with the unfamiliar gold band on his right-hand ring finger. He didn't try to hide, there was no point; the occupants of the house knew full well he was watching them. After all, it was his job.

A car pulled up outside the house and Flynn shifted position slightly to get a clearer view as the front door opened and Michael Collins stepped out into the street and looked around, before plonking his hat on his head. Except for the moustache he now sported, he was the spitting image of the photographs Flynn had seen on RIC circulars and montages of wanted rebels.

He was tall and round faced – every inch the 'Big Fellah' his nickname suggested. He nodded at Flynn and, smiling, climbed into the car. It felt strange standing there watching the man who had masterminded so much mayhem and bloodshed over the previous two years. There was a time when Flynn would have tried to arrest him but everything had changed since the ceasefire in July and, as many Irish unionists feared, it was obvious that the British were doing their damnedest to extract themselves from Ireland on the best terms possible by fêting Collins like some sort of celebrity.

'How times have changed, eh? Mick Collins here in London, who'd have thought it.' The middle-class Dublin tones surprised Flynn here in Kensington and he instantly feared the worst as his hand wrapped around the butt of the gun hidden in his coat pocket. He began to draw as he turned on the speaker. 'There's no need for that, Sergeant Flynn. The war's over, after all.' The man looked about twenty-three but seemed much older, his thin face careworn and tired behind his neatly clipped military moustache. Everything about the man was vaguely familiar, like some distant memory, yet Flynn couldn't quite place the voice or the face.

'What brings a Dub to Kensington?' Flynn asked cautiously.

'Same thing that brought you here, I suspect.'

For a brief moment Flynn thought that the stranger was a policeman, like him; perhaps that was why he thought he recognized him. The front door opened and three men, members of Collins' personal staff, stepped into the street and began to climb into the car. Suddenly, the last man stopped and looked around, scanning the street, until he saw Flynn and his new companion on the corner. 'Emmet! Will you get over here, there's work to be done!'

'I'll be there in a minute, Liam!' the man shouted back and suddenly the penny dropped. Flynn realized who he was talking to. Liam Tobin, the man who'd shouted, along with Ned Broy and Liam McGrath, had already climbed into the car but the fourth member of Collins' team was standing next to him. It had been almost five years since he'd seen him this close but it was him, he knew it was him; he was older but it was definitely him, the young lieutenant that he'd first seen cradling the corpse of Tom Kettle in a fetid trench outside Ginchy. It was Emmet Dalton, Collins' military advisor and head of security.

'It's been a long time, Sergeant Flynn,' Dalton said with a smile, 'and I'm glad you survived it all – the war and this bloody mess. How times have changed, eh? I've heard a lot about you over the last year. You've made quite a name for yourself and it's a shame you'll be out of a job soon. You know where we're going?' Flynn shook his head; he was paid to report what went on at Cadogan Gardens. What went on anywhere else was of little concern to him and as for what Collins and the other Irish delegation did elsewhere, that was well above his pay grade. 'Mick's off to sign a treaty with the British and, if all goes well, it looks like this time tomorrow this bloody war could really be over. Ireland will be free at last,' Dalton said.

'And you think that will be an end of it?'

Dalton looked at Flynn, a flicker of doubt in his eyes. 'Jesus, Flynn, as I live and breathe, I hope so, I truly hope so. Even the unionists up in Ulster might see sense eventually. Sure, there'll be those who won't like it, you know, but if we handle it right, then who knows? Christ, don't we have to try? Nothing's the same anymore. Who'd have thought the British would recognize our right to govern ourselves? Who'd have thought that the snotty subby you saved all those years ago at Ginchy would end up a brigadier general in an Irish army? If there is trouble, I could use good men around me.' He looked at Flynn. 'Just say the word and there's a commission in it for you. Lieutenant Flynn – that's more than the British ever did for you.'

Collins stuck his head out of the car window. 'Oi, Emmet, will you stop gassing with the peelers and get over here! We don't have all day!'

'Think about it, Kevin. It's been good seeing you again. Take care.'

He patted Flynn on the arm and then walked across the street to the waiting car, leaving him alone with his thoughts. Flynn had to admit that he quite liked the sound of 'Lieutenant Flynn' – it had a ring to it.

He looked at his watch, the German watch he'd acquired one night during a raid on a German trench all those years ago on the Somme. For a brief moment he thought about the man he'd killed, the man he'd hacked to death with a shovel on a dark, wet night. Sometimes it felt like it was another life; that it had all happened to someone else. Sometimes he truly wished that it had.

Maguire emerged from the park and walked huffing and puffing over to Flynn. 'What did yer man Dalton want?' Maguire asked as he lit a cigarette. His eye patch reminded Flynn of a pirate, a livid scar slashed across his left cheek like a second smile. 'He offered me a job in the new Irish army,' Flynn said.

'He always was a cheeky little bastard, was our Ginchy!' Maguire said, almost affectionately. 'Look, our shift's over and I could murder a drink. Is there anywhere around here that sells stout?'

'Jesus, Joe, this is Kensington not Kilburn, though I thought I saw a pub down that way that sold Guinness.'

Flynn pointed off down the road and Maguire's face split in a broad grin, his remaining eye glinting in the streetlight.

'All right, let's give it a go but I swear to God if any little gobshite tries to draw a bloody shamrock in the head I'll shoot the little fecker!'